AN ACADEMY FOR LIARS

ALSO BY ALEXIS HENDERSON

House of Hunger
The Year of the Witching

AN ACADEMY FOR LIARS

ALEXIS HENDERSON

ACE ✦ NEW YORK

ACE
Published by Berkley
An imprint of Penguin Random House LLC
penguinrandomhouse.com

Copyright © 2024 by Alexis Henderson
Penguin Random House supports copyright. Copyright fuels creativity, encourages diverse voices, promotes free speech, and creates a vibrant culture. Thank you for buying an authorized edition of this book and for complying with copyright laws by not reproducing, scanning, or distributing any part of it in any form without permission. You are supporting writers and allowing Penguin Random House to continue to publish books for every reader.

ACE is a registered trademark and the A colophon is a trademark of Penguin Random House LLC.

Export edition ISBN: 9780593820018

Library of Congress Cataloging-in-Publication Data

Names: Henderson, Alexis, author.
Title: An academy for liars / Alexis Henderson.
Description: New York: Ace, 2024.
Identifiers: LCCN 2024014067 (print) | LCCN 2024014068 (ebook) | ISBN 9780593638309 (hardcover) | ISBN 9780593638316 (ebook)
Subjects: LCSH: Magic—Fiction. | LCGFT: Fantasy fiction. | Novels.
Classification: LCC PS3608.E52548 A64 2024 (print) | LCC PS3608.E52548 (ebook) | DDC 813/.6—dc23/eng/20240329
LC record available at https://lccn.loc.gov/2024014067
LC ebook record available at https://lccn.loc.gov/2024014068

Printed in the United States of America
1st Printing

Book design by Daniel Brount

This is a work of fiction. Names, characters, places, and incidents either are the product of the author's imagination or are used fictitiously, and any resemblance to actual persons, living or dead, business establishments, events, or locales is entirely coincidental.

This one is for Alice

AN ACADEMY FOR LIARS

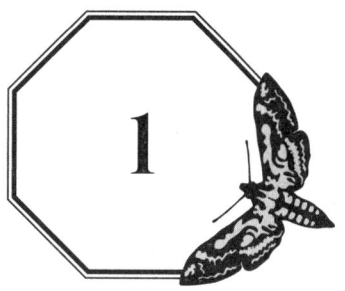

1

THERE WAS SOMETHING in the bathroom mirrors. Lennon first noticed when she was standing between them, preparing for her own engagement party. One of the mirrors hung above the sink behind her; the other hung above the sink in front of her. Standing between the two, she gazed with glassy eyes at the reflections of herself reflecting one another, on and on, shrinking into the dark and distant ether.

Every one of them looked miserable, which was to be expected.

Lennon had realized some time ago that her misery was less a problem with the wedding than with her. She had been in a bad way for months—unmoored, discordant, occupying her own body with a sense of unease, the way one might in an airport terminal or the lobby of a rent-by-the-hour motel. Her own flesh and bone a kind of liminal space.

She'd hoped things would change with the engagement. So she'd attended the cake tastings and the dress fittings, and she'd made a deposit on the venue and secured a film photographer, who would be flying in from out of state for the occasion. She'd sent wax-sealed invites across the country to her family members and a few seat-filler friends. And now here she was, alone in her bathroom regretting everything and so desperate to be somewhere, anywhere, else that she would've almost rather died than face the engagement party outside her bedroom door. It was something of a miracle, then, that she finished her makeup. Her body seemed to perform the act without her, and when it was done, she stared at all of her faces in the mirror and saw someone, many someones, that she didn't know.

And then she slapped herself.

One hand raised—all of the other Lennons in the mirror raising their hands with her—and a sharp pop across her freshly blushed cheek. The slap carried down through the legion of her reflections and then stopped.

One of the Lennons in the mirror didn't strike its cheek. It didn't move at all really, except to smile, its lips pulling up at the edges, as if the corners of its mouth were attached to strings that had been sharply tugged. Then it sidestepped out of line, edging up through the ranks, walking toward her. It was like her in almost every way—bony bronzed arms sparsely tattooed, thin high nose spattered with freckles, long braids unfurling halfway down her back—but there was one glaring difference between Lennon and the defecting reflection in the mirror: she had eyes, but this . . . *thing* did not. It strode toward her, smiling all the while.

Lennon wheeled to face the mirror behind her, saw nothing except the same girl moving toward her, through the shifting ranks of the line. Panicked, she glanced around the bathroom but saw that she was alone.

The defector was edging closer now, stepping gingerly around its peers, sometimes weaving between them, letting its fingers trail along their bare shoulders as it passed them by. It stopped only when it'd reached the reflection nearest Lennon and stepped up onto its tiptoes so that it was an inch or two taller. The aberration in the mirror slid its hands around Lennon's waist from behind, the way that a lover might. It opened its mouth and pressed a kiss into the soft juncture where neck curves into shoulder.

Lennon stumbled, backing into the sink, arms wheeling, swiping a jar of cotton balls off the counter on her way to the floor. It shattered on impact beside her.

There was a beat of silence, followed by a knock at the door. She knew it was her fiancé, Wyatt, checking in on her. She was now more than an hour late to her own engagement party, and she could tell from the strained tenor of his voice that he was running out of patience. "Are you okay?"

"Yes, fine! I'll be out in a second." Gingerly, Lennon scooped up the glass shards and placed them in the trash, risking glances at the mirror all the while. The thing was gone, but she swore she could still feel the wet crescent of its kiss at the curve of her shoulder.

She scrambled to her feet and fled the bathroom.

The house was full of Wyatt's faculty friends from the university where he worked. One of them, a WASPy woman in a tasteful tweed blazer, abruptly stopped whispering when Lennon emerged from the bedroom. She bore the decided stink of significance, which to Lennon smelled a lot like Chanel No. 5. The woman looked at Lennon, slightly startled, as if she were an intruder instead of someone who lived there.

This was the uncomfortable reality of her life in Denver. The obligatory check-ins from vague acquaintances upon the event of a police murder, or the subsequent protests that followed it. The offhanded inquiries about the details of her DNA makeup, her nationality, her place of birth, the texture of her hair, and if it was really hers. Then there were the acquaintances at Wyatt's dinner parties who inquired about the color of her eyes and how she'd come by them and what or who she'd been crossed with. Then came the questions about her parentage, and her parents' parentage, because those same acquaintances now wondered if the parents of her parents had eyes the same muddy hazel as hers. It was a gentle othering, or perhaps more aptly, a distancing, that made Lennon feel it was impossible to connect with others in the close and complicated ways she wanted to. She'd since stopped trying.

Lennon, still badly shaken by her encounter in the bathroom, forced a smile and shouldered her way through the house, a midcentury-style ranch with an interior courtyard, complete with a cactus garden and a large koi pond stocked to capacity. Every year Wyatt forgot to remove the fish before the first freeze of winter. She remembered one of the first nights they'd spent in the house. There was a blizzard raging outside and they'd lost power and were forced to sleep on the floor of the living room, in front of the fireplace for warmth. Come dawn, Wyatt woke with a start and a muttered "Fuck."

He snatched a bucket from the supply closet, shuffled into the kitchen to fill it with warm water from the sink, and took a meat tenderizer from the drawer before staggering outside, trudging through calf-high snowdrifts to the very edge of the koi pond, where he dropped to his knees and began to hammer the thick crust of ice. He removed several heavy plates of ice from the surface of the pond before proceeding to extract each of the eight koi by hand, placing them in the bucket of warm water to thaw. He then hauled them all into the house and put them straight into the bathtub, which he filled with warm water.

Lennon had sat on the bathroom floor, arms folded on the edge of the tub, chin atop them, watching the koi stir back to life. She even touched a few of them, let her fingers skim along their slick spines as they emerged from their slumber. But one of the koi did not rouse to her touch. It floated motionless at the bottom of the tub. Panicked, Lennon plucked it from the water and hastily swaddled it in a hand towel. Cradling the fish to her chest, she carried it to the kitchen, where Wyatt stood, stress-smoking a joint. He took the half-frozen koi corpse from her bare-handed, leaving the damp towel behind, and studied it by the pale morning light that washed in through the windows.

"You know, it's not the cold that kills them," he said, as if to absolve himself. The dead fish dribbled water onto the freshly cleaned kitchen floor. Wyatt didn't seem to notice. Or if he did, he didn't care. "They suffocate. They can't breathe under the ice."

"Can't they breathe the water?"

"They breathe the oxygen in it," he said, rather matter-of-factly, and turned to throw the koi corpse into the trash. It struck the bottom of the bin with an ugly *thump*. "But under the ice there isn't enough."

Lennon began to love him then, foolish as it was. She had been so young then, and it had seemed to her that Wyatt knew everything about everything. She thought him the smartest person she'd ever met and thought herself all the more alluring for being the recipient of his sparing love . . . or if not that, then the object of it. Had he bent to one knee and asked her to marry him then, she was confident she would have said yes, being the bright-eyed little idiot that she was.

As it turned out, she would wait another year before Wyatt proposed (if one could even call it a proposal). He had broached the subject in the front yard, not on one knee but standing beside the empty koi pond. All of the fish were dead and gone, lost to another winter, soon to be replaced by new and expensive imports, long-finned butterfly koi flown in from Kyoto.

Wyatt had no ring at the time, or question to ask. He knew what the answer would be already. He'd simply said that he liked the idea of marrying in the fall.

Tonight, the koi appeared comfortable, swimming beneath the cover of their lily pads, their faint fins moving like fabric in the wind. A few guests—academics and admin whose names she didn't know—stood smoking and sipping cocktails around the water's edge. They waved at her, with some awkwardness, and Lennon waved back as she cut quickly across the courtyard.

She found Wyatt in the kitchen, slicing paper-thin slivers of lime alongside two of his colleagues. He was good-looking, with his shirtsleeves rolled up to his elbows, his forearms shapely and covered in a soft down of curly brown hair. He had wide-set blue eyes, and he was tall and gangly with pale skin faintly freckled; a large, distinctly aristocratic nose; and a boyish, canted smile, which he flashed at her, forcibly, as she stepped alongside him.

"I'm sorry," she said as he pulled her into a hug. "I don't know if it's those new meds or what, but I think I saw something in the bathroom—"

"We'll talk later," he said through gritted teeth, smiling all the while.

Wyatt's closest friend and fellow professor, the blond and wiry George Hughes, stood beside him aggressively shaking the contents of a cocktail strainer. As he worked, he relayed the intricacies of his latest research trip to Russia. A PhD in architecture, he had gone to study some significant brutalist structure there. "It's the most amazing building. The spirit of communist antiquity quite literally made concrete. I had to travel almost sixty miles north by snowmobile to reach it, and I hiked the last half of the journey on foot, limping along with a pair of broken snowshoes that barely clung to my boots, and they still wouldn't let me in to see it."

Beside George stood their friend Sophia, measuring small scoops of ice into their respective copper mule mugs. On that night, she wore her hair—which was the pale beige of a peanut shell—combed carefully over one shoulder. Her sweater was a tasteful gray, half-tucked into the waistband of her slacks. She puckered her lips and kissed the air in Lennon's general direction by way of greeting. "If it isn't the blushing bride."

Lennon made herself smile.

Sophia was good at performing kindness (or maybe she was kind, and Lennon too bitter to admit it). The two of them had been friends once. Or something close to friends anyway. Sophia had transferred into the University of Colorado just after Wyatt joined the faculty. Sophia was married, but her husband often traveled for work and wasn't around much, so in their early days in Denver, Sophia was a constant presence. Lennon hadn't minded this, as she found that she liked Wyatt better when Sophia was there. He smiled more when she was around, and they quarreled less.

But things had changed over time. While Lennon cycled through therapists and endured brief stints at various hospitals and rehab facilities around the city, Sophia (a psychologist) went on to secure research grants, publish papers in well-respected journals, defend her dissertation, and secure a coveted internship at the University of Colorado Hospital, where she worked now.

The two fell out of touch. Wyatt was the only bridge between them at this point, but he seemed increasingly content to observe the separate spheres of his life with Lennon and his life at the university. So Sophia had become less their friend, and more Wyatt's, specifically.

The two confided in each other as colleagues, shared in the varying triumphs and miseries of their respective fields—Wyatt divulging the difficulties of his research, its lack of funding, the grants he'd wanted and failed to acquire, and Sophia sharing the rigors of her life as a clinician, struggling through the last half of her internship, pinning her hopes on the faculty positions that she hoped would open in neighboring colleges. Lennon was largely left alone.

The party settled for dinner on the back patio. Lennon and Wyatt sat at either end of a long banquet table. Over dinner, Lennon watched her fiancé through the faint tendrils of pot smoke that traced through the air between them. He had the kind of startling charisma she had always coveted, a certain thrall that drew people like moths to light and made everyone want to be known and loved by him. She could see it now, as he chatted among his peers, single-handedly commanding the table so that even those on the opposite end of it craned out of their seats and strained forward to catch his every word. They were the kind of people who mistook greatness for its shadow. As long as they were in the presence of brilliance, they too were brilliant by proxy. Lennon knew this about them because she was once the same—struck dumb with awe and utterly convinced that Wyatt's presence alone was enough to elevate her above the murk of her own mediocrity.

Lennon had been a college freshman then—dewy-eyed and jejune—studying English literature at New York University. Wyatt had been a poet in residence at one of the neighboring colleges. She had attended one of his readings, and he'd taken an interest in her because, apparently, she looked like an actress from a French art house film he'd loved as a teenager. Lennon, for her part, had never watched it (and never bothered to either).

Nevertheless, they fell in love the way most people do—which is to say they felt as though they were experiencing love for the first time. It was all so fast and intense, and Lennon had the suspicion that this was the root cause of her unraveling. She had learned, at a young age, that change was her trigger. It could be change for better or for worse—it didn't matter; her body interpreted the stimuli in the same way. So when the panic attacks first began, she wasn't entirely surprised. What did surprise her, though, was their violence. The tears and the vomiting and the vertigo. She stopped counting how many classes she'd missed, lying naked on the bathroom floor, waiting for the waves of terror to subside.

By the end of that semester, the first of her sophomore year, she found herself in a psychiatric ward, where she would remain for eight weeks. Lennon dropped out of college shortly after she was discharged, on the recommendation of her psychiatrist and the urging of her family members and Wyatt, who by this time had become almost as close as family to her. Perhaps they all knew what Lennon only allowed herself to accept months later: she wasn't fit to continue on at college. She was not brilliant in the ways that Wyatt, George, and Sophia were. She was neither an artist nor a scholar nor even a particularly promising college student. She was simply very, very sick.

Her parents urged her to move back home to their house in a Florida retirement community, which sounded like hell to Lennon. So, when Wyatt invited her to move to Denver, Colorado, where he had taken a job as a professor in the University of Colorado's MFA program, Lennon decided to go with him. She moved into his house—carefully slotting herself into the empty spaces of his life—and became, officially, his live-in girlfriend. Or, unofficially, his housewife.

She was twenty.

Lennon plucked a smoking joint from the cinders of a nearby ashtray and toked. Bored, she shifted her attention down the table and noticed that Wyatt and Sophia were nowhere to be seen. This didn't arouse her suspicion at first. It was a casual event; half of those in attendance had already finished their meals and dispersed to different corners of the house. A few professors puzzled over the contents of Wyatt's bookshelves. Grad students stood around the koi pond smoking weed, watching the fish circle. A group of poets huddled together in the kitchen, gossiping over the rims of their cocktail glasses.

Twenty minutes passed. Sophia and Wyatt remained missing.

Lennon dragged on her joint once more and got up to look for them, a part of her knowing already what she would find when she did. She wasn't sure what it was about this night that made her want to confirm her darkest suspicions. But it imbued her with a kind of bravery she had not known before. In the end, it didn't matter what led her to find them together in the primary bathroom—Wyatt hunched over Sophia, his bare belly pressed hard to the small of her back—only that she did.

Sophia's trousers were pooled about her ankles, her lace panties pulled taut between her straining thighs. She was smiling and saying the nice things that men like to hear when they're inside you. The sorts of things Lennon could never bring herself to say about Wyatt, not because they weren't true (though maybe they weren't) but because she didn't know how to say them in a way that made them *seem* true. But Sophia did, and Wyatt responded in turn. They moved together as one, and as Sophia pressed forward the edge of the countertop cut deep into her stomach and her breath fogged the mirror.

It was dark in the bathroom, so neither Wyatt nor Sophia noticed Lennon in the doorway, or the fact that her reflection disobeyed her once again, breaking the tether that bound likeness to master. It was the same eyeless aberration that had appeared earlier that evening, and when it met Lennon's gaze, it grinned.

2

LENNON LEFT THE party. She edged past the koi pond and the grad students who encircled it, down the long driveway, and stepped out into the street, where Wyatt's car was parked parallel to the sidewalk a few houses down.

It was a silver Porsche 911, a hand-me-down gift from Wyatt's father to commemorate his successful dissertation defense. Wyatt had never allowed Lennon to drive it. He didn't trust her behind the wheel or with much of anything, really. To him, everything she did (unplugging the iron before they left to run errands) or said ("I love you, the way you deserve to be loved") was cast in a hard shadow of uncertainty.

Lennon unlocked the doors of Wyatt's car and climbed inside. The leather of the seat was cold against her bare thighs. She didn't check the mirrors before slipping the key into the ignition. But her gaze flickered back to the house. Though she didn't know it then, this was the last she'd see of it for some time.

She began to drive. Aimlessly at first—letting the car drift from empty lane to empty lane—and then with purpose, pressing down on the gas pedal, picking up speed, the suburbs—the trim little lawns and tasteful houses, the organic grocery stores and Citizens Banks, the Mattress Firms and storage facilities—smearing past the windows in a blur. She thought a bit about the aberration she'd seen in the mirror of the bathroom. The girl with no eyes who was her but . . . not. And Lennon wondered what she wanted, or if she was some harbinger of bad fortune, or if not that, then the cause of it.

Her thoughts returned to Wyatt.

What she realized then as she sat in his car was that she had been so obsessed with trying to bridge the gap between them—to prove herself precocious and smart and worthy enough to be the recipient of his love—that she'd made the grave error of mistaking the want of closeness for closeness itself. But one was not a sufficient substitute for the other. Her love—or her yearning for it—was not, and would never be, enough, which is why Wyatt was with Sophia tonight, and not her.

By the time Lennon reached the abandoned mall on the cusp of the suburbs, she knew what she was preparing to do. There were blood thinners in the glove compartment, prescription strength. Wyatt kept them there after suffering a pulmonary embolism—years ago, before he met Lennon—that very nearly killed him. He'd warned her once to make sure that she never mixed them up with her antidepressants—the pills looked similar—because the blood thinners had no antidote. If you overdosed on them, there was nothing any doctor or hospital could do for you, apart from watch you slowly bleed out from the inside.

Surely, Lennon thought, downing a bottle would do the trick.

She decided she would find some bathroom stall or stockroom at the heart of the place where there would be no one to disturb her. No one to intervene, which should've been a good thing . . . but as Lennon stepped out into the deserted parking lot, intervention was exactly what she wanted. A sign, a symbol, the grasping hand of some meddling but benevolent god who would reach down through a break in the clouds and shake her senseless, until she was forced to believe—really and truly—that her life had meaning and that she was destined for something more than mediocrity. She wanted salvation and she found it in the form of a phone booth half-devoured by crawling ivy, standing in the flickering halo of one of the last streetlights in the parking lot that was still shining.

The booth was oak and old-fashioned with yellow stained-glass windows so thoroughly fogged that even if there had been a person within, Lennon likely wouldn't have been able to see them. The leaves of the ivy plant that bound the booth stirred and bristled, though there was no wind that night. As Lennon stood staring, the phone began to ring, a shrill and tinny sound like silver spoons striking the sides of so many small bells.

Lennon decided, at first, to ignore this and started toward the mall with the pill bottle in hand, but the phone kept ringing, louder and louder, as if with increasing urgency. She stopped, turned to the booth, then walked toward it, reluctantly at first, half hoping the ringing would stop before she reached it. But it persisted.

Lennon drew open the collapsible doors of the phone booth, stepped inside, and closed them behind her. Its interior was oddly warm and humid, and there was a sulfurous scent thick in the air. The phone was an old black rotary. Its receiver quivered in its cradle with the force of the ringing. Lennon raised it to her ear. There was a sound like static on the line that Lennon recognized as the distant roar of waves breaking. Then a voice: "Do you still have your name?" it asked, as if a name were a thing that could be misplaced, like a wallet or a pair of keys.

She faltered, wondering if this was some sort of prank call or trick question. "It's . . . Lennon?"

"Lennon what?"

She grasped for the rest of it, but it didn't come. She was really high. "Who is this?"

"This is a representative from Drayton College." The voice on the line was a combination of every voice of everyone that Lennon had ever known speaking together at once. A horrid and familiar chorus—her mother, her sister and first therapist, her high school boyfriend, her dead grandmother. "We're calling to congratulate you on your acceptance to the interview stage of your admission process. You should be very proud. Few make it this far. Your interview will take place tomorrow, at your earliest convenience."

"I don't understand. I never applied for anything. I've never even heard of Drayton before—"

The question was asked again, with something of an edge this time. "Can you make it, Lennon?" The address, someplace in Ogden, Utah, was then given.

At a loss for words, Lennon fumbled for her cell phone, quickly typed the address into her GPS app, and discovered that the location was an eight-hour drive away. It was already nearly midnight: if she were to make it to the interview in time (which was a ridiculous idea in itself), she'd have to drive all night. What kind of program called prospective students the day before their interview? Was this all some sort of twisted prank? Her confusion festered into bitter frustration. "I'm not going anywhere, for an interview or for anything else, until I get some answers about what the *fuck* is going on."

A lengthy pause, and then, in a broken, tear-choked whisper that was unmistakably her own: "He will never love you the way you want to be loved. And if you stay, he will love you even less, until one day you mean nothing to him."

Lennon froze, her hand tightening to a vise grip around the receiver. Her throat began to swell and tighten. "It's you. From the mirror. Isn't it? Answer me!"

"We wish you the best of luck with the next step of your admission process." There was a soft click. The line went dead.

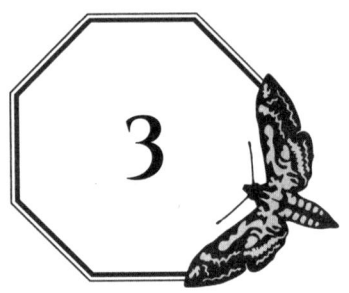

3

LENNON DROVE THROUGH the night, stopping only to get gas, change her clothes (she kept a gym bag in the back seat of the car), and pee at a run-down rest stop in the red deserts of Wyoming. Through the course of her journey, she made a point to avoid using the rearview mirrors (for fear of what she'd see if she did), only briefly glancing at them when she was forced to. It helped that the highway was mostly empty, with only a few semis sharing the road with her. It was nearing dawn by the time she crossed into Utah. After driving for hours, she arrived in Ogden, stiff from sitting for so long. Strangely, she wasn't tired.

As she approached Ogden, she kept replaying the congratulatory phone call from Drayton in her head and she realized that at first, the voice on the line hadn't been gendered. It had sounded almost automated in its neutrality, and she couldn't place it as male or female or anything in between . . . until it had become hers. Which begged the question, *how* had it become hers? And how had it (she?) known about Wyatt's infidelity? How had it known that she was there to receive the call at all? She felt like she was living the loose logic of dreams and wondered for a moment if this *was* a dream—the thing that appeared in the bathroom mirror, Wyatt's affair with Sophia, the phone call, her own voice warbling over the line. Or if it wasn't a dream, then perhaps it was a delusion as vivid and convincing as it was tragic . . . and pathetically grandiose. She wondered if perhaps this was some sort of manic episode like the ones she'd suffered in the past. But those episodes had always been characterized by an unwavering sense of conviction—in herself and the forces that fueled her delusions, be they genius or the mechanisms of fate. But as her hands tightened, white-knuckled, around the steering wheel, she felt only small and helpless, adrift on a dark tide that carried her to what, she didn't know.

Lennon kept driving, following the directions on her GPS. She entered a small historic district in the shadow of a mountain, used for skiing in the wintertime. There, the streets were narrow, canopied by the lush branches of the trees that grew on either side. She found her destination at the curve of a large cul-de-sac: an imposing redbrick mansion set far off the street, half-shrouded by a copse of overgrown hawthorns. Its roof was low-slung over the second-story windows, and it made the house look like an old man frowning at her approach.

She parked in the empty driveway and checked her phone. Seven missed calls (three from Wyatt and four from her mother) and twelve text messages (one from Wyatt, five from her mother, six from her older sister, Carly). Lennon left everything unanswered—the text messages, the voicemails, and the countless questions she'd asked herself through the duration of her drive—got out of the car to rifle through the contents of the trunk, until she found the grease-blackened crowbar resting below the spare tire. She weighed it in both hands, nodded to herself as if to summon what little courage she had to muster, and then slammed the trunk shut.

The yard was large and covered in a dense carpet of grass. The hedges that lined the house were round and well shaped. Lennon tramped through the plush lawn, crowbar in hand, and stepped up onto the porch. The front door was set with a small window of stained glass that distorted the glimpse of the foyer behind it. Hanging on the wall beside the door was a large plaque that detailed the extensive history of the house (apparently it had been owned by some oil baron millionaire from the 1800s).

Lennon knocked three times, hard and in quick succession. A brief pause then footsteps. The door creaked open. A man stood in the threshold, barefoot in a loose linen shirt and pants to match. He was only a little taller than Lennon, maybe six feet even, with lively blue eyes that wrinkled at the edges when he smiled, with all the warmth and fondness you'd expect from a friend who hadn't seen you for some time. He looked to be in his late forties, and Lennon found him to be almost excessively good-looking.

"Well," he said, still smiling at her, his teeth so straight and white they looked like a set of dentures, "you must be Lennon." He glanced down at her crowbar. "Can I take that off your hands?"

Lennon handed over the crowbar with some reluctance. In retrospect, she wasn't sure why she did it. She didn't know or trust this man. She wasn't sure if he was the only one in the house. But when he'd asked that question, and made to reach for the crowbar, her resolve had abruptly softened . . . and a calm had washed over her, as though she'd taken a Valium.

He stooped slightly, leaning her crowbar against the wall. "I'm Benedict. Just like the breakfast dish," he said, straightening, and ushered her inside with a flourish of his hand. He closed the door behind her but didn't lock it.

The walls of the foyer were paneled in the same dark mahogany as the floors, and the house smelled of polish and potpourri. There was an ornate birdcage elevator to the left of the door, just beside the stairs. Benedict led Lennon past the elevator and down a narrow hall. As they walked, the floors groaned beneath their feet, in what seemed like a begrudging welcome.

Benedict led her past the kitchen and through the parlor to a little study off the back of the house, with a wall of windows and French doors opening out onto a small, sun-washed solarium. The study was covered in a grid of shadows cast from the window stiles and bars. Benedict gestured to a large oak desk. There were two chairs drawn up on either side. Benedict sat in one and Lennon sat in the other.

"I suppose I should tell you about Drayton," said Benedict, and his eyes took on the faraway look of someone moved by memory. "I graduated years ago. You might've been just a fluttering in your mother's womb back then. Maybe less than that, even. Little more than an egg and an idea."

Benedict's eyes came back into focus, and he blinked quickly, like he was only just remembering that Lennon was sitting there. "Tell me, what do you know of Drayton?"

"Nothing. I've never heard of it. I didn't even apply."

"Of course you did. Everyone's applied, whether they know it or not."

"But how is that possible? Don't I need to present a portfolio or take some sort of exam?"

"You're already taking it. The first phase of testing begins at birth."

"And the second?" Lennon asked, pressing for more.

"This interview."

"And the third?"

"The entry exam, but you shouldn't worry about that," said Benedict, looking mildly irritated. "Candidates always have so many questions when they come here, but most don't make it past the interview. Besides, there's little I can say to ease your curiosity. Drayton is to be experienced not explained. All I can tell you is that Drayton is an institution devoted to the study of the human condition. At least, that's what they put on the pamphlets they passed out at my orientation. Perhaps its ethos has changed since then. It's been many years." Benedict stood up, one of his knees popping loudly. "Before we begin, let me make you something to eat."

"I'm not hungry."

"And yet you must eat," he said, waving her off. "You can't interview on an empty stomach. Besides, you'll need it for the pain."

"I'm not in any pain."

"It'll come," said Benedict, and a sharp chill slit down her spine like the blade of a razor. Lennon wondered, shifting uncomfortably in her chair, if she was entirely safe in this strange house with this strange man who was supposed to be from Drayton. What if this was all some elaborate sex-trafficking scheme wherein the targets were "gifted and talented" kids who'd never received their magic school acceptance letters and grew up to become depressed, praise-starved, thoroughly gullible adults.

Benedict disappeared down the hall and into the kitchen. There was the clattering of pots and pans, water running and later boiling. Unsure of what to do, Lennon turned her attention to the strange portrait hanging over Benedict's desk. The lower half of the painting was rendered in hyperrealistic detail, depicting a man dressed in a flesh-colored tweed blazer, and a crisp white shirt buttoned up to the throat. But the upper half of the image was distorted, as if the artist had—in a moment of great frustration—taken up a wet washcloth and viciously smeared the thick layers of oil paint, as if to wipe the canvas clean. There were stretched and gaping eye sockets, a ruined mouth, the twisted contour of what might have been a nose, but it was hard for Lennon to say.

"A former student painted it for me," said Benedict. He stood in the doorway, holding a breakfast tray. On it: a delicately folded cloth napkin, a bowl of pasta, a glass of wine, and a small dish stacked with pale cookies.

Glancing at the spread he'd prepared, Lennon realized she must've been gazing at that painting longer than she'd realized. "It's . . . compelling."

"Quite," said Benedict, and he set the tray down in front of her, taking a seat in the chair beneath the portrait. He nodded to the food. "Go on, then."

Lennon ate. The pasta was herbaceous and a little too lemony.

"How do you like it?" Benedict inquired.

"It's very good," said Lennon, chewing mechanically. She hated eating in front of people, and strangers especially, but she didn't want to appear rude.

"You grew up in Brunswick, Georgia," said Benedict, watching her eat. His eyes were wide and grave. "Yours was the only Black family within your neighborhood, a half-built subdivision that went under in the last recession. The movers you hired warned your parents—as a kindness—that families like yours didn't move into neighborhoods like that. Your father was a high school history teacher. He and your mother were both avid bird-watchers. Do you hold these facts to be true?"

Lennon faltered with the fork raised halfway to her mouth. "How did you know all of this? I don't understand."

"You don't understand the mechanics of how a person on one side of the world can take a call from someone on the other. But you trust your own ears and you know that it's true. This is no different. You don't understand the mechanics of how you came to be here, but it is real, and it is happening, so all you need to do is trust that someone, or something, more informed than you must have made this happen."

"So you're saying this is all some type of magic?"

"May I remind you that I'm the interviewer," said Benedict, not unkindly, though his tone was rather firm. "I ask the questions for now."

Lennon fell silent.

"When you were young, you would often wake in the morning to see your father standing on the back porch of the house, peering into a pair of binoculars, bird-watching. One day, he spotted a nest of starlings in the branches of an oak tree. What did your father teach you to do to the starlings?"

"I don't see how these questions relate to my admission."

"You're not meant to. Just answer them as best you can. What did he teach you to do to the starlings, Lennon?"

"Crush their eggs," she whispered tonelessly, her cheeks flushed from the shame of it.

"And what about the starlings that had already hatched—the little ones huddled in their nests among a graveyard of cracked eggs? What did he teach you to do to them?"

"He told me to take their heads between thumb and pointer finger, and twist them, fast and hard, the way you'd turn a bottle cap."

"And why did your father tell you to do this?"

"Because . . . because the starlings were a menace to other birds.

They drove them away, stole their nests, and spread disease. He called them vermin and told me that it was imperative to sacrifice a few to save many."

Benedict smiled, and it was an entirely different expression than the one he had welcomed her with at the door. So different, in fact, that Lennon considered the idea that this was the first moment he had been truly genuine. "You walk down a narrow lane. Someone walks toward you from the opposite direction. The path isn't wide enough to accommodate both of you, standing shoulder to shoulder. Are you the one that steps aside?"

"I—I'm not sure."

"This is a yes-or-no question. Are you the one that steps aside, Lennon?"

"Yes."

Benedict appeared appeased. He nodded to her engagement ring, an heirloom that had belonged to the dead great-aunt of someone significant on Wyatt's father's side of the family. The center stone was nearly two carats, and the band was encrusted with other smaller stones that glittered brilliantly when the sunlight struck them. The first time she'd slipped it on her hand, it felt heavy. "You're married?"

"Not yet," or likely ever—on account of the fact that her fiancé was fucking one of her supposed friends—but she didn't say that last bit out loud. "I got engaged over the winter."

"To Wyatt Banks?"

"Yes."

"Tell me more."

"About Wyatt?"

Benedict appeared, for a moment, disgusted. He waved her off with a flap of his hands. "We don't need to waste any more time on that man. I know enough of the sob story—pretty little girl leaves her dreams and aspirations to become a bauble, an accessory to the life of a man she, *wrongly*, believes is more significant than she is. Does that about sum it up?"

Lennon felt like she'd been backhanded across the face. "W-well, I wouldn't say I was an accessory. I mean, Wyatt and I are engaged—well, we were engaged."

"What happened?"

"I found him with someone else. Just before coming here."

"And how did that make you feel?"

It seemed like a stupid question. How would anyone feel when they watched the life they'd built for themselves unravel before their eyes? Lennon answered anyway. "I mean . . . I wanted to die. In fact, I planned to."

"Was that the first time you've wanted to end your life?"

She shook her head. "I've had my . . . struggles before."

Benedict nodded, knowingly, and with sympathy that seemed neither forced nor pitying. He produced a box of tissues and passed it to her across the desk. Lennon stared at them, confused for a moment, then realized she was crying. She never cried in front of strangers. Ever. The humiliation alone was enough to keep the tears from flowing. She hadn't even cried when she'd discovered Wyatt with Sophia in the bathroom. But Benedict had . . . *dismantled* something deep within her; he'd given her the license to release—grieve, even.

"I want to let you know that you're free to leave if this is too painful for you," said Benedict, as Lennon hastily wiped her eyes. "This is an emotionally harrowing experience, and a painful one at that. Few make it this far, and most who do won't graduate to the final step of the admissions process. If you choose to leave now, you'll follow in the footsteps of many others. But I'll warn you that the questions I ask you today are the same questions you'll ask yourself tomorrow, and the day after, and decades later, in the twilight years of your life. You'll never escape them, which is not to say you'll find answers for them either. But I'm of a mind that the difficult questions should always be asked, whether they can be answered or not. Do you agree?"

"Yes. At least I want to."

The left edge of Benedict's mouth twitched twice. "Then I'm happy to say you've passed the interview and may now proceed to the final step of your admissions process, the entry exam. Take the elevator in the foyer up to the eighth floor."

"But this is a two-story house."

"I'm well aware."

Lennon stared at him blankly. Benedict stared back. "You'd better be on your way," he said. "Drayton waits for no one."

4

LENNON WALKED DOWN the hall, the floorboards groaning beneath her sneakers, and approached the birdcage elevator. It was old and rickety, with brass walls. She stepped into the cabin and dragged the collapsible door shut with a rattle. The buttons on the operating panel ranged from one to eleven. She punched the *8* with her knuckle and a second, inner set of doors sliced shut behind the grate of the birdcage and the elevator lurched into a shuddering ascent.

It was a relatively short trip. Within a few moments the elevator ground to a stop and its doors trundled open. Golden sunlight spilled inside. Lennon, shaking, stepped out of the cabin and into what she first thought was a cathedral. It was rather dim, but there were windows cut into the stone above, pale sunlight bleeding in through them, laying bright squares of daylight that trailed like stepping stones down a wide corridor where both floor and ceiling canted in opposite directions—the former sloping slightly up and the latter down.

To the left was a large wall mural that vaguely reminded Lennon of Picasso's *Guernica*. It depicted a series of grotesque figures—twisted bodies, contused and warped and seemingly seized by the throes of some primal passion. It was rendered in the same spirit as that strange portrait that hung in Benedict's study, and she wondered if they shared an artist.

Stunned, Lennon turned back to the elevator, only to find a wall of stone behind her.

"Welcome to Drayton."

Lennon turned to see a spectacled woman seated behind a long, low desk opposite the mural. She was thumbing through an issue of *Vanity Fair* magazine—just an ordinary human doing ordinary human things—and Lennon realized, with a great deal of relief, that the place was not entirely divorced from her former reality, though it was perhaps only distantly adjacent to it. The secretary lowered her magazine, folded it shut, and smiled.

"Your name?" Her accent, thick and husky, was decidedly southern.

"It's Lennon Carter."

The secretary nodded and keyed something into a wheezing brick of a computer that would've been sorely outdated more than a decade ago. Then she stood. "Do follow me."

Together, they walked down a long corridor where a run of stained-glass windows offered distorted glimpses of the campus beyond. There was a large square, more than two miles across, densely overgrown with live oaks and magnolias, a few scraggly palms growing low to the dirt. Set around the square were a number of old buildings, townhomes and mansions mostly.

It took Lennon a moment to identify what she was looking at as a campus, composed of the square and tall brick townhomes set around it, all of them overgrown with ivy like the phone booth where she'd first received word of Drayton. The other buildings on the square reminded her of the early work of Frank Lloyd Wright, with flat roofs low-slung over wraparound porches. Paths—which seemed like piazzas under the dense canopy of the moss-draped oak trees—threaded across the square like arteries. People—students, Lennon presumed—gathered in the sprawling courtyards between the buildings. Their attire was varied enough to dispel any notion of a strictly enforced uniform, but they were all smartly dressed, in their tailored slacks belted at the waist, well-cut blazers and thick-rimmed glasses, tastefully wrinkled linen shirts with the sleeves rolled up to the elbows.

A few of those gathered on the lawn had spread out picnic blankets and kicked off their loafers, stuffed their socks into their shoes, opting to lounge barefoot across the plush grass that carpeted the courtyards, drinking in what little sunlight shone through the dense canopy of the trees. One girl—a pretty brunette in a dark wool pencil skirt—was in the process of peeling off a pair of stockings, like a snake shedding its skin.

"Do keep up," said the secretary, without turning or even breaking pace. "You'll be late if you don't."

Lennon hastily tore her gaze from the window and kept walking. The corridor forked and she followed her guide down a narrow hall to the right. Here the floor began to slope downward more severely; the ceiling and its skylights seemed farther and farther away. For a long time, there was nothing but the sharp rataplan of the secretary's heels striking the marble floors. Lennon wondered, absently, how old she was and how she'd come to work at a place like Drayton. Surely they didn't host job fairs or run ads online or in the papers.

"This is where I leave you," said the secretary, stopping so abruptly that Lennon very nearly ran into her. She motioned to a small mahogany door near the hall's end. "Good luck."

Lennon dragged the door open and took in the lecture hall that lay beyond it—the walls paneled with hickory, the stairs steep. There were about two dozen students seated there, equipped with pencils and slim test booklets.

A petite man approached her, dressed in loose linen pants and a tunic shirt, embroidered with a tangle of brown vines along the collar. He motioned to a nearby desk. "Do sit down. The exam will begin shortly."

Baffled, Lennon took a seat beside a strikingly pretty young woman with platinum-blonde hair and a silver ring pierced through her left nostril. She was rapidly typing something into her cell phone, muttering—with a raspy vocal fry that made her sound like a pack-a-day smoker who'd come down with a particularly nasty cold—about the fact that there was no reception. Then, as if called by name, she abruptly looked up and smiled at Lennon, and Lennon, a little embarrassed to be caught staring, smiled back at her. She decided then that if they both passed the exam and stayed at Drayton, they would be friends.

She surveyed the others. There was a person with a shaved head and thick eyebrows who sat near her, scowling. A boy with an overgrown military cut sat grumbling Russian curses through his gritted teeth (based on the two semesters of rudimentary Russian Lennon had taken as part of her core curriculum in college, he seemed irritated that the test was taking so long to begin). An impeccably dressed woman—bronze skin, high cheekbones, sharp eyes—chatted in a rapid-fire exchange of whispers with the curly-haired redheaded man who sat beside her. Both looked like the kind of fashionably erudite academics Wyatt would've liked to be friends with.

At the front of the room, a panel of six proctors, split evenly into two groups of three, sat at long tables on opposite sides of the lectern. All had the demeanor of professors fresh off a long sabbatical and possessed a kind of sharkish, academic curiosity that put Lennon ill at ease. One, a sleek-haired man in a perfectly tailored tweed suit, smoked a fat terra-cotta dudeen pipe and passed it to one of his peers, a dark-skinned woman who vaguely reminded Lennon of her own mother. She accepted the pipe and took a long toke and moments later spit a lively burst of fat, dancing smoke rings.

A blonde woman seated among the proctors rose and stepped up to the lectern. She wore an off-white button-down the color of pale flesh, tucked into the waistband of a dark tweed pencil skirt. Her hair was ice-white and cut into an overgrown, but elegant, bob.

When she spoke, the room fell quiet. "My name is Eileen, and I am the vice-chancellor here at Drayton, as well as one of the six proctors of today's entry exam. It's a pleasure to welcome you to our school." A brief pause and Eileen lowered her head, as if trying to decide what she wanted to say next. "Our entry exam begins at birth, and everyone takes it. The test being administered today is merely the final step in your lifelong application process. And I warn you, it will be the most challenging."

A thin boy, who Lennon later discovered was a math prodigy from Iceland who'd bagged his first PhD in number theory at just sixteen, tapped her on the shoulder and passed her a surprisingly heavy metal mechanical pencil and a manila test booklet.

"The final portion of the entry exam is split into two phases. First, the written exam, which is before you now. It's composed of forty-five multiple-choice questions. The second and final phase of the exam is the expressive interview, wherein we will assess your ability to complete a task of our choosing. This portion of the test is not timed, though it will end at our discretion."

Lennon glanced at her peers, wondering if they found this ordeal as bizarre as she did. All of them appeared relatively calm, apart from one frail boy loudly hyperventilating in the front row.

"The fact that a pool of applicants the size of a global generation has been narrowed down to you, who sit before me now, is a remarkable triumph. Should you fail to pass this exam—and most of you will, in fact, fail—then I do hope you'll remember it as such." Eileen extended both hands to the test takers. "You may now begin."

Lennon pumped her mechanical pencil twice and opened the test booklet. There, she saw the grainy image of a young boy with tears in his eyes, taken from the shoulders up, in the style of an ID photo.

What is Nihal's predominant emotion?
a) Yearning
b) Rage
c) Shock
d) Resignation
e) None of the above

Lennon stared down at the question, confused. How was she meant to parse exactly what he was feeling from a single image? She looked up, hoping for some hint as to how she was supposed to proceed, but her fellow test takers seemed every bit as confused as she did, frowning down at their papers, their pencils dancing between answers, circling things only to erase them and try again.

She squinted down at the paper. The boy, Nihal, stared back at her, his eyes wide and watery, a webwork of veins threading through the whites. She examined the image for context clues—he looked to be about nine years old; his shirt was an ill-fitting tank top, patterned with thin stripes; his bottom lip was slightly puckered, as if caught between the teeth. But none of these details gave any indication as to exactly why Nihal was crying. Unsure of what to do, Lennon circled *A* on instinct alone and moved on to the next question.

This image featured a slight woman who appeared to be in her early thirties (give or take a few years) with a pinched, freckled nose and a painted mouth, downturned at the corners. Lennon couldn't distinguish the shade of her lipstick, given that the images on the exam were printed in black and white, but she assumed it was some shade of red. Her pale hair was gathered into a bun at the crown of her head, exposing her large ears, the stretched lobes pierced through with hoops.

What is Bianca's current state of being?
a) Arousal
b) Satisfaction
c) Listlessness
d) Despair
e) None of the above

Lennon selected *C*.

The following question featured an abstract ink painting vaguely reminiscent of the work of Pollock. The brushstrokes were so viscous and heavy-handed it was hard to catch glimpses of the white canvas beneath the smears and spatters of ink.

What is this painting meant to depict?
a) Euphoria
b) Chaos
c) Joy
d) Gluttony
e) None of the above

She circled *D*.

There was another question and an accompanying image, this one of a wizened woman.

What is Maria trying to hide?
a) Contempt
b) Lust
c) Envy
d) Grief
e) All of the above
f) None of the above

Lennon circled *C*.

Lennon pressed on, feeling increasingly disoriented, struggling to parse the expressions of the people in the images or the motivations behind the abstract artworks she was asked to scrutinize. One question featured a woman cradling a newborn baby, presumably her child, to her breast and asked the test taker to distinguish her predominant emotion (Lennon chose malice). Another question featured the crude ink drawing of a Picasso-esque face, with one pupil three times the size of the other. The image was said to represent infatuation, and the test asked its taker to identify the secondary source of inspiration behind the work (she chose *B* for dread and felt sure of her answer).

As Lennon approached the second half of the exam, her nose began to bleed. Fat droplets of blood spattered the edge of question twenty-two, causing the ink to seep and smudge so that the expression of the woman in the accompanying image was badly distorted. She had chapped lips and thinning hair. She looked like she was in her late forties, maybe.

What emotion is Anya experiencing? Choose one of the following:
a) Grief
b) Awe
c) Envy
d) Disgust
e) None of the above

Hastily she circled *E*. Her nose kept bleeding profusely, spattering the pages of the booklet as she worked through the remaining questions, one of which featured a wide-eyed man, thickly bearded, his brows knit together. There was a tattoo beneath his right eye, but the poor image quality made it impossible for Lennon to distinguish what it was.

What emotion is Lyle trying to convey?
a) Obstinacy
b) Confusion
c) Disappointment
d) Frustration
e) All of the above
f) None of the above

Lennon pinched her nose and tipped back her head in a vain attempt to stop the bleeding. It was all she could do not to gag when she tasted the blood draining, hot and thick, down the back of her throat. By some miracle she managed not to retch, and circled *C*.

Finally, she reached the last question: a dizzying image of countless hand-drawn concentric circles shrinking to a near-imperceptible axis at the center of the page.

What is this image meant to convey?
a) Ecstasy
b) Humiliation
c) Gratitude
d) Anxiety
e) Jubilance
f) None of the above

Lennon wiped away the last of her nosebleed and circled *B* with seconds left to spare.

"Pencils down," said Eileen, stepping up to the lectern. As she did, all five of the other proctors rose in practiced tandem, and began to climb the steps of the amphitheater, collecting the test booklets as they went. One boy—broad-shouldered and sharp-eyed and sitting toward the back—kept circling answers in a hasty attempt to finish the exam, and as a result was immediately ousted by the same man who owned the dudeen pipe, dismissed with a hissing whisper and a finger pointed toward a dark door at the top of the stairs that Lennon hadn't noticed before.

There were, in fact, many things she hadn't noticed. Like, for example, the fact that the room had emptied considerably during the evaluation. More than two-thirds of those who were originally present at the beginning of the exam were now, inexplicably, gone. Lennon hadn't seen or heard their departures.

Those remaining were led to a small waiting room up a flight of stairs and down another narrow passageway, this one lined on either wall with floor-to-ceiling bookshelves that were packed to capacity with old leather-bound tomes. The place smelled of dust and horse glue. From there, they were ushered into a kind of parlor. Its walls were paneled with dark wood and heavy green curtains were drawn across its only window. There was a fire dancing in the hearth, though it wasn't nearly cold enough to warrant one.

The test takers were supplied with a few refreshments—small buttermilk biscuits with raspberry jam and pats of butter molded into the shape of flowers, sliced peaches with whipped cream, and sparkling water in ceramic bowls that tasted of rosemary and minerals. Lennon ignored the biscuits but had her fill of fruit and drank several bowls of water in the minutes before she was called into a private testing room down the hall.

Here there were no proctors or lecterns. No fellow test takers. The door groaned shut behind her, and Lennon was left alone in a large, sparsely furnished classroom. The far wall of the room was consumed almost entirely by a clean, green chalkboard. In front of it, an empty chair and a mahogany desk. At the center of the classroom, another single desk and chair, facing its larger counterpart.

Opposite the door Lennon entered through was a stained-glass window left slightly ajar. There were students gathered in the courtyard below, and she caught snippets of their conversation. They were rigorously—and with raised voices—debating some philosophical matter that pertained to the immateriality of the mind.

Unsure of what she was supposed to do, Lennon stalled there by the door for some time, waiting for directions from one of the proctors who'd overseen the first portion of the exam. But they never showed up. Instead, after a few long minutes that felt like hours, a man she didn't recognize entered. He was slim, and tall enough to need to duck a bit when he walked through the door. His jaw was sharp and faintly stubbled with the ghost of a beard, like he'd intended to shave that morning but had forgotten. His hair too was shorn short. His skin was a rich bronze. Lennon guessed he was about Wyatt's age, give or take a few years. He was covered in tattoos. The backs of both of his hands were tattooed with moths, and the imagery was repeated on the hard planes of his neck. The moths on his hands had their wings, but a few of the ones on his neck had had their wings ripped from their thoraxes. The imagery was grotesque enough to make Lennon squirm.

The man drew the door shut, frowning slightly, his blunt brows drawn together. He made no apologies for his lateness. Barely registered Lennon when he spoke. "You have a name?" His voice bore what she guessed was a faint Brooklyn accent, though she wasn't sure.

"It's Lennon."

His gaze flickered to her. He looked, for the briefest moment, startled. But he recovered himself quickly, extended a hand covered in tattoos. "Dante."

Lennon shook it. His palm was calloused. "Nice to meet you."

Dante walked to the desk at the head of the room and shrugged off his trench coat, draping it across the back of the chair. He set his briefcase on the floor beside the desk. His shoes were brown leather oxfords, mud stuck to the soles. He nodded to the other, smaller desk that stood opposite his. "Sit."

Lennon obeyed, and stepped into the center of the room and slipped into her seat behind the desk. It was so small her knees pressed painfully against the underside of the tabletop. It seemed like it was built for a child.

Dante settled himself in the chair behind the desk and reached into the inner pocket of his blazer, withdrawing a crude, fat little pig figurine with three stubby legs (two in the front, one in the back) and deep holes for eyes. He set it down on the desk, facing Lennon. "This is the expressive portion of the entry exam," said Dante. "Your task is to make me lift this figurine without leaving your desk or touching me. Understood?"

Lennon nodded, swallowed nothing. Outside, a drizzling rain began to fall, and the students gathered in the courtyard hastily collected their things and retreated indoors.

"Let's begin," said Dante.

Lennon blinked. At a loss, she said: "Um . . . would you lift the pig? Please?"

"I said *make* me lift it. Not ask me to."

Lennon didn't know what he meant by that (what was she supposed to do, produce a gun from thin air and order him to lift the pig with a finger hooked over the trigger?) but didn't dare ask. Instead, she focused her attention on the pig, wondered at its origins. Its ears were perky, and Lennon imagined its creator forming them, carefully pinching wet clay between thumb and forefinger and affixing its curlicue tail before ushering it into the oven, where it would bake and blacken until the soft earth hardened into scorched terra-cotta.

"You're trying to reach me," said Dante. "Not the pig."

Lennon raised her gaze, observed him the way she had the photographs during the previous phase of the exam. The terrain of his face told stories. There was a silvery scar to the left of his cupid's bow, near the corner of his mouth—a busted lip poorly stitched? Lennon couldn't place his race but could tell that, like her, he was mostly Black but mixed with something else. White, maybe?

Dante endured her scrutiny without expression. His hands remained motionless, palms flush to the desk, flanking the pig figurine. But she noticed a slight fissuring in the stone façade of his expression. He looked almost . . . disappointed. He checked his watch; it was dull brass with a brown leather strap, and Lennon swore its face was painted to resemble a woman. "This is a waste of time."

A sudden pang of anger pulsed through her, so sharp it snatched the breath right out of her lungs.

Everything, she realized then, had been leading up to this. This one chance at a success so great it could make up for her countless failings. All that stood between her and success was the smug man sitting in front of her and that *fucking* pig figurine. Lennon would make him lift it. She *had* to make him lift it. She refused to crawl back to Wyatt with her tail tucked between her legs, fresh off yet another failure. In the moment, her desperation grew so dire she felt like her survival and her success at Drayton were near synonymous. And though she didn't know it then, she was right.

Lennon felt a kind of stirring, a trembling pressure that built behind her sternum, like the drone of bumblebees or a phone ringing on vibrate. It spread through her chest and into her limbs, numbing them, then traveled to her head, thrumming incessantly behind her eyes until her vision doubled, both Dante and the figurine standing on the desk in front of him duplicated, then tripled. Her nose began to bleed again, more profusely than it had the last time, spattering the desk, which was shuddering violently, both chair and table rattling in unison. But then she realized, with mounting horror, that it wasn't the desk that was shaking . . . it was *her*.

Somewhere down the hall, or in the distant recesses of her own mind, she swore she heard the chime of an elevator's bell.

Dante's fingers twitched. He flexed them.

The seizing grew more severe, and Lennon feared she would be sick, or scream, or lose herself to the throes of a passion so complete she wasn't sure she'd survive it. Passion turned to pain. Her ears began to ring, and she realized that this was the pain that Benedict had warned her of. She kept shaking and gripped the edges of the desk with white-knuckled desperation to keep herself from being thrown out of it.

Dante's hand shifted across the desk, inching toward the figurine, and Lennon gritted her teeth so hard she thought the molars at the back of her mouth might crack. Her vision came back into focus and her shaking dulled to a tremor as she gazed into Dante's eyes with silent urging. The intangible force of her will moving across the classroom.

The rain came down harder.

Dante's hand peeled away from the desk and hovered, shaking, a few inches above the pig, then he seized it in a jerky motion reminiscent of an arcade claw machine fastening its metal fingers around a stuffed toy. He lifted the figurine a few inches above the desk, his eyes on Lennon, then dropped it abruptly as though it had burned him.

The pig bounced twice, struck the floor—its snout breaking on impact—and rolled across the classroom, stopping just short of Lennon's sneaker. She leaned out of the desk to pick it up. It was heavier than it looked, and the scorched clay was rough to the touch.

Lennon raised her gaze to Dante again, parting her lips to ask him whether she'd passed the exam, but her tongue remained, limp and useless, like a small dead animal at the basin of her mouth. The exhaustion hit her then and she collapsed back into her chair, dizzy and utterly spent.

Dante eyed her for a beat longer, then nodded, first to himself then at Lennon, as if to admit defeat. In his eyes, something close to contempt. "Congratulations on your acceptance to Drayton."

5

LENNON SUFFERED A series of four seizures in the hours that followed the entrance exam. The first, the worst of the four, on the floor of the classroom at Dante's feet. The second in his arms as he carried her, thrashing, to the infirmary, where she suffered two more. Lennon, for her part, recalled next to none of this. What she did remember came in fractured dreams of scorched concrete and the sour aroma of trash left to rot in the summer sun. In her sticky hand, a thawing freeze cup popsicle, red juice leaking like blood through a crack in the Styrofoam rim. Across the street, in the fuzzy reflection of a car window, the aberration looked eyeless and unspeaking.

The dream changed again, homed in on the campus of Drayton, and she saw a boy, followed him as he walked barefoot across the lush lawn until he reached the porch of a fine house with shuttered windows. He raised a fist and knocked on the doors, over and over again, until his knuckles blackened and split, exposing a glimpse of white bone below.

When she woke the following morning, it was to an entirely

different boy sitting upright in the hospital bed beside hers. He was much older than the boy she'd dreamed of, with eyebrows so thick they very nearly met above his nose and long brown hair, which he wore tucked behind both of his pink ears. Something in his manner reminded Lennon of a very malnourished mouse. There was an old book spread open in his lap; a plastic inhaler stuck out of the middle pages, a kind of makeshift bookmark.

"You're up," he said, without the vaguest trace of concern. "I was beginning to think you were dead. Or dying."

Lennon squinted past him, her eyes slow to adjust to the sunlight. The space—a large room that reminded Lennon of the orphanage dormitories in historical films—had a run of wrought-iron cots, twelve on each side, facing one another. All of them empty. The ceiling domed into a large skylight, warm sun casting in through it.

On the far wall was a bowed oriel window that looked out onto an overgrown courtyard. There were flowers there, flocked with butterflies, and strange statues—the suggestion of a human body, rendered in tangled wire, glass-blown orbs that resembled animals . . . or perhaps organs.

"Where am I?" said Lennon hoarsely. Wincing, she dragged herself into a sitting position. Her body felt like one gigantic sprain. Every movement hurt, even breathing.

"You're at Drayton," said the boy, and he flipped the page of his book. She decided, reluctantly, that he was handsome, but it took some squinting to really see it because he looked so sick and pale. "The doctor will be back soon so you can ask him all of your pressing questions."

Lennon swallowed with a grimace, tasting blood and sour spit. There was a glass of water on the table between the two beds and she reached for it. It had a mineral taste, and it was slightly carbonated, the bubbles burning a bit when she rinsed her mouth, gargled, and spit the water back into the glass. It was rusty with blood. She tested the raw wound on the inside of her cheek with the tip of her tongue and realized she must've bitten it while she was knocked out. "How long have I been out?"

"Not long," said the boy, and he gave a rattling cough, tugged the inhaler free of the pages of his book, and pulled on the mouthpiece the way you'd smoke a pipe. He took a few hoarse breaths, recovered himself. "Dr. Lowe dumped you here last night after your seizure—"

"I had a *seizure*?" That explained the body aches, at least.

"Four seizures, actually. You were out cold by the time you were admitted. I'm not surprised you don't remember. You were in rough shape. But it's nothing to be ashamed of. I had an asthma attack in the middle of my entry exam. Thought for sure I'd failed."

"You're a student here?" Lennon asked.

The boy nodded, didn't look up from his book. "Sawyer. Second year."

"Lennon," she said. "Is there a bathroom around here? Someplace I can wash up?"

"You should really wait for the doctor."

"Well, I'm not going to," said Lennon, swinging her legs out of bed. "I feel like shit, and I smell even worse."

Sawyer nodded to the other end of the room. "Down the hall to the right."

The bathroom, like the infirmary, was empty. There was a run of wood-walled toilet stalls, basin sinks in sterile white porcelain. On a shelf near the showers were towels, disposable toothbrushes wrapped in plastic, crude-cut cubes of lye soap, and other toiletries. In the small mirror above one of the sinks, she caught her reflection. Apart from the blood crusted beneath her nose, she looked better than she'd expected to, given how badly her muscles ached. The bags that perpetually shadowed her eyes had faded considerably. The aberration with no eyes was nowhere to be seen.

Lennon stripped out of her hospital gown and limped into an open shower stall with a slick tile floor. She bathed with a rough washcloth and a heavy brick of lye soap that smelled like jasmine. As she washed, taking care to rinse the blood from beneath her nose, she felt she was slowly reassembling the pieces of her person, but differently than the way she'd been assembled before.

When she finished showering, she stepped out into the empty cavern of the bathroom. On the countertop were the same T-shirt, shorts, bra, and socks she'd been wearing yesterday, folded and freshly laundered. Her sneakers looked like they'd been replaced, the soles scrubbed clean with a toothbrush. Careful to avoid making eye contact with her own reflection, for fear of seeing the aberration, Lennon dressed quickly and returned to the infirmary to discover that Sawyer was gone. In his place was a doctor stripping the sheets off the cot that Lennon had been lying in. He was a willowy man but rather short; his lab coat brushed mere inches above the tiles as he crossed the infirmary and thrust out a hand by way of greeting. His fingers were long and bluish, sparsely furred, with gray hair between the knuckles. "Lennon, good to see you on your feet. I'm Dr. Nave."

Lennon shook it. His grip was very firm.

"Sit, please." He patted the freshly stripped mattress. "Let me have a look at you."

Lennon obeyed, and the doctor took her vitals. He produced a glass thermometer from the ink-stained pocket of his lab coat and held it under her tongue for some time. It tasted slightly sweet, as though it had been dipped in simple syrup. He then pressed two cold fingertips into the soft hollow of her wrist and nodded along to the rhythm of her heart with his eyes tightly shut. "Do you still have your name?" he asked.

"It's Lennon Carter."

Dr. Nave released her wrist and opened his eyes. He held up a finger, just in front of her nose, moved it left. "Follow my finger."

Lennon's gaze tracked left, then cut right again, following Dr. Nave's finger, only for him to move it to the left once again. She was beginning to feel a little dizzy. "You're twelve years old standing on the shores of Edisto Beach, on the coast of South Carolina. What do you see in the distance?"

As he said this, the memory came to her. "A blue heron flying low over the water. It was sunset, I think, and its wings looked touched with fire."

Dr. Nave smiled. He lowered his hand. "Good. Very good."

"What happened to me yesterday?"

"You suffered a series of seizures. One of them a grand mal."

"No, I mean before. When I was taking the entry exam. What was that?"

"From what I hear, you persuaded our Dr. Lowe to pick up a pig figurine. Quite an impressive feat indeed. Dr. Lowe is rather strong-willed—"

"But it was more than that. I *made* him pick it up."

Dr. Nave smiled at her. "So you did."

From the ink-stained pocket of his lab coat, he produced a small pen (pausing to tear the cap off with his teeth) and accompanying notebook and scribbled something indecipherable. "Vitals are good," he said around the cap of the pen. "You're free to go."

"Go where, exactly?"

"Well . . . I'd imagine you'd want to make your way to the assembly. It's mandatory, you know."

Lennon did not, in fact, know. "Where is it? And when?"

The doctor capped his pen, folded his notebook, and slipped both of them back into his coat pocket. He checked his watch. "You'll have missed the first part already. It started at two. But the auditorium is only a five-minute walk from here, so if you leave now you should make it in time to hear the bulk of it. You'll want to take the stairway to the left down to the first floor. Hang a tight left and keep walking down the breezeway until you reach it. It's big; you can't miss it."

Following the doctor's instructions, Lennon left the infirmary and stepped into a crowded corridor. Opposite her was a run of floor-to-ceiling windows that looked out onto a lush campus crawling with students. She watched from above as two orientation leaders, dressed in loose slacks and tweed blazers, steered a swelling tide of incoming first years, clinging anxiously to crumpled maps and instruction pamphlets that must've been distributed when Lennon was out cold in the infirmary.

The orientation leaders were walking backward, pointing at different buildings, pausing to answer questions. Lennon wished she could hear them and wondered how much she'd missed during her stint in the infirmary. Classes hadn't even started yet, and she already felt behind.

After a short walk, she arrived at the doors of the auditorium, which, to Lennon's surprise, took the form of a large stone cathedral. Its interior was like that of an old and ornate movie theater. The seats were a dark and dingy velvet, and almost all of them were taken. The stale air smelled of popcorn and cigarette smoke. On a stage at the front of the room, with her back to the velvet curtains, was Eileen—the vice-chancellor, who had been at the entry exam. At the sight of Lennon, she broke into an easy smile. She was somehow even more beautiful up close. "Ms. Carter, so nice of you to join us."

Dozens of gazes affixed themselves to Lennon.

"Do have a seat," said Eileen. "We were just getting started."

Lennon walked down the center aisle, to one of the only empty seats in the auditorium, about three rows down from the stage. She shuffled sideways past her peers and claimed a seat between two girls she thought she might recognize from the entry exam.

Once Lennon was seated, Eileen raised the microphone to her mouth. "We've prepared a short film for you to watch. Please give it your full attention."

Eileen sidestepped. The curtains parted down the middle and pulled apart, revealing a large movie screen. The lights dimmed, then cut entirely, plunging the room into a darkness so complete Lennon couldn't see her own hands shaking in her lap. An image appeared on the movie screen behind Eileen. It was a black-and-white photograph of Savannah, Georgia, which looked remarkably similar to the Savannah of modern day—though the oaks weren't as large and the cobbled streets were crowded not with cars but horse-drawn carriages.

"There is a pervasive myth that the city of Savannah was built around twenty-four historic garden squares. But that fact is a careful warping of the true history. Savannah is actually home to twenty-five historic squares. Drayton Square, this school's namesake, was not lost to time but carefully extracted from it."

The slides switched to the image of a bearded white man with a well-waxed mustache.

"This is my great-great-grandfather and the founder of our school, John Drayton," said Eileen in that clear baritone of hers that reminded Lennon vaguely of a transatlantic accent. "In the wake of the Civil War, after most of the south was razed down to the very stones of its foundation, John Drayton turned the mansion of Drayton Square into the Drayton All Boys School, a haven for war orphans."

The slideshow skipped to the crude photo of a mansion overlooking a large garden green.

"A philosopher by trade, a Quaker by practice, and a tireless abolitionist"—Eileen delivered this part with a note of pride, the edges of her mouth curving into a small smile as she beamed up at the image of her grandfather—"John Drayton built his school with one goal in mind: he wanted his students to embody the Socratic ideal of a good man. The kind of man who could win the hearts of other men, and in doing so change the world for the better. Men whose great minds and charisma could negotiate peace in times of war, and usher us into a new golden age of liberty, pacifism, and fairness for all." Here Eileen paused, gave the audience a wry smile: "Perhaps he was a little ambitious."

There was a bit of laughter and Eileen changed slides again, this time to a series of grainy photos of the Civil War: raised muskets, fields dotted with bodies, the earth upturned and ravaged by artillery fire.

"To carry out this mission, John knew that he would need a handful of extraordinarily special boys. So, in the years that followed, John recruited what he called 'exceptional specimens' from across the Americas, Europe, and even the Caribbean. His recruits traveled far and wide, seeking young boys of, quote, 'exceptional charisma, great intelligence, and formidable poise.'"

There was a grainy photo of Drayton and his boys—knobby-kneed youths who stood with their hands behind their backs, eyes cut narrow against the sun. None of them appeared particularly charismatic or special. They stood in a line, shoulder to shoulder, unsmiling, like soldiers disguised as schoolboys. All of them were white except for one boy—fair-skinned with brown curls—who stood at the far end of the line, just apart from the others. Unlike his peers, he wore no uniform. His shirt—several sizes too large—looked moth-eaten, and his feet were bare.

"What John learned through the tutoring of these exceptional boys was that there are those among us who possess a particularly keen talent for the art of persuasion. In the same way that some newborns shriek louder than others, and some women possess more beauty than that which others are born to, John discovered that some human beings—whether blessed or cursed I cannot say—possess the rare and heightened ability to persuade the natural world into complying with their will."

The slideshow flashed to the image of one of Drayton's boys, hands outstretched as if conducting an orchestra. Three boys stood in front of him, limbs bent strangely but in a way that seemed to correspond with the placement of the first boy's fingers.

"Through observing some of the most talented pupils at his school, John learned that this persuasive talent could be honed, allowing particularly gifted individuals to force their will not just upon other human beings, but in rare cases, upon matter itself."

The slideshow flickered to the next photo, this one of a boy in a classroom with a small nub of chalk levitating a few inches above the palm of his hand.

"As you can likely imagine, this gift of persuasion attracted the attention of many forces far beyond the bounds of Drayton. John's gifted boys became both a threat and a spectacle, and it seemed that everyone wanted to use the remarkable talents of his students to achieve their own ends. There was talk of war and money, rebellion and discord, demands and arrests and the kinds of threats that manifest in violence. So, to protect his boys, and the sacred forces they studied, John Drayton enlisted the help of one of his most prodigious pupils. A boy by the name of William Irvine."

The slideshow changed to an image of the poorly dressed boy. He had wide eyes and a bleeding nose. He stood in a hallway so long that it looked almost infinite, and there were dozens of identical doors on either side. The door closest to the boy was half ajar, and it opened onto a beach, the sand dark and strung with seaweed. Just a few doors down from that, on the opposite side of the hall, another door opened out onto a snow-capped mountain range.

"William was the first and last student of Drayton with the ability to create entire worlds unto themselves, using his persuasive ability to open doors to new realities and close them to contain spaces, sequester them from the greater world at large. This is exactly what William did here, at the Twenty-Fifth Square. In what is perhaps one of the greatest feats of persuasion ever committed, he erased Drayton Square from the minds and memories of all who knew of it. Removed it from the historical record, and from reality itself. The only memories left intact were those of a handful of trusted pupils and the descendants of John Drayton himself, who were entrusted with protecting this secret and passing it down to future generations and classes of students."

Here, Eileen turned quite grave. The slideshow flickered to a more recent photo of Drayton, taken in a wide corridor between moss-draped oak trees. "This powerful act of persuasion came with a cost. William died protecting this school—channeling all of the energy of his life and spirit into the task of raising the very walls that now fortify us today, within the long-forgotten and forever-hidden Twenty-Fifth Square of Savannah."

The house lights flickered on. The movie screen retracted. Eileen stepped forward as the curtains behind her swept closed once more. There was a smattering of applause as she stepped to center stage. "Here, safe and in secret, we devote ourselves to the continuation of John Drayton's legacy. The study of persuasion."

6

AFTER THE ASSEMBLY adjourned, a handful of upperclassmen led the first years to Ethos College, the residential dorm where they'd be staying. They walked along a slate path, the tiles slippery with moss, cutting through the gardens and the breezeways that ran between buildings. Ethos College sat on a wide fog-washed green overlooking a grove of magnolia trees. It was composed of four conjoined townhomes with slanted tin roofs and tall stained-glass windows. Taking it in, Lennon felt as though she were walking through the trappings of a dream that wasn't hers. It was an odd feeling, to have such a loose grasp on one's own reality. Her thoughts seemed entirely scattered, a fistful of sand tossed to the wind.

The foyer of the college was empty, and dim to the point of being dark, but she was almost immediately greeted with the lively din of conversation, the mingling aromas of fresh bread and cigarette smoke. To the left was a welcome desk, with a girl about her age seated behind it, her face alight with the artificial glow of the computer monitor in front of her. The other students dispersed—heading to their dorms, presumably—leaving Lennon and the girl alone. She called out from across the hall, her voice echoing. "Your name?"

Lennon gave it, edging up to the desk.

The girl, whose name (according to the tag pinned to her lapel) was Allison, keyed something into the computer, her manicured nails clicking as they connected with the plastic buttons. "Welcome to Ethos College."

What followed was a brief overview of the college. From Allison, Lennon learned that Drayton's approach to housing was rather old-fashioned in that each of its colleges (except one) were separated by gender. Those who fell between (there were several genderqueer students among their cohort) were allowed to select the housing they felt most comfortable with.

There were, according to Allison, three residential colleges on Drayton's campus: Ethos, Pathos, and Logos, named after Socrates's three rhetorical appeals. Logos was the smallest of the three, the only coed college and the most exclusive, as it housed only a handful of Drayton's most promising students. It was a self-governing college and as such its inhabitants retained special privileges, like the ability to leave the campus when they wanted to. As a rule, nonmembers were forbidden from entering Logos without a formal invitation from a resident. As a result, few of those in Drayton had ever entered through the courtyard gates. Fewer still had been formally invited to live and study there.

The boys' college, Pathos, was on the southern end of the Twenty-Fifth Square, whereas Ethos was on its northern end. Each of these residences was equipped with a kitchen and dining room, where students could take their meals at any hour of the day (meals at Drayton tended to occur at unusual times—breakfasts were often taken well past midday, lunch in the late hours of the night, and dinner often lapsed into the wee hours of the early morning).

All of the dorms of Ethos College were in the west wing of the building, on the other side of the greater common areas. Lennon walked past a large dining room, with wood-rafter ceilings and a long banquet table. In a small study just down the hall, a few students sat smoking and talking in hushed tones.

The residential wing of Ethos had a decidedly homey quality. Its wood floors were laid with plush Persian runners, the walls lined with well-stocked bookshelves. Allison showed Lennon to her room, at the end of a long corridor. It was sensibly furnished and entirely symmetrical: two beds, two desks, two overstuffed armchairs standing in front of a small hearth. There were even two oak wardrobes, filled with clothes (Lennon would later discover that all of them were tailored to her specific measurements).

Sitting cross-legged on the edge of the bed to the left was a girl that Lennon immediately recognized from the entry exam, the pretty one with the nose ring, which she'd since removed. She had long hair that fell in feathery layers about her shoulders. She was slim, with slightly vacant blue eyes, and she had a gap between her two front teeth that was just wide enough to slide a quarter through. Lennon imagined doing just that, imagined the girl swallowing down the coin, where, in the pit of her stomach, it would be digested. *How might I assist you?* the girl might've asked, in the cheery and robotic monotone of an AI helper.

Looking at her, Lennon thought that almost every girl who had ever lived—every teenager clawing through the bowels of the internet, every middle-aged woman armed with a diet plan and a prayer, every awkward girl who'd sat alone at lunch—had hoped to look like some iteration of her, if only because it would make life that much easier.

"I'm Blaine," said the girl, her voice gravelly.

"And I'm Lennon."

"From the entry exam. We sat across from each other."

"I remember you," Lennon said. Blaine wasn't the type that anyone would easily forget. In fact, no one she'd met at Drayton was. Every person she'd encountered so far fell along the spectrum of peculiar, striking, or egregiously attractive, and she couldn't help but think this was intentional.

"You looked like you knew what you were doing on that exam," said Blaine.

"I have a decent poker face."

Blaine laughed. "How'd you end up here?"

Lennon would come to recognize this question as the standard introduction among Drayton students and alumni, who relished trading stories about the strange and impossible ways they'd first come to the campus. Eager to share her story, Lennon told Blaine about the anachronistic telephone booth in the parking lot of the abandoned mall, about Benedict and the elevator that had carried her up to the eighth floor of his two-story house, how its doors had opened to Drayton.

Blaine, as it turned out, was a hospice nurse who worked at a facility in Chicago. She was French by birth but had grown up in the Midwest. She'd received news of her consideration via a call that came through late at night. The voice of her dead grandfather relayed a series of coordinates that led her to a diner just a few blocks from her apartment. There she was greeted by a woman. "She was old, my grandfather's age, dressed too warm for the weather. Wearing all black. She was expecting me. Said I was late."

Unlike Lennon's interview with Benedict, Blaine's interview was brief, and within fifteen minutes she passed and was ordered to board the L and get off at a stop that, according to Blaine, didn't exist. At least, she thought it didn't exist until the empty train cab stopped, abruptly, at an abandoned platform. When she took the elevator up to what she thought was street level, she found herself in Drayton instead. "I thought I was going insane."

"So did I," said Lennon, and there was a crack of thunder. She looked to the window and saw that it had started to rain. "What was the entry exam like for you?"

"Strange," said Blaine, and she looked a little haunted. "The written portion was weird enough, all of those faces. They started blurring together at the end."

"And what about the second half, the expressive interview? What were you asked to do?"

"Make a man slap himself," she said.

"Did you do it?"

"Nope. I couldn't even get him to raise his hand. But his thumb twitched, and since I'm still here I'm guessing that counts for something."

This was news to Lennon. She'd assumed that everyone who was admitted into Drayton had passed because they'd succeeded in fulfilling the request of their proctor. Dante had framed the final portion of the exam as the only thing that stood between her and admittance. Failure to complete the task had seemed synonymous with rejection. Maybe Dante was particularly harsh. Or perhaps Blaine had scored higher on the written exam, so that her admittance wasn't entirely dependent on passing the expressive portion.

"What about you?" Blaine inquired. "What did they want you to do?"

"There was a man, Dante. I think he's a professor here. He took a pig figurine from his pocket and asked me to make him lift it."

"And did you?"

Lennon nodded. "But I don't know how. Something came over me. Or him. I'm not sure. In the end, he lifted the pig, and I blacked out. Apparently, it was some sort of seizure."

"Damn," said Blaine, but she said it with an edge. Was it jealousy that Lennon saw in her eyes? Or was she mistaken?

In the awkward silence that followed, Lennon half turned to her own bed and saw that there was a thick leather folder, embossed with her name, lying at the foot of it. She picked it up and flipped the cover open. There was a letter for her there, handwritten on thick cardstock, which smelled faintly of ammonia. It read:

Dear Lennon,

It is our great honor to accept you into Drayton College. As part of our admissions agreement, we ask for a minimum of two consecutive years, during which time you will study here on Drayton's campus, under the tutelage of some of the brightest academics in the Western Hemisphere, who will personally oversee your studies.

At the discretion of our faculty but depending entirely upon your academic performance and conduct on campus, your tenure may be either lengthened or shortened. Upon graduating you will receive a large stipend, befitting of a graduate of Drayton's caliber, as well as a position befitting your specific skill set. We trust that with time and dedication to your studies, you will be a worthy addition to our school.

We wish you the best.

Sincerely,
The Chancellor

Lennon flipped to the next page in the pamphlet. It was a map of the campus. Drayton, as it turned out, was more extensive than Lennon originally assumed it to be. Its grounds included several large gardens, an Olympic-sized swimming pool, an observatory, and several other amenities. The next page featured her class schedule. It detailed a rigorous eighteen-credit-hours semester that included courses in abnormal psychology, ethics, mindfulness and meditation, and of course the study of persuasion.

Lennon frowned. The classes were strange, certainly not what she would've expected from an institution like Drayton. And she was disappointed to see the name of the man, Dante (or Dr. Lowe, as Sawyer had called him), who'd administered the last half of her entry exam among the list of instructors.

She held up the schedule for Blaine to see. "We don't get to choose the classes we take?"

"Not during our first semester," said Blaine. "My advisor, Eileen, told me all the first years have the same course schedule. Apparently, the standardized curriculum allows them to evaluate the strengths and weaknesses of the incoming class more objectively."

"Your advisor is Eileen? The vice-chancellor?"

"The very one."

"You must be special."

The girl shrugged. "I like to think so."

Lennon flipped to the next page of the folder and discovered a detailed schedule that accounted for almost every hour of the next several days. Among the listed activities—orientation, campus tours, brunches, luncheons, and a convocation garden party—she had an appointment to meet with her advisor, Dr. Dante Lowe, at two thirty p.m. (sharp). With a wave of dread, Lennon checked the clock hanging on the wall above the desk.

The time was 2:42 p.m. She was late.

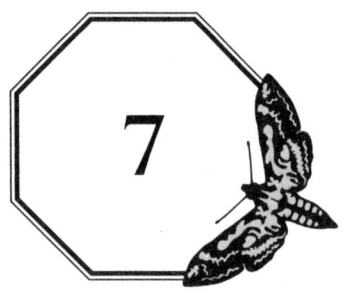

7

LENNON RAN THROUGH the pouring rain and caught Dante just as he was leaving his office. "I'm sorry I'm late," she sputtered. "I didn't get to my dorm until after two, and no one told me we had this meeting—"

He turned to look at her. He had a cigarette in his mouth, which he was in the process of lighting with a match. "What meeting?"

"This one." She opened her folder, which she'd used as a makeshift umbrella as she dashed across the campus, rifled through the damp papers, withdrew the schedule, and held it out for him to see. It was wet, and the ink was bleeding. "It says—"

"I can read," said Dante. "Come in."

He led her down a narrow hall and into a small waiting room where a group of three students sat, talking in whispers. There was a lanky boy with ice-blond hair who was so pale Lennon was actually concerned for his well-being. Beside him, a boy who was his opposite in every way, except in frame and height—dark skin, dark hair, dark eyes, enviably long lashes. Lennon immediately guessed he was Nigerian and was right—she had an eye for these things. Next to him, a scowling girl who glared at Lennon from behind a pair of thick-rimmed, but decidedly chic, glasses. All of them wore the same blue jacket embroidered with an ouroboros.

Their conversation lulled when Dante and Lennon entered the waiting room, though whether this was because of her or Dante she couldn't say.

"Wait here," said Dante, heading down the hall. And then, to the group whispering at the other edge of the waiting room: "Be nice."

The three of them nodded and—still ignoring Lennon—resumed talking among themselves. "Have you decided who you're voting for, Kieran?"

The blond, Kieran, rolled his eyes. "No one if I could."

"Well, George seems like a promising prospect."

"He's a sycophant," said the girl. "Besides, he pissed himself in my first-year persuasion class. Sawyer's a better candidate. Stronger."

"Stronger?" Kieran demanded, raising his faint eyebrows. "You can't be serious. Even if it was possible to pry him out of the library—and that's a big *if*—he can't scale a flight of stairs without triggering a fucking asthma attack."

"Strong in *spirit*," retorted the girl, who was called Yumi. "I mean, I don't like him either—"

"No one does," said the other boy, who Lennon later learned was named Adan. "But that doesn't detract from his talent. If anything, it makes him more impressive."

Yumi rolled her eyes. "He's a waste of time."

They weren't faculty—that much was apparent to Lennon—but they were certainly more self-assured than the average student. The tell was not the ease with which they carried themselves, but the urgency, the decisive air of important people with important places they needed to be.

Adan picked idly at his fingernail. "Emerson said the newcomers have some talent."

"Did she now?" Kieran's gaze wandered languidly over to Lennon. "Is that true?"

Lennon, startled, turned to look over her shoulder to see if he was speaking to someone else. "Me?"

"Yes, you." He repeated his question. "Is it true?"

"Is what true?"

"Is there any talent in the new year?"

"How would she know?" Adan demanded. "She clearly just got here. Who's your advisor?"

"Him," she said, nodding down the hall toward Dante's office.

Yumi's mouth gaped open. She looked absolutely affronted. Personally offended, as if Lennon had just insulted her. "Professor *Lowe*?"

Lennon nodded.

"But the admin office said he doesn't take new candidates," said Yumi, looking as though Lennon had stolen something that belong to her. "I tried to apply to him last semester—"

"Not taking new students and not taking you are two entirely different things," said Adan.

"But I got a mark of distinction on my Persuasion II class—"

Kieran rolled his eyes. "Nobody gives a shit about that. If you're not Emerson, or, I guess, her for whatever reason"—the boy gave Lennon a lingering and contemptuous glare, as if he was struggling to parse out whatever it was that made her so important—"then I doubt he's interested."

Just then, as though on cue, Dante reemerged from his office down the hall and gestured for Lennon. She got up rather gracelessly, collecting her folder to her chest.

Dante's office was more of a tightly contained library, really. Every available inch of wall space, and half of the floor, was devoted to books. There were so many of them, neatly organized into stacks, and Lennon could tell—based on the broken spines and the bare hardcovers without dust jackets—that they'd been read and reread many times over. It was a collection curated out of love, and not for show. There was a hearth, crowded between two bookshelves, more books stacked up on the mantle, a few of them open, others closed over pens and receipts, the flattened boxes of cigarettes and other makeshift bookmarks. In one corner of the room, a well-stocked bar cart. In another, a potted palm. Before the fireplace, a long brown leather sofa, standing low to the ground on wooden legs as thin as pencils. And, of course, there was a desk, with chairs on either side of equal size. Standing at its left corner, in the shadow of a computer monitor, was the three-legged pig she'd compelled Dante to lift during the entry exam.

Lennon sat in the chair in front of the desk, and she expected Dante to fill the seat opposite her, but he remained standing. She was taken with him, she could admit that to herself, and she observed—with an almost clinical detachment—the familiar rhythms of her attraction: the fluttering in the pit of the stomach, a feeling like static in the fingers, a pull toward what she knew she couldn't have, which made her desire all the more intense. But as Lennon examined the sensation of that attraction, she became aware too that she was afraid of him, terribly afraid without really knowing why. She felt caught between the two opposing instincts—attraction and fear—as if shackled by either wrist and dragged apart, until she felt ready to rip down the middle.

Dante finally took a seat on the opposite side of the desk. He pressed a button on his phone. It began to ring. "Do you have any dietary restrictions?"

"I . . . no? But I'm not hungry."

"Yes, you are," he said, and it was rather dickish of him to tell her what she did or didn't feel. But he was, annoyingly, right.

A man's voice sounded over the line. "Yes, Dr. Lowe?"

"Could you bring us up two sandwiches? Whatever they have."

"Of course."

The phone line went dead, Dante eyed her, and Lennon wondered, in passing, exactly what he saw when he did. What did he make of her, and was it any different than what she made of herself?

"Any questions?" he asked. "You look confused."

Lennon was quiet for a moment. "Is it magic? Real magic, I mean."

"That depends on who you ask."

"I'm asking you."

"Then no. I wouldn't call it that."

"What would you call it?"

"The remarkable strength of the human will."

"And that's it? This whole school is devoted to the study of forcing people, and I guess sometimes things, to do stuff?"

"That's a succinct, if facetious, way of explaining it." Dante tapped his cigarette on the edge of the ashtray. He'd been forgetting to smoke it. Lennon took this as a good sign. He was engaged, and that came as a relief, because she felt the urgent need not to bore him. "Persuasion of other living creatures forms the bedrock of what we study here. Most students will never proceed beyond that. However, a select handful of particularly talented persuasionists possess greater abilities. Like, for example, the ability to persuade matter."

"And the people who can do that—the particularly talented students—are they selected to study at Logos?"

"As a rule, yes. Though there are a few students each year without the ability to persuade matter who are either strategic, charismatic, or talented enough to get in without that ability."

Dante flipped open her folder, selected her class schedule, and crossed out her ethics course and replaced it with course ART789: Art and Ego, which was instructed by a Dr. Ethel Greene. It took place in the evening, at the Melgren Art Center on Tuesdays and Thursdays, 7:00 p.m. to 9:00 p.m. Evening courses, Lennon would come to learn, were the norm at Drayton.

Just then, there was a sharp knock on the door, and a slight man, presumably a secretary, dressed in slacks and a blousy peasant shirt, entered the office with a grease-stained paper bag clutched in his hand. He set it on the desk. Dante thanked him and he left, casting a sidelong glance at Lennon over his shoulder as he went. From the bag, Dante removed two large sandwiches: one a Reuben, the other an antipasto, with paper-thin slices of prosciutto, Parmesan cheese, and a generous layering of basil leaves. He extended the latter to Lennon. "For the road."

Lennon took this as her sign that their brief meeting had come to an end. So she took the sandwich, got up, and headed for the door.

Dante called after her. "Lennon?"

She stopped with her hand on the knob, half turned to look back at him. There was a blur, and Lennon felt her own hand animate, watched as it snapped up—as if of its own volition, with speed well beyond the limits of her reflexes—and snatched something from the air. Her palm stung. She looked down: in her hand was the three-legged pig. Dante smiled and as Lennon slipped the figurine into her pocket, she asked herself a question to which she had no answer: Had she caught it, or had he?

8

CONVOCATION TOOK THE form of a rowdy cocktail hour on the vice-chancellor's lawn, which was still soft and muddy from the rain earlier that day. Despite the mud and poor weather conditions, the party was well attended. There were large canvas tents pitched in the yard, people milling about between them, grasping sweaty cocktail glasses, exchanging furtive glances. It was easy to tell the first years from the upperclassmen and faculty, who possessed a distinct ease that the newcomers lacked. The first years clustered together, in odd little groups of three and four. There weren't many of them, especially given that the party was being thrown to welcome them, and Lennon began to wonder just how many of them had even passed the written portion of the exam, and what had become of those who hadn't.

(What she did not know then, but came to discover, was that those who had failed to pass the test had woken in their own beds, at home, wherever home was then. They would've been aware of the fuzzy memory of a dream, or the dream of a dream, and as they rose out of bed and began to brush their teeth or carry on with the rituals that structured their mornings, the dream of Drayton, a dream they had lived and breathed in the flesh, would have been fast and quickly forgotten, the way that dreams often are.)

Somewhere during the course of the party, Lennon began to think of Wyatt. She came close to missing him, which felt like something of a betrayal. Here she was at the precipice of a new life, and all she could think about was the cheating ex she'd left behind in the suburbs. She realized then that she needed to erase him, once and for all, and sought a way to do just that.

After scanning the party once or twice, Lennon locked eyes with a man seated on the far edge of the garden. He was, perhaps, one of the more interesting characters gathered on the lawn that evening. He had a shaved head, and he was, like Lennon, almost worryingly thin, skinny to the point of scrawniness. There were bluish bags beneath his eyes, so dark that it took Lennon more than a minute to realize that the one under his left was actually a bruise.

Looking at him, Lennon thought, simply: *He'll do.*

She approached him with a drink that he accepted. "How'd you find your way here? To Drayton?"

He shrugged and downed his drink in a single large swallow, rosemary sprig, ice, and all. "I couldn't have found my way anywhere else if I'd tried. I'm Ian."

"Lennon," she said, sipping her own cocktail.

Ian, as it turned out, was from Columbus, Ohio. He'd worked as a convenience store clerk and had received the call from Drayton while on the clock. Ian had high cheekbones, a protruding Adam's apple, and a blurry diamond tattooed beneath his left eye that looked, suspiciously, like a coverup for a teardrop. He looked like the sort of boy that Lennon would've dated in high school to piss off her mom.

As she listened to Ian speak—in a kind of drunken ramble—Lennon recognized that he wasn't particularly kind. He spoke with the sort of inflated self-assurance that most deeply insecure people do. She was especially drawn to him for this reason—she had always liked men who had a point to prove to themselves or to her or the whole world—and as Ian rambled, she found herself leaning closer, sipping the froth off the top of her cocktail, posing the unspoken offers people are apt to when they're just drunk and brave enough. Eventually, he asked her a few questions about her past, clearly trying to confirm she was single. And Lennon obliged, offering up the story of her newly ended relationship with Wyatt.

They didn't bother to go back to her room at Ethos, or his at Pathos. Instead, they found a secluded corner of some overgrown courtyard far from the noise of the garden party. Quickly, and in the midnight dark, they did what they had come there to do. There were no words exchanged, no discussion, and it was rough and quick, and Lennon spent the time she wasn't on her knees with her chest pressed painfully to the moss-eaten bricks of the crumbling courtyard wall as Ian moved behind her. When they finished, only a few moments after they'd first begun, Lennon stripped off her sweater and used it to wipe her inner thighs, then she tied that same sweater around her waist (a little gross, but she didn't know what else to do with it), pulled up her pants, and buttoned them.

"This was fun," she said, because it seemed like the sort of thing she was supposed to say after an encounter like that one. In truth, Lennon hadn't had many hookups at all. The ones she remembered she'd been too drunk to say much of anything after the deed was done. She wasn't like Wyatt and Sophia. She didn't know how to be the sort of person who formed hidden attachments behind a front of nonchalance, who kept sex secret and apart from everything else in their lives. But she desperately wanted to be, if only to sever whatever threads still connected her and Wyatt. To prove—more to herself than anyone else—that she could do the same things he did. That she could hurt him too.

Ian broke into an easy smile, tucking himself back into his pants. He really was handsome, in his own way, and she could tell that he knew it. "See you around," he said.

Lennon returned to the party and found that the atmosphere had turned strange and eerie in the brief time she'd been away. A fog hung low to the treetops. Students lay out on the lawn, stargazing and sipping green glasses of absinthe. The professors watched them, looking rather drunk themselves, cheeks ruddy from wine and the thick heat of the evening. In the tent, a few students were attempting to perform the Charleston with varying measures of success.

Several whiskey sours later, as fireworks erupted in the distance, and the last of the partygoers dispersed themselves to their dorms, Lennon stepped into one of the many phone booths scattered about the campus, all of them decidedly vintage, like the one she'd stumbled upon in the mall parking lot the night she'd received news of her acceptance. She dialed Wyatt's number. It took her a few tries to get it right, as she could barely remember all of the digits. Like most people, she had come to rely on her cell phone to remember everything for her—phone numbers, dates, addresses, events. But she hadn't seen a single working smartphone on campus. As far as she was concerned, it seemed like there was no service within the barriers of Drayton, no means for her to reach the world beyond it, apart from these strange black telephone booths. (At a later date, Lennon would realize just how lucky she was that her call had rung through at all. Most didn't, and almost every other time she'd tried to make a call in one of these booths, the line had kept ringing and ringing with no answer, or she'd raised the receiver to her ear in wait of a dial tone but had heard nothing but the roar of static.)

Lennon cradled the phone to her ear with her shoulder, picked anxiously at her nails as she listened to the dial tone ring. Through the windows, she watched the fireworks erupting in the distance, casting the thinning crowds into sharply contrasting shadows.

Wyatt picked up just as she was about to go to voicemail.

"Hello?" he said thickly, and his voice sounded like she'd woken him up out of a dead sleep. She wondered if she had. Wondered what time it was beyond the confines of Drayton. Did time move differently within the campus? She wasn't sure.

"Did I wake you?" she asked, and she hoped she didn't sound as drunk or as frightened as she felt.

There was a long silence. "Len?"

"Yes," she said, and felt the hot pressure of tears in her throat. "It's me."

"Where are you?" he asked.

"I'm at school."

Strangely, Wyatt didn't ask the expected question—*What school and where and what are you studying there?* It was less that he didn't think to, and more that he wasn't allowed to. As though the words that he might've asked with had been suddenly revoked. "When are you coming home?"

"Maybe soon. Maybe never."

She asked him about Sophia.

He didn't answer.

So she asked him again. "I saw you two. In the bathroom together. Why won't you just admit it?"

The static on the line thickened in response to her question.

Wyatt didn't say anything for a very long time. Lennon considered hanging up.

"Are you there?"

"I want you to come home," said Wyatt. "We'll try this all again."

"Wyatt—"

"We'll go to therapy."

"I was already in therapy."

"No, I mean together. We'll go together, and we'll find a way to fix all of this."

It was at this moment that Lennon began to consider the idea that Wyatt had, actually, loved her. Because what was love if not the desperation she heard in his voice? The plaintiveness. She had never—in all of the years she'd been with Wyatt—felt in possession of so much power. Nor had she ever wanted him less. The tables had turned now, and that was for the better. At least, it was better for her. What was better for Wyatt, she could not say. He would have to decide that for himself, alone.

"I need to go," said Lennon, and the glare of the fireworks tinted the foggy panes of the telephone booth gold. "It's late."

"Lennon please . . ." he said, the high-pitched, tear-choked wheedling of a child. A little boy. And she saw then, for the first time, how pathetic he was. Before Drayton, Lennon used to believe that their relationship was a credit to Wyatt—his brilliance and charm, his intellect and singularity. But now she realized it was a credit to her, and her desire to prove to herself that she was worth loving. But no more.

Lennon set the phone back into its cradle and stepped out of the booth. Outside it was muggy. The air sat wet and hot and heavy in the pits of Lennon's lungs. She looked down at her left hand, at the ring on her finger. Then she pulled it off and hurled it into the nearby bushes.

She walked back to Ethos College, through the thickening fog, and spotted Dante cutting across the green. He had his head dipped against the oncoming rain, and he was walking at a fast pace, like he was in pursuit of something, or late for an important meeting. But at this hour? And Lennon could've sworn he was . . . limping. But not in the way people limp when they've broken their leg or sprained an ankle. He limped like he'd forgotten how to walk, or like his leg was half-numb and barely able to hold the weight of him without buckling.

And then his leg did buckle, in the middle of one of his awkward strides, and Dante broke to one knee and caught himself on the cobblestones. He stayed there for a long time, breathing heavily. He shook his head slowly, and while it was hard to make out his expression at a distance, Lennon could've sworn he was smiling to himself. A canted and incredulous grin. Then he tilted his chin up, looked straight at Lennon, and smiled knowingly as though they shared in some nasty and shameful secret. Her throat went dry.

Lennon, who had almost moved to help him up, faltered at the sight of that wicked smile and kept her distance. She watched, breathless and still, as Dante pressed slowly to his feet, brushed his slacks clean of dirt, and, at the same hurried pace, continued on his way.

9

THE FIRST MORNING of Lennon's new life as a student at Drayton dawned without pomp or ceremony. Lennon woke in the wee hours of early dawn, hungover, feeling like she had lead for bones. Upon dragging herself out of bed, Lennon discovered that Blaine was already gone, her bed neatly made, the sheets folded into crisp hospital creases at every corner, the pillows fluffed. She must've left much earlier, or perhaps she'd never come back the night before.

Hastily, Lennon brushed her teeth (she didn't have time for a shower), dressed, then left Ethos Hall a full half hour later than she'd intended to, and had to tramp through the gardens, the ground soft from yesterday's storms, mud sucking at her brand-new loafers as she cut across the campus greens to make up time. The conservatory, which Lennon had initially assumed was a garden, was actually a large wooden overhang on the far western side of campus. It had a flat roof, surprisingly low, and all four of its wooden walls were open to the outdoors. It was striking, and one of the few modern structures on campus.

Lennon arrived only three minutes late, but the rest of her classmates were already there. There were eleven students total, sitting cross-legged on thin pillows arranged in a wide circle. Standing at the center of that circle was a tall woman she took for Dr. Lund, her professor. She was the opposite of what Lennon expected her to be. The image of "professor of meditation" brought to mind tousled hair, prayer beads, and nose piercings. But Dr. Lund was smartly dressed, in a well-tailored three-piece tweed suit, with polished brown oxfords. Her hair was dark, and shaped into a blunt bob, not a strand out of place. Dr. Lund looked and spoke like someone who would wrinkle her nose at the mere mention of anything that related, even vaguely, to the New Age.

Dr. Lund didn't pause her lecture, or so much as register Lennon with a passing glance as she nabbed the only empty pillow in the circle. "Traditional meditational studies emphasize mindfulness and acceptance, but here at Drayton we adopt a different approach to the practice. Our primary focus is control. Our aim, with these studies, is to teach you how to identify and interrogate your every emotion with the intention of giving you full governance of your mind."

And the minds of others, Lennon wanted to add, but dared not say that aloud.

Ian raised his hand. "Will this teach us how to persuade people?"

A dozen eyes affixed themselves on the professor in anticipation of her answer.

Dr. Lund leveled an icy glare. "This is no place for persuasion, Ian. Should it be performed within the walls of this conservatory, it will result in your immediate expulsion from Drayton. While meditating, the mind is prone. It is a violation of the highest degree to breach a person in this vulnerable state. In time, you will learn to bolster the walls of your mind to defend against these invasions. It will be a difficult and at times sickening endeavor, but it is utterly imperative that you learn to do this. Am I clear?"

A chorus of yeses. People nodded their heads. But Ian, glowering, folded his arms across his chest. He looked as if something he was entitled to had been pried from his bony fingers.

"With that said, let's begin."

They were asked to close their eyes and imagine an empty room in need of furnishing. They were allowed to fill this room with the articles of their choosing, totems from their past, memorabilia, keepsakes, and bespoke items that brought them some semblance of comfort. "I will warn you that it is important to adopt a discerning and moderate approach to this curation. Senseless clutter is intolerable," said Dr. Lund, and the insides of Lennon's eyelids briefly went dark as the shadow of the professor slid past her.

Lennon was asked to imagine different objects, to turn them over in her mind, assess their shape, and determine whether or not they aligned with her vision of the space. The features of the room were to be considered too. Would rafters hold the ceilings aloft? Were the walls to be painted? Does the room have windows, and if so, how many? Are they shuttered or hung with curtains?

"Above all else, it is imperative that this room function as a sanctum. By the end of our studies this semester, it should appear more real to you than anything that exists in a three-dimensional space."

Lennon cracked one eye open, frustrated. The task seemed, in that moment, impossible. Try as she might, she couldn't contain her thoughts to the limits of the room. Its details kept changing, or opening out onto memories that flooded her mind, unbidden, no matter how hard she tried to stop them.

"Your homework over the next twenty-four hours is to furnish your room with three items of your choosing," said Dr. Lund. "Be prepared to bring them to our next class and discuss them in detail. I'll see you tomorrow at sunrise."

After meditating, the spillover from the class dispersed themselves across the green, finding their way—dazed and a little dissociative—to a nearby courtyard, perhaps drawn by the scent of coffee wafting from it. Drayton was strange in that each college housed its own dining room, where meals could be taken throughout the day. In addition to this, there was a large central dining hall and several small cafes—or bistros, as the student body referred to them—housed in the cramped basements beneath buildings or in small kiosks scattered about campus, often found in remote or otherwise deserted places where few students ventured to go. Orchid, where Lennon found herself this morning, was one of these. A hole-in-the-wall coffee shop that operated out of a small courtyard that was otherwise abandoned. There were rusty wrought-iron tables and patio chairs scattered across the cobbled courtyard, and students filled them, gathered under the blue cathedral of the early-morning sky, sipping coffee and chewing on sandwiches, working their way through salads, and smoking slender clove cigarettes, which Lennon had quickly learned was one of the favored vices of Drayton's students and faculty alike.

Lennon and her classmates gathered in the far corner of the courtyard, around a rickety bistro table that was far too small to accommodate the lot of them. Ian sat next to Lennon and beside him was a feeble girl with a crucifix around her neck who, halfway through their meditation, had begun to cry and was still wiping her swollen eyes by the time their coffee arrived. Her name—Lennon learned—was Nadine, and she was slight with slick black hair, which she wore in a low ponytail at the nape of her neck. Nadine, as it turned out, had been an aspirant at a convent in Delaware prior to arriving at Drayton. She had felt called to live a monastic life since childhood and was about to become a postulant when she'd first received news of her admission at Drayton.

"I was in confession. The priest's voice suddenly changed, and he told me that I'd be moving on to the next step of the admissions process. At first, I thought he was God talking to me, and then I thought he was the devil."

"And what do you think now?" Blaine asked, sipping on an Americano. She'd had a different class that morning, but had joined their group when she spotted them crossing the campus.

"Now . . . I think this is a test," said Nadine. "A test of faith, that is. I think God sent me here so I can serve him in a different way. For years, I thought I was called to take the veil. But now I see that's not my path. I'm supposed to be here. I wasn't chosen by this school. I was chosen by God."

Across the table, Ian rolled his eyes and stubbed out his third cigarette of the morning. "So let me get this straight, you find out magic is real from a possessed priest, and you *still* believe in God?"

"Of course," she said, smiling in that cautious, rapt way that girls often do when they have the attention of the guy they like. "My faith is even stronger now that the curtain's been pulled back. I see so clearly that I've been blessed with a unique opportunity to touch the hearts of men, to make them understand the love of Jesus."

"Is that what they told you all of this was about?" Ian asked, clearly disgusted. *"Jesus?"*

Nadine gave a little laugh, but it wasn't that funny. "I mean, if not that, what, then? You heard from the vice-chancellor herself. John Drayton was a Quaker, a Christian."

"Everyone was Christian back then," said Blaine.

"He was also an abolitionist," said Felix. He was a dusty blond from Montreal who spoke English with a French accent and had a small pride flag pinned to the lapel of his jacket. He'd been working at a center for gay youth in Canada before coming to Drayton. "I mean, surely that had to be a founding principle behind all of this. John wanted to free people with this power."

Lennon raised an eyebrow. "Free people by controlling them? Does that even make sense?"

As it turned out, each of them had a very different idea about what exactly would ensue upon their graduation from Drayton. This was mostly because they'd all been told different things by their advisors. Ian's advisor, Dr. Alec Becker, told him he'd be placed in a high-powered job of his choosing, with enough money to fund the lives of his children's children. Nadine had been informed that she'd start a Catholic mission in India, where her mother had emigrated from, and a generous donation of more than fifty thousand dollars was made to the charity of her choice after she'd formally enrolled at the school. Other first years had been promised anything from congressional seats to tenured professorships at Drayton and anything in between.

Lennon, however, had been made no promises, a fact that she kept to herself out of sheer embarrassment. Why had she been offered nothing? Was her desperation to escape her former life that obvious to the admissions department? Did they know that anything—even a role as small as a secretarial position in Irvine Hall—would have been far more rewarding than the misery of her failing relationship with Wyatt and a life she was quite literally willing to die in order to escape?

"If this is a ruse, it's an expensive one," said Blaine, peeling apart the layers of a croissant. Something about this made her look a lot younger than she was, a little girl playing with her food. "The clothes they gave us are ridiculously well tailored. And clearly the professors are loaded. I mean, have you seen their offices? Eileen has two Eames chairs. I could almost understand one Eames chair. But *two*?"

"And let's be honest," said Ian, "we aren't expensive. We got a wannabe nun, an aspiring actress, and a college dropout turned housewife." Here he jabbed his thumb at Lennon. She'd told him about the particulars of her past life during the convocation party and, in that moment, sorely regretted her drunk self-disclosures. "Then there's me, working at the convenience store. I don't want to speak for anyone else, but they could've lured me into an unmarked white van with the promise of free rent, beer, and a pack of cigarettes."

That got a long, sad laugh out of the table. But they all knew he was right. In a conventional sense, none of them had been slated for particularly promising futures. They hadn't graduated from Ivy Leagues or accomplished anything worthy of note. They weren't moneyed or from the sorts of families that mattered.

"Is it possible that they're right and that we are somehow . . . innately talented?" Lennon asked, and the table went suddenly very quiet. Perhaps they, like Lennon, hadn't allowed themselves to fully consider this possibility until that very moment. "Maybe we do have some skill that all of the most brilliant people we know simply don't? Maybe we are that special?"

10

P ERSUASION WAS LENNON'S last class of the day, and she arrived just a few moments before the period began. The classroom was already full, students seated behind all but one of the twelve desks in the room. On each of them, there was a small glass cage that contained a single live rat.

Dante stood at the front of the classroom—dressed smartly, in wool trousers and a white button-down, the sleeves rolled up to the elbows to expose tattooed forearms. If he had any memory of their encounter outside of Irvine Hall, he gave no indication. "Lennon, nice of you to join us. Have a seat."

She claimed a desk in the middle of the room, stared into the cage in front of her. The rat on the other side of the glass was dun brown with a little white patch on its left ear. He was shaking.

"I have no idea if you're a boy or a girl, but I'm going to call you Gregory because you look like one," said Lennon in a whisper, and the rat looked up at her, nose twitching, as if he understood.

"What's the difference between training and an act of persuasion?" Dante asked the class, but his gaze lingered on Lennon.

Nadine raised her hand, her arm stiff with urgency. Behind her, Ian rolled his eyes.

"Go on," said Dante, nodding to her.

"Persuasion is forced. Training is taught," said Nadine, and she cut a quick glance back at Ian, her cheeks flushing pink. Was she just embarrassed—Lennon wondered in passing—or was it that even nuns weren't immune to the wiles of tattooed, toxic men?

"An interesting perspective . . . but is that entirely accurate?" Dante picked up a nub of chalk from the sill below the board and sketched the question: *Is persuasion an act of force?*

This question, once written in full, triggered a chorus of murmurs. The class dissolved into a general conversation, no one bothering to raise their hands, people talking over one another, or interjecting in the short breaths between words and sentences.

"Persuasion is the ability to project one's own will onto a being, object, or entity," said Dante, and everyone fell quiet. "There is not a living being in the world that lacks the ability to persuade. It is a gift inherent to all of us. From the smallest microorganism to the smartest humans that have ever walked the face of the earth—every one of us is bestowed with the power to enforce our own will upon the world. I want you to think of a newborn baby, crying for its mother's milk. This early instinct is, for most of us, our first discernible act of persuasion. Now imagine this same newborn baby grown into a man. He goes to a bar, flirts with a woman there, and he ends his night in bed with her. This too is an act of persuasion. But while persuasion is a skill we all possess, our degrees of efficacy vary greatly depending on our social status, natural intelligence, nationality, the money in our bank accounts, even our race.

"Here at Drayton, we believe that a handful of extraordinarily gifted individuals can be taught to command a persuasive ability powerful enough to bend, or even break, the rules of reality itself. This skill is well beyond the natural limits of most people walking the planet. Most who would so much as attempt to wield such a power would either die or go insane. Which is how we come to you, the chosen few." As Dante said this, his gaze again affixed itself to Lennon. She shifted uncomfortably in her chair.

"For the rest of the semester, you will work to persuade—not train—the rat sitting on the desk before you. So I suggest you spend this class session building a sense of rapport with your charge, learning its peculiarities, understanding the subject onto which you intend to impose your will. Cruelty—by way of pain, starvation, or verbal abuse—will not be tolerated. Nor will it help you achieve the kinds of results you'll need to pass this class. Am I clear?"

Lennon nodded along with the rest of her classmates.

"Good," said Dante. "Then let's begin."

What followed was a brutal crash course in rudimentary persuasion. Dante adopted a sink-or-swim approach to the lesson, which Lennon privately suspected was more a test of natural aptitude than anything else, a way to gauge what he was working with. What little instruction he did offer was vague and rooted not in pragmatism but in feelings and intuition. "Think of your will as an extension of your body. No different than a limb. When you extend it to the rat—as you might your hand—imagine yourself expanding around it, the fingers of your psyche closing into a fist. That's how you make first contact and establish control."

Other tips adopted a more athletic approach, focusing more on the body than the mind: "Breathe through the belly, not the chest. Try to keep your hands from fisting up. Palms to the sky. It'll help you relax."

Dante delivered one of the most helpful tips of the evening while standing behind Lennon's desk: "Focus and stress are not synonymous. Try to concentrate without tensing up."

As the night progressed, the class dissolved into utter chaos. There were rats that raced in circles around the perimeters of their cages. Rats that stared blankly into the eyes of their persuaders. Some rats who did nothing but shit and burrow into the pine shavings for a nap. But one, Ian's, convulsed pitifully on the floor of his cage, only to go limp, then startle awake a few moments later. Ian received a sharp scolding from Dante for his heavy-handedness.

Lennon, for her part, couldn't bring herself to impress her will on the timid creature cowering in the cage before her. Gregory was smaller than the other rats—just a baby, really. And despite her best efforts to remain stoic, she felt strangely protective of him. She didn't want to hurt him and couldn't ensure that she wouldn't if she attempted to persuade him.

She hadn't felt the same empathy toward Dante during the entry exam. He had been smug and undaunted and clearly capable—as a seasoned practitioner of this strange magic himself. Besides, he'd asked her to persuade him, so Lennon had had no qualms about doing just that. But the rats weren't the same.

They looked terrified, cowering in their cages. Gregory was especially pitiful—timid and runty, quivering with fear. The idea of forcing her will upon such a small and harmless creature made her want to throw up. She could feel a panic attack coming on, her first since coming to the school.

Trying to get ahead of it, Lennon slid out of her desk and stepped out into the empty hall, making it only a few paces before the terror seized her. Every panic attack that Lennon suffered was slightly different. Some started in the back of her head, a fuzziness like the feeling before passing out. Others began with a wave of nausea that sent her fleeing to the bathroom. This attack began in her chest, a cruel constriction that bent her double there in the middle of the corridor and made it hard to breathe.

"Are you all right?" Dante asked behind her.

"I—I can't do it." Lennon could barely get the words out. "He's so small and weak, and I'm afraid I'll kill him."

"The rat?"

She nodded, dragged a hand through her hair, the feeling of her fingertips scratching along her scalp grounding her some. She sucked in a deep breath. Then another.

Dante came to stand beside her. "You persuaded me just fine."

"You're different."

"How so?"

"You fucking deserved it—"

"So persuasion is something that a person either deserves or doesn't? Like a punishment?"

"I—I don't know, I guess? It's certainly not a gift."

"So during the entry exam, you saw yourself as punishing me?"

"I didn't think about it like that."

"What did you think about?" Dante pressed her. "I want your take."

"I guess . . . I thought you were smug. And I thought you were goading me, intentionally pissing me off, and that made me feel small and . . . and—"

"*And?*"

"Desperate," she said, and realized she was beginning to feel better. Her hands weren't shaking as violently. Her heartbeat had drastically slowed. The floor firmed beneath her feet. Dante had distracted her, talked her down out of a full panic attack without her even realizing it. Damn, he was good. "I felt desperate to prove that I was worth something. Not just to you but to myself. Benedict did the same at his house, during that interview. He dredged up all this shit about my past that made me so ashamed and so eager to prove that I could be something more than what I have been."

"And what have you been, Lennon?"

"Weak."

"Just like that rat back in the classroom?"

She froze, flinched. "Don't you do that. Don't try to get into my head."

Dante only smiled, raised both hands in a gesture of submission. "I won't argue with you about the morality of what we do here. You're too smart for that. But I will say that rats have been used—for decades—in the pursuit of knowledge. There are undergrad psych students who perform more invasive and painful experiments on rats than anything we do here. On a personal note, I'm rather fond of rats, and I can assure you that the ones we keep are about as well cared for as any. We source most of them when they're young, from pet stores where they would've been food for snakes. If anything, they were saved from a worse fate."

"But it's not just the rats," said Lennon, in a quiet voice. "There are human lives on the other end of this. Outside of the classroom. That's what we're training for, right? To change minds by force? Make puppets out of people?"

"That's a harsh way of putting it."

"Well, how would you put it?"

Dante considered his answer carefully, frowning. "Persuasion is morally neutral. It's just a tool, really."

"But what happens when that tool falls into the wrong hands?" Here, Lennon thought of elections and democracy, campaigns of misinformation, nuclear codes and espionage, coups in the dead of night. On a geopolitical level, the power that they wielded here could rise to the level of a weapon of war, if not one of mass destruction.

"It already has," said Dante, "and it will again. But the question we're asking tonight centers around you—your capabilities, your worthiness. Do you trust yourself with this power?"

She didn't have an answer to that yet. How could she? "I just... I don't want to hurt anybody or anything. Okay? That's my limit."

"You can do better than that," said Dante. "You don't want to hurt people, and I understand. Respect it, even. But you can aim so much higher than pacifism. I can teach you how to protect people if you'll let me, how to prevent harm, how to undo it. But if I'm going to do that, you have to grow a backbone and get the hell out of your own way. Do you understand?"

"I—I think so."

"There will always be someone who will use the power they have to hurt those who don't deserve it. That's why it's important that people like you become competent enough to stand between them and those they'd otherwise harm. To let your scruples get in the way of that vital work is cowardice. Now let's get you back to class."

THAT NIGHT, BACK IN ETHOS COLLEGE, LENNON RETURNED to her dorm to discover that Blaine wasn't in. She didn't want to be alone, so she found her way to Ian's room in Pathos College instead. She could tell he wasn't expecting company. When she knocked on the door and showed herself inside, Ian looked more startled than anything else. There was a composition book lying open in his lap, filled with notes from Dante's lecture.

"Where's your roommate?" she asked.

"Don't have one. I got lucky." There was an awkward pause. Ian swallowed, and Lennon saw the bulge of his Adam's apple rise and fall. He looked so young then, so helpless, that Lennon was reminded of that poor rat she'd failed to persuade. "You could stay . . . if you want?"

So Lennon climbed up into bed, sat beside him, drawing her knees up tight to her chest.

"What were you and Professor Lowe talking about out in the hall?" Ian asked, staring down at his journal, all that tangled writing on the page.

"It was less a talk than a debate."

"About what?"

"The rats," said Lennon. "I don't like what we're doing to them. I don't think it's right."

"They're rodents, for fuck's sake," said Ian. "They can't think past eating and shitting. We're practically gods to them."

"Even still," said Lennon. "Something about it doesn't sit right with me."

"Tell me you're not going to abandon all of this because of some inbred lab rats?"

"No. I'm just saying it feels wrong. They don't deserve to be meddled with."

Ian closed his notes. "You ever heard of a rat king?"

"The Rat King? Like from *The Nutcracker*?"

Ian shook his head. "A rat king. The idea is that a bunch of rats get their tails knotted together, and the knot gets tighter the more they struggle to get away. With time, their knotted tails get glued together with all this shit and piss and grime. The filth fuses them together."

"Ew."

"People say they don't exist. They call them some type of cryptid, but I swear to God I saw one. I was in New York, and I stepped out onto the street to smoke and saw what I thought was a cat, but when it crawled out from behind the dumpster and into the light of the streetlamps, I saw it for what it was. And it was fucking vile. It looked more like an arachnid than a mammal, this ball of grimy fur, scrabbling across the concrete. I fumbled for my phone—I was pretty fucking drunk—but by the time I managed to fish it out of my pocket, it had disappeared, back to the sewers, I guess."

"What's your point?" Lennon asked, unsettled and disgusted but still unwavering in her conviction. Rats could be vile—so what? They were still living creatures, and she still felt guilty for hurting them. "Are you saying that because rats are less than us, they deserve to be experimented on?"

He shrugged. "More or less."

"But it doesn't bother you, even a little bit?" Lennon asked, searching his face for some trace of remorse. But she found none. "You don't feel guilty hurting something so small it can't defend itself?"

"I like being good at things," said Ian simply, "and I'm not good at much . . . but I'm good at this persuasion business. I'm not going to give it up just because I feel bad for a couple of rats. Besides, I've got no other options but this."

"I don't believe that."

"It's true. I was nothing back home. I'm not a college dropout; I wasn't even good enough to get in. Didn't even bother to apply. I worked at a fucking convenience store and probably would have until I drank myself into liver failure or found some other way to kill myself. I was nothing to no one. But here things are different. You know what I mean?"

Lennon nodded. She did know. In fact, she empathized with Ian more than she cared to admit. She'd felt the same, until the moment she'd picked up that rotary phone in the booth in the middle of the parking lot. Drayton had lent her the rare opportunity to make something of herself for once, and she knew—just as Ian did—that she'd be a fool to squander that chance. If only she could set her moral qualms aside, like Dante urged her to. But a part of her was beginning to wonder if guilt, or in Ian's case, denial, was just the price of the work they did here.

Lennon had known, since the moment she'd first arrived at Drayton, that in order to become someone she would have to let go of the person she was before. Maybe that meant setting her morals aside, if only for a little while. And what was the harm in it? How guilty was she, really? Lennon hadn't hurt anyone, and all she'd been asked to do thus far was persuade a rat who'd been damned to death anyway.

Ian slid a hand along Lennon's inner thigh. "Are we going to do this? Because if not, I need to sleep."

Lennon nodded, turned to press her lips to his. It was wordless and slow, and while Ian moved within her, Lennon thought of Dante and their exchange out in the hall. The way he'd talked her down out of that panic attack, the moth tattoos on the backs of his hands, the tattered wings that stretched and moved when he flexed his fingers.

That night, in Ian's bed, Lennon slipped into a dream that didn't belong to her. In it she walked barefoot through the Twenty-Fifth Square. The campus had emptied itself. There wasn't a soul in sight. She walked beneath the cover of the live oaks and magnolias, through the fog and dark. The air was wet and heavy, and she felt less like she was walking and more like she was wading through waist-high water, dragging her way through the murk of the fog and heat.

She found her way to the wrought-iron gates of a house half-swallowed by blooming magnolia trees, the blossoms large and monstrous, like the severed heads of white lions, gaping down at her, open-mouthed and starving. The house itself stood proud amid a blizzard of falling petals. On its porch was a boy, barefoot, his back to her. She gazed upon him—the tight frail shoulders, the goose bumps along his nape, the fingers that flinched and shuddered at his sides.

She realized then that this dream was not hers, but his.

The boy turned suddenly. The moment their eyes met, some powerful thrall—like a cold riptide swirling about her thighs—drew her violently through the boy's back, into his body, so that she was within him, housed in the cage of his skeleton, the two of them tragically enmeshed, like rats with their tails tied tight.

The boy turned back to face the house. He raised a hand to the door, pressed his small palm flat against it. Then drew back, clenched his fingers into a fist, and knocked and knocked and knocked. Until his bulbous knuckles blackened with bruises.

No one answered.

11

A WEEK PASSED. Then another. Before Lennon knew it, the second half of the semester was rapidly approaching. Lennon spent most of the time she wasn't in class studying. It was not unusual for her to stay up through the better part of the night, reading material in metaphysics in preparation for their weekly exams, or meditating into the wee hours of the morning. The stress and lack of sleep would've been enough to send her reeling into a series of panic attacks and breakdowns, but Lennon remained surprisingly stable. It was not that she was getting any better—she didn't think she was, or that she ever would. It was just that she was finally channeling her sickness into something that wasn't herself. Her studies consumed her thoughts, so that she had no fuel for panic attacks or compulsions, the dark thoughts that used to send her reeling.

Of all the classes she was enrolled in, persuasion remained the most demanding. Their weekly classes consisted of gruesome exercises wherein they honed their will to a knifelike point and inflicted it on the innocent rats. Under Dante's instruction, they learned how to lull the rats to sleep, calm their racing heartbeats, or drive them mad with rage. Lennon had come to dread these exercises not only because of her guilt about inflicting her will on Gregory time and time again, but because she was so terribly bad at it.

And that thought hung with her—a kind of gray loathing—as she settled behind her desk for class that night. Gregory approached the glass to greet her as he always did, rising up on his back legs, nose twitching, and it was stupid, but in the moment, she swore he was trying to cheer her up.

"Today, you'll learn to lull your subjects into a state of total catatonia, which should not be mistaken with sleep." Dante paced slowly between the desks as he lectured. "Unlike sleep—a state that is familiar, even comforting, to most of us—catatonia has to be forcibly maintained through constant psychic pressure."

What Dante wasn't saying was that catatonia in itself was a kind of torture. Lennon knew that because she herself had once entered into such a state, just before she'd dropped out of college. Her body had frozen in a kind of rictus, and for three days she remained totally despondent. She didn't eat and barely blinked, and her sister, Carly, had to take family leave at the law practice where she worked, to camp out in Lennon's dorm room and ladle broth into her mouth in a desperate attempt to keep her from being hospitalized (Lennon didn't fare well in hospitals).

"Think of catatonia as the bedrock of our practice. It's a versatile skill, one that can be used as a launch point for different persuasive strategies that range from the planting of memories to the removal of them. Catatonia, for our purposes here, becomes a way to manipulate time itself. It allows us to essentially shut down our subjects, subdue them enough to allow for the work we do. Think of it as general anesthesia for a persuasionist."

The students got to work, several of them succeeding almost immediately. Ian and Nadine seemed particularly well suited to this task, lulling their respective rats into a deep and glassy-eyed stupor that seemed close to death. Lennon, however, struggled with the task of subduing Gregory, who was an anxious and unwilling participant. While she was successful in her attempts to suppress his brain function and induce a state of drowsiness, true catatonia remained well beyond her skill set.

"Shit," she muttered, putting her face in her hands.

"You don't want it enough," said Dante. He was frustrated with her, had been for some weeks now, on account of her abysmal performance in his class. And maybe she was sick for this, but it made her skittish and hot when he was angry with her. "You're still too timid."

Lennon tried again. Two bright spots of throbbing pain pierced at her temples. She could smell the beginnings of a nosebleed high up in her sinuses, but she kept pushing, hunched over the terrarium, honing her focus, trying and failing to extend her will to Gregory.

Several fat droplets of blood struck the surface of her desk.

IT WAS RAINING, AND LENNON'S NOSEBLEED HAD SLOWED TO a dribble by the time she returned home to the doorstep of Ethos College. She found Blaine seated at the desk in front of the window, thumbing through the sun-dyed pages of a mass-market paperback from the '60s. Its cover featured a shrieking woman in a metal cone bra caught in the vise grip of a tentacled alien. It was titled *Invasion of the Octopi*. Blaine looked up when Lennon closed the door. Her makeup was smeared and running, like she'd had a good cry and tried to clean herself up with a wad of toilet paper but had given up halfway through.

"What happened to your face?" Blaine blurted, snapping her book shut.

"I could ask you the same question," said Lennon, and she kicked off her loafers. She stripped out of her pants and shirt and changed into one of the soft jersey T-shirts—embroidered with Drayton's logo—that were distributed to all the new students as part of their welcome package. "And if you must know, it was persuasion with Dante—I mean Dr. Lowe."

"You're pushing yourself too hard in that class."

"Well, according to him I'm not pushing myself hard enough. I couldn't even get Gregory to fall asleep."

Blaine raised an eyebrow. "Gregory?"

"He's my rat," said Lennon.

"You named yours?"

Lennon nodded. "I just feel like I'm oscillating between guilt and hopelessness."

"Go easy on yourself. You're still learning. We all are."

"Ian doesn't seem to be having any trouble."

"Too bad you can't absorb his skill by osmosis when you hook up with him."

Lennon hurled a pillow at Blaine's head, which she dodged with ease, laughing. "Shut *up*."

Just then, there was the sharp rap of knuckles on wood. A tall blond boy nudged the door open. Lennon immediately recognized him as Kieran, one of the three students from Logos who'd been camped out in the waiting room outside of Dante's office. Lennon wondered what he was doing in Ethos College. As a rule, the logicians kept to themselves. They were rarely spotted in the central dining hall, even though they had a table reserved for their use only.

Kieran's gaze went to Blaine. "You still coming tonight? Emerson was asking."

Blaine shrugged, noncommittal. "Can Lennon come too?"

Kieran's gaze went to Lennon. "You're Dr. Lowe's advisee, right?"

"Yeah," said Lennon.

"Bring her," said Kieran to Blaine and then he shut the door.

The moment he was gone, Lennon turned on Blaine. "What the hell was that?"

"They're throwing a party at Logos tonight," said Blaine. "Invite only. I think it's a way for them to scope out prospects."

"I'm not going," said Lennon, a little offended that she hadn't received an invite. Not that she would've been expecting one. She knew she was solidly mediocre, if not less than that.

"Come on," said Blaine, "have some fun for once. Don't you want to know what's going on in Logos?"

"Not really. Secret societies full of white people aren't really my thing. Not a fan of the whole *Eyes Wide Shut* vibe."

"It's not like that."

"How would you know?"

"I mean, first off, Adan's a member."

"Is that supposed to comfort me?"

"And secondly, Logos is primarily an *academic* society. They take the best of the first years."

"Did you read that in their welcome pamphlet?"

"I'm just saying it could be fun," said Blaine, and she grabbed for the box of tissues on their shared nightstand, tossed it across the room to Lennon. "Clean yourself up. Let's go out for once."

Blaine convinced Lennon to put on an oversized white button-down, styled as a dress, over a pair of sheer black stockings. Somehow, she'd procured a tube of lipstick, which she used as blush, rubbing it furiously into Lennon's cheekbones, and a pencil eyeliner, which she painstakingly smudged and blurred into Lennon's waterline until she was satisfied.

"It's really not fair," said Blaine. "You look unreal."

Lennon laughed her off. But when she turned to look at herself in the mirror, she saw that Blaine was right. There was something unreal about her. Something changed. A vacancy in the eyes that made her believe, for a split second, that her own reflection didn't belong to her. That the girl in the mirror was not really her at all, but a replacement, like the aberration. But the reflection in the mirror had eyes, and when she smiled it smiled obediently back at her.

"That's it," said Blaine, grinning. "Now you're ready."

It was nearing midnight by the time the girls left Ethos College. Blaine, who linked arms with Lennon, adopted a fairly brisk pace because it was cold out and neither of them was wearing much. Eventually, they reached the deep of Drayton Square, which to Lennon looked less like a garden and more like a dense forest of moss-draped oaks and magnolias.

It was here that Lennon first laid eyes upon the notorious Logos House, standing in a small square clearing. The house was tall and narrow, its red bricks grown over with ivy. It had several large windows, lit from the inside, curtains drawn shut over all of them. The front door was painted with a crest, one Lennon remembered being embroidered on the pockets of the students whom she'd chatted with in the waiting room outside of Dante's office: a snake eating its own tail with relish, one red eye open wide.

"I've seen this house before," said Lennon. "In a dream."

"If you're developing psychic powers I'm going to need some lottery numbers. Quick," said Blaine and she opened the front door and ushered Lennon into a dim foyer with a high ceiling, and dark hickory floors. A pall of cigarette smoke hung blue on the air. For a party, it was surprisingly quiet, the sound of voices was muffled and hushed. From the adjacent sitting room, a record player loosed rambling chords of staticky jazz.

Blaine walked them through the house like she knew where she was going—past a parlor and dining room—and through to the kitchen, where it seemed like the bulk of the party was assembled. There were about twenty students there, some that Lennon recognized, others that she didn't. Ian and Nadine were present, which wasn't particularly surprising given their excellent performance in Dante's class. Sawyer was there too, nursing a watery cocktail at the far corner of the kitchen, his back pressing into the cabinets in what seemed to Lennon a pitiful attempt to make himself small and ignorable.

But there was one person in particular who caught Lennon's eye: Emerson O'Neill, the president of Logos, sitting cross-legged on the dining table. Her white shirt was fastened closed with two buttons, just above the navel, and offered a glimpse of her sternum, the hard plate of bone impressing itself from the underside of her skin, a fossil emerging from limestone.

When Emerson raised her gaze, Lennon would see—through the sharp glare of the glasses that sat perched on her nose—that one of her pupils looked like a pierced egg yolk, the black bleeding into the pale blue of her iris. She held a cigarette pinched between her knuckles and smoke hung on the air around her in tangled ribbons, like the threads of a torn spiderweb. As Lennon stepped into the room, they moved—wending and curling in on themselves—in such a way as to spell out a single word in cursive: *limerence*.

Lennon watched, awed, as the word tore and faded, the hooked *r* that held the word together tearing clean apart, the tatters of the other letters fraying, then fading until all that remained on the air was a faint haze where the word had hung just moments before.

Emerson stubbed out her cigarette on the edge of the table, where there were already a number of charred semicircles burnt into the wood. She flicked the butt into the kitchen sink with frightening precision. "You brought a plus-one?"

"Kieran said I could." Blaine sidestepped out of the way, as if to show her off to the room. "This is Lennon."

"I'm familiar," said Emerson, and then to Lennon: "We share an advisor. Dr. Lowe. He told me about you."

The idea that Dante had been talking about her sent a strange little thrill up her spine. "Good things, I hope?"

"Mostly," she said, and any interest she had in Lennon must've died there, because she turned away and started chatting with Blaine. Feeling awkward—and a little abandoned—Lennon found her way across the kitchen to Sawyer.

"I didn't think this was really your scene," said Lennon, edging up beside him.

"It's not. But I'm not above being courted."

"Is that what this is?"

"Of course, can't you tell? All the drinks and the drugs and the finger foods and finery. We're all being thoroughly groomed," said Sawyer, and then, thinking better of himself, frowned and said, "Well, maybe not you."

It was a known fact that Lennon ranked low among her fellow first years. At Drayton, grades were posted publicly on a bulletin board in the lobby of Irvine Hall, and updated weekly at nine in the morning, just before classes began. Perhaps it was meant to be motivating, but to Lennon it was nothing more than a weekly exercise in humiliation.

"At least you won't have to deal with all of this," said Sawyer bitterly. "All of us sycophants climbing desperately over the corpses of our lessers on the ascent to the top."

"Poetic."

"But sadly true. And it only gets worse with time. The competition. The desperation. I mean, look at them." Sawyer gestured to the throng, milling around the dining table where Emerson sat, a few men engaging Blaine by the fridge. "They're desperate and I can't even blame them."

When a fresh stream of students entered the room, Sawyer nodded toward the back door off the kitchen and Lennon followed him out into the courtyard, where the crowds were thinner.

On their way out, Kieran slipped something into Lennon's hand: a small baggie filled with shriveled fungi. "On the house," he said to her with a wink. "But if you want more, you know where to find me."

They debated about whether or not to take the drugs. It had been a long time since Lennon had done any psychedelics, and she wasn't sure she wanted to risk the headache of a bad trip. Ultimately, it was Sawyer who got them started with a whispered "Fuck it."

He sprinkled a few of the shrooms into his mouth and chewed with a grimace. Then he held out the baggie to her. "Come on, don't make me do it alone."

"This is a bad idea," said Lennon, but she took the shrooms anyway, chewing and swallowing as quickly as she could to get the bitter taste out of her mouth.

"How did you end up here?" Lennon asked, mostly to keep the new quiet between them from turning heavy and awkward.

"What do you mean?" Sawyer asked.

"Like how did you get invited to study at Drayton? And who were you before you did?"

"I worked as a librarian in Connecticut. And that's where it happened for me . . . where I first found out I was being considered by Drayton. I was emptying the returns bin one morning, and on top of the stack of books there was an envelope, wax-sealed, with my name on it. Inside was a letter congratulating me on moving to the next round of my admissions process. I did my interview with Dr. Lowe, actually."

"And how did that go?"

"Oh, it was brutal. He knew everything about me. Worse yet, I felt like he was taking things from me instead of just telling me about myself."

"That's how I felt when interviewing with Benedict," said Lennon. "I became like an object. A box of junk—all these dreams and hopes and secrets—to be rifled through. It was horrible. It hurt."

As they talked, they made slow laps around the courtyard. It was dark, but the waxy leaves of the magnolia tree were limned into brilliance by the moonlight, or maybe it was just the shrooms heightening everything. Walking with Sawyer, Lennon felt a kind of peace that she had only ever associated with being alone. It was as if Sawyer wasn't a person at all, just an extension of her, or she of him. She felt delightfully less than real, like an airy figment conjured up from nothing, free of the horrible weight of being. In the garden she became like a fixture of the school—like the live oaks and the magnolias, the stone face of Irvine Hall half-hidden behind the trees. For the first time since arriving at Drayton, Lennon felt truly at home.

As the night dragged on, they traded stories about their childhoods. She learned that Sawyer had grown up in Connecticut, where his father ran a farm. His mother, a former rare bookseller, had immigrated from Taiwan. They were the only people in their rural town who were anything other than white. In turn, Lennon told Sawyer all about Wyatt and what she'd left behind in Colorado—an engagement and half-planned wedding and a life she was trying to make herself want.

"And what do you want now?" Sawyer had asked her, and his voice was husky, as if he was falling asleep or just waking up. When he laid down on the grass, Lennon laid down beside him, a slightly foolish decision given that the dirt around the green was thoroughly pocked with the hills of fire ants. But Lennon—made relaxed and romantic by the shrooms—did not think of that then. "Who did you come here to be?"

"I want . . . to be significant," said Lennon, and even to her own ear, she sounded drunk. She wondered if she was even making any sense and decided that she didn't care. "I just want to matter. But everyone who matters hurts people. It's like you said . . . all of us tramping on the bodies of others to get to a place where we don't actively hate ourselves."

They went quiet for a while after that, watching the tiny leaves of the live oak trees shift and whisper high above them. Lennon could feel herself spilling out into everything around her, and everything around her bleeding into her. If disassociation was the feeling of being removed and disharmonized from reality, this was the opposite. And Lennon was relishing that feeling—wholly relaxed and satisfied by her own oneness with Sawyer and the trees and the dirt packed hard beneath her back—when the elevator first appeared, with the trill of a bell. Its doors materialized in the garden shed, replacing the single plank of rotten wood that had been affixed to its hinges just moments before.

"Holy shit," said Sawyer, sitting up. He looked at Lennon to confirm that she was seeing the same things. "What the hell is that?"

The golden doors of the elevator opened to reveal an empty cabin, mirrored on all sides. A soft lullaby spilled out into the courtyard, which Lennon recognized as a made-up song her mother used to sing to put her to sleep.

Lennon stood. "I think it's for me."

Sawyer, still sitting, caught her by the sleeve as if to drag her back. But Lennon brushed him off, moving toward the elevator. As soon as she stepped inside, the doors snapped shut, and the cabin lurched into ascent.

12

THE CABIN MIGHT'VE been climbing for several minutes, or several hours for all Lennon knew. But as the elevator began to slow—its gears grinding to a halt with a screech—she realized that her legs, locked at the knees, had gone almost totally numb beneath her. As she squatted and shook her feet, trying to get the blood flowing again, the doors opened behind her with a sigh and a hiss, and a cold wind swept into the elevator cabin. Her ears popped.

What lie beyond the open doors, through a scrim of fog, was not Drayton as she knew it. It was darker, colder, the grass crusted with frost, the trees winter-bare. The wrongness of it all put a pit in her stomach, the hairs on the back of her neck bristling with the creeping sensation that something wasn't right . . . that she was in danger.

In that moment, something became very clear: this was not *her* Drayton.

Lennon pressed the button on the control panel, over and over again, willing the doors to close and take her away. "Shit. Shit. *Fuck.*"

It was no use. After several minutes of panicking, she disembarked and stepped out onto the grass. Lennon turned away from the elevator for a split moment to take in the scene at hand, and when she turned back, it was to the discovery that the golden doors she'd stumbled through mere moments before were gone. She lifted a hand and slapped herself, hard, and when that didn't jar her awake, she pinched her forearm hard enough to leave a bruise. Still, the scene before her, the inexplicable . . . the *impossible*, remained.

In the distance, through the bare branches of the magnolia trees, Lennon spotted Logos House. As she approached it, she saw that its door was open to her. She entered, treading carefully, taking pains not to touch or disturb anything. There was something about the place that forbade interaction, as though this was a museum exhibit, sectioned off by invisible lengths of velvet rope, and she a patron passing through it.

Upstairs, the door to each bedroom was shut, except for the one on the far end of the hall. In that bedroom, there was a young boy sitting on the floor, with his bruised and bony knees collected tightly to his chest.

"It's you. From my dream."

The boy raised his head, and when they locked gazes, she saw that his eyes were filled with blood. Lennon heard a great roaring—like the sound of swarming flies and a thousand TVs turned to channel zero.

She staggered back, turned to face an exit that was no longer there. The door had just disappeared into a featureless wall.

The boy stood up. He held something loosely in his fist; she could see it flickering through the cage of his fingers. Something small, like a baby mouse or a spider. Without really knowing why, Lennon moved to accept it, extending her hand. The boy gave her his gift: a brown moth with tattered wings.

It twitched in the flat of her palm.

In the dark between blinks, an elevator appeared behind the boy. It opened its doors, and music spilled out into the windowless room. Chords of some classical concerto that Lennon should have known by name but didn't. Her gaze went from the elevator to the boy to the moth that now lay dead in her hand. She staggered, took two large steps forward, toward the elevator, dropping the moth in her haste to make it through the door, and collapsed on the floor of its cabin. She was aware, suddenly, of the fact that she could barely breathe. The last thing she saw as the doors drew closed was the boy, crouching on the floor, the moth cradled in his cupped hands.

13

LENNON WOKE TO the gentle crackling of a fire. From somewhere off in the red-washed dark, hushed snatches of conversation: "The elevator appeared out in the garden. According to Sawyer, she said it was for her, walked through the doors, and they closed behind her."

"How long was she gone?"

"No more than fifteen minutes. Sawyer beat on the doors, called for help, but they wouldn't open. I did the same. Then at random the elevator bell rang, the doors parted, and there she was, slumped against the far wall of the cabin. Barely conscious."

"You did the right thing," said Dante. "Bringing her here to me."

"She could've gotten herself, or someone else, killed."

"I know," said Dante. "But we can address that. How many people know what you know? How many people saw?"

"Well, there was Sawyer, Kieran, me, Blaine. A couple people at the party may have seen as well. I don't know. It was all happening so fast."

Lennon's head felt too heavy to lift. She shifted her gaze left and saw two figures standing in the shadows near the hearth, just beyond the reach of the flame's light. There was Emerson with a crust of blood beneath her nose, squinting at Lennon through the bright glare of her glasses, and Dante standing close beside her.

"Give me a moment alone with her," she heard Dante say.

"Sure." Emerson left the office, and Lennon could have sworn she heard the soft click of the door locking shut behind her.

Lennon managed to sit up, bracing a hand on the back of the couch. The room pitched, this way and that, in a sickening wave of vertigo. Dante strode out of her line of vision and returned a few moments later with a small metal wastebasket. He set it on the floor between her feet.

"I'm fine," said Lennon, waving him away. "I'm not going to—"

She retched acid, gagging so violently her throat hurt. Bile spattered the bottom of the trash can.

"Where did you go?" Dante asked, crouching at her feet.

Lennon straightened. Her memories filtered back to her, out of order. She remembered the elevator doors parting open. Emerson dragging her half-conscious from the cabin. She remembered seizing in the corridor with her classmates gathered in a ring around her—a lot of people shouting for nurses and room to breathe and someone who could do CPR, even though she was quite aware of her heart punching furiously at her sternum. Then she remembered the boy and his moth in Logos House. The sprawling campus, the grass crusted with frost.

"I don't know where I was. It was like Drayton but not."

"How was it different?"

"It was cold. There was frost on the ground."

Dante, for his part, looked deeply troubled. "Did you see anyone there?"

Lennon nodded. "There was a boy. A little boy."

Dante stiffened, his jaw locking tight.

Lennon squirmed under his gaze. "Are you going to tell me what's going on or—"

There was a knock at the door.

"Not now," said Dante.

The secretary's voice came through the closed door. "The vice-chancellor's on the phone."

"Tell her to hold."

"She says it's urgent."

"Have Emerson handle it. Tell her to stall."

Dante's attention shifted back to Lennon. "What did the boy look like?"

"He was Black . . . maybe nine or ten. Skinny."

"And where did you see him?"

"In Logos House."

"Did this boy speak to you?"

Lennon shook her head. "He never said a word."

Dante caught her by the chin, tilted her head slightly downward, so they were staring at each other eye to eye. "This school, this place is not what you think it is. It's not a haven or a refuge. And what is about to happen next is going to be ugly. So I'll need you to keep a cool head."

"I'm scared. I want to go home," she said, without really knowing where home was anymore. She couldn't bear to return to Wyatt, even if he would take her back, and she hadn't spoken to her blood relations in many months. For the first time Lennon understood the solemn concept of her own aloneness.

"Home won't shelter you from this," said Dante. "Now listen to me. There's going to be a trial—"

"A *what?*"

"They'll call it a disciplinary hearing, but make no mistake: what you say—or neglect to say—will dictate your future."

"What do I need to do? What should I say?"

"Tell them everything short of the truth. Tell them about the elevator. But leave out the bit about the boy . . . and the cold too. Keep those details to yourself and you'll be all right." As he said this Lennon felt a peculiar sensation, similar to lightheadedness. The memories of her encounter in the elevator scrambled then faded. She shut her eyes, tried to remember, to bring the boy's face into focus, but she couldn't. It was all so terribly fuzzy, like a dream half-forgotten.

"I—I don't understand what's happening."

"You don't have to if you just do what I'm telling you to do. The explanations, the understanding, that'll all come later. My focus now is making sure you live to see that day. Do you understand?"

Emerson entered the room before Lennon had the chance to answer.

Dante turned to look at her. "Well?"

"Emergency hearing," said Emerson.

"When?"

"Now, according to Eileen."

Dante hung his head. "Fuck."

The hearing was to take place in Irvine Hall. Lennon and Emerson walked there together, Dante staying behind to tie up loose ends, whatever that meant. It was a foggy evening, and Lennon felt like the two of them were wading more than walking to Irvine. They were silent until they reached its doors and Lennon, turning to Emerson with a pit in her stomach, asked the question she'd been holding back. "Am I going to be expelled?"

"I doubt Dante will allow that to happen," said Emerson.

"Does he have the power to prevent it?"

"If it's put to a vote . . . perhaps not. But you should know by now that he's incredibly convincing. You don't have anything to worry about. You'll be okay."

Upon entering Irvine, they were ushered up to an oblong conference room on the second floor of the building. It had no windows. There was an oval table at the center of the room. Seated around it were most of Drayton's tenured professors—Dr. Lund from meditation; Dr. Ethel Greene, who presided over Lennon's Art and Ego course; Benedict from Lennon's entry interview, who smiled tightly at Lennon. The vice-chancellor, Eileen, sat at the head of the table. There was a glossy black rotary phone in front of her.

Eileen gestured to one of two empty chairs at the table. "Have a seat, Lennon. Make yourself comfortable. Emerson, you can go."

"But Dante—"

"Is not the one leading this hearing. I am."

Emerson looked at Lennon, gave an apologetic shrug, and left the room. When she was gone, Eileen turned on her. "Perhaps we ought to begin with a verbal account of exactly what it was that you saw after exiting the elevator."

"But Dante isn't here," said Lennon, feeling trapped, like at any moment she might accidentally say something damning. "I was under the impression he'd be present."

"I can't account for his absence, nor can I afford to wait for him. Now answer the question: What did you see after exiting the elevator?"

Heeding Dante's warning, Lennon kept her answer short and simple. "I saw Drayton when the doors opened."

There was an ensuing volley of questions.

"What time of day was it?" Ethel Greene demanded.

"It was night."

Eileen deftly twirled a pen with a ripple of her pale fingers. "Did you see anyone?"

"No," said Lennon, delivering her first lie of the hearing in a careful deadpan.

"And did the campus look the same way you remembered it?" Eileen inquired, pressing for more, but more of what Lennon didn't know. Was she trying to catch her in a lie? Or was there something specific she was fishing for?

"Everything looked the same to me. It's just that I was in one part of campus and the doors opened to another. It was really nothing more than that."

The questions came faster after that, delivered with the urgency of someone trying to squeeze out their last words before a trigger was pulled.

"How did you open that gate?" Dr. Lund inquired from down the table.

"I—I don't know."

A woman Lennon didn't recognize spoke from beside him: "You don't know, or you won't say?"

"I won't say because I don't know. It just happened."

The professors exchanged long and worried glances. Lennon wondered what she'd said or done to make their moods sour even more.

"Nothing just happens," said Ethel Greene. "You must've done something."

"I didn't. I mean, well, I did have some shrooms—"

"So, just to clarify, you *did* do something? You were under the influence of a contraband substance during this encounter."

"I . . . yes. I guess?"

"Would you have described yourself as high?"

"I mean, I was a little high," she said, an understatement stretched so thin it tore and became a lie.

"Allow me to get this straight." Eileen leaned forward, steepling her fingers. Her gaze cleaved down the middle of the table to Lennon. "You were under the influence of a psychedelic drug when the elevator appeared?"

Lennon's cheeks warmed. It had been a long time since she'd felt this small and ashamed. "That's right."

Benedict took over, his line of questioning decisive and cutting. "Is there any possibility that you may have—while under the influence of this substance—mistakenly made a *choice* to call that elevator? Perhaps some part of you wanted it to appear?"

"I don't think so. But I'm not sure."

"What are you sure of, Lennon?"

"I don't know what you mean."

"Let me phrase the question more succinctly: What did you know to be fact when the elevator appeared? We've already established that you were under the influence of a mind-altering substance. But I'd like to know a bit more about your emotional state at the time of the elevator's appearance. What were you feeling?"

"I . . . I guess I was peaceful? I was out in the garden with Sawyer." She wondered then if it was a mistake to say his name, to drag him into this mess. "We'd been talking about how we came to Drayton. All of these hopes and dreams, and I don't know if it was the shrooms, or if I was just sleepy, but when I felt most relaxed the elevator appeared where the door of the garden shed had been, just moments before."

Benedict smiled, as though she'd finally done something right.

Just then, the door opened, and Dante stepped into the room. "Forgive my lateness," he said, draping his coat on the back of the empty chair across from Lennon's. He sat down. "I assume we're done with introductions?"

"I warned you to be on time," said Eileen.

"And I warned you that this hearing was a farce. But here we are."

"Dante," said Eileen. It was the hushed and contemptuous tone of a mother just before she begins to yell.

He raised his eyebrows mockingly. "Eileen?"

"If there's something you'd like to say or argue, you have the floor. Lennon is your advisee, after all."

"I'll keep this brief. Lennon is an asset to this school. Frankly, you're all lucky that your brief tenures have overlapped with her attendance here, because she's the first natural gatekeeper we've had in more than a century."

There was a swell of noise, everyone speaking at once—contradicting Dante, whispering among themselves, a handful of professors who argued for everyone else to be quiet and thus contributed greatly to the noise themselves. The commotion reminded Lennon of a startled flock of chickens.

"What's a gatekeeper?" Lennon asked, but they either didn't hear or chose to ignore her.

Only Dante registered that she'd spoken, his gaze softening some as it met hers. When he spoke across the table, the rest of the room went quiet. "Gatekeepers can open gates, at will, to different places. The last one who lived was Irvine, who first built the confines of this school and shielded it from everyone else."

"Drayton's prodigy. From convocation. I remember."

"Then you may also remember that Irvine gave his life to defend this school," said Eileen, not looking at Lennon, or anyone really, her eyes trained on some random point near the center of the table. "He weighed his own life against the interests and well-being of this school and chose the latter."

"But he was also a student," said Dante. "He learned to hone his gift, and when it came time for him to lay down his life, that was a decision he made himself. A willing sacrifice. Not something that was forced upon him."

Eileen waved him off. "She isn't worth the trouble. Irvine was a prodigy. He'd been taught in the ways of persuasion for years. Whereas Lennon—"

"Hasn't had the opportunity to prove herself," said Dante, cutting her off. "All I'm asking is that you give it to her. Under my instruction—"

"*Your* instruction?" Eileen looked incredulous—baffled, even.

"All right, if not mine, then Ben's. Let him show her the ropes. She has promise, Eileen. The least you could do is give her the chance to prove it."

But Eileen shook her head. "I've heard enough. Let's put this to a vote and be done with it. Shall we?"

"Lennon hasn't done anything dangerous. All she did was open a gate to another part of campus. That's hardly a capital offense—"

Eileen ignored him, turned to address the rest of the room. "All in favor of expulsion?"

All the professors around the table, save Benedict and Dante, raised their hands.

Lennon's heart seized. Just that quickly, with a few raised hands, she had lost *everything*. "W-wait please—"

Eileen stood up, collecting her papers. "Well, that decides it. Dante, as her advisor, I'll leave you to handle this situation in whatever way you see fit. Just make it clean, will you? You know how messy these things can become when a memory is left half-intact."

But Dante didn't move or speak. His gaze homed in on the rotary phone, just a split second before it started to ring, a shrill tinny sound that silenced the room—the murmurings of conversation and the shuffling of papers, the heartbeats and ragged breaths, the buzzing of the bulbs in the old chandelier that dangled above the table—it was a sound that seemed to suck up every other.

Eileen, along with the rest of them, stared motionless at the phone for a few rounds of ringing before—as if emerging from a trance—she picked it up, snatching the receiver from its cradle, holding it to her ear. "Yes. Yes, sir. No. Of course."

Dante locked eyes with Lennon and smiled.

Eileen pulled the receiver from her ear and placed three fingers over the mouthpiece. "Lennon, the chancellor would like to speak with you." She passed the phone down the table, the coiled cord stretching almost taut.

Lennon took it, raised the receiver to her ear. "Hello?"

"You will continue your studies here at Drayton." The voice crackling over the line was the same one that Lennon had heard, weeks prior, when she'd first received word of Drayton. A voice like all of the voices of everyone she had ever known together in horrid synchrony. Her mother, her sister, Wyatt and Sawyer, Sophia and Dante, Blaine and Benedict, the childhood friend with whom she hadn't spoken in more than eleven years, the clerk at her favorite grocery store. And then—perhaps the loudest voice of all—her own. "You will train under Benedict to hone your skill as a gatekeeper, in the service of this school. Do you understand, Lennon?"

A muscle in Lennon's clenched jaw jumped and twitched. "Yes."

There was a rattling sound—like loose change in a cup, or perhaps the clearing of a throat through a storm of static. "I wish you the best of luck with your future studies."

14

LENNON AND DANTE emerged from the hearing to find that the mild showers from earlier had given way to a punishing deluge. They waited for the worst of the storm to pass in a dark and empty breezeway off of Irvine Hall. Dante fished a tin of what appeared to be hand-rolled cigarettes from the pocket of his trousers. The wrappers were black, and they smelled strongly of clove. He offered one to Lennon, and the two of them smoked and watched the rain come down. It was a particularly good cigarette—wrapped tight and thin with a milky clove smoke that, when exhaled, made pale whorls on the air.

"Did you speak to the chancellor on my behalf?" Lennon asked. "Is that why he called when he did?"

"I might've put a good word in for you," said Dante.

"I owe you one."

He waved her off. "You owe me nothing. I'm your advisor. It's my responsibility to look out for you."

That responsibility seemed starkly at odds with what Eileen had asked him to do during the hearing. "I don't think Eileen shares your concern."

"She's just afraid."

"Of what?"

"You, of course." He paused to examine the tip of his cigarette. Flicked away the ashes. "Here at Drayton, we like to think of persuasion as a science. Our founder, John Drayton, believed in developing skill through practice and firmly asserted that mastery could only be ascertained through complete and total control of your own mind and, with practice, the minds of others. But there are some among us whose abilities are more . . . compulsive. Emotional, you could say. John found them threatening because a power like that can't be entirely controlled. It's instinctual and, by proxy, volatile."

"And you think that was what happened when I opened that elevator? My emotion was the trigger?"

"Yes. But you shouldn't be too hard on yourself. There are quite a few of us, actually. And we can do great things if we devote ourselves to understanding the particulars of our own process. Your elevator gate may have appeared compulsively—may still appear that way—but you have a responsibility to learn your triggers and master this power as best you can. Because if you fail to do that . . . there will be repercussions."

"Like you taking my memories?"

He didn't respond.

"Would you have really done that? If Eileen had asked you to?"

"That's the school policy, so yes."

"And if you did that, I wouldn't remember Drayton or the people I've met . . . or you?"

Dante—still staring at the rain—traced the filter of his cigarette back and forth along the line of his lower lip. "If I'd done my job right, yes. I would've taken it all."

"How?"

"That's a lesson for later in the semester," said Dante. "It involves an application of persuasion that's near surgical in its precision and as a result it's incredibly dangerous. If done wrong, you can make a person's mind forget how to execute basic functions like breathing and swallowing. That's why it's considered combative persuasion, the first stage of it anyway. It's one of the ways we kill with the power we wield."

Lennon wanted to ask if that was something Dante had done before—if he or anyone else at the university had killed with persuasion—but she bit the question back. "That sounds . . . a little sick."

"It can be," he said. "But I've seen it used in more merciful ways. There was a professor who taught here a few years ago, Dr. Gordon Meyers. He was dying of spinal cancer, one of the most painful ways a person can go. I and the other professors here took it upon ourselves to induce a state of memory loss, moment by moment—"

"Like laughing gas? Making him forget the pain?"

"Just like that," said Dante. "But more efficient. It allowed him some lucidity in his final days, while also shielding his mind from the worst of the pain he endured. He died with a smile on his face. Imagine that: a man at the end stages of one of the most painful cancers known to man dies grinning. I've never seen anything like it."

"You're still trying to talk me out of my moral qualms?"

"It'll make the rest easier," said Dante. "You'll deal with so much during your studies—neurosis, exhaustion, frustration, burnout, despair—why add guilt to the mix?"

"I can't help it," said Lennon with a shrug. "Symptom of a functioning conscience."

Dante gave her a wry smile.

"There is something I wanted to talk to you about . . . but I didn't know how to bring it up."

"Go on," said Dante, watching the rain.

"I saw you a few weeks ago and . . . you weren't yourself."

She had half expected this statement to trigger some reflexive response from Dante—a stiffening or a look of shock—but he remained placid. "What do you mean by that?"

"I mean you were different."

"How so?"

"You looked at me differently."

Here Dante met her eyes, and it was everything Lennon could do not to cower under his gaze. "And how did I look at you?"

"In a way you shouldn't have," said Lennon, a little frustrated now, and embarrassed to even say this out loud though she knew she wasn't the one who should've felt ashamed. "Or at least . . . in a way you wouldn't have if you'd known what you were doing. And then you just smiled at me, so strangely, and the next day, during class, it was as if nothing happened. I realized then that you didn't remember. That whoever it was I'd encountered wasn't the same you who's here with me now."

Dante hung his head, looking for a moment conflicted. "I'm sorry."

"You don't have to apologize. I knew it wasn't you. But I do want to know who he was."

"I don't know if I can answer that question in a way that will satisfy your curiosity."

"Try," said Lennon.

Dante seemed, for a moment, to search the rain for an answer. "There's a cost for what we do here. That night, you saw that in the form of whatever—or whoever—it was you encountered. I try to keep him leashed, but it's hard at night, when I'm tired. I wasn't able to make it back to Irvine before he broke free of his tether and surfaced."

"Who is he?"

"He's as much me as the man you're talking to now. I just like him less."

"How long has he been with you?"

"Quite some time. But he doesn't mean you any harm." Dante said this in a way that indicated he meant someone harm, but that someone was not Lennon. "Can I ask you to keep this between us?"

Lennon was reluctant to agree to that. "Will he appear again? I mean, surely you can't keep him chained up forever. Can you?"

"I can certainly try," said Dante. "Like I said, I'd had a hard night. I lost composure, but I won't allow that to happen again, which is why I'd appreciate your discretion."

"You have it."

"Good," he said, and looked relieved. "On that same note, I wouldn't speak to anyone about what you saw through the elevator gate. Not even Benedict, if you can avoid it. You'll have to be careful with him, and with everyone from here on out. Your future at Drayton depends on it." The rain abated some. Dante dropped his cigarette and crushed it underfoot.

"Why?"

Dante made as though he hadn't heard her. "You should head back to Ethos. Before the next band of the storm sweeps through. Remember what I said about Benedict and the rest, especially if you want to keep your memories of this place."

"Is that a threat?"

"Yes," said Dante. "But not one from me."

15

IN IRVINE HALL, there was a single elevator, constructed by William Irvine himself. It had ornate iron doors, its cabin was relatively small, and its control panel sported about a dozen buttons, each corresponding to a different location—New York City, Amsterdam, Kyoto, Moscow, Boston, Beijing. With the press of a button, the cabin accessed these different cities as easily as the levels of a building. Unlike the elevator that Lennon had summoned, William's elevator didn't spawn at random. It was a fixed feature of Irvine Hall: reliable, efficient, and perfect in its functionality, despite its old age.

This was the elevator through which Lennon, and many of her peers, had first entered Drayton. It was also the elevator that she was instructed to take back to Benedict's home in Utah for the first of her weekly lessons in gatekeeping. Eileen had wasted no time adjusting her schedule. The night of the hearing, the vice-chancellor had arranged for her first class with Benedict to take place the following afternoon.

The journey to Utah took the better part of three minutes, and

Lennon took this opportunity to examine William's elevator. Apart from the fact that it was a bit old and rickety, the elevator seemed completely normal. Riding in it, Lennon would've never guessed that it accessed different cities instead of floors.

She wondered why the faculty had been so panicked by the elevator she'd opened. What was so dangerous about this means of transportation anyway? As far as she could tell, it was nothing more than a faster alternative to driving or flying. But none of the faculty had treated it as such. There was something she didn't yet understand that Dante and the rest had been either unable or unwilling to disclose the night of the hearing. And Lennon was determined to discover what exactly that was.

There was a man waiting for her in the foyer of Benedict's house when the elevator slowed to a stop. He was tall and broad-shouldered, with brown eyes and a lick of golden-blond hair that swept tastefully across his brow. He had an aquiline nose and high cheekbones.

"I'm Claude," he said without really looking at her, which was a bit awkward because, with the two of them alone in the hallway, there was nothing much else for him to be looking at. He extended a pale hand threaded with delicate blue veins.

She shook it. It was damp and very cold. "Lennon."

"A pleasure."

There was an awkward silence, during which Lennon expected Claude to offer some explanation of who he was and why he was greeting Lennon instead of Benedict. When he didn't, Lennon, a little affronted by his rudeness, said: "And you are . . . ?"

"Ben's apprentice. He asked me to show you in. I'm sorry he's not here to do it himself, but he's out in the garden attempting to behead—or if not that, then poison—the mole that's been digging up his rosebushes. But he'll be in shortly." Claude spoke with a gravelly antebellum drawl that made him sound like a southern aristocrat who'd died and been buried, exhumed, and reanimated.

They sat together in the living room, where—on a large oak coffee table—a selection of hors d'oeuvres had been arranged—finger sandwiches, cut vegetables, and the like. Lennon didn't partake of anything but a small cup of tea that tasted so strongly of roses it was almost unpleasant.

Claude watched her from an armchair across the room, his brow furrowed. His pale eyes possessed a disconcerting intensity that made Lennon feel like she was crawling out of her skin.

"You'll have to forgive my staring. It's just that I expected . . . *more.*" This would've been rude if it'd come from the mouth of anyone else, but Claude delivered this naked truth with an air of nonchalance. As if he was simply too casual to be cruel.

But even though Lennon knew he meant no harm, she still bristled a bit. "More of what?"

"Well, now that I've said it out loud . . . I don't really know. I guess I just expected someone different. Older. But you can't be more than, what? Twenty-one?"

"Four," Lennon corrected him. She drained her teacup, set it down in the saucer with a clatter, and winced.

Claude only smiled, pulling a small flask from the pocket of his blazer. He offered it to her, and when she shook her head he merely shrugged, and poured a generous splash into his own teacup. "It helps with the nerves," he said.

Benedict entered then, or perhaps he'd been stalling in the doorway for some time, waiting for the right moment to make his presence known. He was light-footed, as if he had memorized each of the creaking floorboards of the old house and took special care to avoid them. He wore a wide-brimmed straw hat and a dirty canvas apron.

"Off you go," he said, shooing Claude out of the chair he sat in.

He obliged, winking at Lennon on his way out of the parlor.

"I see you've met my apprentice," said Benedict.

"How is an apprentice any different from an advisee?" Lennon asked.

"Simple," said Benedict, lowering himself into his chair. "An apprentice is someone who's actually going to be something someday. Something more than the average student at Drayton. A professor like myself typically has only one, maybe two, apprentices in a lifetime. That's because, as my apprentice, Claude will take up my tenure. This house and everything in it will become his. He'll be tasked with protecting this gate and by proxy one of the few entrances to Drayton itself. He will, in essence, become me. In choosing him as my apprentice, I've chosen my successor."

Lennon wondered who Dante's apprentice was, if he had one. If not, was there a chance—however slim—that she could be considered for the role?

"Your Dante was apprenticed to Eileen," said Benedict, as if sensing that her thoughts had turned to her own advisor. "He'll one day—sooner rather than later, I suspect—choose an apprentice of his own. I'd thought Emerson O'Neill was a shoo-in for the role, the two of them being so close and her having so much promise. But now that you've come along with your elevators . . . I suspect you may be an upset in her path to succession."

Lennon indulged herself, for a moment, with the idea of becoming faculty. She imagined a corner office, with a fireplace and Eames chair. Faculty cocktail hours and long walks around Drayton Square. Yes, she decided, she did want that. She wanted that very much, enough to rip that dream straight from Emerson's clutched hands. Enough to fight for it. She had no interest in congressional seats or the sort of stupid money that could buy a house in Montecito. She didn't want fame and was too selfish to have a real heart for philanthropy the way that Nadine did. But Drayton would give her two things she desired: power and the skill to use it.

"Of course, you'll have to work hard," said Benedict. "Harder than you have been working. I've looked over your transcript. Your grades are abysmal at best, and I think you know that. But there is hope for you, in the form of that elevator you called. Your special talent."

"But I don't know how I did it," said Lennon. "Dante said emotion might've triggered me—"

"Emotion is not reliable. Nor is it a substitute for skill. You need to approach this pragmatically so that the power you wield remains firmly within your control. Because if you fail to do that, the aftermath of that failure could be both devastating and far-reaching."

Lennon sensed there was something more he wasn't saying, about the gates and their mysterious power. But she knew that if it was something he was willing to share, he would have. "All right," she said. "How do I do that?"

Benedict didn't answer that question directly. At least not at first. "As I'm sure you know by now, there are those whose will is strong enough to shape the hearts and minds of men. But then there are those whose will is so strong it can shape reality itself. You appear to fall into the latter category, as did William Irvine before you."

He paused for a moment, considering what he wanted to say next. "At Drayton, we teach illusion work. Typically, these studies are reserved for second-year students. These illusions are essentially advanced applications of persuasion that warp sensory stimuli in order to convince a subject of a specific reality." Benedict demonstrated this by abruptly changing the scene outside the parlor windows from day to night.

"Oh my god."

"It's quite an impressive little trick," said Benedict, and he quickly restored the windows to their true appearance. "But it can be more than that. When illusion work becomes more advanced than the little parlor trick I demonstrated to you, it enters the realm of theoretical persuasion. The long-held idea is that when you create an illusion so believable that even reality takes it for truth, what you've done, in effect, is create a new reality. That is the skill that both you and William possess in the form of your elevators."

"This is simulation theory," said Lennon.

"You're not wrong," said Benedict. "But let me be clear, you and William Irvine are not the only two individuals who are able to create illusions so convincing they become reality. There have been a number of exceptional practitioners in Drayton's long history—John Drayton and Dante being two of them—whose talent and brilliance allowed them to bend the laws of reality in ways both small and large. However, you and William Irvine are set apart in that your ability to bend reality extends well beyond shaping matter. You appear to possess the ability to bridge space, in the form of traveling across the material plane by elevator. That is what makes you different, special."

"Why do the gates take the form of elevators?" It was a question that had plagued Lennon since the hearing.

"They don't always," said Benedict. "The gate William first opened was, in fact, a single door. Then a hallway with many doors. After he saw an elevator in New York for the first time, he began to spawn those too. My suspicion is that humans need a way to conceive of the inconceivable. The image of the door or the elevator is a familiar one and has been for some time. It creates a sense of liminality that enables us to conceptualize its basic function.

"I would imagine that many years prior, a gate—to someone who had never before laid eyes on an elevator, or before an elevator was invented—might've appeared to them as a stairway, or a corridor like William's, or perhaps a curtain to be drawn back. An ancient human might've seen a field of high grass moving with the wind, offering glimpses of another world behind it. The possibilities are endless, really. The mind makes reality. Your gate manifested itself to you in the form of an elevator because that is an image that both invites use and most accurately conveys its purpose."

"You talk like it's a sentient thing. A creature with a mind of its own."

"It's not. But you most certainly are, and the elevator *is* you."

From there they began to practice, a series of exercises not unlike the ones that Lennon endured in Dante's persuasion classes. Although, unlike in those classes, Lennon channeled her will not toward a rat but toward the empty far wall of Benedict's parlor, trying to summon an elevator.

As it turned out, Benedict was not of much help on the practical end of things. This was not so much his fault as it was the school's. Decades ago, in the days after William Irvine's death, the library had caught fire, and many of the records that William kept on how to raise a gate were lost to the flames.

"If you know how to do it, why can't you just force me to with persuasion?" Lennon asked, frustrated.

"If only it were that simple," said Benedict, staring at her across the table. That crude portrait on the wall behind him seemed to stare down at Lennon too. "The short answer is that you have to learn to do it on your own at first. In the beginning, no one can do it for you."

"But why?"

"It's like if you tried to force a newborn baby to walk. As an adult, you're quite competent, but it's not the same for an infant. Their feet are too round and swollen to stand on, their legs too weak to support them, the ligaments of their necks not yet developed enough to hold their own heads aloft. Even if you forced them into the proper positions, it would be pointless. It's an anatomical impossibility for a newborn to walk at that nascent stage. The same can be said for you now. You have to develop your mind—building its proverbial muscles—in order to endure the rigors of raising a gate reliably. No one can do it for you. At least, not until you learn to do it yourself. It's the same with almost every persuasive skill."

"So you're saying I'm screwed if I can't figure this out by myself?"

Benedict gave her a curt little smile. "How about you try again? This time, replicate your state of mind when the elevator first appeared."

His phrasing made it sound simple, but the ask itself was almost impossible, unless Lennon got her hands on the same psychedelic drugs that Kieran had gifted her that night at the party. After taking them, she'd felt relaxed and dreamy, like her soul was spilling out of her body, but she was too sedated to even care.

Her mindset now was completely different. Under Benedict's careful observation, she felt small and scrutinized and horribly anxious. She'd never performed well under pressure—had loathed public speaking and presentations and anything that required her to deliver a performance in front of an audience of any size. Her mental state couldn't have been farther from the sleepy serenity she'd experienced out in the garden with Sawyer. After several long hours with nothing to show for their efforts Benedict, looking deeply troubled, ended their lesson.

16

THE FOLLOWING DAY, Lennon found Kieran in the central dining hall, sitting alone at the table reserved for the members of Logos. On his tray: a plain, dry hamburger, fries, and a glass of milk. He ate with mechanic pragmatism, chewing slowly, his gaze scanning back and forth across the dining hall as if the scene was something he was reading rather than seeing. But when his gaze met Lennon's, it affixed itself firmly and he smiled.

Kieran was one of the few famous students at the school, for all the wrong reasons. He was a chemistry prodigy who had appeared on the talk show circuit at just nine years old after entering a doctoral program at Stanford. But at age thirteen—four years into his PhD—he was busted for operating a meth kitchen out of the apartment he was supposed to be sharing with his mother (his mother was living with a boyfriend at the time, spending surplus scholarship funds that should've gone into Kieran's trust). Worse yet, the drugs that Kieran cooked in his kitchen were tied to the fatal overdoses of several students on the campus. The media jumped on the story of the chemistry prodigy / media darling turned manslaughtering drug dealer, because if there's anything a news network loves it's a spectacular fall from grace.

But the story of how Kieran came to study at Drayton was far murkier than the well-publicized tale of his downfall. Allegedly, about three years—and several prison transfers—into his eight-year sentence, Kieran enrolled at Drayton, where he had now been a student for more than six years.

Lennon sat down opposite him, trying not to look as intimidated as she felt. "What did you give me at the party?"

"I don't give anything to anyone," said Kieran, his eyes vacant. "I offered you a sample of my product in the hopes that you'd want more. And clearly you do."

Kieran paused to take a small bite of his hamburger, chewed, and swallowed. Lennon found his choice of meal particularly egregious given the selection at the buffet today—deep-fried soft-shell crab; oysters on the half shell, nestled in beds of ice; collard greens with smoked pork; and a large vat of Brunswick stew. She couldn't help but wonder what kind of psychopath would choose a dry hamburger and milk over all of that. "Unfortunately, you're out of luck, because I'm all sold out."

"Well, what do you have?" Lennon asked.

"Something stronger. But of course, that comes at a price."

"I don't have any money," said Lennon. As far as she knew, no one on campus did. They were totally cut off from the currencies of the greater world. The cafes around Drayton were all free, the food unlimited. There was no rent or tuition, and the loans that did exist were largely tacit, everyone operating under the shared understanding that their great work—the contribution that paid their theoretical debt—was the mastery of persuasion.

"Luckily for you, I accept different currencies," said Kieran.

"Like?"

"Favors."

"What kind of favors?"

Here, Kieran leaned low against the tabletop. "There's a professor who confiscated something that belongs to me."

"What's the item and where is it?"

"It's a rat and his name is Antonio, though he doesn't answer to that . . . or much of anything anymore. You'll find him in Dante's lab, in Wharton Hall."

"Wait a minute, are you asking me to break into Dante's lab to kidnap a rat?"

"Antonio isn't *just* a rat. I mean, he was until I gave him a soul. Or at least, I think I gave him a soul. I'm not sure about the particulars."

"How did you give a rat a soul?"

"Crack," he said, and then frowned. "Well, it was sort of a distant cousin of crack that I alternated with DMT and then I laced his water with it at first, which didn't work quite as well as you think it would—look, it doesn't matter. The point is, I need you to kill him."

Lennon's eyes flashed wide with shock. *"What?"*

"A rat with a soul is a terrible burden. I mean, their little minds aren't meant to comprehend the existential. They're intelligent animals, but I pushed things too far, and now that rat exists in a state of complete psychological agony, and it's driving me crazy. I mean, you make a monster and the very least you can do is put it down."

"Well, why didn't you?" Lennon demanded, suddenly very defensive over this sentient rat that she didn't even know.

"I was failing Dante's class first semester," said Kieran. "I knew I had to do something . . . impressive, to bring my grades up. So I gave it a few drugs, opened its mind. It was like a kind of psychedelic therapy, or at least I intended it to be. Anyway, Dante was impressed. I mean, he didn't actually say that, but I passed his class—which had to mean I made at least a ninety-nine on his final—and afterward, he confiscated Antonio and I never saw him again after that."

"Then how do you even know he's suffering?"

"Because I can feel it," Kieran insisted. "There's a tie between me and him. I mean, I can barely sleep. All night I can hear him, like, in my head, thinking these . . . *thoughts*. Philosophical bullshit about time and mortality and the great fallacy of our present reality. It's nauseating, not to mention never-ending. I'm going fucking insane." He slammed a hand down on the table, and his glass of milk leapt an inch or so into the air. "I need quiet. I need to not tranquilize myself to sleep every night. That's where you come in. Dante's your mentor; you can get into his lab on a lie if you're smart enough. Go in, kill the rat, get your drugs. It's that simple."

"If it's that simple, why haven't you done it yourself?"

"Because I don't want to take the fucking risk," he said. "If you're stupid enough to get caught, all you're looking at is a couple demerits and a semester-long suspension if you catch Dante on a bad day. I get caught? I'm finished. Expelled. Dante hates my fucking guts and has for some time. He catches me in his lab killing one of his rats and it's over."

"Why don't you just ask him to kill it, then?"

"He'd never agree. He keeps those rats as experiments. If I told him Antonio was sentient, he'd just have even more incentive to keep him alive and suffering for as long as he could. Thank god you're willing to help."

"I never said I was willing."

"You didn't have to," said Kieran, chugging down his milk. "I can see it in your eyes. You're desperate."

She bristled. "No, I'm not."

Kieran's mouth pulled down at the corners. "Lennon, admitting you have a problem is the first step toward sobriety."

"I'm not an addict."

"Then what is it? Why do you want the drugs so badly? Trouble in class?"

Lennon started to stand up. "You know what? Forget it."

"Don't be like that," he said, and he opened his arms. "You can trust me. I don't expose the personal information of my customers. Your secrets are safe with me. And I already know all about the elevators, so there's no point being coy."

Lennon relented, not because she trusted him but because Kieran possessed a kind of exhausting charisma. He had a way of wearing you down that she found at once draining and highly amusing, and as much as she wanted to dislike him, she just . . . couldn't. It was easier (not to mention more fun) to just play along, give him what he wanted. "That night the gate, or whatever it was, first appeared, it was after I took those mushrooms you gave me. And I haven't been able to open a gate since."

Kieran seemed unsurprised. "You shouldn't feel too bad. Plenty of us need a little chemical boost to get us going. It's why everyone around here smokes so much. And why I have a business."

"Is that what you call it?"

Kieran smiled, choosing to ignore that insult. "The doors of Wharton are locked, but if you're quiet and careful you should be able to tail Dante, or someone else, through the doors and duck behind one of the shelves without being seen. Antonio is the biggest rat in the lab. He's all brown, and his eyes are human. You can't miss him. Just go in, kill him, and be done with it. And don't try to lie and say you've done it when you haven't. I'll know."

"Wouldn't dream of it," said Lennon, and she got up from the table, feeling a little sick and unsteady on her own two feet. She realized that she had never killed anything before. Not really. Not on purpose anyway. Once, though, she'd had a particularly sadistic friend, a little white boy in her neighborhood, a few years older than she, who'd asked her to watch as he poured a pot of boiling water over an anthill. Halfway through the horrible act, overcome with guilt and disgust, she'd caught him by the wrist and tried to stop him, splashing boiling water all over her thighs in the process. The resulting burns had blistered so badly she'd had to go to urgent care, and she couldn't wear anything but dresses for weeks after. She'd hated that, but what she hated even more was that the pot had been half-emptied, and all the ants and their precious eggs boiled alive, by the time she'd worked up the courage to intervene.

17

THE NEXT DAY, after her Persuasion I course adjourned, Lennon lurked in the hall waiting behind a corner. By now, she knew Dante's routine. After every class period, he took the time to speak with any lingering students. Sometimes these exchanges lasted only a few minutes, but on other occasions he'd remain in the classroom for more than an hour, answering questions and tutoring any students who were struggling. On some occasions, these impromptu meetings became small lectures, and half the class would remain just to listen to him. And if that wasn't enough, those same students would appear during his office hours, cramming the waiting room and spilling over into the halls beyond it, leaning against the wall or sitting on the floor with their legs thrown into the corridor, waiting for hours just to speak with him.

And, sure, Dante had a certain star power. At thirty-three he was the youngest tenured professor on campus, and as Eileen's former apprentice, he was slated to take on the coveted role of vice-chancellor someday. But Lennon knew that it wasn't just his accolades that made so many people want a piece of him. It was something else, a charisma, an ineffable quality that made you feel all the better just for being near him and made everyone regard him with a sense of awe that Lennon found, in truth, a little sickening, if only because it was such an ugly reflection of her own susceptibility to Dante's draw, a reminder that what she felt for him wasn't special at all.

Luckily for Lennon, Dante dismissed himself early that night, so she didn't have to wait very long. With a murmured apology about his being double-booked, Dante emerged from the classroom minutes after the last student departed, holding the rats under his arm in their shared transport cage. As usual, he made his way to the exit of the building, and Lennon waited for the sound of his footsteps to fade before she emerged from around the corner and followed him to Wharton Hall, which housed all of the labs on campus.

Lennon herself had never stepped through the doors of Wharton (first-year students like herself never took lab courses), and she almost lost Dante in the labyrinthine halls of that building. But Lennon caught up with him just as he disappeared through the double doors at the end of a short corridor, slipping a key into his pocket before stepping between them. Lennon had to sprint to catch the doors before they closed. She slid inside, casting her gaze about the lab as she did.

Dante, his back turned to the door, had not noticed her.

With a silent sigh of relief, Lennon ducked down the narrow aisle between two tall shelves that were packed top to bottom with more than a dozen rat cages. And there were countless other identical shelves in that long galley of a room just like it. What disturbed her wasn't a lack of care, per se—all of the cages were small but clean, and they each had food, wooden toys, water droppers, a bed of pine shavings, and some sort of structure, even if it was just an overturned yogurt cup with a hole cut into the side. What troubled her was the sheer number of rats in that room. There must have been hundreds on the shelves. The task of finding the one that Kieran had asked her to retrieve was all but impossible, especially with Dante just feet away, on the other side of the shelves she was hiding behind.

Trying to be light on her feet, Lennon paced the aisles searching for this brown, human-eyed rat. It was sheer luck when she found him, only a few minutes into her search, on a lower shelf that she only saw because she'd ducked to avoid being spotted by Dante. He was unusually large, with intelligent eyes.

This was Antonio. She was sure of it.

Lennon slid the cage off the shelf as quietly as she could and, still ducking, retreated toward the double doors at the front of the lab. She was almost there too, her hand just inches from the door handle, when Dante spoke: "Be careful with that one. He bites."

Lennon froze, almost dropping the cage.

She turned to see Dante, standing at a table in the heart of the lab, his back toward her.

"How did you—"

"If you're going to tail someone you should really consider wearing softer shoes or just socks maybe, to muffle the sound. Your footsteps are unusually loud."

Lennon felt the tips of her ears go hot. Embarrassed, she stepped out from behind the shelf and approached him. Up close, she saw that he'd rolled up his sleeves, exposing his tattooed forearms. There was something small and pink in the flat of his palm. A baby rat. He appeared to be feeding it formula with a thin syringe.

"They have to eat every one to two hours at this age," he said, nodding down at that rat in his palm, so small and pink that at a distance it looked more like a grub. "Before I found a lab tech to bribe, I used to keep rats like this one in a paper coffee cup padded with lots of pine shavings. I'd carry it with me from class to class and hope none of my students snitched when I pulled out the syringe to feed it."

"What happened to its mother?" Lennon asked, coming up beside him.

"She rejected it," said Dante, and then, in a firmer tone, "Go ahead and set that cage down."

Lennon, flushing, placed Antonio on a nearby lab table. "You could've just told me you'd heard me."

Dante smiled to himself, never taking his eyes off the rat in his hand. "I could have, but I would've missed out on the joy of watching you attempt to be discreet."

Lennon frowned.

"What do you want with that rat?" he asked, without judgment. If he was angry with her for attempting to steal it, he gave no indication.

Lennon hedged her bets, hastily, trying to deduce the best way forward. She decided, after a brief debate, to be honest. "I need it. To trade with."

Dante raised an eyebrow. "Kieran has his claws in you already?"

She was surprised he knew about Kieran's enterprise, but perhaps she shouldn't have been. Dante, it seemed, knew about everyone and everything that happened on that campus.

Lennon stared down at her hands. "I was high the night I called the elevator."

"And you think that this . . . altered state might've opened your mind? Made it easier?"

Lennon nodded. "That first time, when I was high, it was effortless."

"And you think that's how this should be? Effortless?"

"I mean, no. I realize that I'll have to work for it, the way I've worked for everything here. But the thing is, I tried so hard with Benedict, but there was just nothing on the other end. I think the drugs would open my mind more, make it easier for me to reach whatever it was I tapped into in the garden that night when it first appeared."

"How does the rat come into play?" When Lennon didn't answer (she was no snitch) Dante nodded as if she had. "Oh. Kieran. I assume he wants it dead?"

As he said this, Lennon became aware of how large Dante's hand was and how pitifully small the rat was in comparison. He could've crushed it in a closed fist.

"I thought you didn't want to hurt anything?" Dante asked, pressing her for a real answer.

"I don't," said Lennon. "But if it's suffering—"

"What do you mean by 'suffering'?"

"If it's in pain—"

"Everyone has experienced pain."

"Well, I mean constant pain."

"Constant physical pain or constant psychological pain?"

"Just . . . I don't know, any kind of pain."

"What level of constant pain warrants a moral euthanasia?"

"Agony."

"And how would you define 'agony'?"

"I don't like this line of questioning."

"No one does," said Dante. "But when you hold the power of life and death, it's important that you produce answers. If only to quiet your own conscience."

Lennon swallowed dry. "If someone or something is in a state of constant agony, a state of torment, I think it's a mercy to end that suffering, even if there's only one way to do it."

"And that's why you want the rat dead?"

"I don't want it dead. Kieran does."

"Do you think I would let something suffer like that?" Dante asked. The question, Lennon realized from the earnestness of his delivery, wasn't rhetorical. He wanted her read on him.

"I mean, I don't know . . . I don't think so—"

"Does the rat look like it's suffering?"

Lennon peered down into the cage. Kieran was right—the rat had human eyes—but it didn't seem any worse for it. "Well, no."

"That's because it isn't. Kieran is. And not from some psychic tie either."

"Kieran? What do you think is wrong with him?"

"Nothing. He just has a newly acquired conscience," said Dante, very matter-of-factly.

"So he's just . . . feeling guilty for the first time?"

Dante nodded. "He had antisocial tendencies. A consistent lack of guilt made worse by the fact that the entirety of his childhood was devoted to the role of being a media object. No one expressed empathy toward him—least of all his parents, who enriched themselves on his celebrity—and as a result Kieran never learned to express empathy to anyone else. Until he came here."

"And studied under you."

"Persuasion is often a perverse exercise in empathy," said Dante. "To be good at it, you have to grasp that, and Kieran, one of the more driven students in his class, very much wanted to be good. So there you have it. Kieran meddles in the minds of a few rats and becomes a real boy with the conscience to prove it. It's really kind of sweet."

"Kieran doesn't think so," said Lennon, flushing. Dante looked up at her. Something about being under Dante's gaze always made her want to squirm . . . but in a way she kind of liked it. She'd had crushes on professors before. That had been in a distant way part of Wyatt's appeal. But never quite like this. "He's tormented. He says he can't sleep."

"Is that why he had you come here to kill that rat?"

"I wasn't really going to kill it," said Lennon. "I was going to let it go."

She wasn't sure if Dante believed her. She wasn't even sure if she believed herself.

"You know," said Dante as he took up the syringe again, began to dribble the milk mixture into the baby rat's mouth, "psychedelics can be particularly dangerous for people like us. The wrong drug—or the wrong dose of the right drug—can be the equivalent of cutting a psychic artery. The damage could be incalculable. You're willing to take that risk?"

She shrugged. "I don't see another way forward. I have to perform if I want to stay here."

"And you want to stay?"

"Of course," she said, made defensive not so much by what he said as the *way* he said it. As if he wasn't sure whether or not she had the chops. "There's nowhere else I want to be, and I'll do what it takes to make sure that I get to stay. I want my memories. I want to keep my life here, even if that means—" Her voice broke when she looked at Antonio, those sad human eyes of his, and she cast her gaze to the floor.

"I can respect that," said Dante, and the little rat twitched in the flat of his hand. He picked it up, gingerly, between thumb and index finger and lowered it back into the incubator that stood on the table. "But you should know that it's a dangerous game you're playing now. A game that many have lost before. And I know you think you're different, that you won't get addicted—"

"I am, and I won't," she said, sounding surer than she felt.

"Maybe that's true. But addiction isn't the only thing you should be afraid of. Sometimes when you open your mind you can't close it again." It hurt a little, how flatly he delivered this warning, as if he was obligated to say it but really couldn't care less if she turned up overdosed in a ditch on the side of the highway. But then she saw something in his eyes, a fear in them. Though as soon as he caught Lennon staring, he masked it, withdrawing into himself and shutting her out in the process.

"If it's so dangerous, aren't you obligated to stop me?" she said, almost daring him to do it, daring him to care about her or give some indication that he was invested, if only a little. Her ploy worked, because Dante looked up from the table and they locked eyes. She hated herself for the way she stiffened, flinching, as she met his gaze. Her cheeks warmed and reddened, and she was certain he noticed.

"You have a habit of wounding yourself," he said after a long beat. "I stand in your way now and you'll just hurt yourself again tomorrow. At some point, you have to learn how to deter your own worst impulses, or if not that, then work around them. Maybe this is your way of doing that. And if so, who am I to interfere?"

18

THAT SAME NIGHT, in Kieran's room on the lower floor of Logos, Lennon imparted everything she'd learned about Antonio. She told him that the rat wasn't in pain, and therefore couldn't be paining Kieran. She carefully explained that there was, in fact, no psychic bond at all except for, perhaps, Kieran's own attachment to his newfound conscience.

"I think if you learn to forgive yourself, even a little bit, the insomnia and stress might ease up," said Lennon. She herself knew a thing or two about what a bludgeon guilt could be when wielded like a weapon of self-destruction. In fact, it had been something she'd struggled with every day since coming to study at Drayton, every time she meddled in the mind of Gregory during persuasion class, or thought about how anxious her family must be to think that she'd abandoned her life in Denver to study at some institution they'd never even heard of. "Once you're clear of the guilt, I know you'll feel better."

Kieran nodded, frowning. There was a long silence, and for a moment Lennon thought he wouldn't hand over the drugs. She hadn't, after all, delivered on her end of their deal. But she was surprised when Kieran retrieved a small baggie from a loose floorboard beneath his bed and handed it to her.

"Ideally," he said, "you'll have four people with you when you take this. Two to restrain you, one to intervene psychically if things go awry, and another to distract anyone who might overhear and try interfering. But that's only if things go south, of course. And they probably won't. You seem sane, and as long as you keep calm, you should be all right."

Lennon stared at the baggie in the flat of her palm. Within it were two white tabs. It was hard for her to believe that such a strong psychedelic could be confined to something so small. "Thank you."

"Nothing to thank me for," he said. "We had a deal."

Lennon took that as her cue to leave, but Kieran called her name before she reached the door. She half turned to him. "Yes?"

"If you ever need anything else . . . you know where to find me. Not as a dealer but, you know, as an associate."

"You mean a friend?"

He wrinkled his nose, disgusted, flustered. "I don't have friends. But you know. I'm around."

PER KIERAN'S ADVICE, LENNON GATHERED FOUR OF HER closest classmates—Ian, Sawyer, Blaine, and Nadine—in her dorm room later that same evening and almost immediately regretted the decision. Blaine and Nadine, to her surprise, expressed some mild concern but took the idea in stride. Sawyer, however, was conflicted, and Ian was utterly incensed.

"Let me get this straight," said Ian, pacing the room, "you're going to take drugs you got off a teenage psychopath who turned a rat into a crackhead? Are you hearing yourself?"

"I don't think you're supposed to say 'crackhead,'" said Nadine in a soft voice. "I mean, addiction is a complex issue—"

Ian ignored her. "This is a bad idea, Lennon. A dangerous one. It could ruin your life. Trust me, I would know."

"We took the drugs at the party, and we were fine, right, Sawyer?"

Sawyer, sitting on the edge of her bed, only frowned.

"Nadine's right," said Lennon, unbothered by Sawyer's lack of verbal support. "Don't be such a fucking prude. I mean, didn't you deal drugs?"

"This is different. That kid Kieran has killed people with whatever he was cooking up in his kitchen. And you're fragile—who knows what the hell that'll do to you."

"I'm not fragile, and that was years ago. He was thirteen. He promised me this was clean."

"I really worry about you sometimes," said Ian. He had done a lot of worrying about Lennon recently. Worrying about who she liked or was maybe sleeping with. Worrying about where she was and why she'd come home to Ethos late. Worrying about what she said to him, and more importantly what she didn't.

Lennon had first attributed this new possessiveness to the stress of their increasing workloads—the hours of homework, the hundreds of pages worth of reading, the pop quizzes, and of course the grueling exercises they performed on rats in persuasion. But Ian was easily at the top of their class, securing the highest grades not just in persuasion but in every other course he was enrolled in too. He was all but guaranteed a bed in Logos House. And yet he seemed miserable—edgy and irritable and corrosively jealous in a way that Lennon found at once exhausting and assuring. As shameful as it was—and she was ashamed—she liked the fact that Ian found her worthy enough to be jealous over. After all she'd been through with Wyatt, it was nice to feel like she was something precious that someone as brilliant as Ian had to fight to keep.

"Are you going to say something to your roommate?" Ian demanded, imploring Blaine now.

"I'm not her keeper," said Blaine.

"Maybe not," said Ian, "but you are the only one who she might consider listening to, so how about you have at it?"

Blaine looked to Lennon for a long beat, then back at Ian. "She can do what she wants."

"Fuck." He kicked over the trash can by the desk. Crumpled papers and cigarette butts spilled across the floor. Nadine moved to clean up the mess, and as she leaned over, Lennon noticed that her blouse was open lower than usual (before, every button had been fastened, all the way up to her throat), exposing a pale slice of her chest. She wasn't wearing her crucifix either, and her hair, which she'd worn in a sensible bun at the nape of her neck on every occasion that Lennon had previously seen her, now fell long and loose about her shoulders.

"Mark my words," said Ian, stepping right over Nadine to jam a finger into Lennon's chest, "this is a bad fucking idea."

"Look," said Lennon, squaring with Ian, "I'm taking the tabs. So you can either stay here and watch, or you can leave. I won't hold it against you either way."

He glared at her. "I didn't think you were this dumb," he said, then he turned on his heel and was gone, slamming the door shut behind him.

Nadine scrambled to her feet. "Should I go after him?"

Lennon nodded. "Just . . . try to keep quiet, all right? I don't think he would tell anyone, but if he does—"

"I'm on it," said Nadine, and then she too was gone, leaving just Lennon, Sawyer, and Blaine alone.

Blaine stared down at her hands. "I'm loath to agree with Ian on anything, but what if he's right? What if this is a bad idea?"

"Jesus Christ," said Lennon, "when did you all become such prudes?"

"It's not that," said Blaine. "The last time you took a psychedelic, you were so . . . so—"

"Catatonic," said Sawyer, finishing for her.

Blaine nodded. "It was like a part of your brain had broken for a moment. I really thought we weren't going to get you back. It was terrifying. It almost would've been less scary if you were just out cold. But you weren't. Your eyes were open and you were tracking us, but your expression was so vacant. It was clear that you weren't behind your own eyes anymore."

"Even Dante looked worried," said Sawyer. "And he's never worried. About anything. But you were in rough shape, Lennon. You weren't present enough to see it, but we were. It was bad. Really, really bad. And this drug is even stronger than the last one you took, so who knows what will happen. Is it really worth the risk just to pass a class?"

"It's not just a class," said Lennon. "If I don't prove to them that I have a handle on this whole elevator gate thing, they're going to take my memories of this place and kick me out."

"They said that?" said Sawyer, looking stunned.

Lennon nodded. "So I have to do this. Okay? With or without you."

Sawyer just shook his head, but Blaine—lips bloodless and pursed—nodded.

"All right," she said. "Let's do it."

Following Kieran's instructions, Lennon removed one of the two tabs from the baggie and placed it on the tip of her tongue. She waited for a while, sitting cross-legged and straight-backed at the foot of her bed. The minutes ticked by, and she tapped out a rhythm on her thigh to keep the nerves at bay. Sawyer paced with his hands behind his back. Blaine nibbled at a hangnail on her pinky finger. "A disgusting habit," she said, sheepish, when Lennon looked her way.

Ian and Nadine did not return.

Exasperated, Lennon made to stand. "This is bullshit. I don't even feel—"

The ground rattled. A brief little shudder that reverberated through her bones.

"Did you feel that?" Lennon asked, sliding all the way out of bed. Her legs felt limp beneath her.

"No," said Sawyer and Blaine in unison. Their pale faces had taken on a strange glow that reminded her of those Bible stories where people encountered angels whose brightly shining faces hurt to look at.

"Well, I think it's working," said Sawyer, and when he spoke, she saw a glimpse of pink tongue, the black at the back of his mouth where his throat began. His voice sounded wet and muffled.

"Easy," said Blaine, or the suggestion of Blaine, really; there was no part of her that Lennon recognized as the friend she knew. A white light had overtaken her. Blaine's hand felt hot and foreign on her arm.

"You need to call an elevator," said the voice that belonged to Sawyer. "Hurry before you get too high."

When Lennon nodded, the whole room pitched this way and that like a snow globe shaken. And she was surprised when all the furniture remained in place.

She started chattering, teeth cracking together so violently she bit every word she attempted to speak clean in half, like brittle cookies.

The crumbs of everything she meant to say scattered across the rug at her feet.

"She's not making any sense," said the Sawyer voice, sounding panicked. "We should call someone."

"Just give her a chance," said the one that was Blaine. "She can do it."

Lennon's vision blurred badly at the edges, so she only had a pinhole to see through.

"Go ahead, call the elevator," said Blaine. "You can do it. I know you can."

"I'm trying," Lennon managed to say, though she was not in fact trying to do anything more than stay on her feet and keep from throwing up.

The blurriness cleared some, retracting back to her periphery. And the light in Blaine and Sawyer's faces dimmed along with it. She could see the room again—the dimensions a little warped, as if gazing through a glass tumbler, and she felt her legs firm up beneath her.

Lennon then homed in her vision on a bare spot on her bedroom wall because that seemed like the likeliest place for an elevator to appear. But every time she tried to focus, her gaze kept being pulled back to the door. She felt like if she squinted hard enough, she'd be able to see right through it, see through everything.

"Why does she keep going cross-eyed?" Sawyer asked.

"Don't talk about me like I'm not right here," said Lennon, and her voice didn't come from her mouth but from beneath her feet. The floor shook with it.

Someone in the ground was speaking along with her.

"There's someone under the school," she said, dropping to her knees, flipping up the rug so that she could press her hands flush to the bare wood beneath it. "I can feel it."

"It's crack," said Sawyer then, nodding grimly. "It's *definitely* crack. He gave her crack, Blaine. What are we going to do now?"

"Shut up," said Blaine, and she got down on her hands and knees beside Lennon, her entire presence like the pulse of a heartbeat beside her.

The ground trembled again.

"You don't feel that?" Lennon asked.

"Feel what?"

"The ground. It's moving." Lennon scrambled to her feet and tore through the common room and downstairs, barefoot and in her pajamas. She made several long strides into the green before Blaine and Sawyer—winded and hollering—caught up to her. By that time she was on her knees, fingers sunk deep into the soil, which rose and fell like the belly of a big, hairy man as he breathed.

"It's alive. There's something alive under there," she said, and passed out cold.

19

LENNON SPENT THE next three days in the infirmary recovering from a near-fatal overdose. After Lennon passed out in the middle of the park, Blaine had very nearly broken her sternum with a vigorous—and as it turned out, lifesaving—round of CPR.

"You're lucky to be alive," said Dr. Nave. Every time he made his rounds, he was sure to squeeze in a good scolding. "Are you sure you don't know who gave you those drugs?"

Lennon shook her head. Kieran may have almost killed her, but she was no snitch. "I didn't get his name. He was just some guy in Utah I met at a gas station."

Dante visited several times during the course of her stay. At any point, he could've outed her for her lie, and she was grateful—though not entirely surprised—that he didn't. The first time he'd visited, she'd woken up in the middle of the night to see him sitting in a chair at her bedside, staring at her. It took her a moment to register his worry, and she'd been surprised by it. But the moment passed so fast,

Dante leaning back into his seat, slipping a paperback from the inner pocket of his jacket, that she'd wondered if she'd been mistaken.

On that visit, Lennon had asked him if she was going to be expelled, if this overdose would be deemed a damning offense in the eyes of Eileen and the other governing faculty members.

But Dante shook his head. "You didn't call an elevator compulsively or jeopardize anyone. So no harm, no foul."

He read in silence for the rest of that visit.

On later visits, he came in the evenings. Mostly, he just sat at her bedside, reading or occasionally grading papers, content to sit in silence.

"Are you mad at me?" It had taken her some time to work up the courage to ask the question.

He looked up from his work, and she saw in his eyes that he was. In fact, he was angry in a way that almost scared her, that made her stiffen and brace to be yelled at. But that wasn't Dante's way. "Of course I'm angry."

"You could've stopped me," said Lennon.

"I had hoped you'd have the good sense to do that yourself."

Lennon took the scolding in turn. Tilted her head back against the headboard and stared up at the ceiling. "I couldn't even call an elevator, and my mind didn't open up the way you said it might. It was all pretty stupid in the end. I thought the ground was breathing—"

Dante glanced at her, eyes narrowed.

"What?"

"Nothing," he said.

"It was something. I saw it. You glanced at me."

"I can't glance?"

"Not like that," said Lennon. "Not when you're thinking things about me that you won't share, for whatever reason. What was it?"

"I just found it intriguing, that's all. The ground breathing beneath you. It sounds like you might've tapped into something . . . manipulatable."

"What do you mean?"

He set the stack of papers he'd been grading on a nearby table. "The first step of persuasion is observation. We lend our attention to the subject we want to manipulate; you know this already. But when you're trying to manipulate something inanimate, it helps to find a sort of energy in it that can be bent to your will. Just like a human mind. It sounds like the night you overdosed, you might've done just that. Might've seen a glimpse of life where formerly only its lifelessness was visible to you."

"So you're saying I took a step in the right direction? That my getting high wasn't useless, after all?"

He shrugged. "You tapped into something. If you can learn how to control that, to command it the way you do the mind of, say, a rat, you can learn to raise a gate on command."

"You sound so sure."

"You've done it before. You'll do it again. But only when you believe you can."

AFTER LENNON WAS DISCHARGED FROM THE HOSPITAL, THE days passed steadily. Lennon dutifully attended her classes, managing the workload as best she could, staying up late in the evenings to finish lengthy required readings for metaphysics, sketching a series of crude and, at times, frightening self-portraits as homework for Art and Ego, and generally struggling to catch up and account for the time she'd missed while in the infirmary.

Early-morning meditation remained a grueling chore, persuasion with Dante a challenge. Her days became a blur of classes, punctuated by sessions with Benedict in Utah that proved just as exhausting and thankless as they did before her overdose. If she achieved anything from that near-deadly trip, the rewards certainly weren't obvious to her.

Lennon saw little of Blaine during these dreary weeks. Their schedules misaligned so that whenever Lennon was leaving for her classes in the morning, Blaine was dead asleep or only just returning. And whenever Lennon retired in the evening, Blaine was already gone, often not coming back until the wee hours of the morning, skulking and sneaking quietly into bed, like she was a teenager who'd been out past curfew. So it was something of a surprise when Lennon returned home after a particularly long and punishing session with Benedict to discover Blaine lounging on her bed.

"Where the hell have you been?" she inquired no sooner than Lennon kicked off her shoes. Blaine stared at her now, her brow creased with worry, like Lennon was a slip of tissue paper that could be blown away by the wind at any moment. Sawyer was just as anxious. Lennon often caught him watching her during the classes they shared, and every night he made a point to stop by her dorm and check in on her, as if he thought she'd die alone seizing in her bed if he didn't.

Lennon couldn't blame either of them, given what had happened. But their vigilance was a constant reminder of her own failure, just how stupid she'd been to risk her life to call an elevator that hadn't even appeared, despite her best and most earnest efforts. And there was the guilt to contend with too. Guilt for what she'd put them through, for how scared they must've been that night on the green, when her heart had briefly stopped beating. She'd apologized several times, of course, but it still didn't seem like enough.

"I'm not the only one who's been out," said Lennon, shirking the spotlight. "Where were you last night? And for that matter, the night before that too?"

"You answer first."

"Studying, worrying, descending into complete and utter despair. Your turn."

"I was hanging out with Kieran and Emerson," said Blaine.

"Emerson?" Lennon raised an eyebrow, but in truth she wasn't entirely surprised. It wasn't uncommon to see Blaine dining with the members of Logos House, who seemed almost eerily drawn to her, like moths to a light in the night. So much so that Blaine once expressed to Lennon that it was difficult to befriend anyone else. "Logos is still courting you?"

Blaine gave a noncommittal shrug. "They really want me in."

"But why?" Lennon blurted, and then—realizing just how rude and jealous that sounded—attempted to salvage the question. "I'm sorry, what I meant to say was—"

"That I'm not top of the class? It's okay, Lennon. We all see one another's grades. Nothing's secret here. You can speak freely. I'm not hurt." She said this last bit in a way that argued otherwise. But then she smiled forcibly. "Maybe they just fell prey to my charm."

"Well, we can't fault them for that," said Lennon.

They carried their conversation out through the common area and to the communal bathroom they were all made to share, something that had taken Lennon several weeks to adjust to. Back in Denver with Wyatt, she'd had a large and luxurious primary bathroom with a claw-foot tub and infrared sauna. It was a jarring adjustment to go from that to a dorm lavatory, but Blaine's company made the situation better.

Earlier in the semester, when they saw each other more regularly, they'd made a habit of doing their nightly wind-down together, meeting in the bathroom to perform their skin-care routines (the commissary on campus had a surprisingly good variety of products) and gossip about the goings-on of the day. Typically, they saved their most salacious topics of conversation for the shared shower stalls, where the hiss of the water made it impossible for anyone else to overhear.

But Blaine was uncharacteristically quiet that night. She turned to face the showerhead, her back to Lennon. She looked on the verge of tears.

"Are you all right?" Lennon asked.

Blaine tilted her head to the slick green bath tiles that covered the floor and walls. The water, burning hot the way she liked it, reddened her pale skin.

"I'm fine," she said, turning the water off. It was a remarkably short shower for her, and Lennon had the suspicion she'd ended it early to avoid answering her question. She slipped out of the shower stall, taking her towel off a hook nearby. "It's just . . . sometimes I feel so lonely here, you know?"

Lennon found this statement odd, given that Blaine was inarguably one of the most popular first years on campus. But it was also odd because Lennon felt so different. To her, Drayton was beginning to feel like . . . home almost.

Lennon said none of this to Blaine, wanting to avoid hurting her any more than she'd already been hurt (though by whom or what, Lennon didn't know). It seemed to her that since the day they'd first met, Blaine had been carrying with her some heavy and invisible burden, as if wearing it strapped across her frail shoulder blades, perpetually stooped under the weight of whatever unspeakable thing it was that she refused to put down. And as time went on, either the burden had become heavier, or she had become weaker, or both.

Maybe, Lennon thought, it was the stress of their workload getting to her, the way it was getting to Ian and all of the first years, herself included. Or perhaps Blaine had some secret lover that was slowly breaking her heart—that seemed more likely, what with all the nights she'd disappeared from her bed. But that didn't explain why she looked so sick and sad all of the time. Unless, of course . . . it did.

"Blaine, is someone hurting you?"

No answer.

Lennon frowned, finished rinsing away the last of the shaving cream beneath her armpits. "Blaine? Hello?"

Nothing.

Lennon cut the water, stepped out of the shower stalls, dried herself off, and fumbled into the pair of pajamas she'd brought with her. The bathroom, now empty, seemed dimmer than it had before they'd stepped into the shower. As if a few of the lights had been cut off. Those that remained lit flickered terribly. "Blaine?"

The name echoed through the empty lavatory. Again, there was no answer.

She made her way to the sinks, wondering if Blaine had stepped out of the bathroom, though it wasn't like her to leave without first saying goodbye. Unsettled, she began to apply her shea butter, working it into her elbows and knees. She lifted her gaze to the fog-clouded mirror and saw behind her a figure that she first mistook as the aberration, and then as Blaine. She was wrong on both counts, but before she realized this a black screen of oblivion came down over her field of vision and she felt nothing.

Nothing at all.

20

WHEN LENNON CAME to, she was barefoot, standing shoulder to shoulder with a handful of her classmates—Ian, Sawyer, Nadine, and a few students down, Blaine, her head hanging, cheek cradled against her shoulder, eyes screwed closed. They stood motionless, as though their feet had been tacked to the floor.

Seated before them, behind a long oak banquet table, were members of Logos, among them Claude, who was smiling; Emerson, dragging on a cigarette; Kieran (who winked at Lennon and gave her two thumbs up); Adan; Yumi; and three others. They were all murmuring among themselves over glasses of wine and spent cigarettes smoldering in overflowing ashtrays. The air was blue with smoke. There was a glass apparatus, filled with greenish liquid, that had three spigots. Beside it were eight, frosty glasses, one for each student standing in front of the table, and a candy bowl filled with folded slips of paper.

In the dead center of the room—between the members of Logos and the line of initiates—was a small wooden card table with two chairs, a folded switchblade placed in front of each of them.

Emerson's voice—high and clear—cut through the din of conversation. She was pinching a clove cigarette; it looked like a stick of charcoal burning low between her knuckles. Smoke wafted across the room, the lacy tendrils forming a number of words: *primordial, wiles, ripe, ubiquity.* It smelled, strangely, of burnt tea leaves. "Let's just get on with it."

Kieran stood up: "Fine." He cast his gaze on the row of underclassmen standing before him. "Tonight will most assuredly be one of your worst at Drayton. Maybe one of the worst of your life. I won't say it's worth it, but I will say that none of you are here because you lack the drive you need to succeed. You're all hungry, and that hunger is what got you through our doors tonight. But what will allow you to stay is something more: genius. What you do here tonight will prove whether you've got it or not."

"Is . . . this s-some type . . . of hazing?" Lennon slurred and, to her intense embarrassment, dribbled spit onto the Persian rug beneath her bare feet. Her tongue felt numb, swollen fat behind her teeth.

Emerson stubbed out the nub of her spent cigarette, and immediately fished another from the pocket of her blazer and lit up on the candle flickering in front of her. "I thought you tied them," she muttered around the filter.

"I did," said Kieran, casting the words over his shoulder with a snarl. "It must be wearing off."

"Or maybe you didn't tie her off tight enough?" Claude suggested. "Do you need a refresher?"

"Shut up." Kieran wheeled back to face the students. "Consider this an audition. You have one chance to prove yourself worthy of joining our ranks here at Logos. You step forward. You drink the absinthe." He motioned to the fountain and the glasses arranged around it. "Then you pull a paper from the fishbowl. Read the name of your opponent out loud and take a seat at the card table. The opponent will then step forward, drink themselves, and take a seat. No redraws. No do-overs. Nothing. Understood?"

Nobody spoke. No one but Lennon could, what with the tongue ties still firmly in place.

Emerson tilted her head to Kieran. "Cut them loose, will you?"

"Fine." He snapped his fingers, and the row of students slackened to the point of collapse, falling to their hands and knees. Lennon, for her part, felt as though her legs had gone to sleep. The pins and needles were so severe it was as though her legs had been paralyzed. She thought for a moment she might fall too, but somehow managed to stay on her feet.

"Are any of you familiar with the knife game?" Emerson inquired. "If not, the rules are pretty simple. You're going to splay your nondominant hand on the table, making sure there's space between your fingers. Then you're going to pick up the knife and pierce it into the table between your fingers as fast as you can without stabbing yourself. You'll play two at a time, using persuasion to manipulate your opponent into stabbing themselves. Winners are initiated. Losers are out. Which is to say, half of you won't make the cut. We'll go left to right, starting with Blaine."

Blaine, who stood at the far end of the line, froze. It was the first time Lennon saw her look anything less than entirely composed. She staggered forward, her bare feet scuffing across the carpet as she approached the table. She filled one of the glasses to the brim with absinthe, downed it in a single swallow. Her hand shook as she lowered it into the candy bowl. She withdrew a slip of paper near the top, read the name aloud: "'Felix.'"

Felix flinched and paled at the sound of his name but stepped forward. He drank his absinthe, took a seat, and put his left hand down on the scarred tabletop, fingers splayed wide apart. Blaine did the same, and picked up the knife, and Felix, pausing to wipe a sweaty palm on his pant leg, followed suit.

"Pierce the table to the rhythm of this beat," said Emerson, and she began to strike the table. "One, two, three, four. One, two, three, four. Begin."

They began to stab the spaces between their fingers to the rhythm of Emerson's counting. It started out slow, and Lennon began to relax a little, suspecting that perhaps this game wouldn't be as gruesome as she'd initially expected it to be. But Emerson's counting picked up speed, and Blaine frowned with concentration. Beads of sweat formed above the dip of Felix's cupid's bow. Blaine's attack was quick and incisive: one moment their knives were dancing between their fingers in unison, and the next, the tip of Felix's split through the knuckle of his middle finger with a grisly crunch. He cut a cry that made Lennon's heart seize in her chest, and ripped the blade free of his hand.

Blaine—looking pale and sick to her stomach—pushed sharply away from the table and stumbled to her feet.

"Welcome to Logos," said Emerson, as two other members of the house escorted Felix out of the room. "Let's keep going. We don't have all night."

Kieran stepped forward to wipe down the table and Felix's knife, sopping up all the blood. When everything was clean, Nadine stepped up to the front of the room. She filled the glass of absinthe, pinched her nose tightly shut, and swallowed it down. She looked for a moment like she needed to throw up, but when she recovered herself, she pulled a slip of paper from the candy bowl and her chin immediately wrinkled with the effort of holding back tears. "'Sawyer.'"

Sawyer stepped forward, filled his own glass of absinthe, which he drank down slowly, like it was water. They both sat down at the table, picked up the knives, and the game began again.

"One, two, three, four. One, two, three, four . . ."

This proved to be one of the longest rounds that was played that night. It felt like watching a game of tug-of-war between two people, equally matched.

"One, two, three, four..."

The game picked up speed, and Lennon watched as both Sawyer and Nadine surrendered to a kind of trancelike state, their hands moving of their own volition as their minds toiled away at the great and gruesome work of bending the other to their will. It was Sawyer who prevailed in the end, though: with a strangled little cry he forced the hand that Nadine held pressed to the table a half centimeter to the right. The point of the blade clipped her pinky, and a small bubble of blood welled from the wound and trailed onto the table.

Emerson gave a slow clap. "Welcome to Logos, Sawyer."

Nadine left the room in tears.

Ian stepped up to the front of the room. He didn't look even remotely worried, which made sense given that he was easily the top of their class, and even as a first year was widely considered to be one of the most competent persuasionists on the campus. First, he filled his glass and threw back the shot of absinthe. Then he turned to the bowl, rustling through the slips of paper—a theatrical gesture—taking longer than he needed to select one, given that there were only a couple left. He smiled even, as he unfolded it, but the expression froze on his face when he read the name written there.

"Lennon," he said, his gaze flicking up to her, then casting sharply away.

Lennon felt as though the floor had dropped beneath her feet. When she stepped forward, she thought for a moment that she was being persuaded to do it. As instructed, she filled her glass of absinthe and drank it down. It was strong and herbal, bitter enough to burn her throat when she swallowed. Then she sat down opposite Ian.

"Well, this should be quick," said Kieran with a shit-eating grin that made him look more than twice as punchable as he usually did, which was already quite punchable.

Across the table, Ian could barely look at her. His face—pale to begin with—had drained of almost all color so that he appeared nearly jaundiced in the wan lamplight. Before the game had even begun, he forced a thought into Lennon's mind: *Don't fight. I'll make it painless. Just a nick.*

At the sound of his voice in her head, Lennon flinched and fumbled the knife. It struck the floor, and she picked it up, to a chorus of snickering. Ian withdrew from her mind, but she could still feel the greasy residue of his presence within her, a kind of violation. And who the fuck did he think he was telling her to go belly-up?

"Poor thing," she heard Yumi whisper to Emerson. "I hope this is quick."

Lennon pressed her left hand to the table, spread her fingers so far apart they hurt.

Ian pressed his left hand down. Humiliatingly, he didn't even bother to spread his fingers wide like she had. It was clear he wasn't expecting anything remotely close to a proper fight, and that sparked something in Lennon. It made her angry. It made her want to *win*, not just to earn a bed in Logos but to make Ian eat the very words he'd forced into her mind.

Her hand tightened around the blade. Across the table, Ian—grimacing—gave her a curt nod. Emerson began to count: "One, two, three, four . . ."

Lennon pierced the knife between her fingers, firmly embedding the blade each time. The idea was to get used to the rhythm, to give herself over to the trance of it before she made any attempt to breach the confines of Ian's mind. But her strategy was wholly based around the fact that Ian didn't see her as a threat. He wouldn't seize violent control—he had no need to. She'd given every indication that she would surrender to him, which meant that *she* had the element of surprise. Not him. When Ian's first move did come, it would likely be gentle—he didn't want to hurt her; he'd made that clear. He was expecting nothing less than full compliance. But Lennon knew that the moment she fought back, or even raised her defenses, Ian would realize that she was contending with him, and the ruse would be broken.

She had to act fast, before he knew that she was fighting.

"One, two, three, four."

Lennon summoned her strength, honed her focus—and drove her will toward Ian. She had intended a simple gesture, a jerk of the hand that would've done nothing more than clip the knuckle of his index finger. She was more stunned than horrified when the blade went through Ian's hand—piercing cleanly between the tendons and pinning it to the tabletop. He didn't scream, but his mouth wrenched open, and his good hand slithered from around the hilt of the knife and fell limp to his side. He stared—wide-eyed—at his own hand nailed down to the tabletop, the dark puddle of blood spilling out from under his palm and leaking through his fingers. Ian started to say something and passed out cold. His weight pulled against the knife blade, tearing the wound a little wider. Lennon sprang forward to help him, ripping the hilt free of his hand. Ian slumped low in his chair.

"Holy fuck!" Lennon shrieked, dizzy at the sight of what she'd done. "*Help!* Someone help him—"

But no one moved. Everyone remained frozen there. Even the logicians at the table looked on motionless and in shock. It was Emerson who broke the silence, staring at Lennon with narrowed eyes. "Congratulations on your acceptance to Logos."

21

AFTER THE INITIATION, Lennon found her way upstairs to her new dorm in Logos House. It was dark, and she didn't so much as flip on the lights before climbing into its one and only bed and losing herself to a dreamless slumber. She woke hours later, in the late morning, and by the light filtering in through the curtained windows, examined her new room. It was about half the size of the dorm she'd shared with Blaine, but better furnished. There were bookshelves bracketing the hearth, already filled with belongings from her dorm in Ethos College, though she hadn't recalled anyone coming in last night. The wardrobe was similarly stocked; all of her clothes washed and freshly pressed, the collars starched, her shoes polished. There was a bathroom connected to the bedroom—another luxury—and judging by the narrow, locked door on the other side of it, Lennon guessed that she was meant to share it with just one of her peers. Quite the step up from the communal bathroom in Ethos College.

Mornings at Logos were quiet. In Ethos, each day had dawned with a ruckus, the frenetic energy of students stumbling out of bed and wolfing down breakfast and queuing up for the showers. Logos had no such commotion. In fact, as Lennon stepped out of her room, she found it almost eerie that the only discernible sound in the corridor, apart from her own footsteps, was that of the grandfather clock at its end, ticking. At the opposite end of that hall was a birdcage elevator, just like the one in Benedict's house back in Utah. This came as something of a surprise—she'd wrongly assumed that the only working elevators in Drayton (apart from the one she'd created at random) were located in Irvine Hall.

As Lennon stood staring, the elevator gave a chime, and a cabin rattled to a shuddering stop behind the door of the birdcage. Emerson dragged back the grate and stepped into the hall. She was drenched—stooping beneath the dead weight of a waterlogged peacoat, her cheeks and nose red with cold. "Morning."

"Is that . . . a gate?"

Emerson stepped past her, tracking mud onto the fine Turkish rug that ran the length of the corridor. "Yep. First one William ever raised, actually."

Lennon, without thinking, followed Emerson like a duckling down the stairs. In the kitchen, gathered around a large butcher's block of an island, sat a few senior members of Logos House—Claude and Kieran, among others—picking at the remnants of an elaborate breakfast. Blaine, however, stood over the sink, the sleeves of her shirt rolled up to the elbows, dutifully washing the dishes.

Lennon stalled, not knowing what to do. "Um, is Ian okay?"

"We took him to the infirmary last night. Latest update is that he's been sent off campus for surgery."

"Oh my god." A wave of guilt washed over her. "I have to go to him—"

"No, you don't," said Kieran, biting down on a toast point with a satisfying crunch. He spewed crumbs when he spoke again. "He knew the game he was playing. You won, he lost. Let it go. He wasn't good enough, and that's why you're here and he's not."

"Ian is the best in our class."

"*Was* the best in your class," said Emerson. "But you've unseated him. You should be proud of yourself."

Lennon didn't feel proud; she felt sick. She couldn't stop replaying the moment when she'd overcome Ian, driven that blade through the back of his hand. The flash of hurt that froze his face in a painful rictus as he realized she'd betrayed him.

In the hours that followed, Lennon, along with the rest of the new inductees, was put to work. They scrubbed the grime between floorboards with a toothbrush, dusted and alphabetized the better part of the parlor library, folded the laundry of their more senior housemates. It was grueling, but worse than that it was humiliating because she did it all without complaint.

"I just don't understand," Blaine whined later that day, plunging a mop into its bucket for the umpteenth time. "We're some of Drayton's best students, and they waste our time with this?"

"That's precisely why we're doing it," said Lennon. "They have to cut us down to size. Now keep it down before they give us more to do."

Lennon was only relieved of her duties when it was time for her to attend her weekly lesson at Benedict's house. She rode the elevator in Logos House down to Utah and brisked into Benedict's study.

"I hear you had quite the night," he said.

"I got into Logos," said Lennon.

Benedict gave a small smile. "So I heard. Good for you. You earned that bed."

"I don't feel like it," said Lennon. "I betrayed a friend to win it."

"Even better," said Benedict. "You'll appreciate it more now that you've sacrificed your own virtues to get it. The victory will be all the sweeter—you'll see."

Lennon couldn't help but hear an echo of Dante in these words—harking back to that conversation they'd had out in the hall during her first persuasion class, when she'd refused to force her will on Gregory.

"Any luck with the elevators?"

Lennon shook her head. "I'm starting to think it's impossible. Like maybe I just can't."

Hearing this, Benedict's charm gave way to something far colder. His smile dropped, suddenly, like a painting falling from the wall and crashing to the floor in pieces. "That's not an option, Lennon. You know that. We'll simply have to adopt a different, more experimental approach to your studies. Please sit down."

Lennon sat on the edge of the couch, opposite the roaring hearth, as the fire, burning almost blue-hot, chewed hungrily at a log. It smelled of myrrh as it burned.

"I invite you to enter your safehold," said Benedict, eyes on the dancing flames. "The same state you enter during your meditational studies. Go to the place where you feel safest, and I'll guide you from there."

Outside, it began to rain, a hard rataplan on the copper tiles of the roof. Lennon felt suddenly uneasy, reluctant to close her eyes in the professor's presence. It was the same feeling of turning your back to an open door. Of walking alone through an empty parking lot in the dead of night. Of letting one leg dangle over the edge of the bed while you try to fall asleep.

"The object of this exercise is to remain within the confines of your safehold," said Benedict. "It's a purely defensive exercise. Thus, any attempt to persuade me will result in your immediate failure. For the next seven minutes, I will compel you to stand up and place your hand into the fire burning before us. If I succeed, you fail this exercise. But if you manage to thwart my attack, you succeed." Benedict removed a pocket watch from a drawer in his desk. He set the time. "Whatever you do, you must keep me out. Do you understand?"

"I understand the exercise, but how exactly does this relate to my raising a gate?"

"If it works, then your question will answer itself. Are you clear on the rules of this exercise?"

"I mean . . . I guess?"

"Good enough. Let's begin."

Lennon squeezed her eyes shut. It took her some time to find her way to her childhood bedroom. It was very quiet that night. And her bedroom door was ajar so as to allow a glimpse of the dark hallway beyond the threshold. She closed it in anticipation of Benedict's assault. But there was nothing.

The house was entirely quiet. Time passed differently within the room, but she was quite certain that more than three minutes of their allotted seven had passed. She had just begun to open her eyes when she heard it: a strange and hollow cry that came from outside her bedroom window. Lennon could only liken it to the sound of a distant coyote's howl, carried by the wind.

What followed was among the worst assaults that Lennon would endure during her time at Drayton. Benedict was merciless. He bombarded the walls of her mind with unfathomable malice. She could feel his presence in the walls of the room, pressing against the windowpanes, howling through the halls. She locked the door of her metaphorical bedroom and drew the curtains shut across her windows. The walls of the room seemed as though they were caving inward, and her skull along with them. She had had migraines in the past, cluster headaches even, and a concussion once. But never, *never* had she known a pain like this.

Lennon felt herself stand up. She was ripped mercilessly from her safehouse bedroom and thrust back into the present reality. Her legs snapped straight beneath her so painfully she feared, for a moment, that her kneecaps had broken. There was a force upon her, as if she had weights on her ankles, and had sunk to the bottom of the sea. The remarkable and horrifying will of Benedict was fully forced upon her. And when she cowered before him, when her knees went soft and she began to tremble, he laughed at her weakness. Taunted her. "Come now, Lennon. You must've learned *something* at Drayton."

Lennon staggered. Saw her own hand—hooked and straining, fingers bent at odd angles, as though broken that way—thrown out in front of her toward the hungry flames of the hearth. She tried in vain to retire to the recesses of her safehold, even as her left foot shifted slowly ahead of her right, and her right foot ahead of the left.

In a particularly cruel act of ventriloquism, Benedict forced her to her knees in front of the fire. She dropped from fully standing, busted both kneecaps open on the jagged stone as she landed, and thrust her hand into the flames. She screamed in agony, and as if in answer the elevator appeared on the far wall of the parlor. This one was strange in that it had two sets of doors. The first parted open to reveal the cabin. The second, on the back wall of the cabin, slit open to reveal a pastoral scene: a gray barn with a rusty tin roof overlooking a field of dying crops, the whole scene washed with a thick blanket of fog. Benedict cut Lennon free from the tether of his will.

Lennon kicked back from the fire and bent double over her singed hand, crying and begging for a mercy that Benedict had already afforded to her. But Benedict didn't even look at her. His eyes, filled with tears, were trained not on the elevator itself but on the scene through its second set of doors. The dead field and the barn beyond it.

With Benedict distracted, Lennon got up, staggered, and bolted into the birdcage elevator that would take her back to Drayton, back to safety. She was halfway down the foyer, dragging the elevator grate shut with her good hand, when she heard Benedict cry out her name.

"*Lennon*, come back here! Now."

Panicked, she smashed the infinity button on the control panel, and the cab sank into swift descent.

22

LENNON LIMPED BACK to Logos House in the pouring rain, her burnt hand throbbing a bit, though the pain in her busted knees was far worse. Benedict had only held her hand to the fire for the briefest moment, but the impact of landing on the sharp stones had been enough to gash her kneecaps wide open.

Determined to get home, she kept limping along. What began as a gentle midnight shower exploded into a storm so vicious Lennon wondered if a hurricane was ravaging the coast. It was hard to walk against the wind but the dense magnolias and live oaks offered her some small reprieve. Through the breaks in the trees, she could see Logos House, every one of its curtained windows alight with flickering candles.

She was stunned to see Dante, striding down the walkway that ran parallel to the house, head ducked against the rain, coming toward her. She stopped dead at the sight of him, standing there in the downpour. "There you are. Are you—"

Lennon began to cry.

Dante asked no questions.

He broke toward her and scooped her up, one arm tucked around the small of her back and the other behind her knees, and carried her through the foyer of Logos House and into the powder room on the first floor below the stairs. He set her gingerly down on the toilet seat, leaving the door just ajar.

"Take off your tights," he ordered.

Lennon obeyed, peeling off her torn and bloodstained nylons, tossing them into the wastebasket beside the toilet.

Dante began to rummage through the contents of a cabinet, retrieving a glass bottle of rubbing alcohol and several cotton balls. He crouched before her, soaked the cotton balls with alcohol, and began to dab at her knees. The pain was horrible enough to bring fresh tears to Lennon's eyes, but she furiously blinked them back.

"Are you going to tell me what the hell happened?" he asked.

"Benedict." Lennon managed to cut his name through her gritted teeth.

Dante faltered, froze for a moment, but recovered himself quickly. "What about Benedict?"

"He persuaded me during our lesson. He made me walk toward the fireplace and I—I fell, busted my knees on the stones. When he forced my hand toward the flames an elevator appeared. The pain triggered it, I think."

Something changed in Dante's expression. It was brief but sharp, anger flaring then quickly repressed, like a snuffer clasped over a tongue of flame.

He stood up, rather abruptly, and began to cut thick squares of gauze, which he pressed into the open wounds to staunch the last of the bleeding. Then he wrapped bandages tightly around both of her knees. "I'm going to have a word with Benedict, all right? It's going to be okay."

The tears came again then, blurring her vision so badly she could barely see Dante crouching at her feet. "I don't want to be expelled. I want to stay here. This is the only thing I've ever been good at, and I just—"

"Hey," said Dante, and he took her by the hand, squeezed her fingers. "I won't let that happen. I promise you that, all right?"

Lennon wiped her eyes on her shirtsleeve. "Yeah. Okay."

They emerged from the bathroom to see that quite a crowd had formed out in the hallway. It seemed it wasn't often that a tenured professor darkened the door of the house, and everyone had come to gawk.

"What happened?" Blaine asked, shouldering to the front of the crowd.

"Lennon had a bit of a fall," said Dante. "Can I trust you to look after her?"

Blaine nodded, encircling Lennon with one arm. "Of course. We've got her."

"Good," said Dante, and Lennon expected him to leave through the front door they'd entered through, but instead he scaled the staircase, up to the second floor. There was a pause and then the elevator chimed. She heard the doors open and shut.

Dante had gone to face Benedict.

Blaine tucked herself into Lennon's bed that night, the two of them squeezing onto the narrow mattress, slotting their bodies together to keep from falling over the edge. Lennon told her everything that had transpired with Benedict, feeling as though she had no choice. She seemed to bleed the words more than speak them, and Blaine listened in silence.

"You know, at the very least I thought I'd stop feeling like a failure when I got into Logos," said Lennon, rubbing her swollen eyes.

"You're not a failure," said Blaine. "And what happened with Benedict wasn't your fault."

There was a knock on the door, and it opened before Lennon could even say, *Come in*. She wasn't entirely surprised to see Claude; she'd expected he'd reach out to her at some point, given his closeness to Benedict. But she hadn't expected it to be so soon. The night was still young, and Dante hadn't been gone for long.

"You heard?" Lennon asked him.

"Bits and pieces," said Claude, looking troubled. "Fill me in."

"Ben compelled her to stick her *fucking* hand in a fire," said Blaine, sitting up, angrier than Lennon had ever seen her. "So if you want to know what happened, I suggest you talk to your boyfriend."

Claude actually smiled at this, a cruel grin that made Lennon want to hide under the blankets. "You're one to talk."

Blaine paled a little, half turned to Lennon. "Look, I have to go—"

"I'm sure you do," said Claude, but Blaine chose to ignore him.

"Claude's going to sit with you while I'm gone." Blaine glared up at him. "Isn't that right?"

Claude nodded. "I'll stay with her. Wouldn't want her to die of a scraped knee while you're gone—"

But Blaine was already out the door. Claude sat down on the edge of Lennon's bed, slumped back against the wall. He had a strange thrall—Lennon could never quite decide whether she liked him or not. He could be so rude and yet in the next moment, entirely charming and sincere. It kept her on her toes. She could never be bored around him, but she could never be entirely at ease either. No wonder Benedict liked him so much.

"Dante's pulled a lot of strings for you, hasn't he?"

When Claude spoke, his warm breath smelled of booze—whiskey or something equally strong—which usually Lennon would've found a little gross. But somehow, when it came to Claude, these small imperfections only added to his charm.

"He's a good advisor."

Claude smirked. "I think he's got a soft spot for you."

"What are you trying to say?"

Claude shrugged. "Exactly what you think I'm saying. Don't worry, it's a safe space. I'm not one to judge."

"Well, it's not like that."

"I said the same about Ben, at first. I lived in a state of utter denial that bordered on delusional for months. It was kind of hot. Like sex with a blindfold on. When things came to a head, there was all of this angst and buildup to fuel us."

"How did it start between you two?"

"The way these things always do," said Claude. "I thought he was brilliant. He thought I was precocious, which in turn made me feel almost as brilliant as I believed him to be. You know the story."

Lennon did. She'd lived that story, with Wyatt and half of the other older, emotionally unavailable men that she'd loved and fucked and obsessed over.

"The beginning isn't the interesting part, though. It's what comes after. You probably know that too. You have to come up with who you are and prove it to a person who already knows themselves because they've had all these years to figure that out. But it's unfair because you haven't yet and then you're trying to catch up to them. The whole time you're hoping you don't fuck it up and become less precocious and, in doing so, unfuckable. That's a real risk when you get older. The expectations are higher when you're not young anymore. You go from unusually bright to just . . . pretty smart, or not dumb or whatever, and then before you know it, you're not remarkable anymore. You're nothing special to them or to anyone else."

Lennon had the sudden urge to clamp a hand down, tight, over Claude's mouth. To make him eat the deluge of words he'd just regurgitated onto the bed between them. Why was it that almost everything Claude said—not just then but on other occasions too—was so blunt it hurt? It felt like he was always looking for a bruise to press on, just for the pleasure of watching her squirm.

"I am sorry about Ben," said Claude, relenting a little. He sounded almost sleepy. "He was in a bad way today. I'm sure whatever he said or did, he didn't mean it. You know how it is. The people here, they're not quite right. Ben's no different."

23

IN THE DAYS that followed, Lennon received no word from Benedict. She had half expected to hear from him during her convalescence, to receive something by way of an excuse or perhaps an apology for the cruel way he'd conducted himself. But there had been nothing except a brief notification from the school, slipped under her door in the middle of the night, informing her that all future lessons with Benedict had been canceled. Lennon became certain, then, that she was about to be expelled but heard nothing to that end. She attended classes as usual, and there was no talk of hearings or Eileen or anything else of concern . . . except for Dante's sudden absence.

Lennon had not seen or heard from him since the night he'd bandaged her up at Logos. He had canceled a week's worth of persuasion classes, and when Lennon asked around about his whereabouts she heard a number of conflicting stories: he was away on business, he had been called to New York as a witness to testify as part of a DOJ litigation, he'd been sent to quell (or cause) a coup somewhere in Eastern

Europe, he'd taken a sabbatical—no, he was actually in Budapest as part of his research. But none of these stories explained why he'd left so abruptly, without even checking to make sure his advisee was okay.

Lennon couldn't help but feel she'd been abandoned.

So it came as something of a surprise when—more than a week after her cruel encounter with Benedict, on the first day of November—Dante reappeared. He didn't apologize or account for his absence. In fact, he resumed lecturing exactly where they'd left off, as though he'd never been gone at all. That evening, they focused the bulk of their attention on planting memories within the minds of their rat subjects, a painstaking skill that involved lulling the subject into a state of catatonia, so that the mind and memories could be accessed without interference. Devising wholly new memories was a skill beyond their current capabilities, so Dante had them focus on removing specific memories of events that had occurred and then placing them back within the minds of their respective rats.

The fruits of their collective efforts were abysmal. That evening, many rats forgot how to walk or eat. Several of the rats forgot the stimulus to certain sounds they always responded to—like, for example, the sound of someone shaking their bag of treats. A few rats even forgot life-sustaining actions—like breathing or swallowing—and it was only Dante's skill that kept them from dying on the spot. The class was easily one of the worst of the semester, and Lennon was surprised she was able to spare Gregory from any lasting psychic damage as she carefully extracted the memory of his favorite toy—a red wooden wheel that he liked to gnaw on—and then planted it within his mind again.

"Good work," said Dante, stopping behind her desk to watch her. It was one of the few times Lennon had received his praise, and the significance of the moment wasn't lost on her.

After their daily exercises were done, and all of the rats had been returned to their shared transport cage, Dante resumed his place at the head of the classroom. He leaned slightly on the lectern, studying his class. There was no one that his gaze missed, and Lennon could see the way her peers shrank down in their desks when it was their turn to be examined.

"What's persuasion, in the simplest sense?" he inquired, a question he'd posed several times over the course of this semester. But Lennon had learned that when Dante posed a question like this, it was always because he was genuinely interested in the answer. While other professors seemed intent to herd their students toward a specific conclusion, Dante's approach was more relaxed. He seemed interested in provoking conversation, if not debate, facilitating an exchange of opinions rather than fishing for the one he deemed most right.

Nadine's hand shot up, and she stuttered on a near-unintelligible response about the human will.

Dante turned to the rest of the class. "Anyone else?"

Everyone began to talk over one another, the class dissolving into the recitation of textbook excerpts and reworded snippets of past lectures. The din waned and died completely. Dante frowned and looked down at his shoes. "There's a saying on campus: Good lies are rewarded with belief. Great lies are rewarded with conviction. In my experience, persuasion is a great lie, well told."

Lennon sensed, then, that he was talking to her. But a glance around the room at her other classmates told her she wasn't the only one who felt Dante was speaking to them directly. Everyone looked enraptured, held by him, waiting for what he'd say next.

But Dante cut them loose. "That's time."

The classroom drained of students, Lennon lingering beside her desk as they passed her by. Ian was the last to leave, and Lennon saw that his left hand was encased in a thick cast. Lennon realized they hadn't spoken once since he'd failed to get into Logos. She had intended to reach out to him, but with everything going on with Benedict she just hadn't had the time, and clearly he hadn't made time for her either. She waved at him, but he just glared and turned his back on her.

"Watch that one," said Dante as he gathered his things.

"What do you mean?"

"Exactly what I said. Watch him." Dante nodded toward her bandaged hand. "How are you feeling?"

"Fine. It hurts sometimes, but the burns are healing up quick."

"And your knees?"

She shrugged. "The scabs were gross the first two days, and it hurt to bend them. But they got better. Like I said, I'm fine."

"I'm glad to hear it. I suppose you've heard your classes with Benedict have been canceled?"

She nodded. "He could've delivered that news himself."

"He's been under the weather."

Here, Lennon faltered. "So, what, I'm just not going to learn how to use my elevators anymore?"

"I didn't say that." Dante turned then and rounded his desk. There was an overnight bag in his chair, and he lifted it, slung the strap over his shoulder. "You'll be coming with me."

"Coming with you where?"

"A brief outing. A work trip. I'll be taking over your studies until Benedict is in a better place. This trip is part of those studies. We'll be gone overnight, so pack a bag of essentials and meet me in Irvine Hall. You have twenty minutes."

24

LENNON PACKED IN a hurry, dodging questions from Blaine all the while. "So where are you going again?" she asked for the third time that evening.

"Out," said Lennon, fishing a pair of socks from the top drawer of her dresser.

"With Dante?"

"Yes," said Lennon, exasperated, "with Dante."

Blaine leaned against the doorframe, mixing a clay mask in a mug with a spoon. "And this is some type of . . . field trip?"

"If that's what you want to call it, sure. It's part of his standing in for Benedict. Why do you care so much anyway?"

"It's just weird," said Blaine. "You never leave."

"That's categorically untrue. I had classes with Benedict."

"In Utah, apparently? Which I still don't get. But what I meant was you don't leave to go anywhere outside of your classes. No parties. No social events. Nothing. And now, all of a sudden, this."

Lennon zipped up her duffel bag. "Why is it that when you disappear in the middle of the night, you're not made to account for yourself, but when I do it it's such a problem?"

"That's a false equivalence."

"How so?"

"I go out to work," she said matter-of-factly. It was the first time she'd ever referred to her nightly absences as work adjacent, or referred to them at all really, and it took Lennon by surprise. She'd simply assumed she had some secret boyfriend, maybe a professor, that she didn't want to own up to. Lennon was tempted to press her for more, but Blaine changed the subject before she had the chance. "This *thing* with Dante is different."

Lennon stuffed a fistful of panties into her bag. "Different how?"

"I don't know. A roguish young professor traveling alone with his charge."

"Dante isn't like that."

"And you know this how?"

"I just don't get that impression from him. He's solid."

"Maybe he is, maybe he isn't. But I guess the better question is, are you?"

Lennon looked up, exasperated. "What are you getting at, Blaine?"

"It's just . . . there are already rumors about us."

"Rumors?"

"Rumors about why we got into Logos with the grades we had while others with higher grades didn't. And with you in particular there's the situation with Ian—"

"What situation?"

"Apparently, he's furious that you got in and he didn't. And even more furious, understandably, about how you put a knife through his hand and very nearly crippled him. Lennon, he's saying things about you . . . and Dante."

"What exactly did he say?"

"Nothing to me," said Blaine. "But I heard he's been running his mouth a lot. Saying you two hooked up and that you used him as a stepping stone to get into Logos and that now that you got what you wanted from him you've tossed him out and gone on to Sawyer or Dante or whoever else."

Lennon felt a surge of fury at the thought. She'd known Ian was jealous and sometimes petty, but the Ian she'd known had been honest too. He knew she had talent, and she'd thought he was smart enough to tell that she wasn't the sort of person who got ahead academically by strategically fucking her way up the social ladder. But then she remembered telling him—in the dark of night—about Wyatt and his house and his money and all of the therapies and doctors and treatments that he'd paid for. She wondered if she'd revealed too much, given him the wrong impression.

"That bastard," said Lennon, shaking her head. "I fuck him a handful of times and he thinks I owe him my entire academic career? Fuck him."

Blaine hung her head. Strangely, she looked ashamed. "We have to be careful. No one on this campus thinks we earned our beds here honorably, if you know what I mean. And now that you're running off with Dante—"

"You don't need to worry about me," said Lennon, irritated now. She knew that Blaine was well-meaning, but couldn't help but feel her line of questioning was a little intrusive, especially given her own frequent disappearing acts. "I'm not the one who spends every other night out doing god knows what. You call it work, but I have my doubts."

Blaine flinched, looked away.

"I'm sorry. That was uncalled-for."

"It's fine," said Blaine, in the clipped way that people do when they're wriggling out of further conversation. She forced a smile. "Hope you have a good trip. Bring me back something pretty? I like cheap souvenirs. Bit of a pack rat in that way."

"Yeah," said Lennon, grateful to her for smoothing over the tail end of that awkward exchange. Blaine was good like that, forgiving. "I'll see what I can find."

Lennon left Logos House and found Dante on the stairs of Irvine Hall, smoking a cigarette, which he stubbed out on the head of one of the two gargoyles posted at the entrance. He flicked the filter into the chrysanthemum bushes as she approached. "Let's head out."

She followed him to the elevator that she'd first entered Drayton through. Dante pushed the down button and moments later its doors yawned open. They stepped into the cabin. It was mirrored on all sides, even the floor and ceiling.

"You might want to brace yourself," said Dante, leaning forward to press the 7 button. As soon as he issued the warning, the elevator gave a violent lurch. Dante remained standing with his legs firmly planted, but Lennon staggered, only avoiding crashing headfirst into the elevator panel because Dante caught her by the arm. She managed to find her footing, adjusting to the pressure of the g-forces that seemed to bear down both from above and below at once, which was impossible.

She felt the aberration looking at her before she saw it in the mirrored walls of the cabin. The hairs on the back of her neck stood on end, and a haunted feeling came over her, as though she was on the cusp of some horrible tragedy she couldn't avoid. She turned her head, caught sight of its leering grin out of her periphery—

"Don't look at it," said Dante, his gaze locked on the doors of the elevator.

Lennon stared at him, stunned. "You can see it too?"

"No," said Dante. "But I know you have one. Everyone does."

"Where's yours?"

"It's here," said Dante, eyes fixed on the doors. "Invisible to your eye but present nonetheless."

"What are they?"

"John Drayton believed they were the shadows of our better selves. Freud might've called them images of the id."

"And what do you call them?"

"A glimpse of what we'll become if we lose sight of ourselves," said Dante.

"If everyone has one, why are we the only ones that can see them?"

"The short answer is that we're not everyone," said Dante. "The long answer is that those of us with the ability to persuade are more closely aligned with the ego and, by extension, the id. Some theoretical persuasionists even believe it's the source of our power. According to them, an unnaturally strong id lends us the ability to manipulate on the level that we do. That's also why particularly talented persuasionists see their ids more prominently, why they . . . struggle."

Lennon thought of the other Dante, whom she'd encountered her first night at the school. Had that been his id? A projection of his darkest self?

The doors of the elevator slit open with a hiss and wheeze, as if the cabin had rapidly depressurized. Lennon, reeling, stepped out into the warmth and light of a full day, and onto the cobbled streets of Amsterdam. There were bike bells trilling and the chatter of birds flocking in the trees that lined the canals. The air smelled of grease and pollen and, faintly, cigarette smoke, and the sun was so bright that for a moment after stepping off the elevator, she couldn't see.

"I still don't understand how this is possible," said Lennon, and her own words sounded like someone speaking from far, far away. As her eyes adjusted to the sunlight, the scene before her—the glittering waters of the canal, the tall townhomes with gleaming windows, a smear of blue sky—appeared strange and bulbous, as if she was seeing everything through fishbowl lenses. She began to feel like she was going to throw up, or possibly lose her mind. She staggered.

"Hey. Stay with me," said Dante. "Ground yourself."

Lennon tried to comply, but her breath came fast and shallow. She felt like she was going to pass out. Dante caught her by the elbow, and her heart thrilled a little at his touch. A kind of force—like sharp heat—emanated from his fingertips. It made her feel even dizzier, but she still didn't want him to let go.

Lennon closed her eyes, drew a breath, and when she opened them again, all was as it should be. They were on peaceful cobbled street. A boat moved by along the canals.

Dante dropped his hand.

Amsterdam was one of the most beautiful cities that Lennon had ever seen. Every street they strolled down looked like something from the high-gloss pages of a luxe travel magazine. They passed the brick row houses, walked along canals flocked with ducks. Dante stopped by a small shop and bought them herring sandwiches (which tasted a lot better than they looked), small cups of espresso, and stroopwafels, larger than Lennon's face, still warm from the waffle iron.

Jet-lagged, but hungry, Lennon tucked into her food, eating and observing as they wandered the streets of Amsterdam. She noticed that Dante had intentionally slowed his pace. Later, she would come to suspect that he took the longer, more scenic route to their hotel, to allow her a better view of the city. She even stopped by a small stand where she procured a miniature canal house as a souvenir for Blaine (Dante put it on his card).

It was easy to believe, walking with him through the streets of

Amsterdam, that this was something it wasn't. In fact, Lennon indulged in that very something, allowed herself to imagine what it would be like to be with him. How it would feel to slot her fingers into the spaces between his, or to trace the outlines of the moth tattoos on the backs of his hands. She knew, of course, that it wasn't real, but in the moment, it almost felt like it.

They spent some hours exploring the city before finally checking into a small inn by a narrow stretch of the canal. The suite was on the third floor. It had two bedrooms and a small living room, with a balcony that overlooked the canal. It was the sort of hotel with chocolates on the pillows, the towels folded into the shapes of swans.

Upon entering, Dante stepped out onto the balcony to take a call, while Lennon washed up in the bathroom. It was strange, but despite the fact that the time she'd spent in the elevator had been relatively brief she felt no less tired than she would have after the seven-hour flight it would've taken for them to travel there otherwise.

When she emerged from the bathroom—hair wet, in a cloud of steam, but fully dressed—it was to Dante sitting on the couch in front of the TV, his phone in his hand, forearms braced on his kneecaps, head hung heavy. He looked up at her and she thought she saw something—a flicker of surprise, held in his eyes like the reflection of a flame—before it died into his usual stoicism.

"Is everything all right?" she asked.

"Fine, just family stuff." He pressed to his feet, slipped his phone into his back pocket. "I'm going out for a few hours."

"A few hours? What am I supposed to do, sit here and watch TV?"

"There's a pool downstairs, and if you want you can take a walk. Just be careful—"

"I didn't bring a swimsuit, and we already took a walk. I want to go with you."

"Lennon—"

"You brought me here so I could learn something, right? Tell me, what am I supposed to learn sitting around in a hotel room all night twiddling my thumbs while I wait for you to return from hell knows where?"

"Patience would be a start."

Lennon rolled her eyes. "I'm going with you."

"I don't think that's a good idea."

"You should have thought about that before you invited me."

To Lennon's immense satisfaction, Dante looked rather pissed. She knew then that she'd won this battle of wills. "Fine. We leave in five minutes."

25

THEY WENT TO Cipher, one of those clubs where everyone wears black and people queue for hours only to be turned away at the door. As it was, neither Lennon nor Dante had packed anything black but they bypassed the line and got in anyway. Lennon wondered if this was a trick of persuasion, wherein Dante had pulled a few psychic strings. But if so, it was an extraordinarily convincing act of manipulation, because the bouncer—a Bulgarian man who clocked in at nearly seven feet tall and was built like a linebacker—smiled at them from behind his darkly tinted sunglasses and ushered them in.

"Don't talk to anyone. Don't touch anything. Don't look in mirrors," said Dante, as if she were a handsy and rambunctious child entering an expensive shop full of fragile items to be broken.

"Why did we come here?" Lennon inquired, half shouting over the music. Dante didn't look like he was in the mood for a party tonight. He seemed . . . tense, leveling that thousand-yard stare of his with particular malice, as if he could kill with it.

"Like I said earlier, I have an errand to run," he said, vague as ever.

"What kind of errand?"

Dante's gaze raked, back and forth, across the club. He was looking for someone. "Do you always ask this many questions or are you just making a point to be particularly annoying because you know I'm not currently in a position to send you back?"

They stopped short in a hallway that was mostly empty except for a couple copulating discreetly in the dark. There was a door there, some sort of private room.

"Don't talk to anyone," said Dante. "And stay out of the way."

He opened the door. The room behind it was small and dim. The air turbid with cigarette smoke. The walls padded. There was one woman there, petite with a mawkish smile. She appeared to be in her late fifties and was dressed like a librarian—fuzzy cardigan sweater, buttoned up to the throat, loose slacks, and ballet flats. There was something about her poise that reminded Lennon of the vice-chancellor, Eileen. She realized, a little startled, that this woman was likely a persuasionist.

"Always a pleasure," she said to Dante, ignoring Lennon entirely. The ensuing exchange was shorter than Lennon had expected it would be. Short enough that she wondered why this hadn't happened over the phone.

"Two point five," was all Dante said, flatly.

The woman maintained her placid smile. "One seven," she said. Her accent was British.

Whatever was exchanged next wasn't communicated in words. But Lennon saw, in the set of the woman's expression, and in Dante's, that some sort of psychic contention was occurring in the lapsing silence. It was all very brief and it concluded with the woman standing—she was so short that Lennon loomed over her—and extended her hand to Dante. He took it, a firm fast shake, and gestured for Lennon to follow him out into the hall. The woman slipped out behind them without acknowledgment and disappeared into the crowd.

"What the hell was that?" Lennon demanded, shaken, though she didn't know exactly why.

Dante slipped his hands into his pockets, looked up at the ceiling as though he expected to find a tactful answer to her question in the rafters. "It's a donor system. No different from any other college."

"I don't understand."

"At some schools, if you donate a library, you'll get a box seat at the stadium and an admissions guarantee for your kids, among a number of other perks. At Drayton, a sizable donation could be rewarded with a cabinet seat or a congressional hearing, a sympathetic judge, a ceasefire."

"That's unethical."

"Everything pertaining to politics and business is. I mean, think about it: Presidential candidates use psychological conditioning in their campaign ads. Companies test commercials with focus groups and track the pupil dilation of their subjects to see how effective they are. Food corporations put addictive chemicals into their products to create cravings. Record labels engineer earworms. We're not doing anything that hasn't been done before—we're just doing it more effectively and with tact."

"And that makes it better?"

"I don't care to examine what we do through the lens of morality," said Dante, and something about the way he said it made Lennon believe this was less than true.

"What was it that she wanted?" Lennon asked.

"What most people do," said Dante, "power, in whatever form it comes in."

Just then, a man shoulder-checked Lennon so hard, she lurched off-balance. The ceramic pig Dante had given her—a kind of talisman, the equivalent of Dumbo's crow feather—fell from her pocket and bounced across the floor, disappearing into a forest of platform boots and legs sheathed in fishnet. Lennon dropped to her knees to retrieve it, but the pig was lost in the chaos.

When Lennon surfaced again, she'd ventured farther than she'd realized, and the crowds had thickened considerably. In the distance—and only because Dante was one of the tallest people in the club—Lennon could just barely make out the sharp cut of his profile.

She didn't know how the stampede began, exactly. But she was aware of something triggering within her—a sharp surge of adrenaline, not unlike a sense of doom, as if the entire world was collapsing beneath her feet. She wasn't the only one who felt it; all around her people froze, screamed, and began to run. The urge to flee felt forced upon her. It was a crushing and terrible pressure, but also a familiar one. This was the way she'd felt when under the force of Benedict's will, and Lennon realized then that she and all of the people around her were being persuaded to stampede.

A crush of bodies surged between her and Dante, and Lennon, stumbling over her own loafers, was swept away from him. Someone stepped on her foot. She caught an elbow to the nose and cried out in pain. Another man—tall and broad-shouldered, dressed in a fishnet tank top—moved as if to help her, reaching out a hand, but he too was swept away in the chaos. The music kept playing, but the shouts and yelling, the screams for air, very nearly drowned it out. Someone shoved her forward, but there was no space to fall, her ribs crushed inward, as if tamped down under a boot. She stumbled over something soft, a person, a body on the floor. Time slowed and the air, heavy with the scent of sweat, warmed and thinned. She couldn't breathe it. A black shade came down over her eyes, lit with so many silver stars.

Lennon squeezed her eyes shut. Sucked in a breath of sour air, trying to steal what little oxygen there was left to breathe. She was surprised to discover the room within herself, her bedroom safehold. Its furnishings were all the same. There was rain beating outside the window. The ceiling fan cycled slowly above her bed. She could hear, from downstairs, the clattering of pots and pans. Perhaps her mother was making dinner.

Standing in front of her closet was a boy she recognized. He was the boy with the moth. He looked older now, and less forgiving. "Force them back."

It was the first time Lennon had ever heard him speak.

"I can't. There's too many of them."

"Force them back," said the boy again, and his words—while uttered in the voice of a child—had all the weight and gravitas of a man. There was something, Lennon realized now, that was familiar about him. Though she could not place it. "Get them out of here. Now."

The light in her ceiling fan flickered. Its blades began to whir faster. The pull chains clattering together. Outside the window, rain turned to hail. It cracked the windowpanes.

"Do it," said the boy. "Now. Before you can't."

The windows of the bedroom blew out. Lennon ducked, closing her eyes against the flying glass, and when she opened them again, she felt the force of her will expanding outward, until she occupied all of the people in her vicinity. The ravers and the DJ, the security guards dispersed throughout the crowd. She tasted their emotions and scented their pain. She was present in their minds and organs. She felt her will extend and animate their limbs. She was the air in their lungs and the adrenaline spiking through their veins. She was the voice of their mother, telling them to slow down and look both ways before crossing the street. She was in the quiet between heartbeats and the underground river of their unconscious thoughts. She was, in those sacred moments, everything to all of them.

She felt like a god.

Led by the guiding hand of Lennon's will, the crowds cleared, streaming toward the nearest exits like water swirling down the drain, until the only people that remained were Lennon and Dante. Her knees buckled with relief at the sight of him, and she began to break toward him, when something seized her.

It was an abomination. There was no other word with which to describe it. It was less than human—or maybe more—or perhaps it was something entirely unto itself. A thing that had abandoned its humanness and become . . . what? Lennon didn't know. The thing was almost ineffable. A thin and wretched mouth, lips just apart, a dark razor slit between them. The arms and legs were . . . long and heavy and jointed where they shouldn't have been, as if they were drawn from memory by someone who'd only seen a human being once in passing. But all of these components were . . . wrong. Scrambled somehow. When she met its eyes, her ears filled with the sound of static. She felt the need to vomit, but nothing came up.

Under the flashing strobes the creature moved like something not of this world. The only thing that Lennon could liken it to was the speed and sharp precision of a spider racing up a wall.

"Get back," said Dante, and Lennon saw, with horror, that he was bleeding badly from the mouth. His teeth were slick red, more blood running through the cracks between them when he spoke.

The last of the crowd fled the club. None of them registered the abomination standing in their midst but the crowds parted cleanly around it nonetheless, dragged aside by the force of the thing's will. It cast its gaze on Lennon.

Her heart seized in her chest. It wasn't fear. It was worse. Something anatomical, something *wrong*, like her brain had forgotten how to make her heart pump blood. Like something vital had been severed within her—an artery or a nerve. Her heart skipped one beat. Two. She keeled over, her knees soft beneath her, grappling for her chest. The third beat was a painful palpitation. The next was normal. Then her heart skipped another.

The thing wearing her face grinned. Its expression melted. Its face became someone else's. A boy she didn't know.

Dante yelled from across the club. "Call an elevator, *now!*"

Lennon tried, but her efforts were useless in the face of such power. From inside her head, a horrible voice, at once strange and familiar, leering: *Dante.*

Her heart strained painfully in her chest. She grasped at the hard bone of her own sternum, helpless. Her legs remained weak and soft beneath her.

Dante cried out again, she could hear his voice above the thing that was chanting his name. "Don't let him into your head. Raise your walls. Fight it."

Lennon felt a pull, a sharp kick within herself, as though someone had caught her soul by the hand and dragged her roughly forward, out of the cage of her body.

All at once she found herself in a room, concrete floors, concrete walls, a burnished aluminum toilet burbling in the corner, a small sink set into its top. Some type of prison cell. Overhead, the fluorescents flickered, and a light bulb blew out with a spray of sparks. A brown moth fluttered at the slit of the window of the cell door, throwing itself senselessly against the cloudy glass.

"Stay here." The voice, familiar, seemed to come from everywhere. Dante's.

"Where am I?" she called out into the empty cell. She staggered to the door, stood up on her tiptoes so she could catch a glimpse through the slit window, but the glass was so smudged and dirty she couldn't make out anything more than the flickering light of fluorescents.

"You're safe. I have to go. Stay here."

The concrete floor of the room shuddered. A fissure raced up the wall, but it held fast. Lennon edged toward the hard metal cot bolted to the far wall and sat down, curled fetal, her knees tucked tight to her chest, and stuck her fingers in her ears against the sound of a rising scream.

And then, all at once, Dante was back, coming in through the door of the cell. He extended a hand, and when their fingers met, the walls of the cell dropped around her, falling backward as weightless as playing cards, and Lennon found herself back in the club, Dante's hand tight around her wrist, dragging her along behind him down a dark and empty hall. They cut left, then right, through a doorway and into an empty bathroom.

He shoved her, roughly, into a stall. Lennon, gasping for air, caught herself on the steel toilet pump, and braced there, panting. "What the *fuck* is that thing?"

"Listen to me," said Dante. "I need you to raise a gate and get out of here. Now."

"I—I can't. It's too much. I can't concentrate here—"

"Try," he ordered, putting real force behind the words.

Lennon shut her eyes, grabbed at something deep within herself that felt like power, and tried to transmute the graffitied door of that bathroom stall into an elevator. She gritted her teeth so hard she thought her molars would crack in two at the back of her mouth. Nothing. "I just can't," she said. "I'm so sorry."

"All right, then," said Dante, nodding first to himself, then her.

He reached back into his waistband. He produced a small handgun. Extended it to her. "If it comes through these doors instead of me, you put this gun in your mouth and pull the trigger."

"*What?* No, I can't just—"

He pushed the grip into her palm, folded her fingers tight around it. "That thing out there will do worse to you than a bullet ever could," he said, already backing away, but she reached out a hand, caught him by the arm.

"What was that out there?"

"An ambush," said Dante. "An abomination." And with that he turned and left, leaving her alone in that empty bathroom as the fluorescents flickered overhead. Moments later the room plunged into outright darkness.

Lennon heard sounds, words exchanged, but the interactions stretched—like a recording slowed—becoming incomprehensible. It was almost as though time itself was warping, malfunctioning, the flow of the moments interrupted. She felt the sudden and violent urge to be sick. Then—splitting the silence—a horrible, inhuman scream.

Things went quiet for a few beats after that, and then, footsteps. Lennon raised the gun to her parted lips, fitted the muzzle between her teeth. The barrel pressed her tongue flat against the basin of her mouth. She tasted the bitter tang of cold metal.

She slid her finger over the trigger.

The bathroom door swung open with a groan.

To her shock, it was Dante that stood there, bleeding but alive. She lowered the gun, stunned. In the time that he'd been gone, Lennon had come to terms with the fact that the both of them were going to die there in that club. That she would be slaughtered in that bathroom stall, that the memories of her loved ones would be extracted, and they would not even remember her well enough to mourn.

She ripped the gun from her mouth. "Why the fuck didn't you tell me it was you? I almost blew my head off. I—"

Dante put a blood-slick finger to his mouth, a silent shushing.

"You're hurt," she said, but couldn't see where the blood was coming from. "What happened out there? Are you okay—"

"I'm fine," he said, but it sounded pained. "And we don't have time for this. We need to get out of here."

He caught her by the arm and dragged her sharply down another hallway and through a pair of black doors. They staggered out into a narrow alleyway and started down it, toward a high (it must've been more than eight feet) chain-link gate that cut between the two buildings. It was topped with vicious snarls of barbed wire. Lennon, upon testing the lock, moved to climb over it when Dante, eyes closed, lids twitching slightly, made a motion with his fingers and the bolt—inexplicably and with a sharp click—released and struck the asphalt at their feet.

"It's just an illusion," he said. "One so good that it became reality, if only for a moment."

The gate swung open, and they slipped through, cutting fast down the last of the alley and stepping into the deserted street.

Lennon had expected to see police cars and firetrucks, the emptied crowds of the club and perhaps a handful of news reporters there to cover the scene of the stampede. But there was nothing, no one, except a few pigeons and a plastic bag tumbling like a lone phantom down the long stretch of the road. In the far distance, she saw a bruised girl hobbling down the sidewalk with a cell phone raised to her ear.

"Where did everyone go?" said Lennon, and even though she was whispering, the words seemed loud and grating, like laughter at a wake.

Dante nodded down the street. "Keep pace," he said, so quietly that Lennon wasn't sure whether he'd spoken aloud or if she'd merely read his lips.

They walked with urgency but didn't flee. Kept their hands in their pockets, their heads down. Moved along at a steady but measured pace, entering the Red Light District.

"Are we being followed?" Lennon asked, when she felt it was safe to speak in something above a whisper.

"Yes," said Dante.

"Are we in danger?" she asked, risking a glance up at him. The blood on his hands.

His expression was totally taciturn. "Yes."

"What was that thing?"

"An old friend of mine," he said.

Lennon felt a pricking at the back of her neck, all of the downy hairs bristling and standing on end. It was the feeling of being hunted. "Why is your old friend trying to kill us?"

"I don't have time to explain. Do you think you can call an elevator?"

Ashamed, Lennon shook her head. "I tried back in the club, but I'm too weak. I'm sorry—"

"Do you remember the way to the elevator we took here?" Dante asked, skirting past one of the crimson windows of a brothel. One of the girls in those windows—tall and brunette, standing on platform stilettos, dressed in beige spandex, as if wearing the hide of someone she'd skinned—blew him a kiss as he passed.

"No," said Lennon, ashamed that she was of such little use. That she had begged Dante to allow her to come, only to be such a burden. She hadn't even been able to raise a gate when they'd needed one most.

"That's all right," said Dante. "Here."

Lennon felt something like pain, and then became privy to the transference, a blurry memory, the way back to the elevator returning to her, like a video of the walk played at three times the speed. Dante's memory made hers.

The effort of this act of transference drained him considerably. He staggered, his knees folding beneath him, and caught himself on one of the lampposts that lined the narrow street. Lennon tried to help him to his feet, pressed a hand to his side. When Dante stood and straightened, her palm came away dark with blood. "Dante—"

"Never mind that," he said. "I'll be fine. You know the way now?"

"Yes, but—"

"Then you go. You go back to Drayton. You tell Eileen what happened."

"But I can't—"

"No buts."

"I *won't* leave you."

At this moment Lennon realized something. The street they were standing on, which had been so busy only a few minutes before, had been entirely cleared of crowds. The windows of the brothels went dark, one by one.

"He's here," said Dante, and when he smiled Lennon could see blood filling the seams between his teeth. For a moment she thought he was injured, but then she realized that his gums were bleeding, the same way her nose bled in class sometimes from the intense effects of persuasion.

He began to laugh, and Lennon staggered back, realizing that the man in front of her was no longer the Dante that she knew.

Across the street, from an open window, a baby began to cry. And then it was the pigeons, a flock of them roosting in the arch beneath a bridge, that took to the sky wailing. The lights in the windows of the brothels began to flicker; girls broke to their knees, tearing at their hair, gnashing their teeth, weeping and screaming and dragging their nails along their thighs. Like Dante, they tossed back their heads with laughter—their necks boneless—eyes rolling back to expose a slivered glimpse of white. In the distance, a chorus of shrieking car alarms. The sound of breaking glass. The whole city was under attack, and this time it wasn't the girl from the club, it was *Dante* doing this, destroying everything, conducting this orchestra of chaos and anguish. He was coming undone, and everything in his vicinity was coming undone along with him . . . except Lennon.

"*Dante.*" She seized him by the shoulders, shook him roughly. "You've got to stop this—you've got to come back. Please, you're hurting people."

His bleeding smile only widened. She wanted to slap it off his face. Would that be enough to bring him back to her? Or would that make things worse?

As it turned out, Lennon didn't have the chance to decide.

The entity, that demented aberration from the club materialized behind them, stepping into the center of the street, and Lennon saw—as if a double exposure—a face beneath the one the boy wore. His true face—soft, almost doll-like—was screwed with grief. He seemed younger than Lennon, and he looked . . . *afraid*.

Dante twisted to face him so sharply he tore free of Lennon's grasp and sent her sprawling to the asphalt at his feet. The boy's mouth wrenched open to shape a scream—but the sound was lost amid the shrieking chorus of sirens and sobbing and hysterical laughter. He lunged for Dante, a thick and wicked shard of broken glass clutched in his bleeding hand.

Dante didn't move. The city kept screaming.

Lennon closed her eyes.

After that first night in the garden, every time that she had tried to call an elevator, Lennon had asked a simple question: *Will you please appear?* When the elevator did not answer, she'd grown increasingly desperate. She'd begged and she'd bargained. She'd wheedled like a sniveling child. On her most desperate occasions—like the day Benedict had provoked her with pain—Lennon had cut her psyche wide open and let her own will spill from her body like blood from a wound, her a groveling servant, the elevator a god sneering down at her pathetic offering.

But no more.

This time, Lennon asked no questions. There would be no more begging or bleeding. No bargains to be made.

She commanded the elevator to appear, and when she did she felt something tear open within herself, as she dragged and struggled and grasped for the strength she needed to pull the elevator from the ether. Her nose began to bleed and her eyes soon after, so that she saw the whole scene—Dante facedown on the ground, the monstrous entity prowling nearer—through a blurry red filter.

And then, when she was ready, Lennon cast out a hand.

There was the trill of a bell and an elevator cabin crashed down through the brothel storefront, its windows imploding in a storm of glass. Its doors parted open. On the ground, inches from Lennon, Dante's eyes fluttered open, and he gasped as if he'd been held underwater for some time. He locked eyes with Lennon: *"Run!"*

Dante, Lennon, and the aberration feet from them broke toward the elevator in tandem. Lennon stumbled through the doors first, Dante behind her, the aberration at his heels. Lennon pressed the *Door Close* button just as Dante slipped sideways between them. They snapped shut on the boy's outstretched hand, crushing it with a sickening crack. His fingers twitched, caught between the doors for the briefest moment, and then he ripped them away with a shriek. Lennon punched another button on the control panel at random. The lights flickered. The music died. The cabin plunged into free fall.

26

THE ELEVATOR FELL for what seemed like an eternity, condensed down to the span of a few sickening seconds, and then stopped so abruptly it threw both Lennon and Dante off their feet and against the wall. The buttons on the control panel glowed dully, then flickered out, plunging the cabin into total darkness. The doors remained tightly closed.

"Mother*fucker*," said Dante, and he gave the doors a vicious kick. He hadn't looked scared facing down that entity in Amsterdam, but he did now. Lennon could've laughed. Dante—unflappable, taciturn, and entirely composed—was *claustrophobic*? After all they'd faced in Amsterdam, this was his Achilles' heel?

Dante slit his fingertips into the crack between the doors and pried them apart with brute force. Lennon squeezed her eyes shut against the sunlight flooding into the cabin. Dante stepped out of the elevator, and Lennon staggered after him, making it only two steps before she broke to her knees, bent double, and vomited violently into the dust.

"Easy," said Dante, and he stopped by her side. Put a hand on her back to steady her. "You're all right."

Lennon wiped her mouth clean on the back of her hand. Spit into the dirt. "I am *not*."

"I told you not to come."

"You didn't tell me we were going to be fucking attacked."

"I didn't know. That's kind of what makes the ambush, you know, an *ambush*."

Lennon pushed, rather unsteadily, to her feet and wheeled to face the elevator they'd just emerged from, only to discover that it wasn't an elevator at all, just some sort of industrial shaft jutting up from the dust.

"Mining shaft," said Dante, squinting at it. "Didn't even know these were still in use. How the hell did you conjure this?"

"I don't know," said Lennon, suddenly defensive. "I just knew you were either going to die or kill everyone else—all those girls in the windows—if we stayed. What was that?"

"I pushed myself too hard," said Dante, in the tone of an apology, but he stopped short of offering one. "We should go."

Lennon turned to look around. "Go where?"

Apart from the mining shaft—and the industrial wreckage, old gates, and rust-chewed machinery—as far as the eye could see there was nothing but flat dust. To the east the sky was a stark and startling blue. On the western horizon, a shelf of storm clouds so dark they were very nearly black. A two-lane road stretched out in front of them, but there were no cars in sight.

Dante fished his phone from the pocket of his jeans, but it was dead. The screen shattered. Another casualty of the ambush at the club. "Shit."

In the distance, a threatening peal of thunder. "We should get going before that storm catches up to us."

"It won't give us trouble," said Dante, as if the storm knew better than to test his patience. He started down the road, and Lennon followed after him. They walked for several miles in silence, heading away from the storm. Dante dragged himself along at a steady pace. He was still bleeding and clearly in pain but too prideful to lean on Lennon. It was just as well; he needed more help than what she could offer him then. A hospital—an ambulance, even—if he didn't stop bleeding from his mouth. But when Lennon suggested that he wait by the roadside, let her find help and circle back, he merely waved her off and kept walking.

The storm caught up to them quickly, bringing with it the kind of wind that rips at your clothes and hair, a harsh deluge of cold rain. As they approached the town, nearly an hour after they'd started walking, they heard the whine of what Lennon could only assume were tornado sirens. They picked up the pace, passing an auto shop, and an accompanying gas station, until they reached a run-down by-the-hour motel with a cracked and empty parking lot. Dante staggered up to its doors, opened them for Lennon—a gentlemen even at his worst—and she went through ahead of him.

The girl at the front desk pasted on a smile. "Welcome to Chambers Inn. How can I—"

"Where are we?" Dante asked, limping up to the front desk.

"Um . . . Idaho?"

"Wonderful," Dante muttered, and he wiped away some of the blood collecting in the corners of his mouth. He fished for his wallet, pulled out a hundred-dollar bill. "Is this enough for the night?"

"The *night?*" Lennon demanded. "No. We're getting you to a hospital. Now—"

The clerk's wide-eyed gaze slid from Dante to Lennon, then back to Dante.

"Is it enough?" he asked again, eyes on the clerk, not looking at Lennon.

Mouth agape, the girl nodded, took the money, and gave him change and a room key. Dante snatched both and nabbed a couple of first aid kits from the shelves of the sundry shop on his way out of the lobby. He limped down the hall to their shared motel room, unlocked the door, and Lennon, at a total loss for words, followed.

Dante kicked off his shoe, which was filled with blood, his sock soaked through. "Oh my god, your foot—"

"It's my leg," said Dante, and he made his way to the bathroom, trailing a dark smear of blood behind him. "And I'm fine."

"You're bleeding."

"I noticed. Thanks."

"I think you should go to the hospital."

"Not going to happen," he said, and he stripped out of his jacket, tossing it out of the bathroom and onto the bed. Lennon watched by the door as he peeled up the hem of his blood-damp shirt, muttering to himself as he assessed a second wound, the one on his side. She had never seen an injury quite like it. The skin at his waist had been somehow torn, gashed apart, and deep bruises surrounded the slashes. To her eye it almost looked like something had attempted to claw its way out of him, which was, of course, impossible. She knew he must've been somehow injured during the stampede, shoved along something sharp, perhaps? Or maybe that entity had attacked him with a knife? His injuries didn't look like knife wounds, though.

"This is fucking ridiculous. You need medical attention."

Dante ignored that. "You sit tight. If anyone knocks on the door, don't answer. I don't care who they say they are."

"What if you bleed out?"

"Then I want to be cremated, not buried," he said and shut the bathroom door in her face. She half expected to hear the thump of Dante hitting the floor, but the only sound was a running faucet.

Pissed—but knowing she'd lost this battle—Lennon lay down on the bed beside Dante's discarded jacket. That's when she saw the money, sticking out from an inner pocket. Lennon glanced at the bathroom door and listened carefully to the hissing of the showerhead. When she was certain Dante wasn't about to emerge, she reached carefully for the money and withdrew a thick stack of crisp hundred-dollar bills, folded in half and held fast with a money clip. A quick count confirmed that it was an easy ten thousand dollars, and upon further inspection of the jacket she saw that there was another folded stack of bills in the same pocket, this one in euros, and two more stacks in another, bringing the total sum of money to a cool forty thousand.

"Holy shit," she whispered, shoving the money back into the pockets where it belonged.

Dante finally emerged from the bathroom with the first aid kit in hand, freshly bandaged and looking less pale. Lennon was making coffee in the instant machine and, without asking, she poured Dante a cup too, then they both sat down on the couch and watched reruns of a dog show that was playing on ESPN for a while in silence.

Lennon wanted to ask him about the money but knew she couldn't without revealing that she'd snooped through the contents of his jacket. "So, are you going to tell me what happened back in Amsterdam?"

"Already told you. Ambush."

"But who were we ambushed by? You said it was an old friend of yours?"

He nodded. "A former classmate. From Drayton. We parted on . . . bad terms."

"Why was he like that?"

Dante finished the dregs of his coffee in a single swallow, stared down at the empty mug, which looked small in his large hands, like something from a child's tea set. Lennon could tell her question was one he didn't want to answer. "The power we wield has its costs. If you push yourself past a certain threshold, you can break your mind and lose yourself."

"Will I turn into something like that, if I keep practicing persuasion?"

For a long time, he didn't answer. "Not if you're careful. Drayton will teach you how to kill it. But the catch is that it doesn't stay dead. Every day for the rest of your life you will wake up and wrap your hands around that thing's throat and strangle it. Or it will strangle you." Dante delivered this indictment with his eyes locked on the TV in a dead-eyed, thousand-yard stare. "But this is true both of those who use persuasion and those who don't. Every one of us harbors a facet of ourselves that wants, desperately, to destroy us. A part of us that longs for our own annihilation. It tells you to jump when you stand beside a tall drop-off. It makes you want to put a knife through your own hand when you're chopping vegetables for dinner. It is hungry and it is corrosive, and it will come for your soul and your sanity. Which is why all of us must work actively against it, or else it will succeed." The toll of saying this sapped what little strength he had left. He hung his head.

"You really do need to see a doctor."

"I'll be all right. I rinsed out the wound with alcohol." He nodded to the first aid kit on the nightstand.

"May I have a look?"

Dante sighed. "If you must."

Gingerly, she peeled up the side of his bloody shirt, wishing he had something clean to wear. He'd done a shitty job with the bandaging, though, so Lennon cut it away and started again. The wound below wasn't as deep as it had looked at first. Dante had flushed it thoroughly with alcohol, and while it was slightly swollen it showed no signs of infection. Lennon rifled through the contents of the first aid kit, cut several thick squares of gauze and pressed them carefully to the wound, and held it fast with wrap and strips of tape.

"Where'd you learn to do this?" Dante asked, watching her work. His voice had the husky quality of someone who'd only just woken up.

"My mom was a nurse," said Lennon, carefully wrapping the bandages around his waist. "But more importantly, I was a Girl Scout. A Cadette, actually."

"High achiever."

Lennon shrugged. "I mean, I don't like to brag, but . . . I do what I can."

Dante cracked a wry smile, then winced a bit as she tightened the bandages. "You saved us back there," he said. "Thank you for that. I should've said that earlier."

"You had more important things to deal with."

"Even still. I owe you. I could've killed someone—"

"What do you mean? How?"

Dante seemed reluctant to answer, and she was surprised when he did. "Some persuasionists have the ability to siphon power from those around them. Essentially, they can manipulate the wills of others, use them as a power source. It's dangerous—deadly, even."

"And is that what you did back there? You took too much?"

"I shouldn't have taken anything at all," he said. "I didn't mean to. It was . . . compulsive."

When Dante had told her that he—like her—struggled to contain his own power, she hadn't believed him. He was always so self-contained, entirely controlled. It was hard to imagine him acting on impulse or emotion. But that was exactly what had happened in Amsterdam. He'd lost himself, and the result had very nearly been deadly.

"What matters is that you stopped," said Lennon. "You held yourself back."

"No, *you* brought me back," he said, "with that elevator. But if you hadn't been there—"

"Then you would've found another way to return to yourself," said Lennon, and she wasn't exactly certain who she was assuring: him or herself or both of them.

"The city was screaming," he said, speaking to himself now. "And I knew that I was doing it, but I was as powerless to stop as the people who were under my will—"

"Hey," said Lennon, grabbing at his hand. "Look at me."

He looked.

"You didn't hurt anyone, all right? You didn't."

"You don't know that."

"I do," said Lennon. "I could feel it."

With that, she tugged up his pant leg to examine the wound at his calf, but found that it was much smaller, and Dante had already covered it with a large stick-on bandage. "I did the best I could," she said, sitting again beside him. "But I still think you should see a doctor tonight . . . or at the very least call someone at Drayton."

"Drayton can wait until tomorrow," said Dante, and when he spoke, she saw that blood was still collecting at the edges of his mouth. Was he bleeding internally? "I'm too spent to get to a gate tonight."

Lennon made as though she hadn't heard him. It was clear to her then that he was out of his depth. He needed medical attention, preferably at Drayton. "I'm calling an elevator—"

"Lennon, don't—"

She didn't listen; she was already dredging up the strength she needed to summon it. This time she could tell that the power was within her grasp, but her mind was tired and wounded from the feat she'd performed in Amsterdam. If she called another elevator, she knew it would be at a great bodily, and probably psychic, cost. But for Dante, she was willing to try. She focused her gaze on a bare spot on the wall, cast out a hand, and ordered the doors to appear, but before they did, she felt a small snick within her psyche, and she was abruptly severed from the source of her power.

It took her a moment to register Dante's presence within her mind, impeding her ability to access her own power, tamping down her will, her thoughts, everything. And she was overcome with a horrible weariness that she recognized as catatonia only as she slumped into the couch. "Get out of my head," she mumbled, and her lips felt so numb and swollen she was barely able to form words.

"You need to stop," he said, but he withdrew from her mind. "Just because you can access your power now doesn't mean it's wise to do it whenever you want. You've learned an important lesson, and that's good, I'm proud of you—"

Lennon felt her cheeks flush warm at the praise.

"But there's more to persuasion than blunt power. Now that you've learned to summon an elevator at will, the most important thing for you to practice is knowing when to hold back. Restraint will get you farther than brute force."

Lennon relented, knowing he was right. "I could've done it, you know. If you hadn't stopped me. I can do it anytime I want to now. I've finally got the hang of it."

Dante's gaze remained even. "What changed?"

"What do you mean?"

"I mean what was your lynchpin? How did you unlock it?"

"I don't know . . ." Lennon grasped for words to describe what felt like the ineffable. "It was just different in Amsterdam, more within my control. I felt like I had, or claimed, authority."

"Elaborate on that," said Dante, adopting a tone that was similar to the one he lectured with in class.

Lennon frowned, thinking. "The first time, in the garden, it felt both emotional and almost . . . hapless or accidental. And at Benedict's, I felt like I opened an elevator out of desperation. As if I was, I don't know, begging for it. Pleading almost. But in Amsterdam . . . in a way it felt like for the first time *I* made it happen. It was my will, my choice, alone. Not me being backed into a corner by Benedict or something supernatural happening to me. The elevator in Amsterdam felt like it belonged to me, and me only."

"And you feel changed by that?"

Lennon hadn't realized it until Dante had said it, but he was absolutely right. She *was* different—changed, as he put it. "I guess I feel like I won't be the same after this. Like there was a before and an after. Now I know I can make an elevator appear not because I asked or begged for it, but because I'll make it happen. No matter the cost. Even if I go mad doing it—if I bleed out through my nose or suffer a seizure—I know that I can."

Dante smiled, looking almost impressed. If he wasn't exhausted before, the act of tamping down her will had drained him fully. It was clear to Lennon that he had nothing left to give. If she tried to open an elevator now, she doubted he'd even be strong enough to stop her. And there was something about that fact—his vulnerability in the moment—that she found almost . . . endearing.

"Are you sure we shouldn't try to make our way back to Drayton?" she said, and in what was perhaps too intimate a gesture she snatched a tissue from the box on the coffee table and wiped the blood from the edges of his mouth. "Isn't there someone, anyone, we could call?"

"There is," said Dante, closing his eyes. She'd half expected him to flinch away when she put the tissue to his lips, but he seemed at ease. "But all they'd be able to do is tell us to make our way to the closest gate. As it stands, I'm spent, and I need to rest. It'd be easier to drive down to Benedict's in the morning than make our way to the nearest airport and fly into Savannah."

"But we don't have a car."

"We'll get one," said Dante, stifling a yawn. "We rest tonight and leave in the morning," he said, and she could tell from his tone that they'd reached the end of this discussion, and that he'd reached the end of his patience. He got up and went to the couch, where he would remain, sitting pensive and watchful, through the last of the night.

27

IN THE MORNING they checked out of the motel and walked a few blocks down the street, to a diner called Freddy's. From the outside it looked like a greasy spoon, but the interior was surprisingly quaint. There was a bearded man seated at the bartop who scowled at both Lennon and Dante when they entered. They were the only two Black people in the restaurant, if not the entirety of the town, and had been drawing glances (some of them nasty) ever since they'd arrived.

Lennon edged past the man, who was loudly debating with another one of the diner's patrons about whether or not the most recent school shooting was a government hoax (he argued, most fervently, that it was).

Dante claimed a seat next to a dusty window, and they both opened the laminated menus and skimmed through the offerings in silence. A waitress in a peach dress and matching apron, frilled at the bottom, came to take their order. She eyed Dante with a smile that was, perhaps, a little too urgent. This irritated Lennon, though she couldn't say exactly why.

Lennon ordered a waffle, a poached egg, and a glass of grapefruit juice. Dante ordered a pot of coffee and a slice of pecan pie. They waited for the food in silence for a while, until Dante said: "Do you see that guy?" He gestured across the diner with a slight shift of his gaze. Lennon followed his eyes to the man sitting hunched at the bar, the one who'd glared at them when they entered. He wore a denim vest embroidered with a number of patches—American and Confederate flags, the "don't tread on me" snake, and other patches, pins, and paraphernalia that looked vaguely white supremacist. "You're going to get him to give us his keys."

"Wait, what? Why?"

"We need a ride to Ben's," said Dante. "Consider this today's class."

"I don't think I can do it without hurting him."

"Then hurt him," said Dante, exasperated. "I don't give a shit. Whatever you have to do to make him give you his keys."

"And if I fail?"

"If you fail, then we stay here until you succeed. If not with him then someone else."

Lennon swallowed down her irritation and attempted to will the man, to no avail. He was a particularly difficult target. She began to suspect that either the walls of his skull were suspiciously thick, or he was particularly dense, which—given the patches emblazoned across his vest—was highly likely. By the time the food arrived, Lennon could smell the metallic beginnings of a nosebleed, and all she'd managed to do was make the man frown at his twitching fingers.

"Eat," said Dante, tucking into his pie. It was a large slice, with a generous dollop of whipped cream on top. "It'll help you focus. You can't expect to overcome someone else's mind when you're not fueling your own."

Lennon shook her head. She felt put off her food, nauseous from the effort of intense and sustained concentration. "I'm not hungry."

"Eat anyway."

Lennon cast her gaze away from her unsuspecting target, onto Dante. "Presumably you could just make me eat, right? Force me?"

"Presumably. But I don't like to persuade people to eat things because, while I'm capable of forcing your body to chew, I can't feel the texture of what's in your mouth at a given time. And the mechanics of swallowing are . . . delicate and the risk of choking is high if I screw up. Now stop trying to distract me and focus."

Lennon, with a sigh of frustration, homed in her focus on the man again. She looked for stories in his face, behind that thick beard of his, tried to find weaknesses to exploit, footholds to grasp onto, ways to manipulate. Ultimately, she decided to lean into the conspiracy angle, inspired by all of that bullshit paraphernalia emblazoned on his vest. She figured he'd fall for it, and he did.

The man pushed back from the bar and staggered to their table, his gait strange and unsteady, like a bowlegged baby first learning how to walk.

"For America," he said, and shoved a hand into his pocket, withdrew a ring of keys, and extended them to her. "God bless you. God bless all of us."

Lennon took the keys. "Um . . . thanks? We'll take care of it."

The man nodded, firmly, and trudged back to the bar, none the wiser, and resumed his discussion about whether or not the middle schoolers involved in the shooting were, in actuality, adult actors paid by the government that were just *pretending* to be children. Lennon shook her head, disgusted.

"Creative," said Dante. As soon as she was finished eating, he slipped two twenty-dollar bills from his wallet, put them down on the table, and got up. "Let's go."

The man's car was a black pickup truck hiked on tires that were large enough to be attached to an eighteen-wheeler. Lennon quite literally had to climb up into the passenger seat. The interior was surprisingly clean. The floors looked freshly vacuumed. Lennon offered to drive but Dante, stubborn as ever, waved her off.

It was a three-hour drive to Benedict's house in Ogden. To Lennon's immense surprise, the man they'd stolen the truck from had an extensive collection of audiobooks, and they were able to listen to the better part of a romance novel titled *Prince Charmer* by the time they pulled into Benedict's driveway.

Lennon got out of the truck and rang the doorbell. No answer. She rang it again and knocked several times. Nothing. "Maybe he's out?"

Dante tried the doorknob. It was unlocked. The door swung slowly open. He stepped past it, into the foyer, and Lennon wiped her boots clean on the welcome mat and hesitantly followed after him. The first thing she registered upon entering was the smell of gasoline. The second was that the elevator door was just ajar, the cabin slightly raised, so that it was stuck between the first floor and the second.

"Ben?" Lennon called out into the dark. "Are you here?"
Silence.

Dante started down the hall and Lennon followed him into the kitchen, where the stove burner was on, scorching the bottom of an empty kettle. Lennon switched it off.

And that was when she caught it. A horrible smell, saccharine and decayed and so pungent Lennon stifled a gag, pushing the sleeve of her shirt to her nostrils to block it.

"Go wait in the car," said Dante, but it was too late. Lennon had already crossed into the study, where she found Benedict, dead behind his desk. He was sitting slumped in his chair, which was pushed firmly to the edge of the desk, his head lolled against his shoulder, his mouth and eyes wide open, wrists cut, palms up. On the far corner of the desk was a brass letter opener grimy with dried blood.

Lennon, not fully processing the scene before her, rushed to Benedict's side and clasped a hand over his open arm. His blood was cold and black and thickly congealed. The smell was so horrible her eyes watered. She felt the primal urge to flee but remained there, with her hand clasped to his arm as if there were still a chance she could staunch a bleed that had long stopped.

Dante came to stand behind Benedict. Braced his hands on the back of his chair and hunched over him slightly, hanging his head. He closed his eyes. "Get to the elevator," he said.

"What? No, we can't just leave him here—"

"The elevator, Lennon. Go."

When Lennon still didn't move, Dante forced her, pulling her back and away from Benedict. She took two lurching steps and caught herself on the wall of the corridor before Dante cut her loose from the tether of his will, but he stayed close behind her, as if there were someone else in the house when Lennon knew for certain it was empty. It was a clear suicide. And even if there was foul play involved, what killer stayed at the scene of the crime for days?

"Go straight to Eileen's office," said Dante. "Tell her what's happened." He reached into the elevator and pressed the glowing *8* button on the control panel, then drew the grate shut.

The cabin lurched violently. "Dante, wait—"

"I'll be right behind you."

28

THE ELEVATOR ASCENDED for some time before it came to a stop at Drayton, behind a pair of golden double doors. Lennon staggered through the lobby to the secretary's desk. The woman's eyes went wide at the sight of her, and it was only then that Lennon registered the fact that she was covered in Benedict's blood. Both of her hands were sticky with it, and her shirt was stained too. "I need to speak with Eileen. Can you show me the way to her office?"

"I—I'm afraid the vice-chancellor doesn't receive guests without a formal appointment. Perhaps you could speak to your advisor?"

"My advisor is tending to the dead body of one of my professors. Benedict Barton, who we found dead at his own desk."

"Professor Barton is dead?" The woman's gaze tracked down to Lennon's bloodied hands and shirt. "That's not his . . . is it?"

"I need to talk to Eileen," said Lennon again.

Upon reaching the doors of Eileen's office, Lennon was commanded to wait outside. The secretary went in ahead of her, and she was gone for what felt like a long while. When the door finally opened again Lennon was surprised to see Eileen behind it. "Come in."

Her office was wide but long, a bit like a bowling alley, complete with a run of windows and an expansive view of the Twenty-Fifth Square. There was a large desk that looked more like a banquet table on the far wall of the room. On it, a few personal effects—framed photos and an ornate pen stand—but what caught Lennon's attention was the bust of a little boy—wide-eyed and young, cast in brass—which acted as a paperweight. The child looked somehow familiar to Lennon, something about the set of his mouth.

"What happened?" Eileen demanded. "Tell me all of it."

Lennon, in a shaking voice, recounted the details of what had happened in Amsterdam, the thing—less than human, or maybe more—that had appeared in the club and attacked them. Eileen's face grew drawn and very pale, but she asked no questions, so Lennon kept on talking, telling her about the elevator she'd summoned in the street to escape, and their arrival in Idaho. She told her too about the motel, and the trip down to Benedict's house in Utah. Here, she began to stumble over her words—stuttering in her haste to get them out—her throat swelling with tears, feeling like it might seal shut if she didn't stop fighting them and allow herself to cry.

Eileen digested all of this with her arms folded over her chest, leaning against her desk, legs crossed at the ankles, staring at some fixed point on the floor. When Lennon's story was finished, she said, without expression: "Where is Professor Lowe?"

"He stayed behind. I don't know why. I didn't want to leave without him but he made me."

"That's all right," said Eileen. "You've done nothing wrong. And Dante's tough, I made sure of that. He can handle himself."

"I'm not sure that he can," said Lennon, close to crying now. "He's hurt. Badly. I'm worried about him. There was so much blood."

Eileen raked a hand through her hair. "Thank you for telling me all of this. I want you to go back to your dorm, have a shower, and find yourself something to eat. Okay?"

These instructions were relayed so tenderly that Lennon felt, for a moment, confused. It had been a long time since she'd been mothered, and the last person she would have expected to be mothered by was the vice-chancellor. "But what about Dante? Shouldn't he be back by now?"

"He'll be fine."

"Will you send someone for him?"

As quickly as Eileen had turned soft, she became cold. "What I do in my capacity as vice-chancellor is none of your concern. Nor is the business that Dante keeps. I understand your concern, but right now my primary responsibility is ensuring the safety of the students and faculty I have here. Do you understand?"

Eileen stripped off her cardigan and wrapped it gently around Lennon's shoulders. It was heavy, but strangely cool, as though it had been hanging in the back of a closet, never worn. Eileen buttoned it up to Lennon's throat, like she was a child too young to do it herself.

"To replace your shirt," she said, referring to the bloodstains. "I don't want you alarming anyone as you make your way across the campus."

Lennon nodded. Made for the door.

"And Ms. Carter?"

She faltered, turned back to Eileen. "Yes?"

"Break the news to Claude, will you? He and Benedict were so close."

"I—I will."

Lennon walked back to Logos House, aware of the stares that trailed her as she went. Upon entering the foyer, she climbed the four flights of rickety, creaking stairs up to Claude's room in the attic. She knocked on the door. Claude answered, squinting at her as though staring directly into the sun. "Lennon? What the hell happened to you? Is that blood?"

Lennon had prepared a speech on the way back from Irvine Hall, but in the moment all she could think to say was: "He's dead."

"Who's dead?"

"Benedict."

A half beat passed in silence. Claude faltered—his expression frozen somewhere between a smile and a frown. "Come in. Have a seat by the fire."

Lennon was stunned silent for a moment. She had expected yelling and tears and tearing at clothes, a barrage of questions about who and when and where and how. But what she hadn't anticipated was Claude's complete and utter composure. She stumbled through the door after him. "Claude, wait—"

"What would you like to drink?" he inquired, cheery.

"I—I don't want anything," said Lennon, carefully lowering herself into one of the two armchairs that stood in front of the hearth. "Listen, Claude, I have to—"

"How about something sweet?" He went to a well-stocked bar cart and began to mix what appeared to be two amaretto sours. He took a long time stirring up the cocktails, staring at some fixed point on the wall with a furrow in his brow. "So, you said he's dead?"

"Yes," said Lennon, crying now. "And I'm so sorry. Dante and I found him this morning. His wrists were cut."

Claude turned to face her, his expression blank. He passed her the cocktail with a mechanical motion, and some of the drink sloshed over the edge and spattered the Persian rug. He sat stiffly in the empty armchair beside Lennon. "Benedict wouldn't slit his wrists. He always told me if it came down to it—*when* it came down to it—he'd use a gun. He had one, you know. He kept it in his tea cabinet. An antique, belonged to his father."

Lennon's hands began to shake around the cocktail glass. "Listen, I don't know what happened. That's just what I saw. He's dead, Claude. I'm so sorry—"

Claude hurled his glass across the room. It struck the far wall and shattered on impact. *"Fuck."*

Lennon sprang to her feet, but Claude remained seated, staring at a nothing spot on the floor, his shoulders heaving.

She edged toward him, extending a hand. "Claude—"

He stood up so suddenly that Lennon, startled, staggered back and fell into a nearby bookshelf. Claude caught her by the arm and dragged her out of the bedroom, down the hall, and several flights of stairs until they reached the rickety elevator on the second floor. By this time, those who were in the house had already come upstairs or out into the hall to investigate the sound of breaking glass. Blaine emerged from Emerson's room.

Emerson came out after her. "What the hell is going on, you two?"

"We're going to Benedict's," said Claude, pulling Lennon to the elevator. He dragged the grate aside, stepped into the cabin, and mashed the button on the control panel that corresponded with Benedict's house. He pushed it again and again, but the cabin didn't move.

It didn't seem like a random malfunction; the timing was too perfect. There was no way the elevator to Benedict's home just conveniently stopped working directly after Lennon told the vice-chancellor he'd been found dead. Perhaps Eileen had shut it down, a power that Lennon didn't even think was possible until this moment. The way she saw it, the elevators in the school were reliably simple. They went back and forth between their designated locations on a fixed and unstoppable track. As far she knew, there was no gatekeeper responsible for them who could change their routes or stop them from working. But if that was true, Lennon wondered, then who had stopped the elevator from running now?

"Fuck," said Claude and he kicked the wall of the cabin.

Blaine cocked her head. "What's the rush?"

"Benedict is dead," said Lennon, choking a little on the words. "Dante and I found him today with his wrists cut—"

"Shut up," said Claude and he stepped out of the elevator, dragging Lennon with him. His grasp was so tight her wrist was beginning to hurt. "Open another," he said, motioning to a bare spot on the wall. "I know you can fucking do it. Open an elevator to Benedict's house."

"I'm not supposed to—"

"Do it, Lennon."

"Claude," said Emerson. "Get ahold of yourself."

"I need to see him," said Claude. "And the elevator isn't working. I can't get to him, and I need to, and she's just standing there fucking useless—"

Lennon tried to open a gate, but Amsterdam had exhausted her. Even with her new approach—the commanding nature of her power—she knew she shouldn't call an elevator. She was far too spent, and Dante had warned her about the dangers of depleting herself. For once, she chose to listen to him. "I'm sorry," she said. "I can't."

"Fuck," said Claude, and he slid down the wall in the middle of the hallway, landed hard on the floor, and put his head in his hands. The tears came then, great racking sobs that shook his whole body. The sound of his crying drew more people upstairs. Sawyer came up and sat beside him, drew the shaking man (though in the moment, he seemed more like a broken boy) into his arms, as Lennon fielded questions from Emerson and Blaine and everyone else who wanted to know what had happened to Benedict.

"Who would do something like that?" Blaine asked, searching Lennon's face for an answer. Her eyes were filled with tears. "Who would just murder someone in cold blood like that?"

"We don't know that it was a murder," said Kieran. "Maybe he'd just had enough."

"Ben wouldn't have left me," Claude snapped, his face flushed a hot and angry red. He spit when he spoke. "Someone did this to him, and I'm going to find out who."

29

THERE WAS NO memorial service for Benedict. No mention of his death apart from a small, framed obituary posted on the same bulletin in Irvine Hall where all of the students' grades were announced. It was short and mostly devoid of emotion—detailing in large part Benedict's contributions to the school and his love of gardening. Fittingly, students placed flowers beneath the posting until the arrangement spilled out into the middle of the corridor. No cause of death was mentioned in the obituary, but rumors about how and why Benedict died were thoroughly disseminated across the campus.

A long weekend followed Lennon's return to Drayton. Classes were suspended for the week of Thanksgiving break, and many students returned to their homes for the holiday. Lennon was not among them, though she did call her mom in one of the phone booths scattered around the campus to tell her she was okay and busy with her studies.

"Are you sure you can't come home?" The sound of her mother's voice was enough to make Lennon's throat clog with tears. "Not even for the day? We'll be making all your favorites. Mac and cheese, yams with mini marshmallows burnt dark the way you like."

"I'm sorry, Mom, but I'm too busy. I have to study."

This was a lie.

The real reason that Lennon didn't fly home for Thanksgiving was Claude. He was utterly inconsolable, and in the days after Benedict's death he drank himself violently ill, to the point where Emerson poured every bottle of spirits on his bar cart down the toilet, just to avoid him poisoning himself. With his supply cut off, Claude took to wandering the campus and sometimes even venturing beyond it, sourcing his drinks from convenience stores in Savannah proper by way of the Logos elevator, which allowed access to a floor on the riverfront downtown. Claude's drinking became so extreme that he couldn't be left alone, so the members of Logos divided his care into shifts that lasted all day and stretched on deep into the night, when Claude was most prone to his drunken tantrums. One moment he'd be despondent in his chair, and the next he would rage, throwing things and toppling tables and cursing.

They should've taken him to the infirmary, but when Lennon suggested as much, the cold looks she received from Emerson, Kieran, and even Sawyer were enough to shoot that idea down dead in the water.

"If you take him to the infirmary in this state, they're sure to expel him," said Kieran sharply. "We have to give him a chance to grieve and sober up on his own terms. He'll be fine with time."

But Lennon wasn't so sure.

Things came to a head on a particularly terrible night when it was her turn to watch Claude. He'd been abnormally subdued that evening, and Lennon was beginning to suspect that there was something seriously wrong—that he was succumbing to liver failure or some other malady caused by alcohol poisoning—when he sat upright in bed and looked at her.

"You know . . . Benedict never much cared for Dante."

Lennon looked up from the book she'd been studying, a text on the thin and hazy boundary between psychology and religion, assigned by her metaphysics professor. Finals were just three weeks away, and she had a number of exams to study for, papers to write. "What?"

"Benedict didn't like Dante. Didn't trust him."

"I'm sorry to hear that," said Lennon. She had learned to talk to Claude like a child when he was drunk, a strategy that usually soothed him. But that wasn't the case tonight.

Claude's mouth twisted into a rictus. "You're just so smug," he said. "You open a gate, and you think you have the answers to everything. But you don't know. You don't understand."

Lennon kept her gaze on her book. "You should rest. You're tired."

He tore the textbook out of her hands and hurled it across the room. "Look at me."

Empty-handed, afraid, but too prideful to show it, Lennon raised her gaze. "What is it, Claude?"

"He was murdered. I don't care what anyone says. He was murdered, and Dante did it."

"You're being ridiculous," said Lennon, trying to stay calm even as her heartbeat quickened. "Dante didn't know that Benedict was dead. He was just as surprised as I was. I saw it on his face."

"He's a good liar."

"Not that good," said Lennon. "No one is that good." But even as she said this, she wasn't sure it was true. After all, wasn't it Dante who'd called persuasion a great lie well told?

"He could've been lying," said Claude, seizing on her uncertainty. "You know he could have."

"Let's assume you're right," said Lennon, keeping her voice low and soft and as sweet as she could manage. "Why would he take me to Benedict's house if he knew Benedict was dead in there? If he had killed him, wouldn't he have wanted to cover his tracks?"

Claude made as though he hadn't heard her. He struggled so much with the words he attempted to say next that for the briefest moment Lennon considered the possibility that he was fighting a tongue tie, an advanced persuasive trick that prevented victims from saying specific words or pieces of information. "Because Ben told me he was scared of him before he died. He told me that Dante said horrible things to him. Ben wasn't afraid of anyone, but he was afraid of him."

"Look, I don't know what it is you know about Dante, but I can assure you he wouldn't just . . . I mean, he wouldn't—"

"He wouldn't what?" Claude demanded, cutting her short. "Spit it out. Tell me how surprised he looked. Tell me how he wept. Tell me something that makes him seem anything less than guilty."

Lennon replayed the moment of Benedict's discovery. Dante had remained composed, sure, but Lennon had expected no less of him. Stoicism wasn't a damning offense. Just because he didn't look as shocked as she felt didn't make him a murderer.

"Benedict is dead," said Lennon, and it seemed a risk to say those words aloud in front of someone who grieved him so acutely. As though he would blame her for his advisor's undoing because she'd simply dared to give voice to it. "At some point you'll just have to accept that."

Claude seemed ready to slap her. Gone was the poised young man Lennon had met months ago. He was all grief and malice now.

He began to rage. The way he did every night. He put a fist through the wall. Cleared his bookshelves, textbooks and notes toppling to the floor. He kicked his bar cart and tipped it sideways. Somehow, he broke a window. Lennon didn't see it happen—she was too busy backing away—but when she turned, Claude was half out the window, screaming terrible things about Benedict and Dante and everyone else. He forced himself through the break in the glass, carving up his forearms and stomach as he leaned outside.

Lennon screamed for help, and Sawyer burst through the door seconds later. The two of them attempted to pull Claude back, grabbing tight fistfuls of his shirt. But Claude wasn't small or weak, and he was even stronger when he was drunk. He struggled for a few minutes and threw them both off his back in his desperation to get at the window. Lennon fell against the bed. Sawyer, however, fell harder and cracked the back of his head on the corner of Claude's nightstand.

Lennon had had enough. She cast out a hand and caught Claude in a vicious psychic hold, seizing his limbs and forcing him back away from the window and onto the floor, where he thrashed and struggled and spit at her. So she locked his jaw shut to quiet his screaming.

"Stop," said Sawyer, face screwed with pain, clutching the spot where his head had struck the nightstand. "You're hurting him, please—"

In Dante's class they had spent the past two weeks learning a skill called *anatomical persuasion*. It involved careful interference with bodily functions—orders from the brain that could trigger a variety of symptoms—anything from sneezes to fevers or hives. It was amazing to Lennon just how many symptoms could be induced mentally. This type of persuasion seemed, to Lennon, the closest to real magic. And perhaps that was why she was so damn good at it.

Claude's lips peeled away from his gums in an ugly sneer. "Let me go, you fucking bitch—"

Lennon knocked him out. One moment Claude was thrashing and screaming threats, the next he slumped lifeless to the floor.

Sawyer pressed unsteadily to his feet. "Oh my god—"

"He's fine," said Lennon. "I was gentle."

Emerson, hearing this commotion, appeared in the doorway of Claude's bedroom. If she'd been sleeping at all, she certainly didn't look like it. "Enough," she said, and applied a pressure to the words that cleanly severed Lennon's hold on Claude, something that Lennon was formerly unaware was even possible.

Lennon broke to her knees.

Emerson peered down at her, something in her eyes that was not unlike fear. As if Lennon had been the one raging and breaking things and not Claude. As if she were the violent one, even though all she'd tried to do was subdue him. "Help me get him to the infirmary," Emerson ordered.

Emerson and Lennon dragged a near-catatonic Claude to a bed in the infirmary, where he would remain for the duration of the semester, under a psychiatric hold.

"When he's stable, he'll be released into the care of his family," Dr. Nave assured them on his way out of the infirmary. It was late, and with Claude now sleeping soundly, he looked ready to return to his own bed. "He just needs time to grieve and sober up."

"He won't finish his classes?" Lennon asked.

"Does he look like he's in a condition to do that?" Emerson tossed a hand at Claude, chained to his bed by cloth shackles. "Be serious. He's too sick."

"I've never seen anyone grieve like this," said Lennon softly, worrying about her part in all of this. She'd subdued rats into catatonia before, but never a person. And it felt strange to have cast such a dark spell over Claude, to have dragged him into lifeless slumber against his will, even if it was necessary in the moment. "It's terrible."

"He'll come around," said Emerson, and she stood up. When Lennon didn't rise with her, she half turned. "You're not coming? There are nurses on staff twenty-four hours. You don't need to babysit him anymore."

"I want to sit with him for a while," said Lennon, nodding to Claude asleep on the bed. "I feel shitty about what I did earlier. If he wakes, I want to apologize. Especially if, you know, he's going to be leaving. Who knows when or if we'll even see him again?"

Emerson gave a small nod and left. No sooner was she gone than Claude opened his eyes, staring blearily up at Lennon, his cheek pressed firmly against the pillow.

"You don't want to apologize," he said. "Even if you did, you wouldn't mean it, and I wouldn't forgive you either."

Lennon leaned forward, her voice low. "What did you mean when you said Dante said terrible things to Benedict? What did he say?"

Claude rolled away from her so that all she could see was his back, his once-glossy curls now tangled and matted at the nape. "He said he was going to kill him," Claude whispered. "Dante said to Benedict that one day, someday soon, he was going to fucking kill him. He said it would be August all over again."

"August? What happened in August?"

Claude didn't answer.

30

THE NEXT EVENING, Lennon went to Dante's office, only to find it empty.

"I'm afraid Dr. Lowe isn't in right now," the secretary said when Lennon inquired about his whereabouts. He was the same peculiar man who'd delivered their sandwiches, months ago, during her first meeting with Dante. Looking at him, Lennon realized she couldn't guess his age. He might've been sixteen, or he might've been fifty-six. So many of his features contradicted themselves—the lines that bracketed his mouth contrasting with the baby-smooth alabaster of his skin; his eyes, large and blue, seeming at once to hold all of the innocence of a child and the gravity of an old man. "Would you like to leave a message with me?"

"No need," said Lennon. "I'll come back."

She was turning to leave when she spotted Nadine by the door. Lennon was surprised to see her. She'd assumed that she'd left campus for Thanksgiving like the majority of those at Drayton did.

"Are you looking for Professor Lowe?" she asked.

"Yeah, actually. Have you seen him?"

"Every day," said Nadine. "He spends what seems like half his nights in the chapel and most of his mornings. He's probably there now."

Lennon wasn't even aware that the campus had its own chapel. She'd known there was a chaplain, but only because Nadine spoke so highly of her. Apparently, she was slated to become the woman's apprentice—all but securing the position during the early weeks of her first semester at Drayton. But Lennon had always assumed the chaplain occupied a room in Irvine, like the ones you'd find in an airport or a hospital.

"I'll walk you there," said Nadine, clutching her books close to her chest.

Lennon found the offer strange. She liked Nadine well enough, but she wouldn't have called them friends. And the distance between them—which wasn't small to begin with—had only widened since Lennon had been inducted into Logos and Nadine had not. "I don't want to trouble you."

"I don't mind," said Nadine, starting to walk. "Follow me."

For a long time, they walked without speaking, Lennon staring at her feet and Nadine humming something that sounded like a hymn. They were halfway across campus when Nadine finally broke the silence. "I saw Claude this morning."

"You were at the infirmary?"

Nadine nodded. "I go to pray with patients once a week. Claude included."

"And how did that go?"

Nadine flashed a smile. "About as well as you'd expect. He's the most deeply sacrilegious southerner I think I've ever met."

Lennon laughed. "He's something else. I'm worried about him."

"Me too," said Nadine. "Is it true what they're saying? About Benedict?"

"Depends. What are they saying?"

"That he was murdered. In cold blood."

"I don't know."

"You were the person who found him, right?"

Lennon nodded, wishing they could talk about something, anything, else. She was relieved when she spotted the chapel, the building half swallowed by a grove of blooming magnolia trees and live oaks so large their lower branches rested in the dirt. Here the well-tended lawn of Drayton Square gave way to waist-high grass that moved in the wind. It was so overgrown it looked almost intentionally concealed.

"I'll leave you to it," said Nadine.

Lennon nodded and made for the doors.

"Lennon?"

She turned. "Yes?"

"I slept with him."

Lennon faltered. "Who?"

"Ian."

"Oh."

"I—I just thought I should let you know."

Lennon waited for some feeling—jealousy or possessiveness, insecurity—but there was nothing to that end. Ian wasn't hers, and she'd never wanted him to be. But she was troubled by this, for an entirely different reason. "I thought you were going to be a nun?"

"So did I," said Nadine, and her mouth wavered with the effort of holding back tears. "You know, I used to think that God's greatest gift was His love for us. But I'm not so sure anymore. I think that maybe His greatest gift to us is free will. The ability to choose who and what we are. But if that's true, then . . . is it possible that what we do here is evil? Innately?" She looked down at her feet, as if embarrassed.

"I . . . I don't like to examine things through the lens of good and evil. It's reductive." *Christ*, Lennon thought to herself, she sounded just like Dante.

Nadine ducked her head, nodded. "I'll see you around?"

"Sure," said Lennon, and, a little shaken, she turned to enter the chapel. It was dimly lit, and the air smelled strongly of incense. On a pew in the shadow of the altar sat Dante, legs braced apart, eyes on the cross pinned to the back wall above the altar.

He turned his head when the door opened, stood when he saw her approaching.

"Where the hell have you been?" Lennon demanded, striding down the aisle, and she wasn't exactly sure how it happened—Dante certainly didn't initiate it—but before she had the chance to stop herself, she pulled him into a tight and fast hug. After a half beat, they parted, Lennon feeling the strange and sudden need to cry. She swallowed hard. "I was worried."

Dante pulled away first, motioned for her to sit beside him on the pew.

"Do you think it was a suicide?" she asked.

"That's what it looked like," said Dante.

"Claude isn't taking it well. I thought he'd get better with time . . . but it seems like he's only getting worse."

To this, Dante said nothing at all. But there was something peculiar in his expression. A kind of conflict that put a crease between his eyebrows and pulled at the muscles along his jaw. "Let's light candles. One for Claude and one for Ben."

It took Lennon by surprise. She'd never thought of him as sentimental in that way. "What's a candle going to do?"

"We're in a chapel," Dante reminded her, a gentle scolding. "Have some respect."

He stood and went to a nearby table that was covered in melted candles. Strangely, there were no matches, so Dante fished a cigarette lighter from his back pocket and lit two candles up himself. One for Claude and one for Benedict, and then a third.

"Who's that one for?"

"One of the rats died," he said. "Ian's. I found it chewing off its own leg. He was gone a few hours later."

"Ian must've pushed it too hard."

"No, it's my fault. I should've intervened. But to be honest, we lose a few with every crop of first years. I always try to avoid the inevitable and then I feel like shit when I don't. You were right to be worried at the beginning of this semester. They do suffer." Dante delivered this last bit with his eyes on the candles, as if he was too ashamed to look at her when he said it.

"Why didn't you just tell me the truth to begin with?"

"Because I thought you'd quit if you knew, and I believed—still believe, even more than I did before—that you have too much potential to waste."

This was perhaps the highest praise that Lennon had ever received from Dante. She'd expected to feel proud, but all that welled up in response was the stern conviction that he was somehow mistaken. That she needed to do better, be more, push harder.

"The gate to Benedict's house is down," she said, diverting the conversation. "No one's been able to get back there since the day we found him dead."

"Eileen shut it down," said Dante. "It would be dangerous otherwise. Anyone could get into the house when it's unguarded and come here to Drayton. When we install a new faculty member at the house, it'll open again."

"I thought Claude would inherit the position."

"Is he currently fit to do that?"

"Not now, but . . . he's grieving. He'll get better."

Now Dante looked down at her. "Will he?"

"Well . . . yes. I mean, I hope so."

Dante let it go, but in silence his point was made. The conclusion was obvious: Claude was unfit for the role he was supposed to inherit as Benedict's apprentice. He would be let go.

"Claude said something strange to me. I need to know if it's true."

"Ask your question."

"Did you threaten Benedict's life when you went to speak with him, that day after—"

"After he abused you? It's okay to put a word to what it was. You won't combust if you say it."

Lennon wasn't sure why she was so reluctant to admit what she knew was the truth. Was it because it made her feel weak? Or was she simply sanctifying Benedict out of pity now that he was dead? "He was trying to provoke me. He warned me that there would be pain."

Dante appeared, for a moment, elsewhere. It was like the opposite of what happened when his aberration surfaced all those weeks ago, during her first night on campus. If that was a personality stepping forward, this was a stepping back. In the absence of himself, his face took on a softer quality. It made him look younger and somehow more familiar. "Claude was correct. I told Benedict I would kill him if he hurt you again. He was violent with you and—acting in my capacity as your advisor—I responded in turn."

"Claude thinks you killed him."

"I can understand that, given what he might've heard."

The candles, stubby to begin with, were burning dangerously low now, the wicks threatening to extinguish themselves in the melted puddles of wax.

"I didn't kill Benedict," he said, "if that's where this is going."

And with that he walked back to the pews and sat down. When he was deep in thought, he had a way of pressing his palms together, lining up his fingers. He did this now, staring at the ground.

Lennon sat beside him. "Are you okay?"

He didn't answer that question, but she could feel his gaze on her mouth as she spoke.

Dante had taught her how to infiltrate the minds of rats and men alike, and Lennon had learned dutifully under his careful instruction. But despite her skill, the inner workings of his mind had remained a mystery to her. She'd never been privy to his thoughts or succeeded in her efforts to decode them. Not until this moment, as she watched him want her, for the first time. His desires, previously hidden from her, now took shape in what little space there was between them.

Lennon became aware of a heat between her thighs, and between them also, a charged quality on the air like cracking static. All of the heat trapped within her body went straight to her head, and there it became a thought. That thought was that she wanted to kiss him, or taste him, more precisely. So she shifted a little closer, narrowing that slit of charged air between them, angling her head, her lips parted.

She closed her eyes and was surprised when their brows met, instead of their lips. Dante was angling his head down, so that his mouth was a little lower than hers. When he spoke, she could feel the brush of his lips at her chin. "I'm sorry. We can't."

He drew away and left the chapel.

31

THOSE WEEKS LEADING up to final exams were harried and miserable. It was unseasonably hot and the humidity was thick. Every time Lennon left Logos—to attend a class or study in the library—she became a feast for the swarming sand gnats that amassed in dense, buzzing clouds around the campus. She thought of Dante often and hated herself for it. After their almost kiss, he'd all but cut her off. He delayed their advisory meetings, which were supposed to occur every week. His office hours were postponed indefinitely. In class, he never made eye contact with her and always left the moment he was done lecturing, perpetually double-booked or late to some task that required his immediate attention. Every appointment Lennon tried to schedule with his secretary was promptly canceled. And once, Lennon had spotted him cutting across campus and had attempted to flag him down. But either Dante hadn't seen her or, more likely, had intentionally chosen to ignore her, a slight that stung more than Lennon cared to admit.

But despite this abrupt and cruel shunting, Lennon's feelings for him didn't diminish.

Quite the opposite, actually.

As a rule, she had always despised the feeling of falling in love. Her experience with Dante was no exception to this, but her resentment toward him—a feeling so strong it could almost be called hatred—was an anomaly and she felt so stupid for allowing him to occupy so much of her headspace, especially now that it was so painfully obvious just how little she mattered to him.

Finals week began, and the campus buzzed with the building anticipation of a long holiday break. Everyone but Lennon seemed excited to return home to their families. Blaine would be yachting in the Maldives with hers (Lennon thought it was rather unfair that she got to be beautiful *and* rich, and told her as much). Sawyer would head back to Connecticut to spend the holiday with his father. Claude had been sent home prematurely, to recuperate with his family, and Emerson had plans to go to Europe with her girlfriend of the moment, Yumi. But to Lennon, the idea of folding herself back into a life and family she'd left behind felt strange and unbearable, like shoving her feet into boots several sizes too small and then being forced to go hiking in them.

Finals proved easier than Lennon suspected—almost suspiciously so. Most of her written exams were short, no more than six or seven questions long. Meditation was pass or fail, and based entirely on attendance and participation. Persuasion I concluded with a series of brief persuasive exercises that functioned as their final assessment. Thus, four days into finals week—Lennon was free as a bird. Her one and only test taken, her papers for metaphysics turned in. Her first semester at Drayton came to a soft close.

That same week, Lennon said goodbye to her peers at Logos House and left the school via a car parked in the staff parking lot. The driver was a handsome man who looked vaguely embalmed, as if a statue at a wax museum had been brought to life. He didn't speak and

Lennon, dead tired from a string of late nights and early mornings, fell asleep before they'd even left the parking lot. When she woke, they were at the Savannah Airport, where a small jet was waiting to fly her down to Florida.

Apparently, the school didn't trust her to travel there by elevator.

Three hours after boarding, Lennon landed at the Orlando airport, where her mother—Beverly—was waiting to pick her up. She was slight and tall and beautiful. Her face was very similar to Lennon's, but their energy was unmistakably different—her mother soft in all the ways that Lennon was sharp, and warm in all the ways her daughter was cold. Upon seeing Lennon, she broke into a jog and pulled her daughter into a tight embrace. But she quickly pushed Lennon away, stepped back to get a real look at her. "You look different. Taller, maybe? Or thinner? I can't tell. Have you been eating enough?"

It was a fraught question, but Lennon was happy to have a good and honest answer. "Three square meals a day."

"I believe you," said her mother. "You look . . . well."

"I like to think I am," she said, and meant it.

Lennon's sister, Carly, was in the kitchen when they arrived at the house, her hair heaped atop her head and held fast with a large claw clip. Where Lennon favored their mother, Carly favored their father. She had his heavy-lidded eyes, full lips, and blunt brows that made her seem like she was always frowning a bit. But she was actually frowning when Lennon entered the kitchen that day.

"Hey," said Lennon, that one word breaking the silence that had lapsed between them since their last argument. It had begun after Lennon had called Carly, drunk at 3:00 a.m., just a few days after her big move to Colorado, one that Carly had strongly advised against. Lennon had been crying about her life and all of the things that had gone wrong with it, and Carly had been silent on the line for some time. But she would never forget the way her sister's voice sounded when—ten minutes into the call—she finally spoke in a strained monotone: "You're self-absorbed and annoying and at some point, you'll have to accept the fact that at the center of all of your *many* problems is you. And making those problems everyone else's problem isn't the same as actually dealing with your shit."

Lennon wasn't sure if she'd hung up on Carly or if Carly had hung up on her, but they hadn't spoken since.

"You're smoking again," she said to Lennon.

"No, I'm not," Lennon snapped. But it was a half lie. She'd begun smoking socially a few weeks after she'd begun studying at Drayton, a bad habit she shared with most of the student body and faculty. "Not often anyway."

Carly narrowed her eyes. She was a lawyer, gunning for partner at a big firm in New York, and as such, she was cutthroat, and smart in a way that often scared Lennon. Which is not to say she was unkind, but hers was a kindness that was packaged in a thick wrapping of brutal and incisive honesty. It kept Lennon in a state of perpetual tension, hanging on her every word, waiting for whatever truth would break her, because when it came to Carly, inevitably something that she said would.

"You know me and my nasty habits," said Lennon, the self-deprecation itself a kind of olive branch.

Carly received it as such and dragged her into a tight hug, her bony shoulder cutting deep into Lennon's windpipe. "I'm glad you're here," she said.

THAT NIGHT, THEY ATE DINNER ON THE PATIO OFF THE kitchen, which overlooked a wide swath of lush, green golf course, and a murky pond with a fountain spitting in the middle of it. There was an alligator sunning on its far bank, large and black and fat with possums or deer or the neighborhood dogs that had made the fatal mistake of venturing too close to the water's edge.

Her mother beamed at the girls. "It's nice to have the gang back together, isn't it, Joseph?"

"Sure is," said Lennon's father. He was a quiet man—slight and furtive—but seemed even more ill at ease than usual in Lennon's presence. Had they been apart long enough to become strangers, she wondered, staring across the table at him. Or had he always been so acutely uncomfortable in her presence, and time had just smoothed over the memory?

The questions about Lennon's life came over dessert. They'd spent the whole meal stepping carefully around the elephant in the room that was the abrupt end to Lennon's now-broken engagement and her subsequent enrollment at Drayton. But she'd known it was only a matter of time before her mother or Carly started fishing for details. What she hadn't expected, though, was her father to ask first. "You said you were studying in Savannah?"

"Yep."

"Studying where?" Carly inquired, eyes flickering up from her ice cream. "SCAD?"

"No. You know I suck at art."

Her mother lifted a glass of wine to her lips. "Then where?"

"A place called Drayton."

"Never heard of it," said her father, frowning. He'd grown up in Brunswick, before moving north to Augusta for college. "Is that some sort of unaccredited for-profit thing . . . like that Griffin University or whatever it's called?"

"Of course not," said Lennon, bristling a bit. "Drayton is nothing like that."

"What are you studying there?" Carly inquired, which was really one of the worst questions she could've asked, second only to *Can I visit?* Lennon found herself desperately wishing that the admin at Drayton had offered something by way of advice when it came to handling inquiries (or inquisitions, as the case was then) about Drayton. Something as simple as a brochure or a website to appease anxious parents would've been helpful. But then, Lennon realized that they had already equipped her with everything she needed to handle a conversation like this one. In fact, she'd spent the entire semester's worth of persuasion classes preparing for just such a time as this. If she'd wanted to—with half a thought—she could've shut the conversation down, made them all forget it had ever happened. But the fact that that thought had even occurred to her made her stomach clench with guilt. Who was she?

"I, um . . . I study the human condition," said Lennon.

Carly narrowed her eyes. "So, psychology?"

"Not quite. But it's related."

Her mother looked quite alarmed. "And that's . . . an accredited course?"

"Yes. At least I think so."

Carly raised an eyebrow. "How do you not know?"

"How long will you be in school?" her father asked, chattier than he usually was. More curious. Frankly, Lennon wasn't used to him being interested in the particulars of her life and it made her uncomfortable.

"I'm supposed to stay for at least two years," said Lennon.

There was a long silence at the table, and for a fleeting moment Lennon believed that this portion of the conversation had come to an end. But then Carly spoke up: "And you're sure this isn't . . . you know . . ."

"No," said Lennon, looking up at her sister. "I don't. What are you trying to say?"

Her mother, who could see where this was going, issued a low: *"Girls."*

Carly waved her off, affixed her gaze to Lennon. "You're sure this isn't just another way for you to run away?"

A long and uncomfortable silence settled over the table.

"No. I don't think so."

"You don't . . . *think* so? You take off in the middle of the night—breaking your engagement—and turn up across the country studying at some random-ass school that no one has ever heard of, and you don't think that's running away? Do you hear yourself?"

Lennon realized—with a searing flash of hurt and shame—that her family thought she was lying, thought that Drayton was all some large and elaborate ruse to cover up the fact that she was just, once again, choosing to flee from her problems instead of facing them. And could she really blame them, given her history?

Lennon had run away no less than six times as a teenager. On more than one occasion, after a nasty fight with her parents, she'd fled into the night with no money or belongings, except the clothes on her back and the cell phone buzzing in the pocket of her jeans. When she snuck out to parties, she often didn't bother going home after they ended, preferring instead to wander the streets alone deep into the wee hours of the morning, returning home sometimes days later, in smeared makeup, with her heels dangling from hooked fingers. It was sick, but back then she had liked the power of punishing people with her absence. Of making herself disappear only to turn up again, like some twisted little magic trick.

She liked to think she'd grown up since then. But had she really?

"The night I left Colorado, I caught Wyatt fucking my only friend in the state. And yes, when I saw that I ran. I fled the house, stole

Wyatt's car, and drove off. I ended up in the parking lot of this abandoned mall . . ." Lennon realized she couldn't tell them the rest of the story without risking another involuntary psych hold. "When I found Drayton—or when Drayton found me—I felt like for the first time I had something to run toward instead of from. I still feel that way, and if you can't see it then I don't blame you, because I think to you, I'm always going to be this drunk teenage girl running away from . . . hell knows what. But I'm not that person anymore, and if you give me a chance, I'd like to prove it."

Her mother reached across the table, squeezed Lennon's hand. Her smile was pained and pitying. "If you're happy, we're happy."

AFTER DINNER, LENNON'S MOTHER HANDED HER A LETTER from the mail stack. It was sheathed in a crisp, white envelope. It was addressed to her in filigreed calligraphy and it had a gilded stamp that depicted some sort of gargoyle-like creature. It had no return address.

"What's this?" Lennon inquired, holding it up. But she already knew who it was from. What she couldn't figure out, though, was how they'd known where to send it.

"I don't know. It came in the mail this morning. In fact, the postman knocked and hand-delivered it. Made me sign for it and everything."

Lennon slit the letter open, withdrew a hard piece of parchment paper, embossed with the Drayton letterhead in the left corner. It read:

Ms. Carter,

It is our great pleasure to inform you that you've passed your first semester at Drayton, and we look forward to welcoming you back to campus in the new year. The spring semester will resume on

January 22, and you will resume your studies under the supervision of Dr. Alec Becker, your newly appointed advisor. Please dial the number below to confirm your attendance.

Fondly,
The Drayton Registrar's Office

At the bottom of the letter was a telephone number, along with a list of her spring-semester classes, which she didn't even bother to read.

Lennon crumpled everything in a closed fist, her heart hammering against her sternum. She knew that Dante had been distancing himself ever since their near kiss—that, he'd made painfully clear—but she'd never actually suspected, or even considered, that he would pass her off to Alec Becker, Ian's advisor, of all people. He'd abandoned her, he'd really done it, and he hadn't even had enough care or decency to do it himself, so he'd passed the task off to some admin at Drayton, as if she wasn't important enough to warrant an actual conversation.

And maybe she wasn't.

The hurt came then, her cheeks warming with it, and then the anger after that. The last time she'd felt this betrayed had been the night, months ago now, that she'd found Wyatt screwing Sophia in their shared bathroom. But that betrayal had felt somehow more . . . familiar. Expected even, in its own way. If she was being honest with herself, she had never really expected things to work out with Wyatt. But with Dante it was different. Why was it different? Had she really been dumb enough to assume that he not only shared her feelings, but could reciprocate them in such a way as to actually amount to something like a relationship? Dante didn't even seem like the type, and maybe that was exactly why she wanted him so much.

She hated herself for that. Almost as much as she hated him.

"What does it say?" her mother asked, nodding at the letter, just as nosy as she ever was. But she wasn't the only one watching. Carly was gazing at her from across the living room with a knitted brow, sensing trouble, and even her father had torn his gaze away from his football game to watch the scene unfold.

Lennon shoved the crumpled letter into the pocket of her pajamas. "Nothing," she said. "Just junk mail."

That night, while the rest of her family was sound asleep, Lennon picked up the landline phone on her nightstand and dialed the number at the bottom of the crumpled letter. She decided that if Dante wanted to be an asshole, she would follow suit.

A woman's voice answered after three long rings. "This is the Drayton Registrar's Office. Is this Lennon speaking?"

"Yes. I need to speak to Professor Lowe," she said, and just saying his name over the phone was enough to get her heart racing. She'd rehearsed the conversation several times in her head before she'd actually worked up the courage to call. She'd honed her strategy, refined her threats, decided that she would adopt a tone of cool detachment, just like his.

"Professor Lowe isn't in right now."

Her heart sank. Surprisingly, stupidly, she hadn't planned for this. "Well, then could you give me his home phone number? I really need to speak with him."

"I'm afraid that's not an option."

"Fine," Lennon snapped. "Then let me just leave a message. Will you relay it to him?"

"If it's an urgent matter—"

"It is. Tell Dante I won't be returning to school next semester if he's no longer my advisor. Tell him I'll withdraw."

A long and staticky pause. The voice changed slightly, going deeper, the syllables stretched like a slowed recording. "Thank you for your call."

The line went dead.

Lennon should have gone to sleep after that, but instead she lay awake, fueled by the weak hope that Dante might return her call. An hour passed, then two, and still nothing. She got up and went to the kitchen, made herself a cup of tea and turned on one of her mom's old period pieces, a stylized regency where everyone wore shapeless pastel dresses and little ringlet curls around their ears.

Lennon was a half hour into the movie when Carly entered the living room, dressed in an overlarge sweatshirt she'd owned since they were in middle school. It was a wonder that it was in such good condition, given that it was so old. But it was pristine, like all of Carly's belongings. Everything she owned or loved or tended to was all the better for it—boyfriends, pets, plants, it didn't matter. Lennon was the one exception to this rule, and she knew that it bothered Carly.

"I have melatonin if you want some," said Carly, sitting down on the couch, an awkward distance between them.

"I don't need it," she said, which was a lie.

On-screen, the heroine of the movie ran through a forest of dead trees, her white nightgown billowing behind her.

"You know, as a kid, I always fucking hated this movie," said Carly. "I was sick with jealousy because you and Mom loved it so much and I just didn't get it. I couldn't even admit it was kind of good until I rewatched it as an adult. And even then, it was hard."

"Wait, you were jealous of *me*?" This was new. It had always been

Carly and her mom's closeness that Lennon was jealous of. Perpetually the outsider looking in through the window of their relationship. They were the ones who were more alike, resolute and reliable, so steady and sure of themselves in a way that Lennon decidedly was not.

"Of course I was jealous," said Carly, not looking at her. "Mom might like me better, but she loves you more." Lennon opened her mouth to challenge that statement, but Carly cut quickly to a new topic of conversation before she had the chance. "So, are you going to tell me what you're actually studying at that school?"

"The human condition—"

"Yes, you said that over dinner. But I want a straight answer. What are you really studying?"

"It's hard to explain."

"Try me."

Lennon did try, but when she opened her mouth to speak of the magic of Drayton, its strange curriculum, she gagged on the words.

Carly sprang to her feet and bolted to the kitchen with surprising speed, grabbed a glass out of the cabinet, filled it with water, and returned. "Jesus Christ, what's wrong with you?"

Lennon waved her off. "I'm okay. I guess this is what happens when we try to talk about it."

Carly set the glass of water on the coffee table and sat down. "I don't understand."

"You're not meant to. And if I tried to make you understand, then . . ."

"Then what, Lennon?"

"Then I wouldn't be able to. Something would stop me."

"What the hell is that supposed to mean?"

"Never mind," she said. "Forget it."

"Lennon, I—"

"I said forget it," said Lennon again, and this time she made it reality, erasing the past few beats of conversation, to the moment just before Carly asked her what she really studied at Drayton. It was surprisingly easy entering Carly's mind, for all her stubbornness. Lennon had once heard it rumored that it was easier to persuade those you were already bonded with. Romantic partners were apparently the easiest to manipulate, but family members were a close second. This was certainly true for Carly, whose memories Lennon was able to carefully extract with more ease than the rats they'd experimented on in Dante's class.

It was only when she drew away from Carly that she saw that she might've made a mistake. Carly's chin began to tremble, creasing up the way it always did before she was about to cry. "I . . . I feel like I'm coming down with a migraine or something."

Lennon, sick at the sight of what she'd done, wrapped an arm around her sister and helped her to her feet. "It's okay," she whispered, walking her back to her bedroom. "You're just tired. It's okay. You'll be okay."

32

ON CHRISTMAS MORNING, as they were unwrapping presents, there was a knock at the door. Her mother rose to answer it, whispering about nosy neighbors who lacked the God-given common sense to avoid unsolicited visits on Christmas morning of all days. Lennon, tired and dazed after staying up so late, thought nothing of it and was surprised when her mother returned to the living room moments later, looked at Lennon, and said: "It's for you."

Lennon, Carly, and their father all got up at once, Lennon edging to the front of the group, almost defensively, the other three trailing her as she walked down the foyer to the front door and opened it. Standing there was Dante.

"What the hell are you doing here?" said Lennon. "I mean . . . Merry Christmas."

Her mother glanced back and forth between the two of them. "Is this . . . a friend of yours, Lennon?"

"This is Dante. My advisor."

"Your advisor. At Drayton?"

"Ex-advisor, apparently," said Lennon.

Dante's eyes homed in on Lennon, as if there were no one else there. "We need to talk."

They walked down the tiled driveway to the vintage Audi parked parallel to the street. Lennon stood a few feet away on the curb with her arms folded over her chest. It wasn't that cold, but she was shivering terribly.

"What the hell are you on? You pull me from Christmas morning to handle this?" She'd never seen him this angry, and it was kind of, well, hot, though she was loath to admit it. Either way, it was better than the tacit nonchalance with which he'd abandoned her two weeks before.

"I don't want to study at Drayton if I'm not studying under you," said Lennon.

"Bullshit," said Dante. "This is a fucking power play, and you know it. You think you can force my hand by faux-quitting?"

"Clearly, I can, because you're here. You could've called, you know. You didn't have to come all this way. We could've done this over the phone if you'd had the decency to let me know that you don't want to be my advisor anymore, instead of handing over the task to admin."

"These kinds of administrative tasks are usually handled by—"

"It's not about that and you know it," said Lennon, angry now. Really angry. "This is about what happened in the chapel. You're punishing me for it."

"It's not a punishment—"

"Then what is it, Dante?"

He leveled his gaze, was quiet for a long time. "I am your advisor, and you are my charge. We can't do this."

"I'm not a child—"

"I know that."

"—and I'm not some starry-eyed teen fresh out of high school either. I mean, I've been *engaged*, for Christ's sake. If something was to happen—"

"It won't."

"But let's say it does. Let's say I wanted it to. It's not coercion."

"And how do you know? How do you know that I'm not pulling strings? Persuading you to do what I want?"

"So you do want this."

"That was hypothetical."

"Was it?"

His eyes turned stern and hard, and she thought he might yell at her. But he just dipped his head and smiled instead. Not with kindness or humor but with sheer disbelief, as if he couldn't believe he'd been dragged into this. "Do you know why I came here?"

"Damage control?"

"No. I came all this way because Eileen was deeply troubled by your phone call, so troubled that she began to suspect your mind needed to be wiped clean of every memory you've ever had of Drayton. I came here to assess whether that needs to be done."

Lennon stiffened. "What's your take?"

Dante ignored that question, just sidestepped it like it wasn't even worth his consideration. "You're going back to Drayton. Today."

"Not if you won't be my advisor," said Lennon.

"Don't be difficult."

"There's nothing difficult about this. It's simple. I return to Drayton with you as my advisor, or I don't return at all, and you take my memories. Which one is it going to be, Dante?"

"Lennon—"

"I'm serious. I mean every word. I don't want—" Her voice broke on that lie. "I don't *need* or expect to have any relationship with you beyond advisorship. But if I'm expected to continue my studies—to be this gatekeeper that everyone at the school is so determined for me to become—then I need an advisor who I can trust to guide me. And you're the only person who fits that description."

Dante turned quiet and contemplative for a beat. Staring down at his own shoes as he made up his mind. "If we do this, you and me, we can't be anything. Ever. Our relationship will be strictly contained within the parameters of advisorship. Nothing beyond that. Do you understand that?"

"I understand."

A muscle in Dante's jaw jumped and flexed. She swore she felt his presence in her mind, just the briefest touch, there and gone in an instant. She wondered what he saw, what he was looking for. "Let's get you back to Drayton."

Lennon nodded, trying to mask just how relieved she really felt. "Can I say goodbye to my family? I'll be quick."

"You have fifteen minutes."

Lennon walked back up the drive to see the faces of her family pressed against the windows on both sides of the door. The questions began as soon as she was inside.

"Why is he here?" Carly demanded.

"That man looks like Black Adonis," said her mother. "You said he's your advisor? He doesn't look like an advisor."

"Not with those tattoos," her father muttered. "Did you see the backs of his hands? Anyone who gets tattooed on their hands is an idiot."

Lennon shouldered past her family to the Christmas tree, where she hastily collected her opened presents, which consisted of a few pairs of socks, a silk blouse, and several passive-aggressively titled self-help books. She carried everything back to the guest room, dumping all the presents on the bed.

"What are you doing?" Carly demanded.

"Packing."

"But it's Christmas," said her mother.

"I know. But the term starts earlier than I thought, so I should be on my way."

Lennon packed quickly. She hadn't brought much to begin with so it didn't take long.

"This is weird," said Carly. "You're acting weird."

"According to you, I'm always acting weird."

"Well, you're acting even weirder now. And that guy, Dante, or whatever is name is. He just comes here to collect you? How did he even get this address?"

"I gave it to him," she lied.

"Bullshit. Why would you give your advisor the address of your parents' retirement home?"

Her mother's eyes flashed wide with outrage. "I'll have you know this is a freestanding condo for people of *retirement age*, Carly. My god, you can be so patronizing—"

"Lennon," said Carly, catching her by the arms now. "Listen, if this is some weird sex trafficking cult thing—"

"It's not," said Lennon. "And I love you, and I need to go. And you need to let me."

"No," said Carly. "I'm not letting you go anywhere. And he"—she pointed out the front window of the house, and Lennon was fairly certain Dante could see her—"he can go fuck himself as far as I'm concerned. He's making you do this, isn't he? He's taking you."

"He's my advisor," said Lennon. "The only place he's taking me is back to school."

"Ah, your advisor. Of course. The same way Wyatt was your friend?" Carly demanded now, with a real maliciousness. "And that architecture professor back in college? And before him, in high school, your boyfriend's mom—"

Her mother's eyes flashed wide with alarm. *"Lennon!"*

When she willed them all to silence, it didn't feel like a choice. It was as though someone else had simply sucked their words right out of the air. But her consciousness returned to her when she began to walk them back to the living room. She dragged her parents over to the couch, had her mother offer an open palm, bid her father take it. She tugged at the corners of their lips and arranged their faces into expressions that looked less like grimaces and more like smiles. Of the three, Carly was the most difficult to compel—perhaps because she'd wised up, after Lennon had persuaded her that first time. It took several grueling tries before Lennon was able to settle her, somewhat comfortably, on the couch next to their parents. All of them together there formed the scene of a family, made perfect by the fact that Lennon was not a part of it.

"Something came up at school," said Lennon, and as she said this, she made it an immutable reality in their minds. "I'm going to leave now. Have a good Christmas."

As a parting gift she delivered a feeling of peace, and felt it settle thickly in the minds of her loved ones, turning them all soft and compliant and perhaps a little sleepy. All except Carly, who, sitting stiffly on the couch, gazed at the floor with tear-filled eyes as if betrayed.

33

THEY DROVE THE four hours back to Savannah in silence, Dante compulsively checking the mirrors, the ocean smearing past the windows. Lennon carefully observed the distance between them, hyperaware of her own body and his. She made sure never to reach for her drink, nestled in the cupholder, at the same time he reached for his for fear of their hands brushing. She kept her gaze mostly fixed on the road. Their conversation was contained to discussions about school or the weather or other equally dull topics.

Somewhere along the stretch of highway between Orlando and St. Augustine, Lennon began to wonder how they'd get into Drayton, given the school's immateriality, the fact that its very existence seemed to break the laws that governed the reality they occupied now. Her question was answered when they entered into Savannah proper, exiting off the highway and into the downtown historic district. Dante drove with the windows down, cold wind washing through the car. There was music playing—the bass thudding against the back of her sternum like a second heart—Dante bobbed his head, occasionally mouthing along to the lyrics, but was silent more often than not. Blurring past her windows, Savannah was as beautiful as ever. There was the pink house on the garden square, a man on the curb with a megaphone and a sign that read HELL IS NEAR in bleeding red letters.

They were in the thick of the historic district when—rather abruptly—Dante slowed the car and turned toward a tall wrought-iron gate. It parted open for them.

"Irvine's work," said Dante, reading her thoughts, a thing that he was apt to do with unnerving accuracy. "The last gate he ever raised."

"How does it know to let us through?"

"Above my pay grade," he said.

They turned onto a narrow dirt road. Inexplicably—impossibly, given that they were in the heart of the densely populated downtown—the road was flanked by thick forest. As they drove, the car picked up speed, pinning Lennon to the back of her seat. A dizzying sensation, like motion sickness, scrambled her thoughts and made her wish she had a barf bag on hand, just in case. Her vision blurred out of focus as she turned to Dante. "Is that you?"

He was totally relaxed, gripping the wheel one-handed as the forest trees blurred past the windows. "It's the road itself, carrying us to the campus."

"Like the elevators?"

He nodded. "They're the same. This road just takes a different form. It makes it easier for cars to bridge the gap."

They slowed as a second gate—identical to the one they'd just passed through—appeared at the end of the road. Behind it, a small parking lot came into view. The gate parted open for them and Dante turned off the moving road and they got out of the car, walked up a narrow path through the trees. From around a tight bend, Drayton came into view.

The campus was, perhaps, more beautiful than the memory of it that Lennon had carried with her over the winter break. The Twenty-Fifth Square was resplendent in the reddish light of sunset. The glistening Spanish moss, touched by sun, seemed almost gilded. The shock of the frost-kissed grass, the ice shattering beneath her loafers as she tramped through the Twenty-Fifth Square. She was home, and it felt good.

Dante left her just outside of Irvine Hall, with a hurried goodbye and something about a meeting that Lennon didn't fully catch. So Lennon walked alone across the empty campus until she reached Logos House.

She was struck, suddenly, by how much she'd missed the place.

Lennon went up to her room to discover that it wasn't as she'd left it. Her bed was freshly made, the sheets and blankets changed and laundered, the scent of detergent sharp on the air. At the foot of Lennon's bed, lying on her quilt, was a leather folder, embossed with Drayton's crest. Within was her schedule for the spring semester, which included a sampling of Drayton's core curriculum classes—Metaphysics II, Persuasion II, and Meditation II—as well as courses like Persuasive Thought and Tactical Persuasion I, taught by Alec Becker, Ian's advisor—who would've been Lennon's too if she hadn't convinced Dante to keep her on. Most of these courses took place in the evening or at night instead of the early morning. She would have to become a truly nocturnal creature this semester, to manage the rigors of her course load. This came as something of a relief to her, as she'd come to prefer working at night, if only because her insomnia had worsened considerably in the wake of Benedict's death.

Blaine entered her room then—rosy-cheeked from the cold—and didn't bother to set down her bags before collecting Lennon in a hard hug.

"I thought you were in the Maldives?" Lennon asked when they pulled away.

"I got seasick and came home early," she said, and for some reason Lennon wasn't sure that she believed her. "Yachting isn't for me. Why are you back?"

"Long story not worth telling," said Lennon.

She was surprised when Blaine didn't press her. "Have you heard the news?"

"What news?" said Lennon, unpacking what few belongings she'd brought with her to Florida, stuffing clothes back into the drawers of her wardrobe.

Blaine's voice dropped to a low whisper. "Claude was expelled."

"Expelled?"

Blaine nodded gravely. "He had some sort of altercation with Dante at the end of last semester. Turned up to his office drunk, apparently."

"Dante didn't mention anything to me."

"You were with Dante over the break?"

"Not over the break. But he came to pick me up from my parents' house down in Florida."

"Lennon."

"It's not how it sounds. I swear. Who told you all of this business about Claude being expelled?"

"I heard it from Kieran, but apparently Emerson knows more. She was in his office at the time. I don't know, you'd have to ask her. She's here if you want to. Apparently she and Yumi had it out and she came back to Drayton early, like us."

So Lennon went to Emerson's room to discover that she was hosting something of a Christmas cocktail hour. There were people—

women mostly; women were always so drawn to Emerson—sitting cross-legged on the floor nursing mugs full of mulled wine. Cigarette smoke hung on the air in a bluish pall. Emerson, though, was seated at her desk, her back to most of the guests she was hosting. As Lennon stepped closer, she saw that Emerson was hunched over a spread of papers, weighted down with expensive-looking pens and mechanical drafting pencils. A redheaded girl who was decidedly not her girlfriend, Yumi, was grasping at her left shoulder, working out a knot.

"I take it you had a breakup over the holiday?" Lennon inquired. Though this wasn't entirely surprising. On at least two occasions, Lennon had overheard Yumi and Emerson in the thick of a lover's quarrel.

Emerson flashed her the middle finger without looking up from her desk. "What do you want, Lennon?"

"A second to talk, if you can spare it."

Emerson glanced up from her work. In her left hand, she held a cigarette. There were bluish bags beneath her eyes, and her lips were badly chapped. "That depends upon what you want to talk about."

"Claude's expulsion."

Emerson went back to her work, sheathing the cigarette between her lips. When she spoke, it wagged and rained ashes down onto her papers. "There's nothing to talk about. He's out."

"What happened? Blaine said he had a clash with Dante."

"He was clashing with everyone, as you well know."

Lennon became aware, now, of the attention on her. Everyone in the room had fallen silent, listening in on her conversation with Emerson.

"Could we just go outside for a minute?"

Emerson arched an eyebrow but got up, shoving back her chair so forcefully it very nearly toppled. The girl who'd been squeezing her shoulders stumbled away as she and Lennon stepped out into the empty hall.

"What the hell happened between Dante and Claude?" Lennon whispered.

"Claude burst into his office—drunk—and it went about as well as anything goes when Claude is drunk and belligerent. Dante responded in turn."

"What do you mean by that?"

"I mean Claude got himself expelled. He was breaking things. Saying things—"

"Like what?"

Here Emerson paused, suddenly reluctant to answer. "Why don't you just ask Dante yourself? You two are so close now—"

"Close?"

"Oh, fuck off, Lennon. Everyone knows you're slated to be his apprentice. It's only a matter of time."

"That's not . . . What? No. You're the shoo-in."

"Please," said Emerson, rolling her eyes. "You don't have to pretend not to know to spare my ego. I could give a damn, but it is annoying the way you act like you don't know."

"That I don't know what?"

"That you're the favorite," she snapped. "That ever since you stepped foot on this campus Dante has been pulling strings to protect you, which is exactly why Claude was expelled."

"What the hell do I have to do with Claude's expulsion?" Lennon demanded, shocked that Emerson would even suggest such a thing.

"The night Claude burst into Dante's office, he was saying things about you and that last lesson you had with Benedict before everything went south."

Lennon's heart dropped into her stomach. "What kind of things?"

"I don't know," said Emerson. "I heard Claude say your name—loudly, a couple of times—and then he was cut short. When he emerged from Dante's office he was totally subdued, no doubt Dante persuaded him. The next day I got word from the admin that he'd been expelled. So, if you want to know what Claude said, your best bet is to ask Dante."

34

DRAYTON'S PROFESSORS KEPT private apartments on school grounds. At the distant edge of campus there was a block of townhomes, off-limits to students, where the faculty spent their nights. It wasn't hard to locate Dante's residence, because each of these narrow row houses bore a plaque on the front, designating their ownership. Dante's was a dark brick, half-covered in crawling ivy. Its windows glowed warm in the chill autumn night.

Lennon knocked.

After a long beat, Dante answered. He didn't look surprised to see her on his stoop. "You can't just show up to my private residence in the middle of the night."

"You showed up at my parents' home, uninvited, on *Christmas*."

"That was different."

"How so?"

"For one, you wanted me to come—"

"That's—"

"Don't deny it, Lennon. Second, there was little to no risk of anything when I showed up at your parents'. The same can't be said for you being here. It doesn't look right, me with my advisee on my doorstep in the middle of the night. What if someone saw us?"

"Then I guess you better get me inside before someone does."

His gaze hardened. "We have an agreement, Lennon."

"I know. This conversation won't breach it. It's school related. Perfectly within the bounds of our advisorship."

Dante looked unmoved. "Is that a promise?"

"Of course. I wouldn't lie to you."

He rolled his eyes but stepped out of the doorway, showed her into a small living room—furnished tastefully in the same style as the rest of the campus. A coffee table in front of the couch was covered in at least a dozen white envelopes.

"What is all of this?" she asked.

Lennon hadn't expected a real answer—Dante was always one to keep his secrets—so when he offered one it came as a surprise. "There's a congressional campaign out of Pennsylvania that one of the school's primary donors would very much like me to quash."

Lennon sat down on the couch. "Will it be violent? The quashing, I mean."

Dante sat down on the couch beside her, a careful distance between them.

"Most likely."

"How will you do it?"

"I won't do it. I'm going to refuse them."

"But if you did?"

Dante thought through this carefully. "I'd try my hand at diplomacy. And if that didn't work, and inevitably it wouldn't—that's why they wrote to me in the first place—I'd put a bit of force behind my words."

"Which is to say you'd persuade them?"

"Correct."

"What if they won't bend?" Lennon asked, knowing from her studies that high-stakes targets were often stubborn, married to their own agendas, and reluctant to be put off of them. They might even have persuasive defenses of their own, ways to ward off psychic attacks.

But Dante didn't seem troubled by this prospect. "If they won't bend... then I opt for violence. But only the clean kind. A well-timed stroke. An unfortunate car crash. A suicide maybe, if the circumstances allow for it. It's ugly work, and I don't relish it."

"Then why do it at all?"

"Because it needs to be done," said Dante. "This school, the people who depend on it, we exist in a closed ecosystem, and we all have to do our part to sustain it. This work—these letters—is a part of that. You'll be getting letters like that soon, if you haven't already. But you're not here to talk about work."

"No. I'm not."

"What are you here for?"

"You had a confrontation with Claude the day before he was expelled. What happened?"

"Claude came into my office drunk," said Dante. "He toppled a bookshelf and accused me of a number of salacious misdeeds, including murdering Benedict. I drew the line there."

Lennon swallowed dry. "And by 'drew the line,' you mean—"

"It's clear to me that Claude wasn't going to be able to stay at this school without destroying himself, and I was willing to allow him to do that. But to drag you into the mire of his drunken self-annihilation was a step too far, so I made my concerns apparent to Eileen and the rest of the professors here. A hearing was assembled, and Claude showed up drunk, which I imagine didn't do him any favors. The hearing took a vote, and he was expelled."

"And by 'expelled,' you mean you took his memories of Drayton. Of everyone he met here. Benedict included."

Dante got up off the couch to pour himself a drink. She thought he wouldn't answer the question, but then, staring down at his empty glass, he nodded. "I left Claude's memories intact," said Dante, which came as a surprise to Lennon. She'd assumed all of the students expelled from the school had their memories taken. "I saw no reason to take them. All I did when I removed him from this campus was give him the chance at a normal life, because the one he had here was clearly killing him. Now, I'd call that mercy. But you can make of it what you will."

"What about Benedict?"

"What about him?"

"Did they ever find a suicide note? Something to explain why he did what he did?"

She watched Dante's expression carefully, but he remained as casual as ever. If the mention of Benedict's death provoked anything in him, Lennon certainly couldn't see it.

"There was nothing," he said, and for some reason, she didn't believe him.

35

WHEN CLASSES BEGAN, Lennon decided to pay Sawyer a visit at the Fincher Library, where he worked as an apprentice to the head archivist. Because of that apprenticeship, Sawyer was one of the few people on campus with unfettered access to the files of every student that had ever studied at Drayton. Which meant that Sawyer could tell Lennon where Claude had departed to upon his expulsion, assuming he was willing to help her.

The Fincher Library—named after the head boy of Drayton's inaugural class—was widely known to be the second-most-haunted building on Drayton's campus (the first being Logos House). While the school's official stance was to eschew any belief in the paranormal, its founder, John Drayton, was a paranormal enthusiast, and was said to have hosted a number of drunken séances in the library. Drayton himself didn't believe in ghosts, but he found it highly entertaining to watch feebleminded paranormal enthusiasts succumb to their own anxieties.

Lennon, like Drayton, didn't believe in ghosts, but she did believe there was something strange about the Fincher Library, something in the atmosphere there, like the charged quality of the air just before a thunderstorm. The library was about as grand as the rest of the campus, but with its looming cathedral ceilings and polished stone floors it looked more like an art museum. Nothing in the space invited touch or exploration. There were few desks or chairs, and the books themselves—old but impeccable and packed tightly on the shelves—may as well have been behind glass.

Upon entering, Lennon walked up to the front desk, where Sawyer stood behind an archaic monitor, the screen throwing a harsh glare across his face.

"Have you heard about Claude's expulsion?" she asked him. It was the first time they'd spoken since he returned to campus the night before.

"Of course I heard. It's all anyone can talk about."

"Claude told me he thought Dante killed Benedict," said Lennon.

"Claude says a lot of things, especially when he's drunk and angry."

"But does he lie? In your experience?"

Sawyer paused for a beat, considering. "Not intentionally. But he's grieving and sick and confused. I wouldn't put too much stock into anything he says, given his state."

"So you think there's nothing to it?"

"I didn't say that."

"Then what are you saying?"

Sawyer heaved a sigh, shuffled some papers that were already mostly in order. "I'm saying that when you spend enough time around here, you learn not to involve yourself in the messes of other people. Nothing good comes of it."

"I'll keep that in mind," said Lennon. "And on that note, I was hoping you could pull Claude's file for me? I need his most recent address."

"Lennon—"

"I just need to ask him about something he said before he got kicked out."

Sawyer, staying true to his beliefs about not sticking his nose where it didn't belong, didn't ask for particulars. "You should really leave that alone."

"I wouldn't ask if it weren't important. Come on, please? For a friend?"

"Who's the friend in question here? You or Claude?"

"Both of us," said Lennon.

He considered the request with his head bowed. "Fine."

The archives beneath Fincher Library were strange and cavernous, like a whale's belly or the skeletal interior of some primordial beast. The ceilings were low enough that anyone over six-three would have to duck a bit to keep from bumping their head. The walls were bathed in a flickering, jaundiced light, and the narrow alleys that ran between the bookshelves were so long that the perspective warped a bit when Lennon gazed down them. Even when she squinted, she couldn't see the far wall. "Holy shit—"

Sawyer shushed her. "Keep it down."

He led her through one of the narrow alleys between shelves, muttering softly to himself as he went. When it became apparent that they were alone, he relaxed some, taking the time to point out some of his favorite offerings stored in the archives: a letter penned by John Drayton's mother, wherein she relays home remedies to treat a winter cold (boiled turnips, tallow poultices, mustard with raw onions). A scarred Ouija board that John Drayton was said to favor during weekly séances. A log of all of the school's expenditures that featured a number of strange items, like several sheaves of horsehair, a set of dentures, several miles' worth of thick nautical rope, and other oddities.

"We keep the newer student files at the back of the archives," Sawyer explained, leading Lennon to the back of the collection, where the shelves were steel instead of wood and the files themselves were crisper, the papers stark white instead of yellowed with age. He began to scan through them, still muttering to himself. "One of the archivists told me she updated Claude's file just after he left, so it should be here . . ."

But as Sawyer walked deeper into the newly updated parts of the archive, Lennon stalled in front of a dark cabinet with many drawers. One of those drawers was just ajar, and when Lennon pulled it open it was almost as though someone had persuaded her to do it, the motion detached from her own mind.

Within—behind a sheet of glass—was an arrangement of bones so strange and warped that the species of the creature they belonged to was virtually indistinguishable. But on closer inspection, Lennon saw that the bone shards were human. There was the curve of a skull cap. A rib cracked in half. A small scattering of shattered teeth.

"Oh my god. Who is this?"

"One of Drayton's boys," said Sawyer, visibly disturbed. Not looking at her. "First generation, most likely."

"What the hell happened to him?"

Sawyer blinked quickly, recovered himself. He slid the drawer firmly shut. "Someone must've rearranged things over the summer. This cabinet isn't even supposed to be here—"

"*Sawyer*. How did this happen to that boy? Was he beaten? Run over by something? I don't understand—"

"He pushed himself too hard," said Sawyer. "Or he was pushed.

It's hard to say. When persuasion is practiced incorrectly, the power of a person's will can turn on their own body. It's like an autoimmune disorder, almost, wherein the immune system attacks the—"

"I know how autoimmune disorders work. My mom has one. What I'm asking is how the hell did persuasion become this?"

"It was a seizure, probably. His muscles spasmed so tight around weakened bones and ligaments that they broke. There are records of Drayton's earliest boys falling ill, their bones turning brittle from the effects of persuasion, so that when they seized—sometimes for days at a time—they suffered fractures and other injuries. In one case, a boy was said to have snapped his own neck in the throes of a days-long convulsion."

"Is that like a worse version of what happened to me? The day I first came here?"

Sawyer shook his head. "Not quite. These boys were different. In a letter to his family physician, John Drayton wrote that one of the boys who'd died was still . . . moving."

"What do you mean, 'moving'? Like decomposing?"

Sawyer shook his head, looking drawn and pale. "It was just a few hours after his death, allegedly. John wrote that the room where he died echoed with the cracks of breaking bones. Even though he wasn't alive, his will was still ravaging his corpse. Like it was possessed by something."

"I thought John Drayton didn't believe in ghosts?"

"But it wasn't a ghost," said Sawyer. "At least not in the conventional sense."

"That's horrifying," said Lennon.

Sawyer didn't disagree. "Look, that was then, and this is now. Over the years we've learned more about persuasion and how to practice it safely. No one dies like that anymore. No one is pushed that far beyond their limit, or even allowed to push themselves that far. I would know. Student records are kept here in the library. I key them in myself. What happened to some of Drayton's earliest students is tragic, but stuff like that just doesn't happen anymore." He said this as if to absolve himself.

They were quiet for a long time. The silence between them only broken when Sawyer pulled Claude's file. "Here," he said, and he handed over a thick leather folder.

Lennon flipped it open. Within, there were the expected things, birth certificates and scans of old passports, transcripts from high school and college. But it was the other things that surprised her. The extensive doctor's notes dating back decades, the family photos, and faded Polaroids of Claude as a kid. There were even a few crude drawings in crayon, depicting a stick figure family, each person spaced oddly apart. An assortment of plane tickets and dividend checks and tuition statements and transcripts from a Catholic preschool somewhere in Mississippi. On the following page, therapy notes from a session years prior outlining Claude's "antisocial tendencies" and "combative approach to discussion."

Lennon stared down in awe and horror. It was an entire life flattened and put on paper. It felt wrong to even look at it.

"Do you keep one of these for each of us?"

Sawyer nodded. "We update them roughly once a semester to include final grades or new contact information in the event that someone graduates or leaves, like Claude did."

Lennon paused to jot down Claude's most recent address on a slip of paper. It was a residence somewhere in Manhattan, which surprised her. Given Claude's rich southern accent, she'd been expecting to find him on a plantation somewhere deep in the south. "So you have one on me?"

"Of course."

"What's in it?"

"Why are you so sure I looked?"

"I know you looked. Why wouldn't you?"

Sawyer rolled his eyes. "You're not half as interesting as you think you are," he said, which Lennon noted was decidedly not a *no*.

"What if I asked you to pull Dante's file? Could you do it?"

"No. That information is . . . restricted."

"Why? Because he's a professor?"

"No . . . I can access the files of professors too."

"Then why is Dante's restricted, specifically?"

"Why don't you just ask him yourself?" said Sawyer, exasperated. "The two of you are close. I can't imagine he'd refuse you."

"Then you have a flawed idea of who he is and how much I matter to him."

"My condolences," he said flatly and without a hint of sympathy.

Lennon narrowed her eyes. "You know something. Don't you?"

The flush on Sawyer's cheeks deepened from red to an almost ashen purple. He didn't look at her but didn't deny anything either. "I'm not doing this with you."

"Why not?"

"Because his file basically doesn't exist."

"What? Why?"

"I don't know," said Sawyer. "I only found out because Claude came in asking questions a few days after Ben's death. He kept demanding Dante's file, and I was worried he'd lose it if I didn't hand it over. So I offered to look for it—just to appease him, keep him quiet. But when I found Dante's file there was next to nothing in it. Just a slip of paper that said the contents were redacted."

"Did Claude ever say why he wanted it in the first place?"

"He was drunk and, honestly, less than lucid, so I'm not entirely sure what he was after. But he was determined, and he became furious when I couldn't find it. I even tried to ask the other librarians if they knew why his file was redacted, and they didn't have a clue. Or if they did, they wouldn't tell me. All I gathered was that the redacted files are kept in the vice-chancellor's private library. She's the only one who has access to them."

Something twisted deep in Lennon's stomach. Feeling sick, Lennon nodded and tucked Claude's address into the pocket of her trousers. "Thanks for all of this. I'll tell Claude you said hi when I see him—"

"Not so fast," said Sawyer. "If you're going to see Claude, I'm coming with you."

36

THERE WAS A wildfire burning somewhere up in Canada, and New York was in the process of being smothered under a blanket of smoke when Lennon and Sawyer stepped off the elevator and into the large, windowed living room of a penthouse in New York, Claude's most recent residence, according to his file in the archives. The view should've been stunning, but the jaundiced pall obscured what should have been a sweeping skyline.

The penthouse itself seemed empty and mostly quiet, apart from the sound of water running. They followed that sound across the living room, down a long hallway, and into a large primary bedroom. There was a bath en suite, its door just ajar, and it was there that Lennon and Sawyer found Claude, fully clothed and chest-deep in a steaming bathtub, smoking.

"Rough day?" Lennon asked.

Claude's gaze shifted to hers, half-lidded and lackadaisical. He didn't seem remotely surprised to see them. But, Lennon noted, he didn't seem drunk either.

"No worse than yours," said Claude and gestured to Lennon's bloody nose by wiping at his own. Lennon hadn't even realized she was bleeding. The act of calling the gate had drained her more than she'd realized. "There's gauze in the first aid kit beneath the sinks. Try not to bleed on the bath mats. My mom will have a fucking fit."

Lennon retrieved the first aid kit, rolling several squares of gauze into tight cylinders, which she stuffed up her nostrils to staunch the flow.

"This is your mom's place?" Sawyer asked, as Lennon struggled to stop bleeding.

Claude stared up at the bulbous skylight overhead, which allowed for a hole-punch cut of the flat, yellow sky. "Sort of. It's been in the family for years, but to be honest, it's less ours than Drayton's."

"Wait," said Sawyer, looking stunned. "Your *mom* knows about Drayton?"

"She's alumni," he said. "Most of my family is, actually. You're looking at the great-great-great-*great*-grandson of one of Drayton's first boys." Claude wiggled his fingers for theatrical effect.

It made sense to Lennon that Claude was Drayton royalty. He had that Old South accent and, for that matter, an air of audacity, a kind of confidence that could only ever come from true privilege. She wondered if that was why he'd been able to keep his memories of Drayton despite being expelled.

"So the apartment is a nepotism perk?" said Lennon dryly, trying to sound less intrigued than she really was.

"No," said Claude. "The apartment is ten million dollars of deadweight that's going to keep me rooted here in New York, blackmailing stockbrokers with the intimate details of their own fucked-up personal lives until the school decides to find me some other gainful means of employment."

"That's a harsh way to describe a penthouse overlooking Central Park and job security," said Sawyer, but it came out strained and forced the way jokes often do when you're desperate for them to land.

Claude didn't laugh. He nudged the faucet with his foot and managed to cut the water off after a few false tries. He ignored Sawyer and looked to Lennon again. "You know, I'm surprised he let you come here at all. Dante, I mean."

"Dante doesn't *let* me go anywhere," said Lennon, bristling a little at the implication. "I go where I want to go. When I want to go there."

"Is that what you tell yourself?" said Claude, a smile pulling at the edges of his mouth.

"What is that supposed to mean?"

He exhaled smoke. The gray tendrils festooned his head in a tattered halo. "Only that you mean a lot to him, and he tends to keep the people and things that matter most to him on a short leash. He's careful that way." He ashed his cigarette. "Why did you two come here?"

"We wanted to know if you were okay," said Sawyer.

"Bullshit."

"And we wanted to know what happened between you and Dante."

"We fought," said Claude, looking annoyed. "Dante didn't appreciate my tone, and here we are. It's not even a story worth telling."

"Do you really think he killed Benedict?"

"Why ask the question when you already know what I think?" Claude snapped. "Admit it: you don't want to know if Dante really killed Benedict, you want to know if you're allowed to love him if he did. And you want me to tell you instead of him, either because you trust me more, and for good reason, or because you're afraid that if you hear it from his own mouth, you'll force yourself to hate him like you already should. That about sum it up?"

"I just want the truth," said Lennon.

"No, you don't," said Claude. "Not really. You just want me to tell you a story that gives you license to love him, and I know that because I've been in your shoes before. But you're worried about the wrong thing—don't you see that? It's not about what he did or didn't do to Benedict. It's about what he's going to do to you."

"And what is he going to do to me, Claude?"

"What he does to everyone. He's going to use you for as long as you're useful to him and then, one day, he's going to cast you aside like the broken thing you are. Like he did to me. Like he did to Benedict. And the worst part is you're going to let him."

"Dante can be kind," said Lennon, a soft rebuttal that sounded less pathetic in her head. "I've seen it."

"You've got him wrong," said Claude, shaking his head. "For the longest time I thought he'd just learned to hold poison in his mouth so he could pass for a viper. But then I realized that's not the case. He's just as bad as the worst of them, and Ben knew it. He was maybe the only one who wasn't afraid to say it to his face—"

"And you think Dante killed him for it?" Sawyer asked, sounding less certain than Lennon. More wary. "You think that could've been some type of motive?"

"I don't know," said Claude, sinking deeper into the tub. "And frankly, I don't care either."

"What do you mean you don't care?" Lennon asked, finding it difficult to believe this was even the same man who had raged and broken windows, desperate to discover what had happened to Benedict only weeks before. Dante had claimed that he hadn't tampered with Claude's mind, but now, standing in front of him, Lennon wasn't so sure.

"I've decided I'm done with it," said Claude. "Done with Drayton... or at least as done as I can be for now. I just want to keep the good memories I have, of Benedict mostly, and stay as sober as I can. If I do that, my mind stays my own."

"So you're giving up? You're not even going to attempt to figure out what really happened to Benedict?" Sawyer asked, looking as disturbed as Lennon felt. She could tell he had the same suspicions she did, could tell he was wondering if these words and sentiments were truly Claude's, or if they'd just been planted in his mind to be recited on an occasion like this one.

Claude's eyes narrowed and filled with tears. "I'm tired. You couldn't possibly understand how fucking tired I am."

Lennon could see it in his eyes when he said it—a kind of weariness she'd once seen when she met her own gaze in the mirror, back when she'd lived with Wyatt, when it was a struggle just to get up and face the drudgeries of the day. "Before we go, I have one question, about something you said the night Emerson and I took you to the infirmary. You mentioned something that happened in August, but you didn't say what. What was it?"

Claude was quiet for a long time, staring up at the skylight, the pall of yellow smoke. When he stood—an abrupt and violent motion—water sloshed out of the tub and flooded the bathroom. Both Lennon and Sawyer staggered back, on edge, as if bracing for a blow. But Claude stepped carefully out of the tub, his hands limp at his sides. He looked so sad and frail in that moment, weighted down by his wet clothes, that Lennon had the sudden urge to pull a towel off the rack and put it around his shoulders. But she held back.

"I don't remember saying anything like that," said Claude—a lie. Lennon was certain of it.

37

AFTER THAT MEETING with Claude, the first half of the semester passed in a gray blur. In those weeks, Lennon replayed her conversation with Claude countless times, his warning about Dante haunting her perpetually. She could tell that it was the same with Sawyer, though he never mentioned it once over their weekly coffee dates. They became good at pretending to forget him. So good, in fact, that eventually they did.

Once a week, Lennon had a private course with Dante to develop her gatekeeping abilities. Now that she'd learned to call elevators on command, her studies focused on refining this practice and building her endurance. Each time they met, Dante had her open a gate to a new place—Madagascar, Boston, the tundra in the north of Siberia. He never permitted her to enter these doors, though, only to open them, which she did with increasing efficiency until it was almost second nature to her. Under Dante's careful supervision, she excelled.

By far the most difficult course of her semester was Persuasion II, with Professor Alec Becker. He was a grave man as tall as Dante, and even more heavily tattooed. The entirety of his face, his shaved head, his neck and hands, were covered, allowing only pale glimpses of skin to show through. He had blue eyes that looked almost frozen over, as though he were staring through a thick sheet of ice. His eyebrows were so white they were barely visible. Next to Dante, Alec was the youngest tenured professor on campus. He was known to be both exacting and kind, though Lennon had never particularly warmed to him, or he to her. Alec—amiable toward his other pupils—regarded Lennon with a kind of coldness she found strange, given how well she performed in his class. She wondered if Ian had poisoned Alec against her, and, if so, she couldn't fault him for it, not after she'd put a knife through his hand.

Alec was difficult to impress. It seemed like every class he taught was a challenge to be met, an exercise to complete, a test to pass or to fail. Every class period, they were made to spar with one another, brutal battles of will that often ended with teary eyes and bleeding noses, burst blood vessels that turned the whites of their eyes an eerie red. Adan even cracked a molar in the middle of their sparring exercise and had to depart for the infirmary halfway through class because of the pain.

When the weather allowed for it, Alec liked to hold these grueling matches outside instead of in their classroom in Irvine Hall. That was the case on this night. At Alec's bidding, they formed a tight circle on the ground. The task at hand was a simple one. Each of them was given a small article, chosen at random—a rock, a seashell, a dead leaf, a splintered tree branch—which they placed on the ground in front of them.

"I'll call the names of two individuals in this circle. Upon doing so, each will strive to persuade the other to pick up the object in front of them. The first to do so wins the exercise. I would caution you to spend as much time fortifying the walls of your minds as you do persuading your peers. Both skills are integral parts of your success in this exercise. Now, all of you will have had some experience in the realm of fortification. If you've been diligent about your meditational practice—as I'm sure all of you have—then you will have fortified a room within the confines of your mind, a safehold. The walls of this mental space should, if bolstered correctly, defend you against the persuasive will of your opponent. But whilst maintaining that shield, you will still need to find a way to reach and persuade your partner. This is the central paradox of this task."

The hours that followed were brutal. Lennon watched as her classmates contended, one round after the other. The first pitted Nadine and Adan against each other. Nadine gritted her teeth with the effort of forcing Adan to lift her acorn off the ground. Adan staggered to his feet, took two large steps, and emptied his stomach at the base of a magnolia tree just a half yard outside their circle. He returned moments later, wiping his mouth.

In the rounds that followed, other students suffered similar, crushing defeats at the hands of their fellow classmates. One boy's nose began bleeding so profusely in the aftermath of his swift defeat, Professor Alec dismissed him to the infirmary. Another student, a girl, suffered a panic attack a mere thirty seconds into her round and snatched the magnolia pod in front of her of her own volition.

By the time it was Lennon's turn to contend, she had seen almost half of her classmates cow to their opponents. Most of the Pyrrhic victors—who seemed about as spent and sick as those they'd beaten—were visibly uneasy with their hard-won wins. Those who were unfazed, Lennon noticed, had been so efficient, so brutal and competent in their persuasion, that they seemed entirely impervious to, or unbothered by, the pain that they had inflicted upon their opponents.

Alec clapped his hands. "Lennon and Ian. You're up next."

Lennon's stomach dropped. This wasn't a coincidence. Ian had been waiting for a chance to humble her since that gruesome night at Logos when she'd put the blade through his hand. And tonight, Alec was giving him just that.

Ian cast his gaze on Lennon and smiled widely—like he'd already won—and Lennon saw clearly that any affection he'd once had for her had rotted into hatred.

Ian's assault was quick and brutal, with a force that reminded Lennon of being pinned to her plane seat, amid a particularly punishing takeoff. Only it was much heavier than that. Lennon might've picked up the pebble in front of her immediately—if his intention had been only a bit more clear, more specific.

But Lennon resisted, refusing to pick up the pebble.

This frustrated Ian, who perhaps recognized the limits of his ability. He was strong, yes, but he lacked a kind of artistry, the gentle touch of technique. It was all brute force and no precision. So he forced harder, pushing her to the brink. Lennon realized then that his intent was not to make her to lift the pebble. He simply wanted her to collapse under the force of his will. His aim was not to control her, but to *break* her. And Ian wanted her to know it. He leered at her, his lips tearing into a hideous grin.

The pressure behind her eyes built. Lennon felt something pop high up in her sinuses. She caught the metallic stench of blood and felt it trickling hot and thick down the back of her throat moments later. She tried to search Ian's face for something she could use against him, some weakness to manipulate, but her vision blurred so badly she could barely see him.

She realized she was crying.

Alec might've said something, but she couldn't hear it over the ringing in her ears. The pressure built within her head until it became pain. Ian's assault was relentless. He'd only grown stronger over the winter break. His was a frightening power, a kind of contained and channeled chaos. It made her feel as though she was going insane, as though Ian could bleach every memory from her mind, suck out the color and the meaning of every significant event that had ever happened to her and make it all null. A fate worse than death.

She panicked, lashed out with everything she had. Which, as it turned out, was quite a lot.

Ian froze, stunned by the viciousness of her attack. His fingertips skimmed the rock on the ground, Lennon pushed harder, and he grabbed it.

Ian's eyes went wide, first with shock, then rage. "Fucking *whore*—"

Lennon didn't make the decision to break his nose. Or even to strike him. It just . . . happened. Her body, for the briefest moment, severing from his will, animated and sprang to action. Her hand locked into a painful fist, her arm drew back, and she punched Ian so hard the force of the blow shunted the knuckle of her middle finger out of its socket.

Ian reeled backward and clutched his nose, blood streaming through the cage of his fingers. He looked up at her and lunged before anyone could drag him back. Lennon caught a blow to the face that might've been a backhanded slap, but in the chaos of the oncoming assault she couldn't be certain. Ian, who had no preoccupations with valor or chivalry, fought with a viciousness that Lennon, in her anger, matched. And the two abandoned any psychic exchanges in lieu of blows and biting and pulling hair. They scrapped like children, like starved dogs.

And Alec allowed this to continue for some time before he stood up, fixed his cuff links, and—with a toothy smile and the flourish of his fingers—paralyzed both of them so thoroughly they froze where they stood, as though their muscles had, in the span of an instant, calcified and turned to bone, Ian with a fistful of Lennon's hair and Lennon with her fingernails a half centimeter shy of his open eye.

Alec clapped his hands. He was grinning. "That will be quite enough."

38

LENNON WALKED, BY the force of Alec's will, to Dante's office. The hold of her persuasion professor slackened only when the door snapped shut behind her. Weak in the knees, Lennon stumbled forward and caught herself, sloppily, on a nearby bookshelf, clearing half of its contents with the violence of her near fall. A set of brass bookends, a picture frame, and a tin of cigars clattered to the floor.

"I'm going to let you start," said Dante from behind his desk.

Lennon, stepping tersely over the mess she'd made, recovered herself enough to make her way to the empty seat in front of Dante. "Ian is a dick."

"And you were sloppy."

To this charge, Lennon—slumped low in her seat—said nothing. She pushed at a molar with the tip of her tongue. It was loose, so she opened her mouth wide and pried it free. It looked small and jewel-like in the flat of her palm, a malformed pearl slick with blood and spit.

Dante got up and went to the cocktail cart beside the fireplace. He poured her a glass of something dark and set it down on the desk in front of her. "Rinse."

Lennon didn't touch it. She dropped the tooth into the drink with a small splash. It sank down to the bottom of the tumbler, a few tendrils of blood ribboning from its root.

"How did it start?" Dante asked.

Lennon wiped blood from the corner of her mouth. "You want a blow-by-blow?"

"No," he said, looking bored. "I want to know how and why it started."

"He called me a whore and I hit him," said Lennon, and she realized this was the only part of her fight with Ian that she really cared about. "When he said it, it felt so . . . pointed, I guess? He could've called me almost anything else and I wouldn't have cared."

"But you did care about that one word, specifically. Why?"

"Does it matter?"

"It does if it provokes you to violence."

Lennon narrowed her eyes. "Look, am I in trouble?"

"Not with me," said Dante.

"Then why can't we just let it go? We fought; it's over—"

"But the memory isn't. And come morning everyone will be discussing the blow that *you* threw to begin the fight. You made him look weak, and now he has a target on his back that can only be removed by putting you firmly in your place. Which is exactly what he'll attempt to do before the semester's end. That's why you need to be ready. And not just for him, but for everyone who is beginning to grasp what I've known since the day we first met."

"And what is that?"

"You're dangerous."

Dante was one of many men who'd said this to her. The first time she'd heard it, she was thirteen, and walking home from school. A man had winked at her and said just that—"Well, aren't you dangerous"—and men had been saying that to her ever since. When they said *dangerous*, Lennon knew they meant she was jailbait, a guilty pleasure, a potential homewrecker, someone who could derail their life. But Dante said it differently, without smugness or innuendo. When he called her dangerous, it was stated like a simple fact. Her eyes were hazel. Her hair was curly. And she was dangerous. It was as simple as that, and yet Lennon found that she liked the way he said it, so much so that she almost wanted to ask him to say it again, just so she could watch his lips move around the words.

Dante didn't make her call any elevators that evening. Per his instructions, she left his office, with the tooth in the cup of brandy, and went straight to the infirmary. A talented persuasionist, Dr. Nave was able to refit the roots of the tooth and constrict her gums tightly around it, both stopping the bleeding and holding the tooth roughly in place. It would've been almost agonizing, but he numbed her mind to the pain of the procedure, kept her comfortable.

"Ice it and stick to soft foods for the next few days," he said, sounding exasperated. She could tell he'd seen more of her than he would've liked between her overdose months before and now this.

Upon being discharged, Lennon stepped out of the infirmary and collided almost immediately with Blaine. On that night, she wore a cocktail dress, riding up high. Her makeup was smeared and running, like she'd had a good cry and tried to clean herself up with a wad of toilet paper but had given up halfway through.

"What the hell happened to your face?" said Blaine. "Are you okay?"

"Ian and I fought. With fists. What about you?"

Blaine blinked rapidly, picked a crusty bit of mascara from the inner corner of her eye, and flicked it away. "Boy trouble."

It was as close as she'd come to confirming Lennon's long suspicion that she was conducting a secret affair with someone that she couldn't, or didn't want to, claim. More than once, Lennon had considered the possibility that she was involved with one of her professors. A married one, maybe. But if that was the case, she wondered why Blaine had never confided in her. Surely she knew her secret would be safe. After all, Lennon had divulged to her in detail about her not-relationship with Dante, had even told her about their near kiss. And Blaine had nodded and listened and comforted her through it all, while never breathing a word about her own romantic situation.

"Do you want to go somewhere?" Lennon asked as they stepped outside. She was surprised by the urgency behind her own words. She'd meant to be casual, but it landed more like a need than a want. As if she were asking Blaine to jump her car or give her a last-minute ride to the airport.

"That depends," said Blaine. "Where do you want to go?"

"Down to River Street, maybe?"

As a rule, students of Drayton were not permitted to go beyond the bounds of the school. But the members of Logos had special privileges. Their elevator could take them to a number of locations, including several within Savannah's historic downtown. Of course, Lennon could've called her own elevator. But she was drained after her spar with Ian. Tonight she craved the ease of a quick trip and a drink strong enough to ease her worries, take the edge off the pain of her throbbing tooth.

"You want to get into trouble," said Blaine, looking equal parts delighted and aghast. "What? Fighting with Ian wasn't enough?"

Lennon shrugged. "I'd rather be drunk than sober tonight."

"We can get drunk on campus."

"Sure we can," said Lennon. "But it won't be half as fun."

They decided to go to one of those tourist-trap bars on the riverfront that served oversized daiquiris in light-up cups. Despite the fact that it was freezing outside, Blaine persuaded a man to buy her some god-awful tequila slushy that stained her mouth a monstrous blue, and then followed that up with several rounds of shots, goading Lennon to drink along with her. Which she did, with some reluctance. She wanted to get a little drunk, not totally wasted, but she downed two shots anyway.

"Attagirl," said Blaine, and she stamped a fat, wet kiss to the apple of Lennon's cheek.

Sometimes, when she was around Blaine, Lennon got the distinct impression that they were playing at closeness. Pretending to be honest with each other, to be the sort of confidant that they needed in order to survive the constant stress and bewilderment that was their time at Drayton. But the truth was that Lennon knew very little about Blaine, and not for lack of trying. Whenever she attempted closeness—real closeness—Blaine held her just apart. She dodged questions artfully, wriggled her way out of vulnerability. With Blaine, Lennon never quite knew what she would get. It was part of her charm, and Blaine knew it.

"No one does coke anymore," said Blaine, looking suddenly disappointed and very sad. "My ex-husband always got the best coke. That was one thing he was good for. He could be in a new city for less than an hour and he'd find the right dealer, at the right price. It was a real talent. Maybe his only talent."

"Wait, you were married?" Lennon knew that Blaine was four years older than her, but it still took her by surprise that she'd ever been married. The construct seemed to suit her even less than it did Lennon. "To who?"

"Doesn't matter," she said, waving her off. "I don't like him half as much as I like you. In fact, I think I almost love you. I definitely almost like you in a way that I shouldn't."

Lennon blushed despite herself. She'd never had feelings like that for Blaine, but you couldn't listen to someone as attractive as she was say something like that without getting at least a little hot under the collar.

"What's stopping you?" said Lennon. "From liking me in a way that you shouldn't?"

"We're too similar," said Blaine. "If we ever got together, it would be more out of comfort and narcissism than any real attraction. Which is not to say you're unattractive, because you're not, of course—"

"In what way are we similar?" said Lennon, cutting her off. Blaine had a way of ranting when she was drunk, and she was extremely drunk tonight.

Blaine considered this question for a long time in silence before she deigned to answer it. "You and I, we like to play with people, don't we? But we don't like being played with."

Blaine stared down into her shot glass, looking sad suddenly. It was Lennon who'd wanted to go out, but Blaine was outdrinking her more than three times over, and she looked all the worse for it. Maybe it had been a mistake to take her out when she'd clearly been in a bad way. Lennon had thought the drinks and the noise might cheer her up, but if anything, she looked worse, not better.

"I lied to you about how I came to Drayton," said Blaine, in a soft voice. "I mean, not really. It was less a lie than a half-truth."

"What do you mean?"

"Before I came to Drayton, things with me and my ex-husband were sort of . . . volatile." Blaine ran her index finger around the rim of the shot glass until it whistled. She smiled. "He used to hit me. But the night I left for Drayton—the night I got the call—I finally hit him back. Just once . . . on the back of the head. With a brick."

Lennon tried to mask her shock.

"He twitched on the floor for a little while. I've never seen anyone move like that. And then the blood, under his head, it just opened up, and this is weird, but do you know those old cartoons—like *Tom & Jerry*, *Looney Tunes* stuff—where a hole opens up in the floor? Well, that's what his blood looked like against the tile. It was so dark and the puddle was so crisp it looked almost fake, and I just couldn't bring myself to believe it, you know? I couldn't get myself to believe what I'd done."

Lennon swallowed dry.

"Anyway. I just stood there in a daze, watching him bleed out. I was just frozen there. I didn't do anything."

"It sounds like he had it coming."

Blaine only shrugged. "The call from Drayton snapped me out of it. I remember stepping over him to answer it. I put my cell to my ear, and I heard my husband's voice over the line, which didn't make any sense because my husband was lying unconscious at my feet, bleeding out. I knew then that either what the operator was saying was true, or I was really going insane. Something I'd suspected for some time, to be honest. When they asked me to go for an interview, I said yes. I left my husband on the floor, packed half my stuff, and I just, I don't know, I just went. They said if I passed the interview and entry exam, everything would be okay. And I did, and it has been."

"What happened to your ex?"

"Oh, he's alive. I think he lives in a care facility now. Somewhere. So it all worked out. I think that brick might've saved him from drinking himself into an early grave." She said this like the brick just up and hit him itself, like the situation had no affiliation with her.

Lennon reached across the sticky bartop to squeeze her hand. "I'm glad you told me."

"Why?" Blaine asked, looking up at her. "So you know what you're dealing with?"

"So I know you," said Lennon. "I'm not afraid. And I don't judge you. I just . . . I just want to understand where you're coming from, you know? And tonight, I feel like I do."

"Do you?" Lennon could tell that Blaine took this as an insult. She hated being known, pinned down. "If that's true—if you really understand me—tell me what I'm thinking right now. If you get it wrong, drink." Blaine pushed another shot toward her.

"Are you inviting me to enter your mind?"

"Only if you can," said Blaine. "But if you know me so well, you shouldn't have to."

Lennon squared her shoulders, tried to sober up enough to get a proper read on her. She began with the features of her face. Her lips were wet, and her breath smelled of malt and sugar. Her eyes were glossy, her pupils swollen fat so that they were barely limned by the blue of her irises. There was an urgency in them—Lennon was inclined to call it desperation—this desire to be seen and understood without having to say anything at all. After that, it became easy to sift through her thoughts, find the one that she wanted Lennon to see. But she was still surprised by what she found.

"You want me to run," said Lennon.

Blaine's expression fractured as soon as the words left her mouth.

Lennon often found that when she went out, there was a moment when the night went south, when whatever horrible outcome had been set into motion and the evening was doomed to end with her vomiting all over a curb or waking up beside someone who was about three times uglier than she'd thought he was when she was drunk.

This was that moment.

"I need to sober up," said Blaine, and she appeared to go boneless, sliding off her stool. "Let's take a walk."

The two of them stepped out into the biting cold. There was a sharp wind blowing west off the river, tossing the greenish water into frothy whitecaps. Underfoot, the cobblestones were slick with slush and ice. It was one of the coldest nights Savannah had seen in some time, and Lennon's knit sweater felt pitifully thin. She shoved her cold-stiff hands into her pockets, rounded her shoulders against the wind.

"So did I guess right?" she asked, shivering.

"More or less," said Blaine, not looking at her. But it wasn't that Blaine was avoiding Lennon's eyes; it was as if she was seeing another, second Lennon, somewhere down on the ground among the cobblestones. "What I really wanted to know was if you'd run away with me tonight, if I wanted to go. Would you leave Drayton behind?"

"Why would you want to do that?"

Blaine didn't answer.

Lennon took her by the hand. Her fingers were ice. "Why, Blaine?"

"Forget it," she said, stealing her hand away. "We should be getting back anyway. It's late."

They walked back to the narrow alley that housed the Drayton gate. As they did, two drunk men began to tail them. They were subtle at first, but when Lennon and Blaine turned down the alley, they did too.

"Let's hurry up," said Lennon, and turned to face the rotting wooden door that concealed the elevator. But when Lennon drew it open, there was nothing behind it but a brick wall slimed with algae.

The gate that was supposed to take them back to Drayton was gone.

Blaine—eyes alight with panic—slammed the door shut and opened it again.

Still no elevator.

"What the hell?" she said in a thick whisper, her breath a white bloom of steam on the air.

The men at the mouth of the alley came closer, calling after them, waving. Lennon turned to face them.

"Whatever you want, we're not interested," she said, but the quiver in her voice undermined any authority she tried to channel with those words.

"We just want to talk a little," said one of the men, leering. He held a cup of beer, and when he gestured at Lennon some of it sloshed over the rim and splattered the sidewalk. "You don't like to talk?"

He was close enough now that Lennon could smell him, all beer and musky cologne. They were both relatively well-dressed—leather shoes, expensive watches flashing on their thick wrists. They looked like stragglers from a bachelor party. In their wake, Lennon felt like a small mouse, held between two cupped hands large enough to crush her. It was the same feeling she'd had that very night while sparring with Ian as he'd violated her mind and humiliated her in front of her peers. The same feeling when he'd told her to go belly-up, the night they'd been called to Logos.

"Look, we're just trying to get home," said Lennon, adrenaline spiking through her. Blaine kept fiddling with the door.

"There's something wrong with the gate," she said, panicking less because of the threat of the men, Lennon realized, and more because she couldn't get back to Drayton. Here, in the real world, they were stranded until someone thought to look for them. But if she and Blaine couldn't get into Drayton, there was a good chance that those inside of Drayton wouldn't be able to get out either. Everyone would be trapped on campus, which to Lennon seemed preferable to being trapped outside of it, removed from the only world she'd ever wanted to be a part of.

"You two shouldn't be out here alone," said one of the men. They were imposing and tall enough to blot out the light of the streetlamp at the alley's end. "Savannah's not a safe city anymore."

"Leave us the fuck alone," Lennon snapped.

And one of the men, the taller and drunker of the two, screwed his face into a boyish frown. "You don't have to be so aggressive about it. We just wanted to invite you out for a drink. Can a man invite two ladies out on a Friday night, or is that not allowed anymore—"

Lennon strangled him. There was no other way to say it. She induced a reaction that was not unlike anaphylaxis, a cruel application of persuasion that Lennon had picked up in Dante's class. One moment the man was on his feet, the next he was doubled over and turning red, with a series of desperate, raw gasps. The artery running up the side of his neck fattened to the point of bursting. He opened his mouth, and Lennon saw that his tongue had swollen to the size of a crab apple, lodging itself so firmly against the roof of his mouth there was no way for air to pass through.

He dropped to his knees, his cup falling through his hand, beer splattering all over Lennon as he fell. His friend dropped beside him, smacking him on the back frantically as he writhed and gasped for air, scrabbling helplessly at the cobblestones.

Lennon stepped past both of them, shooed Blaine away from the fallen gate, and attempted to call one of her own. But when she extended her mind to Drayton, there was nothing on the other side. As if the school itself didn't exist.

Panic washed through her and then rage after it. She gave the door a vicious kick, and the wood broke and splintered. *"Goddamnit."*

"Lennon," said Blaine, putting a hand on her arm. "I think you're killing him."

Lennon turned to see the man unconscious, his face gone blue, froth collecting at the corners of his open mouth. His friend was on the ground beside him, fumbling with his phone.

"Fuck," said Lennon, and she stepped right over him, snatched the phone from his hand, tossed it to the ground, and stomped on it, shattering the screen. She cut the choking man loose. There was a long silence—and for a moment Lennon thought she might've actually done it, that she may actually have killed someone—but then he stirred to life with a juddering breath.

"He'll be fine," said Lennon to the other man, who burst into great blubbering sobs of relief. "And you're going to forget this ever happened." She made this true as she said it, snatching every memory of what had occurred in the alley, putting him to sleep beside the dumpster, curled fetal against his friend so the two of them would be warm enough to sleep through the night without any danger of freezing.

"Look," said Blaine, and she pointed to the door. The birdcage elevator had appeared behind it, the bands and whorls of iron forming its door.

Lennon drew it open and the two of them stepped into the cabin.

39

LENNON AND BLAINE stepped off the elevator and back into Logos to find the house empty, the lights on despite the late hour, all the doors along the hall flung open. A cold breeze gusted in through the front door. Lennon and Blaine exchanged a horrified look and wordlessly raced down the stairs and out of the house to find the campus in total chaos. People stood outside their dorms bleary-eyed and wrapped in blankets, huddled close together to keep warm. The church bells were tolling.

"What the hell is going on?" Blaine asked, looking around in a daze.

"I don't know," said Lennon, wondering if there had been an ill-timed fire drill or perhaps a false alarm. But if that was the case, she had no idea why every building on campus seemed affected. Lennon also noticed that a few of those buildings had broken windows, and a couple of the magnolias around campus, and one of the live oaks, had fallen.

The two walked until they spotted the bulk of the first years, standing in the lawn outside of Ethos College. There was Ian, shirtless despite the cold, his arm slung around Nadine, who appeared to be wearing his shirt as a dress. Blaine approached, but Lennon, feeling uneasy after the fight with Ian, trailed after her with some reluctance. She was relieved when Nadine ducked out from under Ian's arm and met them halfway, as if making a conscious effort to keep Lennon and Ian apart.

"What happened?" Blaine asked her.

Nadine half turned to face Blaine so that it was obvious she was only talking to her when she said, "The gates malfunctioned and there was some sort of quake—you didn't feel it? The whole campus was shaking."

"We were out," said Blaine. Her expression was flat and blank, almost like she was wearing a papier-mâché cast of her own face. She half turned to face the trees, as if looking for something specific, and very nearly lost her balance.

Lennon reached out to steady her. "What do you mean they malfunctioned?"

Nadine very pointedly didn't look at Lennon. She crossed her narrow arms tight over her chest, stomped in place to pump blood into her feet. She was only wearing socks, Lennon realized. "I don't know. The ground started shaking and the church bells started ringing and we all came outside because we thought there might be an earthquake. Windows started breaking and it was so loud it woke everyone up and then the RAs came in and alerted everyone that we needed to evacuate to the center of the square. When we asked what was going on they said the gates were failing or something? That didn't explain the shaking, though."

"What did they mean when they said the gates were failing?" Lennon asked.

"I don't know," she said. "But I'd barely made it out to the square when there was this feeling of . . . dropping or moving. It brought everyone to their knees. A couple people even got so dizzy they threw up."

"How long did it last?" Blaine asked, and she looked on the verge of tears.

"Not long," said Nadine, and she began to rub slow circles into Blaine's back. "It was nothing, really—everyone's fine. No one got hurt, and only a few buildings have broken windows. I did hear that a downed tree might've clipped the chapel. But no one was hurt, and I think things are stabilized now, so—"

"Why did the gates start to fail?" Lennon asked.

"No one knows," said Nadine with a shrug. "And the faculty aren't answering any questions." She nodded a few yards away. A small crowd of professors cut down the sidewalk, striding from their townhouses and moving across the campus, in the same direction that Blaine was staring. Dante and Eileen led the pack, their heads close together, talking in a rapid-fire exchange of whispers. They didn't look at Lennon, but the rest of the professors did, their gazes snaring on her briefly as they passed by. Watching them go, Lennon realized they were heading toward the chancellor's mansion, which took the form of a large plantation house on the far edge of the campus.

Lennon took off after the professors, running a little to catch up, and was winded by the time she matched Dante's long strides.

"Hey," she said, catching him by the arm. "What's going on?"

"Not now, Lennon."

"What happened to the gates?"

Dante stopped then. Eileen cut a glare over her shoulder that could've curdled milk but kept going with the rest of the faculty close at her heels, a few professors jockeying for the place by her side that Dante had abandoned.

"I don't have time for this tonight, all right?" he said. "Go back and wait with your classmates."

"Did the gates go down?" Lennon asked again. "And if so, is there any way I could—"

"No," he said, the scrape of a whisper, unusually harsh. "You stay clear of this."

"What do you mean stay—"

He turned and left before she could finish the question, catching up with the others in just a few long strides. Eileen immediately caught him by the arm and resumed their conversation. Frustrated, Lennon turned and walked back to her peers.

"What was that about?" Nadine asked, and it was clear she wasn't the only one wondering. At least a dozen of her classmates were looking on, arms folded tight across their chests, murmuring among themselves.

"Nothing," said Lennon, edgy, defensive though she didn't know why—something about all those eyes on her then, and not in a good way. A couple of people—most of them from Ian's clique—even cut her dirty looks and whispered behind cupped hands as if afraid she'd read their lips.

"It didn't look like nothing," said Nadine, and Lennon wondered in passing when she'd become such a bitch, or if she was just pretending to be one in defense of Ian. As if he needed any real defending.

"I was just asking about the gates," said Lennon. "But he wouldn't tell me anything."

"Hm," said Nadine, lower lip ejected, slightly, beyond the upper. "You two really are close, aren't you?"

"I mean, we have to be. He's my advisor."

"But it's not just that. Is it true you vacationed with him?"

"It wasn't a vacation," said Lennon. She could feel her cheeks going red, and not from the cold. "It was a work thing—"

"A work thing?" Nadine raised an eyebrow. "What kind of work thing?"

"Why do you care so much?" Blaine asked, sobering up enough to defend her. "Are people asking?"

Nadine only shrugged and retreated back toward Ian, who was watching. He smiled at Lennon, his split lip tearing open a little wider as he did.

40

THE LAST DAYS of March came and went. April brought with it the warm promise of summer, and a new wave of anxiety that rippled throughout Drayton's student body. In the days leading up to final exams, Lennon became increasingly reclusive, locking herself away in her dorm to study and train. Preparations for her persuasion course with Alec proved particularly challenging. Comprised of both written and combat portions, the final exam would take place over a four-hour class period that culminated with a pass-or-fail sparring match. Unless you scored almost perfectly on the written portion of the exam, it was almost impossible to pass the class if you lost your spar.

The night before the final, Lennon stayed up to study. She was dead tired, and her notes blurred and doubled as she scanned through them. She closed her eyes, tempted by sleep, and when she opened them again—what felt like mere moments later—it was not to her textbook, or her cluttered desk, but to the wan and dappled light of the moon, filtering down through the branches of the magnolia trees.

Lennon wasn't in her bedroom anymore. She was standing in the middle of the Twenty-Fifth Square. She had no recollection of how she'd found her way there. The last thing she remembered was resting her head on her desk, letting the tide drag her out to the deep sea of dreams.

Two feet from her, grinning at her through the thickening fog, was Ian.

"Why am I out here, and what the hell do you want?" Lennon asked, in a white huff of steam. It was cold, and she had on nothing but a thin T-shirt and shorts, which offered little reprieve from the cold. "Wait, did you persuade me to come here?"

"You want to know what I like about you, Lennon?" Ian began to walk around her in a slow circle that became something of a spiral, drawing nearer with each completed revolution. "You don't know when to leave well enough alone."

"Go fuck yourself."

"Kneel," he said, and Lennon broke to her knees there, in the middle of the square. Ian's will was nothing if not demanding. His strength had more than doubled since the last time she'd contended with him. She realized, with a wave of horror, that he had been holding back during their spar. "What do you want?"

"I want your total compliance," he said, with a smile. "And I know how to get it."

Ian forced her to her feet and walked her, slowly, to the chapel. To anyone else, they might've appeared like two lovers taking an evening stroll. Every time she tried to break pace, or speak, or lock eyes with one of the students she passed, she was overcome with a wave of nauseating pain that spread from her brain stem down her spine and into her legs. She might've limped to ease the pain, favoring one leg or the other, but Ian maintained control of her limbs, kept her gait steady.

They entered the chapel through a door off a small apse and took a flight of winding, rickety stairs up to the clock tower, the tallest structure on Drayton's campus. At the top of the stairway, they stepped through a battered door and into a cramped octagonal space, all raw wood and cobwebs, moonlight shafting in through slits in the planks. There were beer cans and cigarette butts strewn about the floor, the leavings of parties past. On the far wall was a shuttered window, which Ian opened to the night. Lennon expected to see a stunning view of Savannah—the city lights, the estuary lapsing out to sea—but as it was, there was only an ocean of black treetops as far as the eye could see.

Ian walked her to the window, forced her to climb up onto the sill. She stood there, one hand braced against the splintered wall, clutching the wood with numb toes. He allowed her to tilt her head so she could take in the sickening drop more than five stories below.

"No need to be afraid. You won't die from a height like this," said Ian. "That is, unless you land wrong. Try to aim for the hedges and you'll be all right. Probably."

Ian loosened her tongue, so that she was able to get a few words out. "What do you want from me? An apology?"

"I want to see you fly," he said. "On my call, you jump."

Lennon gripped the sill with her toes so tightly they went white and bloodless, then blue after that. She felt a wet warmth in her shorts and realized—with horror and humiliation in equal parts—that she had wet herself. "Ian, please. I'm sorry—"

"Begging now, are we?" he asked, and he sidled up close to her so that she could feel his breath, hot at her ear. "That's a good look for you, Lennon. I'd like to see more of that in the future, after we're done with this. You know, if you're up for it."

Lennon's legs began to tremble beneath her as she stared down at the sickening drop. The thin strip of bushes. The cobblestones.

And then, in the silence, a shrill bell ringing.

Lennon and Ian turned to see, in place of the stairway door, a golden elevator. She leapt down from the sill and lunged for it but only made it a few strides before Ian recovered himself and pursued her.

By some miracle she made it to the doors, which parted open for her, and burst into the cabin. She turned to the control panel and frantically pressed the infinity button just as Ian took his first step inside. He was going to kill her if he got his hands on her—she could see it in his eyes and feel him in her mind, his will like a severing knife, a scythe cleaving through the wheat field of her thoughts. If she didn't save herself—didn't act now—she would die under the force of his will.

It was either her life or Ian's.

Lennon threw out a hand, mashed the *Door Close* button.

The doors clamped shut on Ian with the sickening crunch of breaking bones. He cut a dry and withering cry, his rib cage crushed between the elevator doors. The two of them locked eyes for just a moment, and Ian stretched out his hand, as though he wanted her to take it, pull him out from between the clamped doors. She thought for a moment he was going to beg, or apologize, even. But all he did was point at her and say: "You're nothing."

Lennon nodded. To herself, then to him.

And the cabin plunged into free fall, tearing Ian in two.

41

LENNON WOKE IN the infirmary with Ian's blood matted into her hairline and Dante sitting in a chair beside her bed, his forearms braced on his knees. The memories of what had occurred in the clock tower flooded back to her. She remembered Ian's torso, crudely severed from his legs, the tangle of intestines at his ravaged waist, the way that he'd slipped, twitching, to the floor and how he'd struggled there for a few excruciating moments before passing, the elevator lights dying when he did, and how they'd fallen together for some time in the darkness, before the cabin had slowed to a stop in the upper hallway of Logos House. It had been Emerson who'd found her, staggering over the viscera of Ian's remains, slick with his blood and numb with shock. Her memories had faded into nothing after that, and how she had come to be in this bed, with Dante keeping vigil at her side, was a mystery to her.

"I'm sorry," she said, and began to cry.

"Hush," said Dante, not unkindly, and he took her hand and held it between both of his. She could've sworn the moths tattooed on the backs of his hands beat their wings. "Tell me honestly, was it an accident? If you lie, I'll know, and so will they."

"He attacked me," said Lennon. "And I . . . I made the doors close on him, then I sent the cabin down while he was still trapped between them. I don't know why I did that. Why did I do that?"

"Listen to me," said Dante, lowering his voice now, "I'm going to get you out, but you should know that the position you're in right now is dangerous." He nodded to the doors of the infirmary, and Lennon saw that there were two people posted outside, men she didn't know.

"We'll have to be quick," said Dante, talking now to himself more than to her. "They'll be looking for you. Not just them but anyone else on the campus who got the same memo I did. All the faculty, admin, even the custodial staff. Word will be spreading through the student body as well, by way of Ian's friends. I can momentarily wipe clean the minds of anyone who sees you, but I can't hold them all forever, or make them all forget what they know to be true. So you'll have to raise a gate quickly. There's no time to waste."

"I can't call another elevator."

"Lennon—"

"I won't. It's too dangerous."

Dante contemplated this. Spoke after a long beat. "You know the parking lot where I dropped you off at the start of this semester? Can you reach it on your own?"

"Yes . . . but what about them?" She nodded to the men at the door. Somehow, they seemed oblivious to her and Dante, as though the former was still asleep, and the latter wasn't there at all. And Lennon found herself wondering if Dante had cast an illusion, drawn some sort of shroud of obscurity around the both of them, to hide the fact that they were talking.

"I'll handle them. Now hurry up. We're running out of time."

Lennon got out of bed. Dante lent her a jacket, which she slipped on over her hospital gown, and—barefoot—she tiptoed toward the doors of the infirmary. To her shock, the men parted to make way for her, and as Lennon moved past them, she saw that their eyes had rolled back into their sockets, showing only the whites. Their mouths had fallen open, and their lips were slick with spit. They looked familiar in the way that a relative does, lying in a casket at a funeral, their faces waxy and drawn.

As Lennon moved past them and through the halls of the infirmary, and outside into the school grounds, the gazes of almost everyone slid over her slick as oil. Those who did register her—the administrative assistant in the lobby of the infirmary, the custodian sweeping the corridor—paused only briefly before casting away with a violence, as though she were an abomination, too terrible to be looked at. Such was the power of Dante's illusion.

There was only one person who seemed unaffected by the illusion Dante had cast: Alec Becker. He strode through the campus at a rapid pace, toward Lennon. She froze there in the middle of the breezeway and raised the walls of her mind, which felt about as flimsy as soggy cardboard in the wake of Alec, a man who could bring her and half the campus to heel with a passing thought. He was the only person at Drayton, apart from perhaps Eileen, whose power could rival that of Dante's. But to her surprise, Alec didn't register her. His gaze slid over her as he brisked past, heading—Lennon noted—toward the infirmary she'd just left. Where she and Dante had parted.

The moment Alec disappeared from her periphery, Lennon broke into a run. Upon reaching the faculty parking lot, she paced through the assortment of vehicles—rust-eaten pickup trucks, sleek electric sports cars, an Airstream camper bus—until she found Dante's Audi. The door unlocked of its own accord as she approached. She slipped into the passenger side and sank low, flattening herself against the leather seat to avoid being seen.

Dante appeared minutes later with a bleeding nose and the deranged and exhilarated air of someone who had successfully robbed a bank. He slammed the door shut behind him and didn't bother to buckle his seat belt before fitting the key into the ignition and peeling backward out of the parking lot. They turned out onto the road, and the trees smeared past the windows in a blur. Lennon—pinned to her seat and weeping silently—could not help but think that this was all too easy, and that someone, or something, had decided to let them go.

42

THE SUN HAD set by the time they arrived at Dante's home, on a ragged stretch of the South Carolina coastline. It was a ranch with a low-slung roof, half-overgrown with ivy and great flowering tangles of honeysuckle, flocked by wasps. The living room looked like an extension of Dante's office back at Drayton. There was a well-worn leather couch, sagging a bit in the middle. On the edge of the coffee table was a metal ashtray fashioned into the shape of a large fly. The eastern wall of the living room had a run of floor-to-ceiling windows that looked out onto the black and glistening waters of the ocean. Unlike Dante's townhome in Drayton, this place had a decidedly lived-in quality. It smelled like him, felt like him in a way that immediately put Lennon at ease.

Dante showed her into the guest room. It was quaint, with a queen-sized bed bracketed by two barrel nightstands and French doors that opened out onto a small, private patio. From that patio led a narrow path that threaded through the marsh and down to the beach.

"I'll give you some time to wash up," said Dante, and he set a stack of folded towels on the bathroom countertop. "Holler if you need anything."

Alone, Lennon took a long shower in the adjoining bathroom, relishing the steam and the heat of the water, scrubbing herself clean and raw. She climbed into bed and fell asleep to the gentle rush and draw of the ocean, the sound of waves storming the ragged scrap of beach beyond the dunes. In her dreams, there were dead things in the water—limbs and viscera drained of blood; bones picked almost clean by crabs and the other things that scuttled and lurked in the dark of the ocean, waiting to subsume the corpses.

She woke up screaming, with Dante by her side, her hand held firmly in his.

"You lied to me," she said to him, her voice thick both with sleep and the tears she was holding back. "All those months ago, you said I wouldn't have to hurt anyone. You lied. Why did you lie to me?"

"I thought I'd lose you if I didn't," said Dante. "And even back then I knew a talent like yours was too great to waste."

"But you knew I'd hurt people?"

"Yes," said Dante. "I had a feeling."

"I should've never been allowed to stay at Drayton. You should've extracted my memories like Eileen told you to. If you had, Ian would still be alive."

Dante merely shrugged. "His life isn't worth half as much as yours is."

"He was brilliant."

"And possessive and unhinged, and he would've been a thorn in your side for as long as he was alive to hurt you." Dante pressed to his feet, dropping her hand. "You did what you needed to do."

Lennon wanted to believe that was true, but her thoughts kept returning to Ian, one hand outstretched, in his final moments. If she'd pressed the button to open the doors—or if she'd never pressed the button to close them in the first place—Ian wouldn't have been torn apart. Deep down, she knew she hadn't acted solely out of necessity. Ian wasn't dead by accident or ambivalence. He was dead because she *chose* to close the doors of that elevator.

"What happens now? Is anyone going to come for me?"

"Not if you stay here," said Dante. "Drayton is their domain. This house is mine, and they know that. You're safe here."

But Lennon didn't want to be safe. What she wanted—even after all of this—was to return to Drayton, the only place where she'd ever really belonged. "I want to go back—"

"Lennon—"

"I have to go back. Take me back now. I'll face the hearing, or Eileen. I'll do whatever I have to, but I can't risk expulsion—"

"It's not safe for you there. You need to be patient."

"*Patient?* You don't understand. At Drayton I'm something. But out here, without it, I'm nobody. Nothing. I won't go back to that. To being pathetic, to being no one."

"I do understand," said Dante. "Better than you know. But this isn't the end for you—"

"I killed someone."

"We all make mistakes."

"But will those mistakes be forgiven? I mean, I don't know if you've noticed, but things don't normally turn out well for people who look like us when we fucking kill white kids—"

"He wasn't the kind of white that matters."

"Jesus Christ, *Dante!*"

"It's true, and you know it."

"Ian was at the top of our class."

"Until he wasn't, and remind me, who was it that replaced him? Who was it who put the blade through his hand and secured a bed in Logos?"

Lennon hung her head.

"Look at me." Dante crouched in front of her. Lennon looked down at him. "At Drayton—and in other places too—some lives are worth more than others. That was the case when the school was founded, and it's still true now, a century later. It just looks different now." He straightened, drew away from her. "Ian was a persuasionist of middling talent, from a family of no consequence, who if left to his own devices would've died of an overdose before age thirty. As far as I'm concerned, you sped up the inevitable."

"That's fucking cruel."

"Maybe. But it's true," said Dante. "He wasn't your equal. You have a power that comes once every few generations, and you're going to prove that to them, in time."

"But what if someone comes for me?"

"They won't," said Dante. "I'll see to that. All you need to do is lie low for a little while, let the dust settle, and then when the time comes, you'll return to Drayton and continue your studies." He said this with so much confidence it was like he was writing the future as he spoke it aloud. "And sure, they'll hate you, but they hate you already. Now they'll just have a way to justify what they've felt all along."

"So that's it, then? This is how I get away with murder?"

"This isn't the first time a student has died on Drayton's campus at the hands of a peer. It won't be the last either. You're not special in that respect, you're just indispensable and lucky because of it."

"But what about that hearing where everyone was so up in arms about me and what I might do? What were they so afraid of if not this?"

Here Dante went dark, his eyes out of focus. "It's easier to lie when you don't know the truth. Benedict used to tell me that. He called it strategic ignorance, said it was one of the greatest skills to have in your arsenal."

"What are you trying to say, Dante?"

His gaze went to her, and behind it she saw a glimpse of his aberration, as if his real eyes were just lenses that it was gazing through. "We're both tired. We should get some rest."

43

LENNON SPENT THE bulk of those first weeks at Dante's house ravaged by a guilt so ferocious it felt a lot like grief, replaying Ian's final moments, turning the memory over in her mind until she'd rehearsed it so thoroughly, she felt as though she was reliving it. Sometimes she saw him—halved at the waist—drowning in the great gyre of her nightmares, his mouth filled with seawater, screaming alone in the deep dark of the churning currents, his entrails floating in loose spools about his arms. In those horrid nights, she often woke screaming, to Dante at her bedside, coaxing her awake, and talking her through the dream's aftermath on the bathroom floor, where she dragged herself upon waking from the nightmares, to lie on the cool tiles and ground herself. It was not uncommon for her to lie there until sunrise.

The days, though, were better. Lennon slept late into the morning, and when she woke it was usually to Dante swimming out in the ocean. She could see him making the crossing between the coast and a small island about a mile and a half offshore. He threaded through the water with strong, sure strokes, back and forth, lap after lap. But by the time Lennon got up—showered and brushed her teeth—he'd be in the kitchen, making breakfast, as if even out in the water he knew the precise moment that she'd woken up.

Dante, as it turned out, was a more than competent cook. Each morning, he made a small spread—French omelets, johnnycakes, and fruit were daily staples, but sometimes there'd be fresh bread or occasionally pastries too. When he was done in the kitchen, they'd eat together in the breakfast room. Dante would sip his coffee, looking up from his own plate to encourage Lennon, with a nod or a gesture, to eat as much as she could. And Lennon found the silence between them to be every bit as satisfying as a stimulating conversation.

"How do you feel about camping?" Dante asked her one morning, passing a cigarette across the table to her.

Lennon shrugged. "I've done it a couple of times. Why?"

"I thought we'd go out to the island," he said and nodded out the kitchen window. "We could even stay the night, pitch our tents on the beach?"

The request caught her off guard. She hadn't taken Dante for the camping type. But what surprised her even more was her own response. "Why not?"

Hours later, they took a skiff boat—loaded with tents and sleeping bags and other camping supplies that Dante had hauled down from the attic—and headed out to the island during high tide. As they approached the island's shore, Dante climbed out of the boat and into the waist-high water. He dragged the boat ashore, pulling it high up the beach with a rope as Lennon, trying to help, shoved it from behind, her feet piercing deep into the wet sand. She slipped several times in the process, and Dante, laughing, eventually waved her off and told her to wait on the beach.

The island was no more than four or five acres across and, apart from the narrow beach, was heavily forested. While Dante made camp, Lennon explored, gathering armfuls of firewood as she walked. Because the island was so small no matter where she was, she could hear the sound of the waves crashing ashore, catch glimpses of the water between the trees. But the farther she ventured, the more disoriented she became and her thoughts returned—as they always did—to Ian, trapped in the maw of the elevator doors, his hand outstretched, a moment before she tore him apart.

Tears came with the memories, but she fought them back, doubled over, a hand pressed flush against a tree to steady herself. She took a few deep breaths but sucked the air in too fast, and before long she was panting, hyperventilating alone in a copse of scraggly pine trees, wondering how she'd made such a mess of things and wishing that she'd just jumped when Ian had ordered her to.

After all, she could've recovered from broken bones. But she couldn't unsee him, torn in half at the torso, twitching on the elevator floor.

By the time she returned to the beach, Dante had a tent pitched on either side of the fire pit. He was sitting on a large rock near the tide pools, a speargun in his hand, which he was in the process of loading, the butt end wedged against his sternum, his arms straining with the effort of drawing back the rubber. He looked, Lennon had to admit, almost annoyingly hot. Straining in the sun, his brow slick with sweat, shirtless and barefoot and more relaxed than Lennon had perhaps ever seen him.

"You all right?" he asked without looking up at her. She wondered if the reason he couldn't fall for her the way she had for him was because for Dante, there was no mystique. He could see through to the core of her so easily. There was nothing she could hide from him, no part of her that felt truly private when she was under the weight of his gaze or even just standing beside him.

"I'm fine."

He stood up, made for the skiff boat. "Good, give me a hand."

The waters just off the coast of South Carolina were murky, which made spearfishing a challenge. But Dante employed a few psychic tricks to maximize his efforts. His strategy was simple: he would circle the boat and extend his will in a kind of radius through the nearby waters, luring fish closer. Lennon was to do the same, and when any particularly promising marks swam close enough, Dante would dive down to spear them.

Persuading fish and crabs, as it turned out, was entirely different from persuading rats. And it took some time for Lennon to really get the hang of things. No two creatures were the same, she learned, and crustaceans, for example, had an entirely different psychic structure than mammals, which made them incredibly challenging to manipulate. Rats were a fairly easy mark in comparison. Their innate curiosity opened their minds to psychic interference. While crustaceans and fish weren't as intelligent—in the conventional sense—they had strong flight instincts that were at times difficult to supersede. As Lennon lured fish closer to the boat, they often snapped free of the tether of her will and retreated at the sight of Dante.

But even when she messed up, which was often, Dante would surface to take a big breath of air, push his goggles back to the top of his head, and smile at her. A full, deep-dimpled smile. Nothing held back, no joy that was hidden from her. She'd never, not once, seen him look even remotely as happy at Drayton, and despite all of her guilt and grief she was grateful to be the person who got to see him like this, even if she wasn't the only one, even if he didn't want her in the way that she wanted him.

During those long hours on the water, Lennon slowly improved, and by the time they were done for the day Dante had speared a few striped sheepshead, several flounder, and a Spanish mackerel. Lennon, for her part, scooped up several of the blue crabs she called to the surface of the water with one of the nets Dante kept on the boat. She placed the largest of the bunch in the cooler and let the small ones go, per Dante's orders.

That evening, they started a fire on the beach. Dante gutted the fish and boiled the crabs, and they ate their fill on the sand. The fish—grilled whole, seasoned, and spritzed with fresh-squeezed lemon—was, Lennon thought, one of the best meals she'd ever had. It was also the first time she'd eaten a full meal in one sitting since Ian had died, and she felt guilty for every single bite.

Dante gazed at her from across the fire. "You need to go easy on yourself."

She looked at him, and away, picking a bit of meat from a fish bone.

"I'm not telling you to forgive yourself, but at some point, you'll need to set your guilt aside. Allowing yourself to be eaten alive by it won't bring Ian back."

"You don't understand," said Lennon, staring at the ground, so ashamed she couldn't even bring herself to meet his gaze. "I deserve to feel guilty. Back in the elevator, I made a choice. It wasn't an accident. I chose to rip him in half. The least I can do is feel guilty for it."

"Look at me," said Dante, and Lennon looked as her eyes filled with stinging tears. "You have nothing to apologize for. Okay? Nothing. So when you return to Drayton, and you will—soon, I'm sure of that—you give people two options. They can either respect you or fear you. But don't let anyone make you question yourself. You did what you had to do. Am I clear?"

She didn't speak.

"Lennon, am I clear?"

"Yes."

"Good." He got up and went to stand at the water's edge. "Come here."

Lennon stood and followed. The tide was out, and gentle waves licked the shore. It was a bright night, thanks to the near-full moon, its reflection shattering into bright shards of light on the black surf.

Dante cast a hand out, and Lennon watched, enthralled, as he held the little waves back, interrupting their rhythm for no more than a few moments, before releasing them again. "This is how I settle my mind when things start to feel like too much. Try it. Just focus on the water."

Lennon did try, but the most she could do was send little ripples across the surface.

"How do you do it?" she asked him finally, exasperated by her own ineptitude. What was meant to ease her nerves had quickly devolved into a humbling lesson about brushing against the limits of one's own power. But that was better than her wallowing in guilt. And perhaps that was Dante's design.

Instead of explaining how to hold the waves back, Dante decided to show her. It was the first time that he had ever opened his mind to her, and what she experienced in those moments took her breath away: The scope of his power, the way that it expanded through the facets of reality itself. The fact that one man could extend a hand and just seize it all, like it was his.

44

THERE WERE FIGURES on the shore when Lennon emerged from her tent the following morning. Nine of them, standing along the beach behind the house. Dante had eyes on them already. He was sitting near the ashes of last night's fire, staring at them with his elbows braced on his knees.

"It seems we have a few uninvited guests waiting for us back home," said Dante, and Lennon considered that word, *home*. It was a strange way to refer to a place she'd only been for a few weeks. But it didn't feel facetious. She couldn't deny that here, on what seemed like the very edge of the world with Dante, she felt safe in a way that she didn't anywhere else. Not even Drayton.

Lennon came to stand beside him. The sun glared so sharply off the water that it almost hurt to look at it. "Do you think they're from Drayton?"

Dante nodded. "When we go back, I want you to say as little as possible. And stick close to me, if you can, unless I tell you otherwise."

"You don't think they're going to try to take me back to Drayton, do you?"

"I don't know," said Dante, his eyes narrowed against the sun.

They packed up in a rush, loaded the boat, and made their way back to the house. Upon docking the boat, they were approached by the men at the shore. Lennon recognized Professor Alec, who led the pack, and none of the other eight, though she could tell, immediately, that they were graduates of Drayton—something about their demeanor, the way they stood. On instinct, she firmed the walls of her mind against any potential invasions. But if the men were projecting their will, Lennon couldn't feel it.

"Send the others away or we don't speak," said Dante to Alec, tying up the boat. She noticed, though, that Dante kept his speargun close, which she found almost funny because the real weapon was, of course, his mind. He was the best of all of them. Lennon guessed that with half a thought he could bring all the men on the beach to heel, with the exception of Alec, perhaps, who might be able to hold his own against Dante. But even then, for how long? No one was Dante's equal, as far as Lennon was concerned, and the men who had come here today were more of an intimidation tactic than any tangible threat. At least, that's what she wanted to believe.

Alec nodded to the other men, and they dispersed, disappearing around the sides of the house and back, no doubt, to their vehicles. When the last of them was gone, Dante motioned for Alec to follow him into the house, and Lennon trailed after them both.

"How do you like your eggs?" he asked Alec, gesturing for him to sit at the same breakfast table where he and Lennon had taken most of their meals thus far.

"Scrambled hard," said Alec, and he settled himself, rather too comfortably, in the chair that Lennon usually sat in. Lennon, not knowing what else to do, sat awkwardly beside him.

Dante nodded and began to crack a few eggs into a bowl one-handed, tossing the shells into the sink as he worked.

Alec appraised Lennon, giving her a small grin. "Well, you've done well for yourself. Haven't you?"

Dante cut a glance behind him. "Alec."

"What? She looks amazing. The ocean air must do her good." Here, he shifted his attention to Dante. "Quite a stunt you pulled to get her here. Was it worth it?"

Dante didn't deem that question worthy of an answer. He set two plates of breakfast on the table—one for Alec, his eggs scrambled hard like he'd requested, and one for Lennon, her eggs poached soft, the way she liked them. There was toast and fruit too.

"If I'd known you were coming, I could've prepared the guest room," said Dante, sitting down.

"Oh, I won't be long. I'm only here to impart two things, really. The first is for you." He pointed at Lennon with his fork. "Ian's been laid to rest. Or what remained of Ian anyway. I figured you'd want to know."

Lennon had, actually. She'd thought about what had been done with his remains many times over the past few days, wondering how they'd spun the story of his gruesome death to inquiring students, or any family he had outside of Drayton. A part of her wanted to ask for more details, but she couldn't think of a way to phrase the question without sounding mawkish or, worse yet, gloating.

"I'm truly sorry" was all Lennon could think to say in the moment. "I know you two were close—"

"I've had advisees before, and I'll have advisees again," said Alec, a dissonance between the coldness of the statement and the placid smile he wore as he said it. "You owe me no apologies for his death. He did, however, have a family. A mother back in Ohio. A younger sister who misses her older brother very much. She's eight years old. Too young to even process such a loss."

Lennon thought of her own sister, Carly, and found it hard to breathe around the lump in her throat. "I didn't know. He never mentioned them. What did you tell them?"

"We worked with local law enforcement to communicate a story about Ian's remains being discovered in an abandoned building." Alec spoke through a mouthful of toast and eggs. He had a disturbing way of mashing together the contents of his entire plate, so that it was almost impossible to distinguish any one component. "You know the story: strung-out junkie stumbles down an elevator shaft, where he's found rotting and crushed days later. Given the gruesome nature of his death, we strongly advised his mother against viewing his remains. She heeded that advice, and Ian was cremated in Savannah. Then his ashes were delivered to his family. I don't think there was a funeral. They seem like private people."

Lennon swiped a tear from the corner of her eye.

"I find it difficult to believe that you'd come all the way up the coast, with eight men accompanying you, just to antagonize Lennon about a man who's already dead." Dante cast a hard glance across the table at Alec. "Why are you really here?"

Alec turned now on Dante, flashed a dazzling smile. Lennon had never noticed before, but behind all of his tattoos, she saw what was an entirely classic, almost eerily symmetrical, face. Strong nose, full lips, straight white teeth. "You didn't think I would miss your birthday, did you?"

Lennon looked to Dante, surprised that he hadn't told her, but his gaze was set very firmly on Alec. Alec leaned out of his chair to reach for his briefcase and removed a gift, wrapped in plain brown paper, tied off with a bit of twine.

"What is this?" Dante asked.

"Open it for yourself and see."

Dante was clearly reluctant, but he took the package and tore off the paper. Inside a small shadow-box frame was a pinned moth.

"A birthday gift," said Alec, beaming. "From the vice-chancellor."

Dante set the moth on the table. He'd spared it no more than a passing glance, and yet he seemed . . . shaken. Something in the set of his mouth, a small crack in his composure. "Lennon, can you give me a moment to speak with Alec alone?"

She nodded, retreated to the guest bedroom. But not before she heard Alec ask a question that froze her blood: "Does she know what you are?"

"Alec—"

"I'm just wondering," he said. "I mean, honestly, I thought it was something you two could bond over. You know, given everything with Ian. Who better to support her through this than you?"

"You're acting like a child."

"Am I?" A harsh laugh from Alec. "You do know that you're going to have to tell her eventually. One day, she'll have to see you as you are. You worried about that?"

"Outside. Now," said Dante, in a whisper so low Lennon barely heard it.

There was the groan of the patio door opening, followed by footsteps as they left the house. Lennon retreated back to the guest bedroom, shutting the door. Through the window she saw the two of them, pacing along the narrow strip of beach. Dante with his hands clasped behind his back, eyes on the sand, more listening and nodding than contributing. Alec, though, was animated. Eyes alight, talking so fast that Lennon couldn't read his lips, even though she tried hard. Occasionally, he would fling out an arm and gesture back to the house, and Lennon—startled—would drag the curtains shut so she wouldn't be caught spying.

This lasted for the better part of an hour, and then it was over. Alec leaving with the other men, in dark cars with tinted windows. Lennon emerged from the guest bedroom and raced to the front of the house to watch them all drive away. When she returned to the living room, she found Dante sitting on the couch, his back to her. On the coffee table in front of him was the pinned moth in the shadow box. Dante wasn't looking at it, though, or much of anything, really. But from the deep crease that cut between his eyebrows, she could tell he was thinking hard.

"You didn't tell me it was your birthday."

When she spoke, Dante stirred, startled almost, as if she'd shaken him awake. He clapped his hands together, nodded, and stood up. "I'm going to talk to Eileen and see if I can make sense of all of this stuff with Alec."

"Do you think she'll even be willing to speak with you, given what happened?"

Dante had a way of simply stepping around questions he didn't want to answer, and he did this now, as he walked to the foyer, took his keys off the hook where they hung. "I'll be back in a few hours. Don't open the door for anyone," he said, and was gone.

Startled by this abrupt departure, Lennon returned to the living room, sat down on the couch where Dante had been just moments before. She picked up the shadow box, squinted through the glass at the moth within. It was large and brownish with spots that looked like eyes on its wings. In most of the taxidermy that Lennon had seen, the pins were carefully placed, so as to appear invisible. But the brass nails that secured this moth were thick and conspicuous, as if the person who'd placed them had wanted them to be seen.

While Dante was gone, Lennon pulled together a birthday cake, more to distract herself than out of any real altruism. Alec's visit haunted her as she assembled the cake, following the instructions written in one of Dante's cookbooks. As she mixed the batter and whipped up a bowlful of buttercream, she kept replaying Alec's words, wondering at what he'd been alluding to and if she could find a tactful way to ask Dante about it, without revealing that she'd been eavesdropping. Claude's drunken accusations were easy to dismiss. But it was harder to brush off Alec, whose statements, while more lucid, were still so like Claude's both in tone and conviction.

When the cake was baked and frosted, Lennon settled herself in the living room to watch TV, hoping to keep her mind occupied. The pinned moth was on the table in front of her, and she picked it up again, this time flipping it over to discover a small, open envelope affixed to the backing of the frame.

Lennon knew she shouldn't pry but couldn't resist.

Within the envelope was a small white card on Drayton letterhead, the paper faintly scented with the smell of what Lennon knew to be magnolias, just past the peak of their bloom.

The card read:

My Dearest Dante,

This moth reminded me of you. I know that this has not been an easy summer. But I so appreciate the work that you do.
   I think of you often. Stay the course.

With love,
Eileen

45

LENNON SLIPPED THE card back into the envelope, got up, walked very slowly to the kitchen—as if to keep herself from running—and called her sister.

Carly answered after four long rings. "Who is this?"

"It's me," said Lennon, whispering even though there was no one in the house to hear her. She was safe, but she didn't feel like it. Alec's veiled accusations had unsettled her, yes, but the letter from Eileen had almost disturbed her more, for some reason. Something ominous in the way it was written, a promise there, a threat that she couldn't yet decipher. But it was undeniably present, like the ghost of magnolias scenting the paper. A kind of darkness behind her words that Lennon didn't yet understand.

"Where the *hell* have you been?" Carly demanded. "We haven't heard from you in weeks."

"Do you remember that man who showed up on Christmas? My advisor?" Lennon asked, uncertain. When she'd persuaded them on

Christmas, she'd been careful to leave the memory of Dante untouched, wanting to avoid as much interference as possible.

"Face of Adonis with the eyes of a serial killer? How could I forget?"

"Dante, yes. I'm at his house for the summer."

Carly gave a dry, hard laugh. "Of course you are."

There was something about the way she said it that made Lennon's cheeks burn with shame. She had the sudden urge to defend herself and Dante, to tell Carly that the situation between them wasn't what it seemed like. She wanted to tell her about how for once she had been chosen and how that meant something, even if Carly was unwilling to see it. But she swallowed all of that ego down, suppressed it.

"So," said Carly, "you want me to do some digging?"

"What?"

"I mean, that is why you're calling, right? We've been through this before, Lennon, with Wyatt and the others before him. You start dating a new guy. At first things are great, but then it goes sour, you get suspicious or afraid, and then you call me."

"I'm not suspicious of Dante."

"But you are afraid?"

"I'm not afraid or suspicious," she snapped. "I just . . . I want to know more about him."

"That's what internet stalking is for."

"That won't work. He's a bit of a ghost online." She'd checked over Christmas break, thumbing through her phone (all cellular devices had been returned, dead, by the school for the duration of Christmas break). But she'd found next to nothing on Dante, or for that matter any of the faculty members at Drayton.

"If I was going to dig—"

"I'm not asking you to," said Lennon hastily.

"But if I was, what kind of digging would you like me to do?"

"I don't know..." said Lennon, and this much at least was honest. "Just, you know, find whatever you can."

"What I find depends on what you already know."

"I know his name is Dante Lowe. He has a house here, on the coast of South Carolina, at least I think he does. I mean, I guess it's possible the house belongs to the school—"

"Do you have the address?"

Lennon gave it.

There was the sound of a pen scratching over paper as Carly wrote it down. "What does he drive?"

"An Audi. Something old. Vintage, I think. I don't know the model."

"Can you get me a license plate number?"

"Not now. He took the car."

"Took the car where?"

"I don't know."

There was a long pause. "Lennon?"

"Yes?"

"Are you in any danger?"

"No."

"When you say it fast like that, it makes me think you're lying."

"I think I'm telling the truth," said Lennon.

"You think?"

Lennon heard the garage door open.

"I have to go. If you need to reach me, call this number, and if I don't pick up or I'm not here, just hang up, okay? Don't leave a message, and don't call back unless I call you."

"And if I don't hear from you? What then?"

"Then I'm probably dead."

"Lennon, that's not funny—"

"We'll talk later," said Lennon, just as Dante entered the house. She hung up the phone and went to greet him in the foyer.

"Who was that on the phone?" he asked, looking tired.

"Carly. I figured I should give her a call, so she knows I'm alive."

"How was she?" he asked, and Lennon couldn't tell if he was fishing for information or just trying to make conversation.

"She's still not particularly enthusiastic about you," said Lennon, trying to make a joke of it. But it landed wrong, and neither of them laughed. But the mood lightened when they found their way into the kitchen, where the cake was on display.

"Happy birthday," said Lennon, scrambling to light a match. "I know it's lopsided and the frosting looks like shit, but I did my best."

Dante, caught off guard at first, smiled and blew out his candle. They ate large wedges of cake for dinner at the breakfast table.

"So, what did Eileen say?"

"She apologized for the rude intrusion this morning and we were able to discuss the circumstances of your return to Drayton. The conversation was . . . surprisingly productive."

"What do you mean by that?"

Dante stared down at the floor, as if in search of the answer to that question. "The school wants some assurance that they haven't misjudged you. There is . . . mounting concern that your existence is a threat not just to the school and the students in it, but to reality itself."

"Because of Ian?" she asked, a pit in her stomach. She hated that even after killing one of her own classmates, she was worrying if the offense was bad enough to result in her expulsion, as if she didn't deserve to be expelled for what she'd done.

"Yes, but also because as of leaving the campus, you're no longer under the school's jurisdiction," said Dante. "And apparently, the chancellor isn't entirely impressed by your progress thus far."

"But I've done everything they've asked of me," said Lennon, her voice cracking on those words. "I've been at the top of most of my classes, I've learned to call elevators on command—"

"You lack discipline," said Dante, cutting her short. "I've told you as much myself. But their concerns are farther-reaching. According to Alec, it's not just your gatekeeping capabilities that have been called into question. It's your personality, your conduct with your peers at school, namely Ian but others too. Your mental health history was also a point of concern, as was your past promiscuity. In general, the school's opinion is that you're chaotic, unreliable—"

"And a bit of a whore?" Lennon snapped, her cheeks flushed hot with shame and anger. "Do you agree with their assessment?"

"Not all of it," said Dante. "I do believe you lack discipline. Your feelings are intense, and they often dictate your behavior against what I believe is your better judgment. As for their concerns about your health history and who you choose to sleep with, they can shove it up their ass."

Lennon relaxed, immediately, with that assurance. The faculty could loathe her. Her peers could hate her. But if Dante was in her corner, that was enough. "So what now? They're not going to let me return, are they?"

"I don't want you to just return," said Dante. "I want you to go back to Drayton and graduate by the fall semester's end."

"*What?*" She was stunned. The thought of graduating from Drayton hadn't crossed her mind once since she'd come to Dante's house for the summer. Any hopes of graduating had died along with Ian in that elevator. "How am I supposed to defend my right to graduate when the majority of the school thinks I'm rash, incapable, and violent—"

"You prove them wrong."

"But how, Dante?"

He was quiet for a moment. "Do you know why we were all so afraid when you opened your first gate?"

"Because it was dangerous," said Lennon. "I mean, look what happened to Ian."

"Surely you didn't think that hearing was because we were worried you'd turn an elevator into a guillotine? You had to know there was a greater thing we feared."

Lennon racked her brain, trying to think of an answer, but came up short.

"Your gates are more than just a means of transportation through space. Or at least, they could be more. Some gatekeepers possess the ability to open channels not just through space but through time also. The consequences of such an act can be both deadly and far-reaching. That's why everyone was so wary of your power . . . and potential."

The hairs on Lennon's arms bristled, stood on end. She was overcome by the feeling of being followed, like something terrible was lurking just behind her shoulder. "Well, they don't have anything to worry about. I've never opened any channels through time, and even if I could, I wouldn't. I mean, why would anyone risk dabbling with that when the cost could be so high?"

"Because the school is in danger," said Dante. "The gates that currently surround it are failing. Soon they will fall and expose Drayton to the world."

"I'm not following. Like at all."

Dante heaved a sigh. "Look, for as long as you and I have been alive, the gates around the school have been weakening. You know this because you've seen it yourself. There have been more quakes since we left. The elevators malfunctioning. Officials at Drayton have been doing their best to stabilize the situation, but the school's power, the power of the faculty who serve it, has its limits. They can't keep the school stable for long. One day, the gates around the school will collapse entirely and expose the secrets of Drayton to the world. As you can probably imagine, the effects of such a collapse would be devastating not just to the school but to the world at large. What do you think will happen when nations start wielding persuasion like a weapon?"

"I—I don't know—"

"Take a guess. What will the world's worst people—the rapists and the warlords, the billionaire CEOs and the corrupt politicians—do with the power we possess?"

Lennon felt sick just thinking about it. "They'll use it to their own ends."

"Violent ends," he said. "The results would be far-reaching if not world-ending. But I believe you can prevent that."

"Why? If you and Eileen and the rest of the faculty can't figure out how to keep the gates up and stable, then what can I possibly do?"

"You can raise a new one. You're the only one who likely can."

"But how? I open gates that move through space. But the boundaries around the school are different. Illusionary. They just shield it from the outside world. That has nothing to do with my elevators."

Dante shook his head. "You've got the wrong idea. Drayton isn't static. It's alive. Moving through space *and* time."

"What do you mean by that?"

"I mean that the boundaries that protect it from the world aren't illusionary. They're not keeping it invisible. Drayton is a reality of its own. You can think of it as a ship, moving along a river through space and time. The elevators we use to access it—even that long road that marks the end of campus—all of them are like small lifeboats carrying us back and forth between the reality on campus and that of the present."

Lennon felt, with no small amount of discomfort, her mind stretching to accommodate this new information. "So you're saying that the campus itself is kind of like one big elevator cabin?"

"Exactly," said Dante. "And when that elevator fails, the cabin of the campus will fall back into the present."

"Why the present? Why not the future or the past?"

"The future doesn't yet exist. The past has already happened, so we would know if the campus had been revealed. By that logic, it makes sense to deduce that there's no place for Drayton to land but the present reality, whatever that is at the time that it falls."

As Dante said this, the truth came slowly into focus. The precarity of this new reality. "What makes you so sure I can even do this? My elevator cabins are small, and I can only sustain them for so long. But something on the scale of Drayton's campus? I mean, that would take an impossible amount of stamina, not to mention skill that I don't possess—"

"You don't possess it *yet*. But I can help you," said Dante. "It's important to remember that your elevator gates are something more than what they appear to be. They only take the form of an elevator because that's the easiest way to communicate the concept, a way for you to comprehend and express the ineffable. But the cabin itself, it doesn't exist as a concrete reality. It can change forms, expand to become something different."

"Like William's doors did," said Lennon, thinking back to one of her first lessons with Benedict. "His gates manifested as a hallway."

Dante nodded. He had that light in his eyes that he often did when he was lecturing and was particularly riveted by the material. "If you can reach beyond the scope of your own understanding, if you tap into enough power, you can expand the uses of your elevator and change the way they manifest."

"I can create a gate around the school," said Lennon, understanding, "just like William did."

"Exactly."

Lennon humored the possibility, with some reluctance. But the idea still didn't sit right with her. She couldn't imagine herself as the kind of person capable of wielding that much power, with care and competence. She'd struggled to climb to the top of her class, unlike William, who was said to have been a known prodigy. And then there was Ian's death, a scar on her name forever, a demonstration of her own weakness and volatility and, worse than that, the violence that seemed almost inherent to her. A kind of corrosive chaos within.

Lennon was no hero. And she wasn't even sure she had the spine to call herself a villain.

She was just a coward. And she was very afraid.

"Something's bothering you," said Dante. "What is it?"

"It's just . . . it doesn't add up. If I have the potential to save the school with my power, then why did Eileen seem ready to expel me when she realized that I had it? Surely, she must've known that I had the potential to be useful."

"She did," said Dante. "But at the time it was just that: potential. Nothing more. To her you weren't a particularly promising student. You almost killed yourself trying to raise gates through space, and raising them through time is an even greater feat and one that, to be frank, I don't think she believes you're capable of. Also, at the time of that hearing, Eileen didn't have a dire need for the talents of a gatekeeper. The quakes hadn't begun yet."

"But now that the quakes have begun and she knows that she needs a gatekeeper, she never once asked me to intervene. Why? What are her reservations?"

Dante seemed reluctant to answer at first. "Eileen has never enjoyed sharing the spotlight, and she likes sharing power even less. If you become the person I think you can be—if you save the school and we're all indebted to you—she'll be forced to cede some of her power. To Eileen, I think that idea is almost as horrific as the school being exposed entirely. She doesn't trust you, she doesn't like you, and I don't think she's yet accepted the reality that she *needs* you. We all do."

"But what if she's right to be wary of me? If I begin to tamper with time, you say that the repercussions could be devastating, even deadly. It would be one thing if it was just my life that I was gambling with, but there are others at stake too. Do you really trust me with that after everything that's happened? After what I did to Ian—"

"That was once and you had your reasons."

"But what about all the other times I've screwed up? All of the times I've failed in your class, that I've come up short. I put a knife through Ian's hand months before I killed him and felt so little in the aftermath it scared me. I scare myself. In the mirror, sometimes I can see what I am. I mean, you said it yourself: I'm dangerous. Why would you trust a dangerous person with the fate of the school, or for that matter, the world?"

"The gates will fall eventually. Maybe not this year, maybe not even in your lifetime. But they will fall, and you're not the only dangerous person in the world, Lennon. What happens when all of the other dangerous people have access to the same power that you do? What will they do with it?"

Lennon swallowed dry, considering. It was a horrifying proposition. Her mind went to those two men in the alley that she and Blaine had encountered that night in Savannah. What would they do with the power of persuasion, if they could wield it?

"You should have told me about all of this months ago," she said, beginning to process for the first time the hurt and betrayal over everything he'd been keeping from her. All this time she'd believed that the walls between them were slowly lowering, that they were growing closer. But in reality, Dante was just as cagey and distant as he had always been. She wondered what else he was hiding and how it could hurt her.

"I would have told you if the decision had been up to me, but it wasn't," he said, and while Lennon wanted to believe him, she wasn't sure that she could. Even now—as Dante seemingly splayed his cards across the table—she had the distinct impression that there were still some things that he was holding back. "Eileen wanted to keep a lid on things for as long as she could. It was only today that I convinced her to consider this new possibility. She agreed to give you a chance at this, but now it's your turn to decide what you'll do with it."

Lennon paused to consider her possibilities: a reality where the gates fell and Drayton was exposed to the world, or a reality where she did something to stop it. She had come to Drayton looking for a savior, and now she had the chance to become one. And if she did, perhaps it would be some small way to atone for what she'd done to Ian. To cement herself as something more than a killer and a coward. A chance to redeem herself.

Lennon looked to Dante. "When do we begin?"

46

WHEN IT CAME to the practice of opening gates to the past, Dante adopted a new pedagogical approach. For one, the majority of their classes took place out on the beach, or if not there, then on the island beyond it. They woke early each morning, well before the sun came up, and began their sessions with meditation, during which time Lennon would lower the walls of her mind and Dante did the same.

"I want you to try to expand your will beyond the confines of your mind. Release any constructs it holds on to—your name, your identity, propriety, even time."

As he said this, Lennon felt his presence within her, a cold fog settling down over her thoughts. It made her almost sleepy. Immediately, she relaxed, legs going so slack beneath her that she had to put real thought behind the effort of sitting upright.

With Lennon as his only pupil, Dante had the liberty to adopt a more direct approach to the teaching of persuasion. Instead of lecturing, like he usually did, Dante used the force of his will to manually instruct her, imparting what he'd learned over his years of practice, entering her mind to deposit different images and emotions, attempting to relay the ineffable.

It was an intimate way of learning that felt a lot like Dante was holding her by the hand, guiding her through the metaphorical library of his vast knowledge. When Lennon had questions, Dante answered them with the full breadth of his wisdom, pouring into her all at once. He never made her feel cowardly or stupid. He was never harsh or unkind. And yet it hurt—all of it hurt so terribly—the knowledge vast and complicated and filling her up until she felt like the walls of her skull were about to crack from the pressure building from within.

Under Dante's instruction, Lennon learned how to tune her mind to the quiet frequencies of the past. She learned how time could be manipulated, folded double, and then folded again like pastry dough until it formed the many layers of reality itself. Then he taught her how to work it, how to navigate all these layers of the past and access them through elevators, which could cleanly cut through time like a sharpened knife. But understanding the basic theories was different than putting those theories into practice by calling an elevator to the past, a feat that Lennon continued to struggle with despite her best efforts and Dante's.

"When William first created a gate—long before he'd ever even seen an elevator or knew that elevators existed—his gates manifested as a hall with many doors, each opening onto a different point in time, the hallway itself running through it. For you it's an elevator. But the principle remains the same."

"Let's say I do move through time and I go back into the past—what happens then? Can I change things there? Affect the outcome in the present?"

"Yes and no," said Dante. "The past creates the present. So even if you went back and tried to interfere, things would turn out the same. In fact, your interference may well create the very circumstances you're trying to change. That's why it's best not to involve yourself. Why it's dangerous."

"So you're saying that if I went back and tried to stop myself from killing Ian, he would still die? Everything would unfold the same way?"

Dante nodded. "Perhaps if you went back, your presence in the past would be the very thing that provoked him to attack you that night. It's impossible to say. But what we do know is that the present is an immutable consequence of what happened before."

"And what about the future? Could I travel to it?"

He shook his head. "You can't travel to what doesn't yet exist. What hasn't happened."

Initially, this made little sense to Lennon. But slowly—over days, and then weeks, of study—Lennon began to understand, and then she attempted to put that understanding into practice. She pushed herself to the brink of utter exhaustion, and then—with Dante's encouragement—further still. She began to lose her grip on the present, as a concept. Even the limits of her own body felt loose and viscous, like skin and bone were no longer enough to contain her soul.

It was grueling work, hard on the mind and the body, but the nights offered some reprieve. The sessions ended each day at sundown, and afterward both she and Dante would retire to their rooms to scrub away the sweat and sand and recover from the toils of the day. They'd reunite in the kitchen for dinner. Dante always had something warm and delicious at the ready—fried soft-shell crabs, Brunswick stew, fish he'd caught fresh that day.

But it was what came after dinner that Lennon really looked forward to. The lawless games of Scrabble, each of them rowdily accusing the other of cheating with sleights of the hand and clever illusions that changed the letters printed on the pieces. They watched horror movies and military documentaries and pretentious art house films. Or, when they were in the mood for something particularly trashy, they'd opt for reality television—deserted island dating shows where tanned contestants wore swimsuits and cowrie shell necklaces—and binge-watch half a season in the span of one night.

But Lennon's mood would turn contemplative and somber as the night stretched longer. She would find her thoughts returning to her struggles, raising a gate to the past, replaying their lessons over and over, wielding her failures against her own mind like a bludgeoning club.

"Where did you learn everything you're teaching me?" Lennon asked Dante one night. It was rare that they discussed their work with the gates after their sessions ended, some unspoken agreement between the two of them that the exhaustions of the day shouldn't impede on the sanctity of the nights, that some part of their lives should be decidedly set apart. But this question—about the breadth of his knowledge and how he'd first attained it—had been troubling Lennon since the day they first began their studies.

"There was a time when the school thought I'd be their next gatekeeper," said Dante. He was shaving in his bathroom when she asked the question, lathering his jaw with cream, working the razor with quick, decisive strokes. She had taken to following him around the house like a second shadow, trailing him from one room to the next. Dante, for his part, didn't seem to mind the company, even on nights like this one, when she tailed him all the way into his bathroom as he went through the motions of his nightly routine. "I trained with Eileen and later Benedict before I called it quits."

"Why? What went wrong?"

"I was too mired in my own past to be of any real use to them."

"What do you mean by that?"

"I was only able to open one gate," said Dante, "always to the same fixed point in time."

"And what was that point? Was it important?"

Dante shook his head, wiping the last of the lather off his face. "Not to anyone but me."

SEVERAL WEEKS INTO THEIR RIGOROUS LESSONS, LENNON BEgan to feel like the slop of her consciousness was spilling out of her tired body, as if she was being drained almost. Each day seemed that much harder than the last. Like she was losing a little more of herself every time she tried to call an elevator.

"It's useless," said Lennon, crouching on the floor of the living room, utterly spent after hours of trying to call an elevator that would carry her back to the previous day. Her nose bled steadily, droplets splattering across the hardwood floor. "I can't do it."

"You can," said Dante, and he extended a hand and helped her to her feet. "I want to try something different. This time, you take what you need from me."

"Siphoning?" she said, thinking back to that terrible night in Amsterdam, when Dante had compulsively begun to drain the city. She remembered those poor girls in the red-light district, screaming. A feeling like death. "You said that was dangerous."

"And it is, especially when it's compulsive. But this will be different. Intentional. I'm going to lend you some of my power, my will, and you're going to take it and channel it into the task of calling an elevator to the past."

"I don't like this," said Lennon, shaking her head.

"Well, it's not a forever thing," he assured her. "I'll just tide you over until you build up the mental muscles you need to be able to do this on your own. I promise I won't let you hurt me. Let's just try it, see what happens."

Lennon complied, if only because she was out of energy and ideas and too tired to protest properly. She stood up, her legs feeling soft beneath her, and fixed her gaze on the wall of the den. Nothing happened, and she was about to give up, when she felt it. Dante's mind within her own, his power channeling through her, a force so strong it snatched the air out of her lungs.

"Wait," she said, not wanting to hurt him even as she drank of his power. Let it fill her.

"Take what you need from me," said Dante, but his voice sounded weak and so far away. "I'm all right."

Lennon's knees softened beneath her. There was a ringing in her ears. Dante's power thrummed through her body in a steady current, and she couldn't tell his will from her own. His every thought and feeling was privy to her. He was in her body, and she was in his, their psyches entwining.

A brilliant light cast across the wall. There was the smell of ash. The elevator doors, white-hot and glowing, seemed to brand themselves into the plaster. Its bell sounded different than the others, warped somehow, as if slowed and played in reverse. It was unlike any elevator she had ever called before. And Lennon knew, knew without a shadow of a doubt, that she'd done it.

She'd raised a gate to the past.

47

THAT NIGHT THEY celebrated on the back porch of the house with small glasses of champagne and a lobster boil. The air was thick with humidity, but the sky was clear of storm clouds, and there was a red sun setting into the ocean.

"My sister used to say sunsets like this one made the ocean look like it was on fire," said Dante, staring out at the waves. He was drained from all of the energy he'd siphoned into Lennon that day. His nose had only just stopped bleeding, and he had deep bags beneath his eyes, as if he hadn't had a full night's rest in weeks. But he looked happy as he spoke of his sister, relaxed. The last time Lennon had seen him like this—so open and at peace—had been weeks ago, the day they'd camped on the island.

"I didn't know you had sisters," said Lennon, surprised, a little hurt even, that he hadn't told her.

"I have two."

"Any brothers?"

"No," he said.

"Are you the oldest?"

"The youngest, actually. But not by much. My mom had all three of us back-to-back, no more than fifteen months between us."

"Trying for a boy?"

"For better or for worse," he said.

"Do you see them often? Your sisters, I mean."

"Not anymore." He paused. She thought that he wouldn't continue and was surprised when he did. "My oldest sister died of colon cancer four years ago."

"I'm sorry."

He waved her off. "The last time I saw my other sister, she was curled up asleep below an overpass. High out of her mind."

"Oh my god."

"She struggled. She'd been struggling for some time, and for years I tried to help her. Get her clean and stable. On my last attempt to get her off the streets, I . . . well, I bent her mind to my will, brought her here. She was angry, of course, but I managed to talk her down, subdue her, or at least that's what I thought. I kept her safe in the house, mostly, but sometimes we'd walk along the beach or run errands around town. I thought I was saving her; I thought that I could. She was as happy as I had seen her in a long time. She'd put on weight. Got sober, even. And then, one night, I woke up and she was gone. I found her a few miles down the road and forced her to come back to the house, where we fought. I told her that she was going to get herself killed and she told me that that was her right. And I don't know . . . that unlocked something in me. I think I realized that night that the greatest gift I had to give her wasn't sobriety, or safety: it was freedom. The choice to live her life on her own terms even if that meant I would lose her. So I let her go."

"Do you know where she is now?"

"No," he said. "And I think that's the way she wants it. I can't blame her, given what I did."

"You were trying to save her life," said Lennon. "I'm sure she knows that. You could always reach out to her—"

"No," he said. "If I do that, I'd have to let go of what I have left. The good memories, they get tarnished by the bad. I've got this image of my sisters I really want to keep. They're young, we're all young. It's summertime and the sun is half-set, its light shining through the breaks in the buildings along our street. Someone's pried open a fire hydrant, and my sisters are running through the spray, hand in hand. That's how I want to remember them both."

"That's a good memory to hold on to," said Lennon.

He nodded. "One of the few."

They were sitting close now, their arms almost brushing, so that Lennon could feel the heat of him, and all she wanted was to be closer. But once again, Dante pulled away, leaning back into his seat with his eyes on the water. His sudden withdrawal might've stung, if not for what he said next: "If we're going to do this, at the very least, we should talk about it first."

A thrill skated down her spine, as if she'd been grazed by the edge of a razor. "Okay. Let's talk."

"I don't think you understand the way things will change if we do this. Likely for the worse."

Lennon fought the urge to roll her eyes. "You keep acting like I'm a child, and I keep telling you that I'm not."

"I know you're not," he said. "But you are someone that I've been entrusted to care for, and to pretend like our . . . affiliation wouldn't in some way compromise that is naïve."

"The way I see it, we've been caring for each other. It hasn't been one-sided."

"I didn't say that it has been. But I have a responsibility that you don't, and it would be wrong—"

"In the conventional sense—"

"Wrong," he repeated again, "if I engaged you."

"Well, I think it would be wrong if two consenting adults denied ourselves the chance at something that could be good, great even, if we let it. Why doesn't that count for something? Why doesn't the pain of our own denial factor into your moral assessments?"

"I feel like you want something from me that I'm not sure I can give you."

"Then give me what you can," said Lennon.

And so he did.

Dante cupped the side of her neck, his fingertips carefully aligning with her artery. When they kissed, it didn't feel like the first time. He lifted her out of her seat, splitting her thighs apart, and hitched her firmly onto his hips. As he carried her to the bedroom, Lennon kissed that moth tattoo on the hard plane of his neck, the corners of his mouth, and the soft hollow below his jaw.

On the bed, he fitted himself between her open legs and she pushed up his shirt as far as she could and then he tugged it off the rest of the way. He was even more heavily tattooed than she'd realized. The moth imagery carried down from his neck, became something of a swarm across his chest and sternum. There were other images too: a hand with a dagger pierced through it (a nod, she assumed, to the Logos initiation process) and another with an open eye embedded in the palm. Lennon spotted the ouroboros of Logos House. A spread-winged starling with an arrow through its head. But it was a small tattoo along his rib cage that caught Lennon's attention. It read: *August*.

Claude had said that word months ago: *It would be August all over again.*

She'd thought he was referring to the month. But she realized now that it was a name.

"Something wrong?" Dante asked, peering down at her, sensing, from the feel of her body alone, the shift in her energy. That was how enmeshed they'd become. That he could feel her emotion, even when she kept her expression contained.

"No," she said, pushing all of the thoughts of Claude out of her mind. She didn't want them here, haunting her. Not now. "I'm fine."

From then on, they did what they did in silence punctuated only by the rhythm of the headboard beating against the wall. As Dante moved within her, his hip bones bruising against her own with each thrust, she kept her hand clasped tight over that *August* tattoo on his side, as if the name were an open wound and she was trying to staunch the bleeding.

48

FOR A WHILE after that, things were good. As the summer came to an end, and the fall semester approached, Lennon mastered the ability to open gates to the past with an amount of stamina and skill that, frankly, startled her. She spent her evenings with Dante, largely in darkness, the two of them twined together on the couch or in bed or in the ocean once, on one of the hottest days of the summer, when even in the dead of night the rolling surf was as warm as bathwater.

"I misread him before," said Lennon on the phone to Carly, one Saturday morning while Dante was out swimming his laps. He'd encouraged her to keep in touch with her family, something that surprised Lennon given the strict school policies at Drayton that largely discouraged any outside contact. "He's . . . kind. Really kind. I want you to meet him someday, properly."

Carly was quiet on the line. "You're really happy, aren't you?"

"Yes," said Lennon, smiling as she said it. And then: "All of that stuff I wanted you to look into, you can just drop it. Actually, I think it's best if you do. I think it was just the stress of school getting to me. But things are different now. Better. I think they're the best I can ever remember them being."

"If you say so," said Carly.

As the days passed, Lennon very pointedly thought of Drayton less and less, wanting to preserve her time with Dante—the precious minutiae of a simple and, yes, even tedious life well lived, where she got to be the kind of person she'd always hoped to become: stable, confident, and entirely fulfilled. But despite her longing for things to remain the same, Drayton beckoned.

"You're ready," said Dante that evening, as they prepared to leave for Eileen's house, where Lennon would demonstrate all that she'd learned that summer to the vice-chancellor. Both she and Dante had dressed up for the occasion, Dante in a collared shirt and Lennon in a pair of well-ironed slacks and a blouse they'd purchased from a shop in town.

"But what if I make a mess of it?" Lennon asked, putting words to the anxiety that had plagued her since the day Dante had first put forth the idea of her opening gates to the past.

"You won't," he said. "You're their hope of salvation, and tonight you'll make Eileen see that clearly."

After dinner, they drove up the sun-scorched coast to Charleston, a trip that took just shy of two hours. Eileen lived in a waterfront neighborhood downtown. The house itself was tall and white, its windows reflected the light of a fiery sunset, which made it look as though it was burning on the inside.

Dante knocked on the door and another Dante answered—at least that was what Lennon first thought when she saw the boy who stood opposite them. It took her a moment to even register their differences—the fact that he was shorter, with lighter skin. In fact, he was so alabaster pale that Lennon could see the green veins tracing delicately across his furrowed brow.

Seeing him in the threshold, Lennon felt her heart launch itself to the pit of her stomach, where it remained, pounding so violently she was certain that both Dante and the boy could hear it. What was a boy—who Lennon knew with crystalline certainty was Dante's son; she would've known it if she'd just passed him on the street—doing in Eileen's house? She looked to Dante for an answer, but he betrayed nothing. Didn't even look at her. His son did, though.

When his gaze fell to Lennon, she was staggered by the force of his will. If she hadn't known he was Dante's son from first appearance, she would have sensed it the moment his searching mind made contact with hers. It took her breath away. In the wake of him, Lennon felt like a nesting rabbit in the path of a lawn mower.

"Where's your mom?" Dante asked the boy.

And it was then that Lennon put it together: this boy was Dante's and *Eileen's*. No wonder his will was so formidable. He was the child of two of the most powerful persuasionists alive. And, for some reason, Dante had kept him hidden from her.

It wasn't a lie, exactly, but it was certainly a betrayal.

And to make it worse, Dante kept complete composure, as if this were entirely mundane and not a cruel shock.

Just then, a man stepped into the foyer. He was handsome, in a leading-man-of-a-toothpaste-commercial sort of way. At the sight of Dante, standing in the foyer with his son, an expression passed over his face that Lennon couldn't quite parse. Like he'd thought something nasty and quickly smothered it. "Professor Lowe, if I'd known you were coming tonight, I would've chilled one of the good bottles of port."

The two men clasped hands and dragged each other into an embrace that would've appeared warm if not for the expression of pain that twisted across the man's face when Dante pulled him near. He locked eyes with Lennon. "Is this . . . ?"

Dante sidestepped, nodded. "My advisee. Lennon."

"So it is," he said. "Lovely to put a face to a name. I've heard so much about you."

Lennon snapped to attention. Set her feelings aside. She knew if she wanted to return to Drayton, now was the time to perform. "Most of it bad, I assume?"

"All of it, actually." He laughed from the belly. "You've caused my wife quite some trouble. I'm Anthony, by the way. And this is Oliver."

Lennon shook his outstretched hand. "Nice to meet you."

"You should send her up," said Anthony to Dante. "Only way out is through."

"How is she?" Dante asked.

"She's been better. But you're here now, and that'll cheer her."

"I doubt it." Dante turned to Lennon then, said nothing, but the strangest sensation came over Lennon's mind—prickling pins and needles, like a limb with no blood flow—and she heard a voice that was like Dante's but not speak clearly from the recesses of her mind: *Say as little as you can.*

Anthony, perhaps a little rudely, gave Lennon directions to the room where Eileen was waiting for her instead of showing her himself. Lennon walked upstairs alone, hung a tight left at the hall's end, and found her way to the primary bedroom through a tall, haint-blue door. The bedroom was so dark that for a moment, before her eyes adjusted, Lennon could see nothing but the black silhouette of a person sitting in a chair across the room. The figure shifted; a lamp clicked on, and there was Eileen nestled in a large armchair, a quilt drawn over her lap, in a small sitting room just off the bedroom.

"Lennon," she said, with a smile. She extended a hand, her fingers as long and elegant as the rest of her, and motioned to the empty chair beside her. "Come in, please. Sit with me."

Lennon sat down in the empty armchair beside her. It was printed with a black-and-white toile pattern that—upon closer inspection—depicted the antebellum south, women in hoopskirts with their hair piled high and behind them, sparsely rendered, the dark figures of what might've been slaves in the distance. Though the sketches were so small, and the room so dim, it was impossible to tell.

"I do apologize for the lack of light," said Eileen, smoothing the blanket drawn over her lap. "I get these headaches, clusters. They're terrible, and the light makes them worse."

"I don't mind the dark."

"Dante said the same the first time he came here. My headaches were bad that year. We used to spend the entirety of our class period in total darkness, just so that the pain was manageable enough for me to speak."

Eileen leaned forward to tug open the drawer on the side table that stood between them, withdrew a pack of cigarettes and a lighter, carved to look like the head of a snake. She lit a cigarette without offering one to Lennon, and for a while they dwelled together in silence, Eileen spitting smoke, and Lennon looking at Eileen, then the floor, and then nothing at all, allowing her eyes to blur out of focus. She suddenly felt so tired.

"Dante was the first student I ever mentored," said Eileen. "One could also argue he was the student that all but passed me the keys to the vice-chancellorship, but that's a story for a different evening. We're not here to speak about him or me. We're here to find a solution for the problem of you."

Lennon shifted uncomfortably in her chair.

"The call is deceptive," said Eileen, and at first Lennon took this to be figurative but then quickly realized that it was a literal reference to the call she'd received all those months ago in the parking lot of that abandoned mall. The call that had first brought her to Drayton. "It seems like an easy thing at first. It was the same for me. For everyone, really. People like us, we've been waiting our whole lives to be told we're special. But soon after starting at Drayton, you learn that our path is not one to be taken lightly. There is sacrifice demanded, to access a power like ours. It is a painful, at times terrible, thing. And this is truer of you than it is any of your classmates. I do pity you for that. But what I think you fail to realize is that your position at Drayton is a gift, too. One that few receive. You should consider yourself immensely lucky to have it."

Eileen delivered the last of this statement with a jagged edge of anger. "That gift is the only reason you will be allowed to return to Drayton next semester. There, you will continue to perform your duties at Logos, in accordance with your station there. Whatever core curriculum classes you have yet to complete, you will. And you'll do all of this with the gentle pacificism of someone who knows that *any* act of violence—however small—will result in the deadening of their brain stem. Am I quite clear?"

"Yes," said Lennon, in a husky, tear-thick whisper. "I understand."

"And are you ready to show me the fruit of your efforts this summer?"

Lennon nodded and began to call an elevator. But Eileen stopped her before she had the chance, entering into her mind with a strange sensation that began at the base of Lennon's spine. It was pleasant at first, a sort of humming or trilling that sang through her nervous system, building as the moments passed. Her legs went soft beneath her. Her pelvis numb. She felt herself slide—as if turned to liquid—from the chair. The seizing began as soon as her head struck the floor, a series of racking convulsions over which she had no control, her limbs thrashing with a violence that felt near to bone-breaking. Her lungs seized up; she couldn't breathe, and still Eileen took and took and took from her, turning through her memories of the summer with a violence, like a person flipping through the pages of a book so hard that they ripped and tore in half, splitting the spine. Any attempts she made to keep secrets—like her affair with Dante—were futile.

Eileen saw and took it all.

It was a strange feeling but a decidedly familiar one. And Lennon wondered just how many times Eileen had glimpsed within her mind without her ever knowing it. How many of her secrets had been exposed? Was there any part of Lennon left that Eileen didn't see or know?

"Eileen, enough." Dante spoke from the shadows. "You've seen what you needed to see. You know she can open gates to the past."

"Just a little more," said Eileen. "She needs to understand."

"She's suffocating."

"Let her."

Lennon, looking up, her face screwed with pain, saw that Dante had come to stand behind Eileen's chair. He braced his hands on her shoulders, hunched over slightly, his figure backlit by the lamp. He lowered his lips to Eileen's ear. Said something that Lennon couldn't hear. But whatever it was made Eileen stiffen in her chair, her hold on Lennon slackening, then releasing completely. Lennon, gasping and trembling with pain, cowered on the floor.

Eileen stood then and stepped over Lennon as she made for the bedroom door. "I look forward to seeing you at the start of our next semester."

49

WHEN EILEEN WAS gone, Dante helped Lennon off the floor and downstairs. Lennon caught a glimpse of his son—emerging from the dark of the foyer—and blacked out. She came to minutes later, strapped into the passenger seat of Dante's car. It was dark, and they were driving through the thickly forested back roads that snaked along the coast.

"How did it start between you two?" she asked in a small voice.

Dante's hands tightened, bloodless, around the steering wheel. "You should rest."

"No," said Lennon. "None of that. Don't patronize me. I want the truth. Why didn't you tell me you had a child?"

"I intended to . . . when the time was right."

Lennon couldn't tell if that was a lie. She was beginning to question whether she'd ever been able to tell. If any of her reads on him were reliable. If she even knew the man sitting next to her at all. "How did it start between you two?"

"Do you really want to—"

"Yes," said Lennon, cutting him off. "How did it start?"

"Same way it started with us. Only I was the student, she the advisor."

So this was the real source of his reluctance. Lennon had sensed it was something more than the usual trepidation but had not put the pieces together until now. Dante himself had been in a relationship like this one, and if his tortured expression was any indication at all, he'd suffered for it.

Lennon didn't want to ask the question that followed. But some dark suspicion prompted her to ask it anyway. "How old were you when it first began?"

"Lennon—"

"How old, Dante?" Lennon said this gently, afraid that she might wound him.

"I was turning sixteen."

"So you were fifteen?" Jesus Christ, she thought, he was a baby. Just a child himself. Younger even than the son he had now, by the looks of it. The idea of it filled her with revulsion and rage on his behalf.

Lennon didn't want to ask the question that came next. A part of her felt like she had no place to. But she had to know—after seeing them together, the way Dante had held Eileen's shoulders—she had to have an answer, even if it broke her to bits. "Are you . . . still with her?"

"Lennon, you have to understand—"

"Just answer the question," she said, her voice breaking a little with the effort of both trying to be gentle and holding back her tears. "I need to know. When was the last time you were, you know, together?"

A muscle in Dante's jaw jumped and spasmed. "Six months ago."

"So since you've known me?"

"Yes."

Lennon felt like she might fall through the floor of the car. "Do you love her?"

"She's the mother of my son."

A gaping silence opened like a wound between them.

"Are you going to . . . keep being with her?"

He kept his eyes on the road. "I don't want to. I haven't wanted to since you and I . . . began. Maybe since before that, even."

This, at least, came with some measure of relief. "You could've told me—"

"I did," said Dante. "I told you many times that we shouldn't proceed. You didn't listen."

"This isn't about me," said Lennon. "This is about you and the secrets you've kept. How you weren't honest with me, or, I suspect, anyone. Not even yourself. You're acting like this was a relationship between two people who could actually consent to one. But Dante, you were a child with a grown woman who had no right to . . ." Lennon cut herself short. She couldn't get the words out.

"Don't pretend this is about that," said Dante, and he brought the car around a tight bend. "If you have something you want to accuse me of, then say it."

"I don't have anything to accuse you of. But I do have questions."

"Like what?"

"Like why is it that I bare so much of myself to you while you always keep me at arm's length? You never let me close enough to understand you. When you're at your weakest, you shut me out. Is it that you don't trust me—"

"That's not it."

Lennon felt close to tears now. "What, then?"

"I can't care for you in the way you want to be cared for," said Dante. "I warned you in the beginning, and you wouldn't hear it. You didn't want to believe me, and frankly, neither did I. I wanted things to work because I wanted you. I still do. But that isn't enough to blind me to the truth."

"And what is the truth, Dante?"

"This needs to end. It needs to end because it should've never started in the first place."

Lennon received these words like a backhanded slap. It all came to her so clearly then, as if she'd woken up from a dream. She had been naïve and stupid in falling for Dante. And Dante had used her, the way men are apt to do. It had been the same with Wyatt and all the others Lennon had loved and slept with. She had given them everything, and they'd taken and taken and taken. And when she had nothing left to give, or when they just grew bored of her offerings, they discarded her like she was nothing at all.

"I defended you," said Lennon. "When Claude accused you of killing Benedict, when people began to believe him, I stuck up for you. Always. I've been on your side this entire time, and now I see that I was a fucking fool for that because clearly I don't even know you." She was crying now—hot, angry tears that cut tracks down her cheeks. "Maybe Claude was right about you—"

A boy appeared in the middle of the road. Eyes wide, refracting the light of the headlights. He had a long pale neck slashed open just above the collar.

Dante wrenched the steering wheel a split moment before he would've struck him.

The car careened off the side of the road, toward the gully that ran along its shoulder. Dante slammed the brakes so hard that Lennon snapped forward, gagging as the seat belt cut deep into her throat. A beat passed. The boy in the road lunged across the left lane and disappeared into the dark of the tree line. Lennon unclipped her seat belt even as Dante caught her by the arm and begged her to stay in the car.

Lennon wriggled out of his grasp, kicked open the car door, stepped out into ankle-deep mud, and dragged her way up the side of the ditch to the road where she'd seen the boy just moments before. He couldn't have gotten far, not in the condition that he was in. But when Lennon staggered across the road and peered down into the gulley, then past it through the trees, there was no sign of him anywhere.

He'd just . . . disappeared, like he'd never been there at all.

And then, with a sinking feeling as though the ground had opened beneath her feet, Lennon remembered. She had seen this boy before, back in Amsterdam. She recalled the way he'd moved and glitched like a thing not human. The way that even when Lennon tried to bring his blurred and twisted body into focus, she couldn't, no matter how much she strained her eyes. She'd blamed the strobe lights and darkness in the club, but what if it was something else? Something inhuman?

"That boy back there," said Lennon, turning to Dante, who now stood in the street. "He's the one from Amsterdam, isn't he? The friend on bad terms."

Dante gave no answer, which was confirmation enough. "Lennon, I need you to get back in the car. It's not safe out here."

"Who was that boy, Dante?" Her voice was rising now, shaky and hysterical. She didn't sound like herself. She couldn't get the image of the boy's open throat out of her mind. The fear in his eyes.

"His name is August. He was a student of Benedict's and a friend of mine, or at least he was. A friend of mine, I mean."

So this was August, who Claude had referred to. The name of the boy tattooed along Dante's ribs. The apparition from Amsterdam. "What happened to him? What happened to his throat?"

Dante didn't answer. But his expression said what he wouldn't.

"Did you hurt him? Is that what Alec was referring to?"

"We can talk about this later," said Dante.

"That's not an answer."

"Well, it's the only one I can give you tonight," he said, and he looked tired then. So tired that if his knees had buckled right out from under him, if he'd fallen there in the middle of the street, Lennon wouldn't have been remotely surprised. "Get in the car. We can talk in the morning."

Lennon—stunned, shaking—got back into the car.

They drove home in silence. Dante retired to his bedroom and Lennon to hers. But come morning, Dante was gone, back to Drayton. He left a note on the dining room table: *I was called back to campus. I'll be home in the evening. We'll talk then. Breakfast is in the fridge.*

Lennon crumpled the note and tossed it into the trash. After the events of last night, she had no appetite, no energy to do much of anything really except sit, listless, in front of the TV, thinking over all that had occurred last night at Eileen's, the apparition of that boy with the slashed throat who had spawned in the middle of the road.

The phone rang. And kept ringing.

Lennon let it go to voicemail twice before, on the third call, she sprang up from the couch, frustrated, to answer it. "Dante isn't in right now—"

"It's me," said Carly. "I'm in Savannah, in the bar of the Clark hotel. I have a flight out at eight tonight, so we have to meet quickly. When can you come?"

"Why are you here?"

"I did some digging on your boyfriend," she said, and Lennon could tell both from her tone and her spontaneous flight to Savannah that whatever she'd dug up had been bad.

"I thought I told you to drop that—"

"You did," said Carly, "and that's precisely what prompted me to start sniffing around. You're a terrible judge of character. Always have been. So I need you to come here now. Faster than now, preferably. Trust me when I say you'll want to see this."

"Give me fifteen minutes."

"Make it five if you can," said Carly, and she hung up.

Lennon got dressed, shut the door of her bedroom—paranoid even though Dante said he wouldn't be home until the evening—and called an elevator to Savannah. Apart from visiting Eileen's, Lennon had rarely left Dante's house since she'd first arrived there at the beginning of the summer, and she found it so strange and dizzying to be out in the world again, with all of its noise and traffic, the trolley buses packed to capacity with tourists, the flocks of pigeons, and people thumbing texts into their phones.

Walking through Savannah, Lennon found that she no longer knew how to make her way through the world. She'd forgotten simple things, things she would've thought indelible, like how to move with a crowd of people, how to blend in. Now she felt as though gazes trailed her as she made her way through the streets. As if the people flooding the sidewalk along with her sensed—bristling—that she was not like them. And she felt the creeping paranoia that she was about to be outed or attacked or otherwise ostracized.

Lennon was relieved when she spotted the Clark Hotel. Inside she found Carly at the bar, nursing a martini and carefully avoiding eye contact with the guy who was chatting her up. Lennon willed the man away as she approached, a mental tug that pulled him—in a sharp and wooden movement—from the stool he sat on. He lurched out the door without paying his tab, oblivious to the bartender, who called after him as he went.

Lennon sat down on that same stool. "What did you find?"

"Hello to you too," said Carly, gazing after the man with a furrowed brow. "What did you do to that man?"

"What do you mean, what did I do?"

"He left so abruptly."

"And how does that have anything to do with me? I've never even seen him before."

Carly narrowed her eyes. "You need to get better at gaslighting if you plan on making a habit of lying to everyone all the time." She reached into a stiff leather tote bag resting on the stool to her left and produced a laptop. "I found something on your Dante."

"He's not my anything." Not anymore.

"I would certainly hope not." Carly opened a file on her laptop that looked like a cross between a spreadsheet and a PowerPoint presentation, complete with a photo of Dante, a professional-looking headshot, like what you'd expect to see on a university's landing page. But as she scrolled lower, there were other photos too—grainy clippings of newspaper articles that blurred as Carly scrolled past them, and at the bottom of one page, a small baby picture. "It was tough, at first, to find anything on him. Our database at the firm is extensive, but it almost seemed like someone had wiped or locked every known record relating to him. What little I managed to scrounge up was almost entirely derived from secondhand sources, so bear with me."

Lennon glanced down the bar to make sure no one was listening. Nodded for her to continue.

"The man you now know to be Dante was born in Harlem, New York, to a Loucille, or Lou, Fredericks. But he had a different last name before. I wish I could give it to you, but it's been redacted from every file I can find."

"Redacted? How is a name redacted?"

"I don't know," said Carly. "But what I do know is that everything

I gathered on him, I had to find by going backward. I started with who he is and tracked back to who he was. Somewhere along the way, it's like he lost his name. He was Dante . . . and then as I went back in time he simply wasn't. In every prison record, every file, every article, every letter and birth certificate, all I could find to identify him by was a blank space where his first name should've been."

"What? That doesn't even make any sense—"

"Let me finish," said Carly. "We don't have a lot of time, I have a flight at eight, and I think you'll want to hear this. The father, Martin Fredericks, was out of the picture. CPS removed Dante from his mother's home at age five—"

"Why?"

"He showed up to school covered in bruises."

"And he didn't say who gave them to him?"

"He didn't say anything at all. According to his file, he was mute for the entirety of his childhood. After CPS took him from his mother, he went to live with his great aunt, Rosetta Lowe, near Beaufort, South Carolina, for several years."

"Is her house the one I've been staying in?"

Carly shook her head. "That home was demolished, the land sold to a homeowner nearby who absorbed it as part of their property. That is the home you've been staying in, I think. Dante purchased the entire estate fourteen years ago. I was able to find a deed with his name on it, the name you now know him by, Dante. He bought the house when he was nineteen for two million, cash."

"What?" The idea Dante had purchased a property like that at just nineteen staggered her. Drayton must've rewarded him well.

"That's not even the half of it." Carly scrolled lower, highlighted a chunk of text from a police report. "After Rosetta Lowe's passing, Dante was released back into the custody of his mother, who was living with a man who would later become his stepfather. There were whispers of alleged abuse, a domestic violence charge that didn't go anywhere. The police were allegedly called to the house a few times. None of those rumors can be corroborated with evidence. What we know is that at nine years old he beat his stepfather so badly that he was almost decapitated internally; by the time the police found him in the bathroom he had no pulse. I have no idea how a nine-year-old kid was able to do that to a grown man almost three times his size. But they were the only two in the apartment at the time. There was no weapon. No one else to blame. He was immediately placed in juvie, in the aftermath of that assault."

"What happened to his stepfather?"

"Paralyzed from the neck down for the rest of his life. Died in a care facility four years ago."

"My god."

"It gets worse," said Carly. "He was held in a maximum-security prison called the Pendleton Juvenile Correctional Facility. The week he first arrived there, the first riot in the prison's thirty-year history broke out. And these riots continued for the months that he was there. Weirdly, each of the boys who'd had a hand in inciting these riots—inmates with good behavior, no citations, who abruptly turned violent—had had strange interactions with Dante just prior."

"Strange interactions? But I thought he didn't speak?"

"He didn't. Not out loud. The boys all claimed, and later a few of the prison guards too, that they could hear Dante in their heads. Speaking without a voice."

A chill carved down her spine. "And what did he say to them?"

"That's the thing. No one knows. None of the boys could remember. What we do know is that he was placed in solitary confinement in an effort to contain him from the rest of the prison body. And this is where things get weird. At midnight on his eleventh birthday, he was *released*. Or at least they think he was. All that's known is that he disappeared from the prison that night. There were whispers that the guard on duty, a woman by the name of Judy Parker, might've aided some type of escape or prison break. She was questioned but remembered nothing of that night except that he had had a visitor."

"A visitor? Who?"

"She either didn't know or couldn't say. Eventually, after no evidence of her interfering was found, they let her be. She died a few years later. A stroke. As for your Dante, or the boy that became him, his criminal record was expunged a year after he disappeared from the prison. Then less than a decade later, he graduated from Drayton College with his doctorate, making him one of the youngest PhDs in the country. And one would think that, given the strangeness of this story, given his past, there'd be some curiosity, some media coverage, *something*. But it's almost like a gag order was placed, like his record wasn't the only thing that was expunged. It was his history too. His birth name—I think that's when it disappeared from all the records. Even physical ones. Look at this." Carly fished through her bag and withdrew a yellowed newspaper. She opened it flat on the bar top and pointed to an article at the bottom of the page. There was a grainy picture of a prison, and an article beneath that talking about a juvenile inmate. The rest of the article was riddled with empty spaces where a name should've been, like the ink had been bleached from the paper.

A little lower down was a blurry school photo of the boy who had been haunting Lennon's dreams from the day she'd first stepped foot on Drayton's campus. In the photo he wasn't smiling, but his lips were parted wide enough to see that he was missing his two front teeth. His eyes were large and solemn.

"Is this all you found?" Lennon asked.

Carly nodded.

"I want you to forget this happened," said Lennon then, with real force behind the words, making them a reality as she spoke out loud.

Carly shifted in her seat, looking pained. "What do you mean . . . I—I don't feel well."

"It's okay," said Lennon. She felt sick with guilt over what she was doing but couldn't run the risk of someone else tampering with Carly's mind. If, somehow, Dante discovered that Lennon had been looking into his past, she had no idea what he'd do to her. But she was certain he wouldn't hurt Carly if she posed no threat to him. Now, if he glimpsed into Carly's mind, he would see that she had no memory of what she'd done or why she'd done it. If he wanted answers, he'd simply have to find them with Lennon.

"I think I'm drunk," said Carly, disoriented, eyes screwed shut.

Lennon, in a quick sleight of hand, grabbed her sister's laptop and the folder that contained all the information about Dante. She would destroy both of them later, burn the papers and remove the hard drive from the shell of the laptop, break it into pieces and then cast those pieces into the sea, erasing the last bit of evidence that could possibly tie Carly to Dante.

"You're not drunk," said Lennon, squeezing her sister's hand.

"I think someone put something in my drink."

"It's okay. You're safe with me. No one is doing anything to you."

Carly turned to look at her sister, a fat tear spilling down her cheek. "Why are you lying to me? We never used to lie to each other."

Lennon squeezed her eyes shut, reached deeper into her sister's mind, retrieving the memories one by one the way someone plucks out splinters with a pair of tweezers. It was painstaking work, painful for the both of them.

"Just try to relax," said Lennon, squeezing her fingers.

But Carly snatched her hand away. "What are you doing? You're hurting me."

Here, Lennon choked back tears of her own. "I'm sorry—"

"Just tell me the truth."

One memory left. The one of that first phone call at Dante's house, when Lennon had asked for her help. What a mistake that was, to drag her sister into all of this mess, to put her through this. She had so many regrets, but that was the one thing she regretted most. At the time she'd felt like a child, wanting her big sister to fix her mess. But she had been careless, selfish, to drag Carly into this.

"Stop it," said Carly. "Just please stop. Be honest with me—"

Lennon ripped the memory free of her mind. Carly stiffened. A slick of blood trailed from her left nostril and filled the dip of her cupid's bow. Lennon grabbed a few damp cocktail napkins and tried to wipe up the mess, but Carly slapped her hand away, stood up so sharply her stool rocked back and clattered to the floor of the bar. She gazed at Lennon, confused, disoriented—not even remembering why she was there in the first place. All Lennon had had the time to do was extract her memories pertaining to Dante, but she hadn't had the time to replace them with new, false ones to explain why Carly had come to Savannah at all. There was a wound in her memory, raw and open. Needing to be sutured shut. But Carly wouldn't let her.

"You ruin everything, you know. Everything you touch it just . . . it goes to shit."

"I know," said Lennon, through tears. "And I'm sorry."

Carly snatched her bag, light without the folder and laptop that Lennon had stolen. She didn't seem to notice, though. She slung it over her shoulder and made her way to the doors of the bar. "I have a flight to catch."

50

FROM THE HOTEL bathroom, Lennon took an elevator back to Dante's. She gave the house a quick pass—just to make sure it was empty, that he was still at Drayton—before locking herself in her bedroom. There, Lennon spread all of the papers from Carly's file across the floor, arranging them chronologically. When she saw it all together, it painted the picture of a broken and violent man. The man that Claude had warned her about. A man she didn't know.

Lennon thought back to Claude's accusations in the wake of Benedict's death, those drunken tirades she had been so quick to dismiss. As much as Lennon wanted to believe that the dark rumors weren't true, that Dante wasn't in fact the troubled boy turned violent man she feared him to be, there were certain things she could no longer deny. Namely, that Dante had been lying to her. He had been lying about his child. He had been lying about Eileen. He had probably been lying about what happened to August too. She couldn't shake the image of him, with the open throat and the fear in his eyes. It was obvious that something unspeakable had happened to him. And while she had not ever asked about—or pried into—the particulars of his past, these files made it clear that that too had been kept from her.

What if he was keeping secrets about Benedict's death too?

What if he'd been lying to her about his involvement?

Claude had been so convinced of Dante's hand in Benedict's death—a murderer, he'd called him. Even Alec had his sneering suspicions, which he'd expressed in fewer words when he'd visited weeks ago. Lennon had been so quick to dismiss it all, to cling to the lies she told herself just to keep believing that Dante was the person she needed him to be.

But as she sat on the bedroom floor, staring at the array of evidence, the truth she'd denied for so long took shape before her eyes. A portrait of a disturbed and dangerous man who'd left bodies in his wake. A man who had lied to her, a man who had killed before and likely would again.

She could see it now: Dante towering over Benedict's desk, forcing him to take up the letter opener and cut his own wrists. His formidable will bearing down on Benedict with such a force that even a persuasionist of Benedict's skill didn't stand a chance. And if anyone had suspected his involvement, Eileen had both the means and incentive to clear his name. They had a child together, a relationship developed over years. Was that why Eileen had redacted the particulars of his file? Kept these secrets locked away in her office, so that no one could see them or speculate? Had she done the same when Dante had killed Benedict? Cleared his name and kept the faculty from investigating, even though it was obvious to everyone that something horrible had happened?

Lennon wasn't sure about a motive, but it was obvious that there was bad blood between Benedict and Dante. And it was clear to Lennon that Dante had a penchant for discarding those who stood in his way. Claude had warned her of as much, and Lennon hadn't listened because she'd wanted, so badly, to let herself love him. But now the truth seemed so clear to her that she couldn't believe she'd ever been blind to it.

Still, there was one question Lennon couldn't get past: If Dante knew that Benedict was dead, why would he have taken her to his house after he'd died? Why hadn't he removed the body? Burned down the house? He was cunning, so surely he could've staged a more convincing murder. He could've made Benedict pen a suicide letter. Altered his behavior over a period of weeks, or even months, leading up to his demise. Benedict lived in a relatively rural area, so at the very least, Dante could've compelled him to leave his house and die in a place where his body wouldn't have been discovered for some time. It just didn't make sense. If Dante was the mastermind of Benedict's death, why had it all been so sloppily executed?

There was, Lennon realized now, only one real way to answer that question. Something she'd been too afraid to test before. If Lennon opened a gate to the past, she could discover what really happened to Benedict the night he died, and she would know once and for all if Dante had been lying to her about this too.

So there, alone in her bedroom, Lennon raised a gate to the past. It was her first time doing it without Dante's aid. Her skill and stamina had advanced considerably over weeks of practice, but it still took hours for her to call the elevator, its doors charring the wall as it appeared. Lennon, bleeding from the nose, stepped into the cabin. Its doors drew only partially shut behind her, an inch-wide slit between them.

The elevator cabin began to sink, down into the past. At first, it was a slow descent. Lennon saw a blur of light in the narrow slit between the doors, glimpses of sunlight and grass, the warped sound of distant voices speaking in reverse. But as the cabin picked up speed, the light between the doors intensified, grew so bright that it hurt to look at it. Lennon squeezed her eyes shut and saw nothing but the hot red of her inner eyelids. She felt stretched and pulled, the cabin screaming as it plunged through time itself.

And then, when Lennon was convinced she was about to die, the elevator slowed and came to a stop with the screech of metal on metal. The doors didn't open, but through the crack between them, Lennon saw a sliver of Benedict's foyer. She gritted her teeth, pried the doors apart, and slid sideways through the slit. The elevator disappeared as soon as she left the cabin, and she heard a voice she would've known anywhere. Benedict's: "You're just in time for tea."

51

LENNON ROUNDED THE corner to find Benedict in the kitchen, preparing two cups of tea. His hand shook a little as he filled the strainers with heaping spoonfuls of oolong. He spoke without looking at her, but she felt him enter her mind as soon as she stepped into the kitchen. It felt nothing like being examined by Eileen. His was a soft presence within her, like cold fingers skimming along the plain of her psyche. But even though Benedict wasn't particularly probing, he must've seen something within her that disturbed him, because he flinched, as if she'd struck him, and a spoonful of tea leaves scattered across the countertop when he did.

"You're not the Lennon I know, are you?" he said.

Lennon came to stand behind him. She wondered what he'd seen to make him so afraid of her. Was it Ian crushed within the doors of the elevator? The culmination of all that she'd become since they'd last spoken? A gatekeeper? A murderer? "No," she said. "I'm not her."

Benedict nodded, poured water into the teacups, stared down into the blooming steam. She wondered if it was shame or fear that kept him from looking her in the eye. He set sugar and a small pitcher of cream on the tea tray, then nodded down the hall. "Let's talk in the study."

They sat on either side of the large oak desk where Lennon had first been interviewed all those months ago. As soon as Lennon settled into her seat, she noted the golden letter opener on the left side of the desk. It was the same one she'd found crusted with blood the day they'd discovered Benedict dead.

"Are you all right, Lennon? You don't look well."

Benedict's gaze was arresting and almost painfully harsh, like staring directly into the sun. "I'm fine," she said.

"You didn't sleep well." It wasn't a question.

"I slept fine," she said—a lie. She'd stayed up half the night thinking about August.

Benedict narrowed his eyes. "You're here because you have a question. So why don't you ask it?"

The question she most wanted to ask, Benedict didn't yet have the answer to. So Lennon settled on another. "Who is August?"

Benedict lifted his teacup, took a small sip. "Dante didn't tell you about him?"

"All he said was that August was a friend of his and a student of yours. Apparently, they had a falling-out? And I've heard rumors—"

"Rumors from who?"

"Claude." Here Benedict's face pinched into a frown, as if he was angry at him for disclosing something he shouldn't have. "Alec mentioned something too."

"Well," said Benedict, and he leaned back into his chair, "August was a brilliant boy. One of the kindest you could ever meet. You would've loved him, Lennon. Everyone who met him did. He was an artist. He painted the portrait behind me." Benedict gestured to the gruesome portrait on the wall. "He painted one for everyone he held dear, which frankly wasn't very many people at all. He was shy, so he didn't have many close friends. He didn't like to open up. But August always found ways to express just how much he cared. For his friends. For the world, even. He was good. Or at least he was at first. You see, August—like you—was particularly gifted. And he—again, like you—possessed a very important ability. He could open doors that led from one space to another."

"He was a gatekeeper too?"

"A brilliant one," said Benedict. "Better than you. Better than Dante. I began training August and Dante both. August immediately excelled. But over the months of our training, he grew . . . reclusive, paranoid, disturbed, even. This was the price of his talent, I think. Because as August slowly began to lose his mind, his power grew exponentially and in a way that frightened me, a way that *should* have frightened everyone else, but they were greedy. They could only see the golden potential of what he could do for the world, not all the ways he could harm it. The ways that he intended to."

"I thought you said he was kind."

"I said he *was* kind. But this power—when pushed to a certain point—is corrupting. And that's what happened to August. That sweet boy turned violent and demented."

"Demented how?"

Here Benedict paused for a moment, considering. "It was his mind. Something went wrong with it. First it was animals, rats turning up dead in the labs where he worked. Dying by the dozens. I didn't want to believe it was him at first, but then his housemates at Logos began to express . . . complaints."

"What kind of complaints?"

"They felt that August was . . . preying on them. The girls were the first to raise the alarm. They were having nightmares that were... particularly twisted, violent in nature. Some might call them harassing, even sexual."

"And you believe August was the source of these dreams?"

"I didn't at the time. But then, during one of our lessons, August... snapped. In a moment of frustration he attacked Dante, put his hands around his neck. It all happened so quickly. Dante was young then, and startled, I'm sure. Even then I don't think he was ready to believe that August was as sick as he was. But I knew, in that moment, that something had gone horribly wrong. So I looked into his mind and what I saw there was... perverse, like glimpses into the psyche of a serial killer. What I saw within him aligned with everything I'd feared. The dead rats. The nightmares plaguing his housemates. All of it."

"It sounds like he needed help. Psychologically."

"He did," said Benedict. "But there was no doctor who could've put his mind back together. Not after the way it was broken. August was powerful, you see. And he didn't just lash out with his body, he lashed out with his will too. During one of his tantrums he would siphon power from anyone around him. His will would rend through the air with such a force that windows broke. The house shifted on its foundation, cracks racing up the walls." He gestured to one of them, a faint discoloration in the paint, so that if you squinted you could see where the plaster was patched over. "But none of that was what really scared me. It was that look in his eyes, a kind of hatred. Like he knew he could do worse and wanted to. I knew then that I'd lost him, that he was going to kill someone, probably many people, if someone didn't try to stop him. He was that sick.

"Desperate—and frankly hopeless at that point—I went to Eileen for help, and told her that August needed to be removed from the school. But she wouldn't hear of it. August had done great harm, yes, but he'd learned to endear himself to the people that mattered. Eileen included. He remained at the top of his class, one of the most promising students that Drayton had produced in several decades. Eileen thought he was a genius, and perhaps more importantly she thought that he—much like Dante—was wholly loyal to her. So, per Eileen's request, I set my reservations aside and continued working with August, and August kept growing worse. More dangerous. The situation grew untenable, as I knew it would, and so I was forced to make a decision. I confided in the only person who could see what I saw. A person who knew August well, who had his trust and through that trust the ability to stop him."

"Dante," said Lennon.

Benedict nodded. "He was the only one who could do it. I asked him to make it seem like a suicide and to make it as painless as he could. It broke his heart, but he knew he had to do it. And then he did."

So this was what Claude and Alec had been alluding to. The great crime that Dante had committed, though not alone, perhaps not even of his own volition. Benedict had cursed him with the task of killing his best friend. And Dante—whether forced or not—had complied.

Lennon began to shake, and as she did, she felt Benedict begin to occupy her mind. The first time he'd persuaded her—months before, when he'd tried to force her hand into the fire—he had been utterly brutal. But this time, Benedict entered her mind gently. She could feel his presence within her, like a cold stream of water flowing down from her mind, into the hollow cavity of her chest and then pouring through her limbs as if his will was blood and her heart was pumping it through her, the effect less painful than paralytic.

"You're so like him. August, I mean. You're both so brilliant. So dangerous."

"What are you doing?" she demanded, fighting against a blackout.

"I won't stand by idle and watch another one of my former students succumb to their own demons at the risk of everyone around them. I won't let you become August. And if Dante is too stubborn to handle this himself, then I will."

"I'm not August," she said, and it was a struggle just to speak. When she attempted to stand, she discovered that her legs were stone-numb, senseless.

"But you are," said Benedict. "I know what you've done to Ian. I see the chaos and violence in your mind, eating away at it like a cancer. Admit it, Lennon, you're out of control. You don't even trust yourself."

"You can't do this," said Lennon, her voice weak. "The gates will fall without me."

"I'd rather take my chances with the greater world than entrust Drayton to you alone," said Benedict, and his efforts redoubled. His will crushed her psyche.

Lennon raised the walls of her mind, fortifying her psyche in the safehold of her childhood bedroom, just as she had been taught to do. But Benedict's will was inescapable. It compromised the doors and the windows, filled the room like a flood.

"If you resist, this will only be worse for you," said Benedict. "I want this to be fast and painless, but you're making that difficult for me, Lennon. And I don't think either of us wants this to be difficult. Try to go to sleep."

The letter opener blurred and doubled before her eyes. Her limbs felt heavy. She couldn't speak. She realized that even if she'd wanted to stand up, she wouldn't have been able to. She couldn't feel her legs or arms or fingers. She couldn't swallow or blink. Her eyes were burning, filling with tears. Her entire body was paralyzed.

Panic, real panic, seized her, even as logic told her—in an ever-softening whisper—that she had no reason to be afraid. She already knew the outcome of this clash. She would not die here, with Benedict, because she'd lived long enough to discover *him* dead. Because the only body they'd found in that house was his. Because he would—Lennon believed—never leave the chair he was sitting in, which meant that someone was coming to save her, that or Benedict would interrupt himself. Whatever it was, this could only end one way: with Benedict dead and her alive. So she decided to wait, to hold on for as long as she could, until someone or something intervened. Because she knew that someone had to.

"There you go," said Benedict. "Ease into it. I promise it won't be so bad. People make a big deal out of these things, but the reality is that our bodies are made to do this. It's the most natural thing in the world. Surrender to it and it'll be just like sleep. Better, even."

Her heartbeat was slowing. But her brain was so suppressed that there was no panic, no adrenaline spiking through her veins. In fact, Lennon wanted to sleep, wanted to give in to it. She was so terribly tired; she had been for a long time, even before coming to Drayton. And there was nothing about Benedict's presence in her mind that felt painful or sinister. To cave in to him would've been as easy as falling into the kind of deep sleep that Lennon had been craving for years.

"That's it," said Benedict. "There you go. Rest. It'll be all right. I know you've wanted this for some time. I saw it in your eyes the day we first met."

Lennon was about to give in when her slowing heart stuttered.

It was hard for her mind—weak under Benedict's influence—to

even form thoughts. But in that moment, as her failing heart struggled to beat, these words crossed her mind: *No one is coming.*

She was out of time. Her vision began to fail.

Something had gone horribly wrong, and she was going to die.

Unless she saved herself.

Lennon's gaze homed in on the desk, on the golden letter opener.

"I'm not going to do it with that, if that's what you're afraid of," said Benedict, sensing that she was fighting him once again. "I wouldn't hurt you in that way. I'm not cruel like that. I just want to keep you comfortable. That's my aim."

Lennon closed her eyes and all at once, she was back at Logos House, and it was Ian sitting across the table and not Benedict. And they each had a knife.

Lennon was surprised to hear herself speak: "You're not going to hurt me."

Benedict went very still. "What?"

Lennon was crying now, as she met Benedict's gaze. "I said you're not going to hurt me. You're not even going to live to leave that chair."

Benedict's eyes went wide.

Lennon's mind clamped down like a rattrap around Benedict's, every part of her overcoming every part of him, seizing control when he least expected it.

"You're going to pick up that letter opener," she said.

Benedict's hand twitched, like a thing possessed, and slid across the desk. He fought it, fingers fumbling, but Lennon forced them into a fist around the handle just the same.

"Stretch out your left arm."

He extended his arm, stiff as rictus, his joint bending in such a way that for a moment Lennon thought his elbow would simply snap under the pressure of her will.

"Put the letter opener to your wrist."

Benedict moved its sharp point to his forearm. His mouth was open. Tongue pressed against the backs of his teeth. His eyes were wide and wild with fear and shock. He tried to speak, to plead, but Lennon wouldn't let him.

"Do it," she said. "Do it and make it quick."

The tip of the letter opener embedded itself between two blue veins. His skin gave way with a pop. There was blood. Then the letter opener disappeared into the wound.

"It's okay," she said, as Benedict's blood slicked the desk. "It's going to be okay."

52

EVERYTHING THAT FOLLOWED Benedict's death was blurry. Lennon remembered calling an elevator back to the present and boarding when it appeared. She slumped against the far wall of the cabin in a daze. When the doors parted, it was to her bedroom in Dante's home. It was as she'd left it—the door closed, the papers from Carly's folder splayed all over the floor. But Dante was sitting on the edge of her bed, staring down at his steepled hands. He looked up at her when she stepped off the elevator, and took in—no doubt—Benedict's blood, flecking her forehead and cheeks. He was always so good at reading her, so he must've known it was bad, from the way she looked at him, from the way her legs buckled the moment she stepped off the cabin so that she had to catch herself on the dresser just to keep from falling.

"Did you know that I killed him?" she asked at last and was surprised by the sound of her own voice, clear and unwavering. She had fallen apart, lost her mind very nearly, after killing Ian. But this felt different . . . expected almost. As if a part of her—a part that she had denied and reviled—had finally surfaced fully. "Did you know that it was me who killed Benedict?"

Dante didn't answer that question. He just patted the foot of the bed, gestured for her to sit beside him. She did sit, but was careful to keep some distance between them.

"Why did you do it?" he asked.

"Benedict attacked. It all happened so fast. I was just trying to defend myself, I think?" She paused, then shook her head. "But I didn't have to kill him. I could've called the elevator back, but I was so scared, and I knew he'd come after me, so I didn't see another way through it."

"You did what you needed to."

"Did you know?" she asked again. For some reason, she couldn't let go of the question. She needed to know if he'd seen this coming, if he'd known all along that there was something deeply wrong with her. If he was as afraid of her as she was of herself.

"I had suspicions," he said, not elaborating.

"And did you know he planned to kill me?"

"Of course not," said Dante. "If I had, I would've never brought you to his house that day, after Amsterdam. Prior to his death, Benedict and I exchanged some harsh words, sure, Claude wasn't lying about that. But it was normal for us. We've always feuded."

"Claude said you threatened him."

Dante stared down at the floor. "I thought he pushed you too hard, to the point of breaking. I told him that if he hurt you like that again I would make sure that he regretted it. Benedict responded in turn; he claimed that he had been testing you, to see if you would break under pressure. To see if you were dangerous. He did warn me, then, that he thought you were . . . unstable. Unteachable, even. But it was just that: a warning. I didn't think there was anything behind it. Benedict didn't seem afraid of you the way he did . . ." Whatever he was going to say he didn't finish. "I must've misread him."

"Maybe you didn't," she said. "When I first encountered Benedict in the past, he immediately entered my mind, and I could tell that whatever he saw disturbed him. He believed that I'd become something . . . dangerous, like August. I think that's why he tried to kill me while he felt he had the chance."

Dante was quiet.

Lennon wiped away tears. "What if he's right?"

"We're not good people, Lennon. None of us. Not you. Not Benedict. Not me. Good people don't wield power like this. We're all dangerous. You should know that by now."

"He told me about August," said Lennon softly. "How he changed. What you and Benedict both did because of it."

Dante very pointedly did not look at her. It was the only time she could recall seeing him look ashamed. No, worse than ashamed: devastated. Disgusted, even. "You know he's stayed with me. August, I mean. I have these attacks sporadically, when I'm in crowded places, when I'm stressed out, sometimes when I'm just . . . tired."

"You mean like panic attacks?"

He nodded. "In a sense, I guess. But mine are different. When they happen my mind turns against me and I spawn things, ghosts rendered in the flesh. The war in my own mind manifesting itself, tangibly, violently."

Lennon thought back to Amsterdam. The abomination that had appeared in the club that terrible night. August. A memory. A ghost. A figment made flesh. Lennon had known that Dante was powerful, sure; she'd never taken that for granted. But this was something else entirely. A power that even after all of her studies at Drayton—all that she'd been privy to—she would've thought impossible.

It was the power of compulsive creation. The power of gods.

Such a shame, she thought, that the only way he could access it was through pain and anguish.

"My attacks have gotten worse, more violent, these past few months. I feel like I'm losing my grip. Becoming him. I guess it was only a matter of time before my demons caught up to me, just like his did."

"Don't say that."

"It's true," he said. "I'm succumbing to it, Lennon. I've known for a while now. What you saw back in Amsterdam, when I drained those people. That was the beginning. But if I go on like this I think I'm going to lose myself entirely. Just like August did. I've seen it before. I know how these things go—"

She caught him then, cradling his face in both of her hands, forcing him to look her in the eyes. He seemed so fragile in that moment. She could feel his torment. His grief.

"We won't let each other destroy ourselves. I'm going to take care of you, and you're going to take care of me. All right? We'll be okay. We have to hold on to that. We need something to—"

The phone rang in Dante's office down the hall. Not a normal ring, but the chattering bell of an old rotary. It was a sound Lennon had heard only twice before: once in the abandoned parking lot of the mall the night she'd intended to kill herself, and then a second time at the academic hearing that had very nearly resulted in her expulsion from Drayton.

At first, neither of them was willing to move, as if by ignoring it they could escape the caller. But the phone kept ringing and ringing, and it was Dante who moved first, stalking down the hall to answer it. Lennon, as if surfacing from a trance, stirred and followed after him. By the time she reached Dante's study, he was already lifting the handset from its hook.

"What is it?" he said. Lennon heard another voice over the line, the sound muffled against Dante's ear.

"What are they saying?" she asked, impatient to know, but his expression betrayed nothing.

"All right," he said after a few long minutes of listening, and hung up the phone.

"Was that from Drayton?"

He nodded. "There's been another series of quakes. We need to return to the campus. Tonight."

53

DANTE WANTED TO take his car back to Drayton for the semester, so they decided to drive down the coast instead of opting to travel via elevator. Lennon packed what little she'd acquired during her time with Dante. A few books he'd given her—novels mostly—a handful of particularly beautiful shells she'd plucked from the beach, and a few items of clothing.

It was a long and solemn drive down the coast. Halfway to Drayton, Lennon fell asleep, and she woke to rain on the windshield and the wrought-iron gate swinging open to them. The campus—behind the sheets of pelting rain—looked small and toylike. The little people darting through the downpour, hollow miniatures made from wax or wood, empty of thought or will, just dolls animated with the stuff of spirit. Objects to be moved and persuaded, at will.

"Stay in Logos and keep a low profile if you can," said Dante. "People are still edgy after what happened to Ian."

Lennon nodded and they both got out of the car and went their separate ways. She was relieved to make it across the mostly empty campus and all the way to Logos without being stopped or even noticed. She stepped through the front door to the familiar aroma of must and books and cigarette smoke. The hallway was a mess of shattered glass, half of the contents of the curio cabinet strewn across the floor. The chandelier dangling overhead was still swinging, casting strange and watery reflections across the wall.

There were students, a lot of them, huddled in the parlor. Their conversation died into stone silence at the sight of Lennon standing in the foyer.

For a breathless moment, she wondered if they could see her for what she was. Ian's killer. Benedict's. A violent person, perpetually teetering on the brink of her own ruin and everyone else's.

But then Sawyer broke forward and Kieran and Emerson after him, the three of them seizing Lennon in a hug so fast and fierce that it knocked the air out of her lungs. Blaine, surprisingly, was the last to approach. She had always been slim, but there was something frail and decrepit about her now. Her collarbones protruded painfully; her eyes retracted into the deep hollows of her sockets. When Lennon dropped her bags and embraced her, Blaine flinched.

"Why did they bring you back here?" Blaine asked. She was the first to pull away.

Tears came to Lennon's eyes, and she blubbered a bit about being sorry and how shitty she was for failing to keep in touch, about how she had regrets over what had happened with Ian and that if they all hated her now, she would understand and accept it.

"No one hates you," said Sawyer.

"I mean, I'm pretty sure Nadine does," said Kieran. "I think she actually wants to murder you. I heard her—"

"Ian was a violent prick, whether Nadine wants to admit it or not," said Blaine, cutting him short. Her voice was thin and strained.

It seemed like, in the span of that summer, she'd wasted away. Lennon wanted to ask her if she was okay, but it didn't feel like the time, what with the crowd of her other housemates surrounding them. "But Kieran is right, Lennon. I'm not sure that it's safe for you—"

Just then, another quake. The ground rattled with a violence. A window cracked and shattered, glass blasting across the living room. Everyone rushed for the doors, separating Lennon from Blaine as the quake grew more severe. A sheet of plaster fell from the ceiling and crashed in front of her, followed by a thorough pelting of bricks. A rafter upstairs crashed down through a wall and tore a gash in the floorboards. More students fled into the halls and out of the building, and by the time Lennon had shouldered past them and out onto the lawn, there was no sign of Blaine anywhere.

The ground gave another violent roll that brought Lennon to her knees. She looked in horror as one of the largest oaks in the square canted sharply to the left, uprooted with a roar as the ground rippled beneath it, and fell. And when it did, Lennon saw her: a flash of blonde hair streaking on the wind as Blaine dashed, stumbling, falling, crawling on her hands and knees as the earth rolled beneath her, toward the chancellor's mansion.

By the time that Lennon reached its doors, Blaine had disappeared through them and the rolling quakes had waned to a series of shivering tremors. The moment Lennon opened the door and stepped past the threshold, her vision went blurry at the edges and she felt weightless and woozy, like the softest wind would be enough to carry her away.

Her faculties returned to her quickly, though, as she stepped into a warm bath of candlelight and soft jazz music. Overhead was a crystal chandelier, shivering with the aftershocks of the quake.

To her left was a dining room. To her right, a small, dark den.

Both rooms were empty, but from beyond the dining room Lennon could hear people talking in grave and hushed tones. One of the voices was familiar. It belonged to Dante, and she thought she heard him say: "She needs more time."

Despite the pull that Lennon felt toward the dining room, to Dante, Lennon decided to go right to avoid being seen. The den had greenish carpet on the floor and heavy drapes drawn over the windows. It was mostly empty, apart from the tightly packed bookshelves that lined the walls, the books themselves filmed with dust. Behind a polished desk was a door. It was narrow and limned with light that shone so brightly it was hard to look at it without the backs of her eyes aching a little bit.

When Lennon took hold of the doorknob, it was strangely warm. She turned it, dragged the door open—it was heavier than it looked, much heavier, as if something was attempting to suction it shut on the other side. She managed to slip through the crack and into a hall that was impossibly, dizzyingly long. For a moment, Lennon thought it must be some fun house trick, but as her eyes adjusted to the light she saw that it wasn't.

The hallway—long and lined with countless doors on either side—ended with another door, this one backlit, just like the one she'd entered through. The other doors along the hall were distinctly different. One looked like the door of a bank vault, another was graffitied and chipped, and a third was just a bloodstained bedsheet, nailed to a threshold and billowing in a breeze Lennon couldn't feel.

Lennon opened the door nearest her—it was short and brown and unassuming, but it opened out to an expanse of the coastline, the stink of the marsh, salt grass rolling with the breeze. In the distance, two figures—a boy and a man, featureless under the bright glare of the sun—dragged a crab trap from the water.

It was the same with every door on the hall. One opened to the parlor of Logos House, where a handful of logicians that Lennon didn't know sat drinking tea. Lennon brushed past the bloodied curtain to see a pregnant woman, laboring alone on a narrow, wooden cot.

It was a hallway of memories, she realized, each of the doors opening out onto a different place or point in time, a feat of persuasion so complex that it took her breath away. Lennon walked until she reached the door at the hall's end. She showed herself inside and was stunned to see Blaine bent over the bedside of an emaciated man, her lips at his brow, his broken hand held loosely in hers. A thrumming energy emanated from the man in nauseating waves that made Lennon's head pound and her vision blur in and out of focus. There were so many pipes and tubes and machines affixed to him. He seemed less man than machine.

The smell of death was a stain on the air.

"Blaine?"

She turned, her eyes—filled with tears—flashed wide with shock. "Lennon? You can't be here."

From the bed, a horrible sound: bones shifting and popping. The man gave a congested groan, and when he did the floor groaned too, bowing a little beneath Lennon's bare feet, the give so slight it was almost imperceptible.

It was a familiar feeling. Months ago, when she'd gotten high, she'd sensed the same thing, had been convinced that the ground itself was breathing. She felt this again now, as she stared at the man, and realized in awe and horror that the floor was moving in time with his rattling breaths.

A shivering rise.

A sharp fall.

The house, the entire campus, was breathing with him.

"Who is he?" said Lennon, staring at the man on the bed.

"This is William," she said. "Our chancellor and gatekeeper."

Another one of William's bones broke with an audible pop. He writhed, and Lennon was surprised he even had the strength to do that, given how gaunt he was.

"So this is what it means to be a gatekeeper," said Lennon, and all of the pieces slotted neatly into place. Dante's insistence that she learn to open gates to the past. Eileen's keen interest in her. Benedict's keen investment in her education, as if the whole world depended on her ability to raise gates, because *his* did. The campus needed a gatekeeper, an engine to keep the gates up in perpetuity.

Persuasion was a living power. If Lennon passed out, her elevator gates disappeared. If she lost focus, the tether of her will snapped like a broken thread. Someone, some gatekeeper, had to be alive to keep the gates around the school raised. And here he was—a shell of a man, his bones breaking under the power of his own will—the engine that kept the school running.

Because power like that didn't come for free. Someone had to suffer for it.

First it was William.

And when he died . . . her.

"This is why you asked me to run away with you," said Lennon, turning to Blaine with tears in her eyes. "You knew. You've known all along what they wanted me to become. This is where you go every night. Isn't it? This is what you do? You sit here and you tend this corpse—"

"Don't call him that."

"—knowing that I'll be the next one."

"I wanted to tell you. I tried even, but . . ." Blaine's mouth wavered, and she choked, gagged, when she tried to say more. Lennon realized, horrified, that she'd been tied. It wasn't that Blaine didn't want to tell her—it was that she *couldn't*.

Blaine clamped her jaw shut, and stalked across the room. She snatched a pen and a slip of paper from the bedside table and attempted to write, and Lennon watched as her hand tightened, bloodless, around the pen, her fingers spasming, pressing down on the nib so hard it snapped and ink spilled across the page.

But Blaine didn't give up. Face screwed with pain, she dragged a knuckle through the ink, smearing a single word: *run*.

54

LENNON FLED DOWN the hall of memories. The doors blurred on either side of her, and the hallway's end seemed to shrink farther and farther into the distance the longer she ran until she collapsed, panting. And that was when she saw it, the only door on the hallway left ajar, a glimpse of stairs behind it. She drew it open, slowly, and immediately sensed that this passage wasn't a gate. The energy on one side of the threshold and the other was the same. When she stepped up into the stairwell, she didn't feel dizzy the way she did when crossing between places and times.

The stairs were steep and uneven. With every step, Lennon had to pause a moment, to shore up her footing and regain her balance before proceeding. She was grateful when she emerged from the passage into another wide hall on the upper floor of the house. She turned and faced a large wraparound balcony. Dante was standing there, leaning against its railing, a cigarette in his hand.

"How much do you know?" he asked, as Lennon approached.

Lennon, who could barely speak for the tears, just shook her head.

But he nodded, like she'd actually answered. "Who told you?"

"I figured it out myself."

The ground gave another tremor. The glass panes of the windows shivered in their casing.

"You brought me here to replace him," Lennon managed to say.

"It's more complicated than that," said Dante, and she waited for him to elaborate but he didn't. Perhaps he sensed, like Lennon, that there wasn't much left to say.

"How is he still alive?" she asked.

Dante turned back to look across the campus. The house was so tall you could see above almost all of the trees on the square. There was Irvine Hall in the far distance; closer was the sharp spire of the chapel piercing above the oaks, and the glossy leaves of the magnolias looked slick and wet in the moonlight. She could see the small figures of the students mulling about the center of the square, bracing for the next series of quakes. Up high and from afar, the whole campus looked like something that could be crushed easily underfoot, and Lennon wondered why it had taken her so long to grasp the fragility of this place, the tenuous nature of its existence. Now, as the boards of the balcony trembled underfoot, as the only man that kept this school protected lay below, dying in his bed, she saw just how naïve she'd been to mistake Drayton for anything more than ephemeral.

"Like the school, this house exists within a pocket of time," said Dante, carefully. "It's extended William's lifespan well beyond its natural length. But that also means that he's lived to suffer longer than any man ever should. Gatekeeping on that level does horrific things to the body and the mind. William has weathered this burden better than anyone ever imagined he could—and he's done it for decades—but he can't go on any longer. He's going to die soon, and without him the gates will fall."

"Which is where I come in. Right?" It felt good to put words to that betrayal. "To replace him? That's why you brought me here. Without telling me the truth, that if I do this I'm going to suffer just like William?"

"It's not as simple as that. I promise you. I wouldn't—"

Just then, clipped footsteps, someone turning the corner of the wraparound balcony.

Eileen stepped into view.

"We can't find . . ." She stopped short at the sight of them. "Oh. There you are." Her gaze bounced between Lennon and Dante. But when she spoke, it was to the latter. "We're getting close, so you'll need to hurry."

Dread pooled like bile in the pit of Lennon's stomach. Her hands went cold and clammy, began to shake, as she realized the reality of her situation. She was standing between two of the most powerful persuasionists alive. Any hope she'd had of running had disappeared the moment Dante had laid eyes on her, if not the moment she'd entered the house. Even if she called an elevator now, they'd have her knocked out cold before the doors opened. She was trapped.

Another tremor rocked the campus. Eileen sidestepped, almost falling out of her heels. A second, more violent quake struck before she could regain her footing. Dante lunged toward Lennon, dragging her back and crushing her against his chest, shielding her with his own body. A few feet from where they stood, just shy of Eileen, one of the beams on the porch collapsed and split through the floor.

There was a horrible moment in the aftermath of the shake when Eileen—eyes wide with astonishment—stared at Dante, at Lennon cradled in his arms. "Get her ready. Now."

"Just give us some time," Dante snapped, and for a moment she really thought she was safe. Thought that he would protect her from this, as he had protected her from everything else. But Dante, releasing her from the cage of his arms, took her by the shoulders and said, very quietly, "I'm going to try to make this painless."

As he said this, a shade of black descended from her upper periphery.

"You should know that your sacrifice won't go unnoticed," said Eileen, flatly, like it was something she needed to say to keep her hands clean. "We're all indebted to you for this."

"Dante." Lennon was crying now, trying and failing to struggle to her feet, her knees giving way beneath her each time she attempted to rise. Her vision contracted to little more than a pinpoint. She fought to stay conscious. "Please don't do this."

A fissure appeared in the stone mask of his expression. Behind it, she saw something, not regret but fear, or pity maybe, and then his will came down upon her in a wave of vertigo, smearing the night into a blurry spiral. She pitched forward, blacking out. As Lennon slumped to the floor, the last thing she saw, materializing behind Dante, were the golden doors of her elevator closing and opening helplessly.

55

"I OWE YOU an apology," said Dante. They were sitting in the same small classroom where Lennon had first met him. She couldn't remember how she'd come to be there, or really anything after losing consciousness on the balcony of the chancellor's mansion.

Lennon tried to speak, but her tongue was swollen, fat and useless behind her teeth, spit pooling at the back of her throat. She had just enough autonomy to swallow, but it was a great effort to work the muscles of her throat without choking.

Her entire body felt like a limb she'd slept on wrong, tingling and unbearable, numb from loss of blood flow. She managed to blink, the effort of closing and opening her own eyelids was equivalent to pulling the cord on a pair of heavy wooden blinds. Even thinking was difficult, but with great effort she strung together a few thoughts, taking stock of her situation. Someone had her in a psychic hold, that much was obvious. It was keeping her body and mind sedated, her instincts suppressed.

Lennon managed to lower her gaze, saw her own hands bound in her lap, her ankles tied to the legs of the desk she was sitting in.

"An unnecessary precaution," said Dante. "I told them you wouldn't run."

Lennon tried to move her hands. Her fingers twitched, and then, very slowly, her hooked middle finger rose just above the rest of her clenched knuckles and straightened itself.

Fuck you.

Dante saw and smiled. "You still have fight in you. That's good. You'll need it."

He sat down on the desk in front of her, and she was surprised to discover that even here he still smelled like the sea. Hot tears welled at the corners of her eyes and slid down her cheeks.

"Hey, none of that," said Dante, but with a fondness that sounded sincere. He wiped at her eyes. "It's okay. I'm going to tell you what happens next, and you're going to listen, all right?"

Lennon managed to straighten her middle finger a little more.

"It's going to be just like we practiced, with the gates to the past. As the chancellor dies—they say he doesn't have a lot of time left—you're going to raise them around the school. I'll be right there with you the entire time, all right? There's nothing to be afraid of. You can trust me if you do it *just* the way we practiced, okay? Like that first time? At my home. When the time comes, you just imagine that you're there, you open that gate to the past, and you keep opening it, okay? You keep pushing until the walls of the cabin surround the entire campus."

Lennon tried to plead. To beg. To curse the day she'd ever met him.

But all that escaped her was a tangled whimper.

"I know," said Dante. "It's going to take a lot out of you. More than you have to give. You saw William. I know that you know. And I'm sorry that I didn't warn you . . ." He cut himself short. "This isn't what I wanted for you. Everything I've done so far has been to try to spare you from this. I know you won't believe that right now, but it's the truth."

Dante stood up, began to pace the narrow aisle between desks, staring at his own feet. "I'm not a good person, Lennon. I'm not a moral one. But I am loyal. I know that you probably don't believe that in this moment—why would you, coming fresh off a betrayal like this one? But for some time now, I've harbored the belief that you could master your own abilities. And by that, I mean I believe you're stronger than William. Strong enough to take on this task without being consumed by it. That's what I trained you for. That's what I hope for you. And I still believe you can do it."

The door opened. Eileen's secretary ducked her head inside. "The vice-chancellor wants a word."

The door shut again.

"Hold on to your hatred; it'll serve you better than sadness," he said, and was gone.

After a few moments, the feeling began to return to Lennon's hands and feet, so that she could move them a little, though she wasn't strong enough to break her bonds. She needed help, but who could she turn to? Blaine and Dante had betrayed her. The rest of her friends and housemates likely didn't even know where she was. If she wanted to escape, she would have to save herself.

Lennon shut her eyes. She felt her will leave her own limp body like a bleed and spill through the classroom and then beyond it, trickling through the long corridors of Irvine Hall and down to the ground floor, then across campus to the labs in Wharton. From there, it wasn't long until she found her mark: the storage room where all of the rats were kept. She entered their minds like a parasite, overcoming them one by one.

Blood bubbled from her left nostril. Filled the seam between her lips.

She kept pushing further into their minds, leaving her own body to enter theirs.

Her vision split and fractured like the multifocused eye of a fly, a shard of each rat's perspective held within her mind. She drew them all to the fronts of their respective cages, pressed their little pink paws flush to the glass, and then—with a knot of guilt in her stomach—forced them forward. Cages rocked and shifted, tipping off shelves, splitting open as they hit the floor.

A few of the rats snapped free of her will and fled, but Lennon—bleeding profusely now, from her mind and from her nose—corralled them back, reestablishing control as she herded the horde through the doors of the lab.

A tech shrieked and fled at the sight of them.

It was no easy feat to control such a large herd of rats, and despite Lennon's best efforts, they began to scatter. By the time Lennon called them up to the second floor of Irvine Hall, where she was being held, the last of the horde had dispersed, with the exception of just one rat.

Gregory.

Lennon—defeated, bleeding, slumped in her chair—only noticed him when his teeth pinched her skin as he gnawed at her binds. He was bigger than he had been the last time she'd seen him; his teeth were white and long, and he made quick work of the thin binds that bound her wrists together. She cried, seeing her little friend, who had come all this way to help her, and not because she'd forced him to, but because she'd asked—more pleaded, really. She'd made her need known, and he had come to help her.

Gregory gnawed the bindings thin enough for Lennon to pull the rope apart and snap it.

From there, she managed to untie the binds at her ankles, working as quickly as she could, her fingers still stone numb and clumsy from the suppression. When she was done, she scooped up Gregory and tucked him carefully into the front pocket of her hoodie.

Still too weak to call an elevator—the suppression warping her mind and making her weak—Lennon resolved to escape across campus on foot. With all the elevators in Irvine Hall heavily guarded—and Eileen's secretary permanently posted behind her desk—Lennon determined that her best chance at escape was the elevator in Logos House. If she was careful and lucky, she could slip in unnoticed, hide in her room or one of the storage closets along the hall, and then, when the coast was clear, take the elevator to one of the locations it accessed in Savannah and then make her way from there.

She didn't think much of what she would do once she left the campus. Where she would run, or who would help her. In the moment, all she thought about was herself, and Gregory squirming in her pocket.

Irvine Hall was mostly empty that evening, and Lennon made it down to the first floor without being seen, ducking into empty classrooms when she heard footsteps ringing through the hall behind her. She moved quickly, knowing it likely wouldn't be long before they realized she'd escaped. Or maybe they knew already, the person who held her suppressed having realized that the tether had been cut. She braced for an alarm—the toll of a chapel bell—ringing through campus to alert everyone that a fugitive was on the loose. But there was nothing. At least, not until she emerged from Irvine Hall, through a side door that allowed her to avoid the lobby, where she would've surely been spotted by the secretary.

She hid in the bushes as two professors, Dr. Lund and Eileen, approached.

"How did she wriggle out of your hold?" Eileen demanded;

Lennon had never seen her so unkempt. Big patches of red on her cheeks, hair hanging loose and damp about her shoulders, as if she'd been interrupted halfway through a shower.

"I don't know," said Dr. Lund, and he too seemed frantic. "Ask Dante. He was the last to see her."

They disappeared through the doors of Irvine Hall, and Lennon, crouching in the bushes, waited a full ten seconds before she sprang to her feet and ran. She was almost halfway across campus when the church bell began to toll, though it wasn't the top of any hour and it rang longer and louder than it ever had before.

Lennon kept running. She'd almost made it to the middle of the square, ducking behind trees and hiding in bushes, successfully keeping out of view, when she first spotted Alec a few hundred yards away. Panicked, she enclosed herself in a nearby telephone booth, covered in ivy.

She clamped a hand over her mouth, tried to muffle her ragged breaths.

A shadow slid past the fogged glass of the phone booth, broken to fractures by the gaps in the ivy. Then it doubled back, stalled by the door. Lennon, pressing herself against the wall of the phone booth, held her breath.

The door opened. Alec stood in it and clucked his tongue with mock sympathy. "Oh, Lennon. I'd hoped it wouldn't come to this."

Lennon could feel him entering her mind as he said this. Under the force of Alec's formidable will, she was helpless.

She felt herself losing consciousness. Fighting back wasn't an option, so she retreated, leaving the confines of her body as Alec took hold of her.

She was only vaguely aware of her own body, slumped uselessly against the back wall of the phone booth, Alec barring her exit, their faces inches apart. She felt like she was watching this happen to someone else.

Panic tore her mind farther from her body, and she felt herself fanning out—spreading thin across the campus. Racing across the lawn and through the brush. And then she found them, the rats that had scattered, gathered together in a shaking horde in the bushes a few yards out.

And an idea took form.

Lennon entered their minds, called them forth—a forceful coaxing—and then the horde began to run. There were shrieks and screams and yelps at the sight of the rat horde skittering across the campus, their little paws tramping across the sprawling green with surprising speed, until they found their mark.

The rats spilled into the phone booth and set upon Alec, clambering up his pants legs and ballooning through his shirt. He staggered back with a yell, foot catching on the bottom of the phone booth. He hit the ground, consumed by the writhing horde of rats. There were dozens of them, wriggling through his clothes and consuming his face. He gave a strangled cry.

Lennon lunged out of the phone booth and ran, her legs weak and leaden beneath her, half falling through the bushes as she struggled to drag herself across the Twenty-Fifth Square. But she was still so weak from the psychic suppression, and her pitiful attempts to firm up her knees were less and less successful. She was slowing down. If she kept pushing she knew she'd lose consciousness.

"Lennon!" Blaine stepped out onto the path ahead of her, waving her down. "This way!"

Lennon stopped dead.

When she still didn't come, Blaine went to her, caught her by the arm, and dragged her along, keeping her on her feet. And it was a good thing that she did, because the moment Blaine's arm encircled her, Lennon felt her legs go soft. It was Blaine who dragged her off the path and behind a live oak as several professors rounded the bend and advanced down the sidewalk Lennon had just been standing on.

"Why are you helping me?" said Lennon, panting and breathless.

"Because I'm finally brave enough to do what I should've done before," Blaine whispered, and gripped her hands. "I'm sorry. I don't deserve forgiveness, but I hope this is enough for you to know that it wasn't all bullshit. That I do . . . regret not warning you sooner. I didn't know anything for sure—I want you to know that. But I did know enough to suspect you were in danger. I just didn't want to have to choose between losing you and losing my life at Drayton because I knew if it came down to it . . ." She couldn't finish, just shook her head. "I hate myself."

"It's all right," said Lennon. "It's not your fault."

But even as she said this, the betrayal stung anew. The reality that Blaine and Dante and almost everyone at Drayton she'd thought she could trust had participated in this cruel ruse, in one way or another. Were they all complicit? Because if Blaine had known, then who else? How many others? Eileen and Benedict were obvious answers, but what about Emerson, Sawyer—hell, even Nadine and Ian? Had they all been privy to this secret and iced her out? Her life the price of their admission to a world that they loved?

If she'd had to make the same decision, would she have done any different?

"Logos is crawling with faculty," said Blaine. "They think you'll go there first. So our best bet is getting you out through the gate in the faculty parking lot. I don't think they're expecting you there." Blaine shifted Lennon's arm tight across her shoulder, keeping her upright. They were moving slower than what was safe or prudent. But Lennon was too weak to go any faster. She was so relieved when she saw the gates of Drayton emerging from the fog that her legs went limp beneath her, and Blaine had to drag her the rest of the way.

The gates didn't open automatically the way they did when Dante's car approached them, so Blaine had to pull them open, mostly alone despite Lennon's best attempts to help her, teeth gritted, shaking hands wrapped white and bloodless around the rusty pickets. Blaine had them open almost wide enough for Lennon to pass through, when Lennon first caught sight of Alec approaching.

His face was a ruin of bleeding rat bites. His lips were so badly bitten that when he attempted to speak, he spat blood, and Lennon couldn't even tell what exactly he was saying. Gregory twisted in her pocket as Lennon attempted to wedge herself through the gate, while Blaine pulled and struggled, panicking.

When Alec's will came upon her, it felt like a heart attack. She immediately began to black out, would have if Blaine hadn't offered an immediate counterattack, lashing out her will, intercepting the connection between Lennon and Alec, distracting him just long enough for Lennon to wedge herself into the break in the parted gate. But she was only half through when the gate closed suddenly, swinging shut on her chest, crushing Gregory deep into her stomach, the poor rat writhing and panicking as the metal tamped down on him. He gave a pained little shriek, wriggled free of her pocket, and fled for the bushes.

"Gregory!" It came out in a raw gasp, the gate crushing against her sternum making it almost impossible to speak or even breathe.

Lennon's vision went. Her bones shrieked agony. For a moment, she was certain she was going to die in the maw of that iron gate. But with the last of her strength, and a strangled scream, Lennon managed to drag herself free, landing firmly back on the Drayton side. Alec had advanced considerably, and he had Blaine on her knees now, bleeding from the ears with the effort of holding him back. She twisted to look at Lennon, helpless, in pain.

And that was when Lennon heard a shout from across the campus. She craned her head to see Sawyer, Kieran, Emerson, and the rest of her housemates from Logos charging for Alec. They attacked him as one, brought him to his knees, severing his hold on Blaine.

Sawyer, bleeding from the nose with the effort of containing Alec, turned to Lennon and yelled: "What are you standing there for? *Run!*"

Lennon turned and broke for the trees, ran until her legs gave out beneath her. She dropped to her hands and knees, panting in the dirt. In the distance she could see the chapel and she started toward it, hoping to hide there for a little while and catch her breath, maybe regain the strength she needed to call an elevator.

"There you are." She looked up to see Nadine emerging from the trees. "The whole campus is looking for you."

"Nadine, I can explain—"

"Why did you kill Ian?" she asked, so softly that Lennon barely heard her speak. It was then that she saw it, a bit of metal clenched in Nadine's left hand. A knife.

"It was an accident."

"An *accident*?" Nadine's eyes flashed bright in the dark. "Lennon, you tore him apart. They wouldn't even let me see what was left of him. They had to send ashes back to his family because what was left to bury was so gruesome they were worried what would happen if they gave them anything more. And you stand here telling me that was an accident?"

"Listen—"

"Shut up," she snapped and thrust a pointed finger in Lennon's face, spitting a little as she spoke. "He had a little sister. He had family. He had *me*."

"I am sorry," said Lennon. "But I can't bring him back."

"I was in love with him," said Nadine, as though she hadn't even heard her. "I'd been in love with him. I loved him even when you used him as a good lay and then cast him aside the moment that you found a better bet with Dante. I didn't want to let myself feel that way for anyone, but I did, despite my faith, despite everything. I sacrificed so much to feel that. And the moment I was brave enough to admit it, to let myself love him, the moment I won him over, you had to take him for yourself. If you couldn't have him, then no one could—"

"That's not true."

"Don't you lie," said Nadine, hysterical now. "I saw it that night, on the way to the chapel. I saw it in your eyes. You didn't like the fact that I was with him. You were jealous—"

"I wasn't—"

"—and competitive. You always have been. Even with Ian, you always had to be the best. That's why you put that knife through his hand the night he was supposed to be initiated into Logos. We all saw you do it. I swear it looked like you were fighting a smile after you nailed his hand to the table. It was sick. You're fucking sick, and if the school won't hold you accountable, I will."

With that, Nadine lunged at Lennon across the field, that knife sheathed in her clenched fist, her will a wicked thing that cleaved through the space between them and seized upon Lennon like the mouth of a snake. Lennon staggered, then hit the ground, extending her own will as she fell. Nadine crashed atop her, the blade of her knife embedded itself deep into the dirt, inches from Lennon's head.

Nadine ripped the knife free of the dirt and raised it again, and Lennon caught her by the wrist as the blade's tip hovered, inches from her abdomen. Nadine was stronger than she looked, much stronger, and Lennon couldn't fend her off for very long. The knife pierced into the soft of her belly, and blood soaked through the waistband of her trousers. Her arm spasmed. Her grip failed. The knife cut deeper, and she could feel the tip biting into her hip bone.

A sharp trill cut the silence of the night.

An elevator bell.

The ground firmed and hardened beneath her back.

Lennon managed to shove Nadine off her just as the doors of the elevator split open behind her, and she fell into the cabin, crashing against the far wall with an impact so violent she very nearly lost consciousness. The doors closed. She slid down the wall as the cabin descended.

Gritting her teeth, she peeled up her shirt to examine the stab wound. It was deep enough to need stitches, but she didn't think the knife had punctured deep enough to do any internal damage. She clasped a hand over the wound to slow the bleeding.

The elevator jolted—stopped—but its doors didn't open. After a few long minutes, she began to panic, beating on the doors, and frantically fitting her fingers into the crack, breaking nails in her desperate effort to pry them apart. She had just begun her first attempts to scale up the walls of the elevator and push at its paneled ceiling when the cabin began moving again. Slowly at first, grinding into motion with a sound she'd never heard before, like a can being crushed in a fist. And she could feel the walls of the elevator trembling almost, as if threatening to give under the pressure.

Again, Lennon wedged blood-slick fingers into the crack between the doors and tried to pry them apart, to no avail. The lights flickered and the elevator bells began to ring, as if in warning. But then the sound distorted as the cabin slowed. It was at this time that Lennon collected her thoughts enough to determine that someone had gotten hold of the elevator and was dragging it off course. Dante, perhaps?

Water began leaking through the elevator doors. A small trickle at first, thickening to a rivulet that washed across the floor and flooded over the tops of her loafers.

The cabin filled fast.

Up to her ankles.

Her knees.

Her hip bones.

Lennon tried to pry open the doors again. But if it was difficult before, it was impossible now, with the cold water spraying in and blinding her, making it impossible for her fingers to gain purchase between the slick metal doors.

The water climbed up to her collarbones, and she began to take deep breaths, trying to saturate her blood with as much oxygen as she could. Her feet lifted above the floor of the elevator, the water climbed higher, and her head wedged against the ceiling.

The lights flickered then died.

In the darkness, Lennon took a final breath.

She thought of Dante.

Her lungs swelled and burned.

She thought of Carly and what this would do to her.

She thought of Blaine.

The doors didn't open. The elevator didn't move.

When Lennon realized that this was the end—that she couldn't hold her breath for even a moment longer—she decided to make things quick. She opened her mouth, inhaled a lungful of water, and blacked out.

56

WHEN SHE WOKE, it was to the twisted shriek of rent metal. She opened her eyes to see the elevator doors parting open, all of the water draining out of the cabin. Writhing in a puddle on the floor, she attempted to breathe in a series of gags and gasps, garbled by water and vomit.

With her lungs clear, she was able to ground herself. The walls of an office took shape around her as her vision came into focus. Big windows, glaring in the sunlight. A butcher's slab of a desk—on it, the bust of a young boy cast in brass. A man knelt on the floor beside her. His eyes were closed, and he was bleeding from the mouth. He looked familiar, and she tried to reach for his hand, but her limbs had not yet come to life. But she could hear his voice in her head: *Lennon*.

Lennon. Yes, that was her name.

And this room, it was in Irvine Hall, on Drayton's campus. She recalled it from the scent—wood polish and cedar. The glimpse of magnolias beyond the windows, a steeple piercing high above them. A woman stepped into view. Pale skin. Thin ankles. Leather pumps.

Eileen. "Do you still have your name?"

"Lennon," she spat out, repeating the name the bleeding man had placed into her head.

"Very good. And who is the man lying to your right?"

Lennon tried to remember his name, but it didn't come to her. "It's . . . he's—"

"Don't strain yourself," said the woman. "His name won't be of much importance anymore. Better not to trouble yourself—"

"Dante," she said, decisive if a little clumsy when it dropped from her lips. And with his name came the memories—of his kindness, of his knuckles brushing her cheek, the word *August* tattooed in the hollow between two of his ribs, the taste of him, the sound of his voice. It was Dante, beside her.

"You people have such a rage in you," said Eileen, shaking her head. "I've never quite seen anything like it. You have no inhibitions or restraint. There's no line of propriety that you won't cross. No building you won't burn. No institution you won't attempt to dismantle."

"What have you done to Dante?" Lennon asked. Her voice was so weak. She didn't sound like herself.

"Dante is fine. Or at least he will be if you listen carefully and do as I ask. Our sitting chancellor, William Irvine, has suffered a massive stroke. The doctors don't think we have long now, and by 'not long,' I mean we're counting his life in hours, not days."

"I'm not going to be your sacrifice," said Lennon.

"I know. You've made your stance quite clear, but I was hoping that Dante might change your mind." When his name dropped from her lips, Dante gave a cry of pain. Lennon thought she might've heard the hollow pop of a bone breaking.

"Stop it."

"I will, if you raise the gates," said Eileen. "Your service in exchange for the freedom of the man you love. And to clarify, you do love him, right? That's what all these theatrics are about?"

"Let him go."

"I've just told you that I would," said Eileen, laughing a little, incredulous. "Don't you see? You sit at the helm now. You've singlehandedly made yourself the most important person on our campus. A kind of rising chancellor, in everything but name. If you want to save Dante, that's well within your power. You just have to cooperate."

"Don't . . . do it," said Dante, too weak to even raise his head.

Lennon reached for him, but Eileen paralyzed her arm so violently her elbow overextended with a gnarly crunch. It felt close to breaking. She cried out.

"All you have to do is let me into your mind and I'll guide you. I don't possess the ability to move through time, as you do, but I've spent many years of the vice-chancellorship dwelling in the mind of William Irvine. I've learned enough from him to be able to perform the act of raising the gates myself, through you, of course."

"You just want my mind," said Lennon, understanding for the first time. If William was the machine that the school ran on, Eileen was its conductor. All of these years while William had lain in agony, it had been Eileen siphoning his power, using it to sequester the school.

"I'll be gentle with you," said Eileen. "It'll be as easy as going to sleep. You won't feel anything."

"She's lying," said Dante, on all fours now, struggling and failing to push to his feet. His arms—corded with muscle—were now so weak they couldn't even support his weight. "Don't listen to a word she says."

Lennon attempted to push to her feet and go to him, but the wind was knocked right out of her lungs when Eileen dragged her down again, her ankle rolling painfully beneath her.

Dante extended a hand to her, his fingers twitching as they dragged along the floor. A fresh mouthful of blood spilled between his lips and slicked his chin.

Desperate, Lennon extended her mind to his, and what she found took her breath away. It wasn't just Eileen who was suppressing Dante. The full weight of half the faculty on that campus bore down upon him, bursting blood vessels and breaking bones. Lennon sensed Alec's signature—a venomous force that corrupted Dante's nerve endings and contracted his muscles, so that every time he attempted to push to his feet they spasmed and stiffened. There was Dr. Lund, holding his thoughts submerged under a cold tide of catatonia. And there were others too that Lennon didn't know.

It was torture.

They were torturing him.

But why?

"Why are you doing this to him?" said Lennon. "He's on your side. He did everything you asked. He tried to get me to raise the gate."

Eileen turned on a heel to look at Dante, perplexed. "You didn't tell her?" She laughed aloud, and Lennon thought it strange that such a pretty sound could come from such a horrible person. "It was Dante who helped you get out. He attacked Alec and half of the faculty, myself included, to ensure that you were able to flee. Because of him, we very nearly lost you."

Lennon looked to Dante, wondering if it could possibly be true. All of this time, she'd thought he'd betrayed her, but was it possible that he hadn't? That this was by design, that he'd been working in secret to save her life while pretending that he'd turned against her?

"It's all quite romantic," said Eileen, but she sounded irritated.

"Though I did warn you that it would end badly, Dante. If only you'd listened to me. I wanted to be gentle. To do this in her sleep—"

Dante raised a hand and the words caught in Eileen's throat, died into something that sounded like a whimper.

Eileen went expressionless with shock, her eyes flashing wide. But she recovered herself quickly, with a knowing little smile. "Th-there he is."

Dante still didn't raise his head. Blood dribbled from his mouth and nose and spattered his pants. "Leave her alone."

"If only I could," said Eileen, and Lennon cut a scream as pain racked her body. It felt like her bones were being crushed from within, the hollow structures of her marrow collapsing in on themselves, imploding almost. She heard a sharp crack as her clavicle bowed, snapping cleanly in two, the jagged shards of bone piercing up through the underside of her skin.

Her vision went and the worst pain along with it.

And she was lost for a while in the murk of unconsciousness.

When she came to, she saw that Dante was on his feet between Lennon and Eileen, making a shield of his own battered body, barely able to stand but protecting her nonetheless.

Eileen's expression morphed from contempt to ecstasy to childlike delight. But she sounded like a mother when she gazed at Dante with tears in her eyes and whispered: "I'm so proud of you."

Dante faltered, froze, as if locked within his own body. Blood leaked from his nose and spattered the floor between his planted feet. His breaths were shallow and congested. Each of them escaped with a rattle.

Eileen was killing him.

Lennon pushed to her feet, an effort that very nearly sapped her of all the strength she had left. She cast out a quaking hand and with the raw force of her will snatched Eileen's legs out from under her, dragging her back and away from Dante. Eileen, stunned by the viciousness of the attack, redoubled her efforts. Shifting the brunt of her will from Dante to Lennon, who staggered back, as if slapped across the face. Lennon watched as her hand seized up, rictus stiff, and wrenched to the left with the hollow pop of a broken bone. She heard herself scream, her vision graying out into the static of stars. She swayed, trying to stay on her feet as the waves of pain emanated from her wrist.

Eileen smiled with mock sympathy, and Lennon raised the walls of her mind a split second before she invaded.

Eileen's will took shape as a storm that battered the tiny windows of her childhood bedroom and ripped holes in the ceiling, so that rain bled down through the walls and soaked the carpet. She could hear Eileen's voice in the wind: a culmination of all of her deepest fears and miseries, her greatest sins and the worst of her self-loathing. She occupied all of the space in the house and infiltrated all of the corners of Lennon's mind: the bedroom safehold contained in her psyche, her memories and desires, her greatest fears.

There was a terrible crack, like a tree felled, and the walls of her bedroom collapsed in the wind, burying Lennon under the wreckage of fallen plaster, downed support beams, and toppled furniture. The rain came down in heavy torrents and flooded what little crawl space there was beneath the debris. The water rose to her chest, then her chin, and all at once she was drowning, buried and alone in the dark of her own psyche.

When she surfaced again, it wasn't to Eileen's office or the fallen walls of her own mind. She was in Dante's house. His den took shape around her, even as the winds of Eileen's will battered the windows, like the torrents of a hurricane sweeping in off the sea. In the far distance, against the cut of the horizon, the finger of a waterspout threaded down from the churning clouds. And yet the walls of the house held firm.

Lennon cast her eyes toward the storm of Eileen's will, ravaging the coastline. She opened the back door and screamed into the howling wind, "Get the hell out of my head!"

The storm winds receded and Lennon returned to the present. Somehow, she was still on her feet, but her knees were locked to the point of pain. As she slowly regained consciousness, her nose began to bleed, gently at first, and then in a thick torrent that clogged up her nostrils and made it hard to breathe through her nose. Her mouth gaped open, she heard herself snatch a gasping breath—her lungs on fire with the rest of her. She tasted her own blood hot and thick as it slicked her tongue and ran down her throat in rivulets. She inhaled it into her own windpipe, began to sputter and choke.

Dante lay motionless on the floor. If he was breathing, she couldn't tell.

A scream tangled in Lennon's throat.

"Easy," said Eileen, seated comfortably behind her desk, one leg draped over the other. Dante lay motionless in front of the desk, a few feet away from Lennon. "Don't make this any harder than it has to be."

In the window, Lennon saw her own reflection. Spine bent back, mouth wrenched open, blood pooling in her cupid's bow and spilling down her chin. Her heaving chest and fingers grasping at nothing. And then she realized it was not her own reflection that she was looking at, but the aberration's. It was smiling at her, laughing. Her chest wasn't heavy with the effort of breathing, it was laughter that racked her. Great bellowing, rip-roaring, throat-stripping peals of hysterical *laughter*. In the dark window, Lennon saw the aberration staring back at her. For the first time, they moved in perfect tandem.

Eileen's will snapped. Like a thread cut.

Lennon slackened, went limp, still laughing, and seemed for a moment to swoon, pitching forward toward the desk, where she grabbed the brass bust of a little boy, a makeshift paperweight, and raised it high above her head.

The first strike caught Eileen at the temple and sent her to the floor. Her eyes were wide with shock, as though in all of her brilliance she had never, not even for a moment, considered that Lennon would be capable of actually harming her. Lennon crashed down on top of her, with a brutal volley of strikes. Here the screaming began, cries for help and shrieks of pain—as Lennon beat her, bringing the weight down on her forearms again and again as Eileen struggled and scrabbled and tried in vain to defend herself from the blows.

Down the hall, the clash of footsteps.

Dante pushed to his feet. "Lennon, get us out. *Now.*"

Lennon tossed out a hand and called an elevator. It appeared in the wall, its battered doors dragging only halfway open, so that Dante had to pry them apart just to get her through. They stumbled into the cabin just as Alec breached the office.

Lennon slumped to the floor, still laughing, and the cabin fell with her.

57

LENNON'S LAUGHTER HAD died to a soft tickle at the back of her throat by the time the cabin slowed to a stop in the foyer of Logos House. Her intended destination had been somewhere—anywhere—beyond Drayton's campus, but she didn't have the stores to get them that far. She and Dante stepped cautiously out of the cabin and edged into the living room, where Lennon was shocked to see not only her housemates, but the better part of the student body crowded there, the room so tightly packed that there was barely enough space to stand. The kitchen and foyer were crowded too. As was the stairway, students sitting huddled together on the steps.

Blaine and Sawyer stepped forward to hug her, a fierce embrace. Upon pulling away, Lennon took in the surrounding crowd, saw the bleeding noses, the broken bones, the faces blank with shell shock, and the glazed eyes with burst blood vessels, the whites gone red. She noticed that toppled bookshelves barricaded both the front and back doors of the house, students standing guard by them, a few watching the windows too through the slits between drawn curtains. The house looked like the scene of a war, and that, Lennon realized, was exactly what this had become.

"Why did you fight?" Lennon's voice sounded distant, to her own ears. A thing apart from herself. "Why would you all risk it just to help me?"

Blaine looked genuinely surprised, and then hurt. "I mean . . . we're your friends."

All of this time, Lennon had thought she was alone. Betrayed and abandoned. Rejected and loathed by the greater student body, but she saw now that this wasn't true.

"So you all did this just to help me?"

Sawyer nodded. "To help each other. It's no more than what you would've done for us."

Lennon wanted to believe that was true. But she wasn't sure anymore. When she'd first come to Drayton, she had been desperate and afraid. Even then she had known her own darkness, had seen it leering at her in the mirrors, but she'd rejected it. Or tried to. And was successful until the night she'd put the knife through Ian's hand, since then the violence she'd harbored within her had been cast outward to devastating effect.

And it wasn't just Ian crushed in the elevator, or even Benedict dead at his desk. It was all of her other, smaller crimes. It was Carly's eyes filling with tears as she ripped memories from her mind. It was straddling Eileen on the floor of her office, bludgeoning her with glee. She told herself that Eileen, at least, had deserved this. But the truth was, Lennon wasn't sure she would've been able to stop herself if she hadn't. The vice-chancellor—for all her hypocrisy—had read her right: Lennon had a rage in her. A darkness that she couldn't control.

And yet, as she looked at the faces around her, drawn with fear, hanging on her every word—she felt something stir to life within her, like a flame struck alight. A bright desire to protect them all, these people who had stood by her when she couldn't even stand up for herself, her friends who'd risked everything to defend her, knowing it was an impossible fight. How could she turn her back on them now, when they needed her most?

Lennon began to wonder if this was destined in some way. The night she'd first received the call from Drayton, she had wanted to die. But maybe it wasn't a want at all—maybe it was prophesy. It made sense that if she could travel through time, she could see through it too, sense what was coming down the line. Maybe Lennon had known, deep down, that it would end this way. Until this moment, death had been the thing she'd seen in the mirror, something to escape and run away from. Now, though, she wondered if it was mercy. If perhaps this was a way for her to atone for the person she'd become.

Dante now looked to Lennon and spoke as though he'd been reading her thoughts. Perhaps he had. "If you raise the gates on your own, without Eileen's interference, you can use the school itself as leverage and put an end to all of this violence. You can protect them if you can keep the gates up. No one could hurt you after that. You'd have the whole school as your leverage against Eileen and the rest of the faculty. You could tie their hands."

"You know I'm not strong enough."

"You are with my help," he said. "We need to get you to the chancellor before he dies and the gates fall. You have to be in the room when it happens. If we miss our window to act, the gates could fall entirely and expose Drayton to the world. There is no margin of error. We have to time it perfectly."

"And we don't have long," said Blaine softly. "William is dying. If things are as bad as they seem, then he only has hours left."

"Can you call another elevator to the chancellor's mansion?" Emerson asked. Of everyone in the room she seemed the most pensive.

"She shouldn't," said Dante. "She needs to save her strength for the gate. She's already expended too much energy. We can't risk getting into that room only for her to start seizing."

"But we can't risk going on foot either," said Emerson. "If we just march up to the chancellor's front door, we'll be obliterated by the faculty."

"Those aren't our only two options," said Kieran. "There's a network of tunnels beneath the school. We can take them straight under the chancellor's house."

"How the hell do you know that?" Lennon asked.

He shrugged. "I have my ways. I'll show you. I can get you anywhere."

So they went down to the basement of the house, where a few students shoved aside a large shelf to reveal a child-sized iron door. It looked like something you'd find in a bank vault. And it was so tarnished that when Dante cranked the handle, rusty flakes scattered across the floor.

A sulfurous and moldy stink wafted from the dark of the tunnel. Blaine gagged. "Jesus Christ, it smells like a fucking sewer."

Dante, Emerson, Kieran, Sawyer, and Blaine all climbed down the ladder and into the tunnel. Lennon was the last to descend, struggling on account of her broken collarbone, the pain white-hot and constant, sharpening whenever she attempted to move her arm. In the end, Kieran and Dante had to hold her, lowering her down into the tunnel as gently as they could.

Under the glow of the flashlights, Lennon could see an oily layer of scum across the surface of the waist-deep water, and the ceiling was so low that Dante couldn't stand at full height. The floor of the tunnel was slippery with scum and whatever else coated the bottom, so that several times Lennon slipped and had to catch herself on the wall to keep from going under.

"You don't think there's, like . . . snakes or alligators in this water, do you?" Sawyer asked.

"I've only seen two, maybe three snakes max," said Kieran. "And only one was poisonous."

Emerson glared at him. "You're not helping."

"Keep it down," said Dante. "The campus floods into these tunnels via sewer grates." He pointed to one ahead, a slat of filmy white light falling down through the iron slats and across the black water. "If we're too loud someone might find out we're down here, and if that happens—"

"We're fucked?" Kieran offered.

"Pretty much."

They kept walking, sloshing through the muck, the waters rising and falling as they went. Sometimes the water climbed as high as Lennon's chin, but another bend might take them through tunnels so shallow that the water barely came up to their knees. They were close to the chancellor's mansion when Dante, who had been walking just ahead, threw out an arm and motioned for silence. He pointed up at one of the dripping sewer grates, and they heard a familiar voice speaking from above. Alec. "Eileen wants the girl alive, of course. The rest are collateral."

"What about Professor Lowe?"

"Eileen wants him too. Of course."

The men walked on, but it was a long time before Dante gave them the go-ahead. The six of them edged carefully around the sewer, their backs flattened against its scummy walls, as they slid past and continued on their way. Lennon felt almost crushed by relief when the waters shallowed and gave way to a run of slick stone stairs.

Sawyer opened the door and checked to see if the room was empty and gestured them all through. They emerged into what was a glorified crawl space, so low they had to bend double and inch their way to the cellar door leading up to the first floor of the house. The six of them emerged into a dark pantry. Overhead, the sound of footsteps. Voices in the halls.

"Can you take them all?" Lennon whispered, looking to Dante. It was one of the only occasions that she'd questioned his ability. Dante was strong, but so were his fellow professors, and she wasn't sure he could take them on, given that he was still so weak from the torture, and the clash with Eileen.

"We can take them," said Emerson, perhaps sensing, like Lennon, that Dante lacked the strength. "Kieran, Sawyer, and me. We'll divert their attention so that you can get to William's room."

"Out of the question," said Lennon. "You heard what Alec said. If you offer yourself as bait and get caught, it's over for you."

Kieran shrugged. "What's a few memories anyway?"

"Kieran, no."

Emerson looked to Dante. "What do you think?"

Dante thought for a moment, then nodded. "Distract them as best you can. Lennon, Blaine, and I will make our way to the chancellor."

The three left. Only seconds later, shouts, footsteps, the sound of glass breaking.

With the diversion underway, Dante, Blaine, and Lennon fled from their hiding spot unseen. They made it to the hall of memories in moments. It stretched out in front of them, dozens of doors on either side, the one that led to William impossibly far away.

They weren't even halfway there when Alec stepped into the hall. "You really are clever. I have to give you that."

Dante placed himself between Alec and the girls.

Alec smiled. "You think you're so chivalrous, but look at you. Dragging them into your own personal vendettas. It wasn't enough to kill Benedict. You just had to tear the school apart brick by brick and get these little soft-minded idiots to help you do it. When are you going to learn to leave well enough alone?"

As Alec spoke, Lennon could feel Dante's will charging the air like static. It made the hairs on her arms bristle and stand on end.

Alec felt it too and responded in turn, advancing down the hall. As he drew closer, Lennon's vision began to fail, black encroaching from the corners of her eyes. Blaine must've felt it too, because she staggered back, blinking rapidly.

Lennon lost her balance, crashed back into the wall, and it was Dante who kept her from falling, lashing out at Alec with the full force of his will. But it was clear that Dante, in his weakened state, didn't have the stores to put up a fight.

And Lennon saw—from the smile that curved Alec's lips—that he knew it too.

Alec was rallying his next attack when someone appeared behind him.

Emerson's will carved through the air like a scythe, and Alec—stunned by the sudden attack—broke to his knees.

"*Go*," said Emerson. "I'll hold him off for as long as I can."

While Emerson clashed with Alec at the hall's entrance—a vicious battle of wills—Lennon, Blaine, and Dante raced to William's quarters. The door was locked today, but Dante made it give with a sleight of his hand, a motion that usually would've demanded little of his strength, but Lennon noticed the way his knees buckled the moment the bolt slipped out of place.

The three of them rushed inside, Lennon first, then Blaine, Dante coming from behind. Lennon had expected a team of doctors and nurses to be in the room, but it was just Dr. Nave from the infirmary. Lennon managed to wrestle him into submission with her will, capitalizing on the element of surprise and knocking him out before he could launch a counterattack.

As Lennon subdued Nave, Blaine locked the door and Dante dragged furniture—an armchair, a table, a few detached oxygen tanks—in front of it as a makeshift barricade. It wasn't enough to keep anyone out for long. Whatever happened next would have to happen quickly.

Dante turned to Blaine. "It's time."

Blaine's chin quivered. She went to William's bedside. He lay, gaunt and waxen, in a nest of pillows. His mouth was wrenched ajar, and the floor and walls of that horrid house trembled with his death rattles. If the bed wasn't nailed down, it probably would've skittered across the floor like the rest of the articles of that room, the side tables and the armchair by the fire, humming in place, sliding. A Holter monitor measured the rhythm of his heart, which was both sluggish and erratic, like water glugging from a bottle with a narrow mouth. The long breaks between each beat, the sputtering palpitations.

Blaine took him by the hand. The floor shuddered.

Lennon wondered, then, about the nature of what Blaine shared with William. The bond between them was a palpable thing, not unlike love. Nor was it one-sided. It became clear to Lennon in that moment that William could sense and feel in his own way. And as Blaine held his hand for the last time, tears slicking her cheeks, she wondered if he knew he was going to die.

If he was relieved to be set free.

"We're running out of time," said Dante, a gentle urging, and for a moment Lennon thought that Blaine had lost her resolve. She saw the conflict in the way her brows drew together, the way her eyes scanned back and forth across the floor, searching for the answer to an impossible question.

Dante turned to Lennon. "I would ask you if you're ready, but I think we're out of time. Either you do this now or you don't do it at all. On your mark?"

Lennon nodded and looked to Blaine. "Let's go."

Blaine nodded back and shifted her hand to William's heart, and Lennon knew at once what she was going to do. It was a cruel lesson that Dante had taught them, months ago, demonstrating on a rat that had cancer, a way to manipulate the mind into creating a lethal arrythmia.

An ordinary persuasionist would have the power to fight back against an attack like that one, to regain control of their own mind and body, defend themselves. But William—lying comatose in his bed—was as helpless as a newborn child.

When Blaine seized his beating heart, he didn't struggle.

The heart monitor shrieked, and the room gave a shake so violent that a crack tore the floor open. Lennon flinched back, but Dante steadied her, taking her by both hands, rubbing his thumbs in circles in the middle of her palms the way he used to when she was falling asleep at night. "I'm going to be with you through every step of this, all right? You just have to listen to me. Can you do that?"

Lennon nodded.

"Good. Now I want you to focus on grounding yourself."

"That's a difficult feat when I'm just trying to stay standing."

"Try for me."

She did, centering herself with deep breaths, even as the floor swayed beneath her feet and sheets of plaster rained down from the ceiling. If the rafters gave, they'd be crushed beneath the rubble. But she tried not to think about that, or about anything apart from Dante's voice.

"Now I want you to call your elevator, a cabin that can move through time. Then, when the gate is present, channel your energy into stretching it larger, to encompass the campus."

"I'm not strong enough for that."

"I've got you. You're going to take what you need from me."

Lennon realized, with a start, that this was his plan all along. He had never intended for her to become like William, or for Eileen to seize control of her mind and body. It was always him who was going to absorb the risk. It was Dante who had planned to make the sacrifice, in the hopes that they would both be freed by it. "No—"

"It's going to be okay," he said. "I promise you that. Just call the elevator."

Lennon did as he asked. It wasn't easy work, what with the ground rolling beneath her feet, the wound at her side still bleeding, her broken collarbone and twisted wrist. She'd expended so much energy calling the elevator in the midst of Nadine's attack, but she had Dante to draw from now, which she did, readily. She could feel his will channeling into her body, a kind of transfusion, filling her stores. He was stronger than she'd given him credit for. And she saw that he had been saving up for her, holding back in anticipation of this moment, waiting to give her everything.

An elevator branded itself into the wall of the bedroom with the warped ring of its bell.

But before its doors parted open, the floor shuddered, and then seemed to drop beneath Lennon's feet with a scream and a feeling of free fall as the campus plunged through time itself. Blaine cried out, and it wasn't just her that was screaming. The house gave a horrible groan, as if its walls were about to give way.

"Open the doors. Center yourself," Dante yelled above the bedlam, spitting blood as he spoke. He was barely on his feet now, Lennon having taken so much from him. And she could see in his eyes—the whites gone red, the pupils shrunken to pinpoints—that he didn't have much left to give her. "Keep opening them. As wide as you can. Give it everything you have. Everything that I have too. Just take what you need from me."

Lennon tried. She tried as hard as she ever had. As the campus fell through space and time, she gritted her teeth—jaw locked, a molar at the back cracking with a burst of pain so intense she almost fell to her knees.

As William's gate came down, the doors of Lennon's own elevator dragged open, wider and wider, retracting into the walls of the cabin, and then the cabin itself stretched wider and taller, until it consumed the entirety of the wall, and then beyond it, opening onto the green, and then stretching farther still.

The gate she opened ripped a hole in the fabric of reality. It was a great and terrible gash, a gate opened in grief and panic and fear. A maw that had consumed the campus whole and swallowed it down through time itself. And as it did, Lennon felt something terrible open within herself. She could hear her own bones breaking, but she felt no pain.

Dante sank to the floor beside Lennon, screaming, his mouth open so wide she feared he'd broken his jaw. He was weeping blood, and she could see it pooling in his ears too, slicking down both sides of his straining neck, painting over his tattoos with red. He was giving all of himself, and even still, Lennon demanded and took more of him.

When the gate fully encompassed the school, she could feel it. Lennon could account for every brick and cobblestone. The grasping roots of the live oaks, the rats that scuttled through the underbrush, the students and the faculty cowering out on the lawn, she could see through their eyes as if through a pair of lenses. She was a part of them all.

And she knew then that her work was done.

With a brutal jolt that broke every window in every building on the campus, the gates firmed, and the free fall stopped. They had done it. The gate had been raised.

"You did it," said Blaine, she was on the floor beside her. "You stopped it. You raised the gate."

Lennon smiled, stunned that she'd actually done it. She turned to Dante, laughing in total disbelief, and saw him lying on the floor, curled fetal. There was blood, so much blood leaking from his mouth, forming a dark puddle on the ground beneath his head. Both of his hands were broken and his legs skewed at sickening angles.

She dropped to her knees at the sight of him and had to crawl across the floor to his side.

The house was already threatening to give, cracks racing up its walls, plates of plaster shattering on impact with the floor. It wouldn't remain standing for long. If they didn't get out soon, they would die there under the rubble.

"We have to go," she said, attempting to lift him up. But with his broken legs, it was a near-impossible feat and she didn't have the strength to drag him. In fact, she could barely walk herself. After several false tries, her own legs gave out. They both crumpled to the floor. "Blaine, don't just stand there. Help me lift him. Please—"

"Lennon, stop," said Dante, his voice so weak it scared her. "Look at me."

"Don't you do this."

"Look at me, Lennon."

She looked at him. Really looked. She took in his broken body. The fear in his eyes, the bloody tears collecting in the corners of them.

"I've got to go now, and you've got to let me."

Lennon shook her head. "You're not going anywhere."

"Hey," said Dante, pressing his knuckles against her cheek despite the pain. "Come on, now—"

"You can't. I won't leave you."

"You have no choice." His voice weakened, his words garbled by blood. There was so much of it, slicking his neck and staining his shirt. "Let me go. I'm ready."

"No. You can't just leave."

His pupils swelled to subsume his irises, then shrank down to pinpoints. He gazed just past Lennon's shoulder, and she realized, in horror, that his vision was going.

"Dante, stay here—"

His eyes came back into focus, homing in on Lennon's. He looked so terribly afraid. "You have . . . to save the school. Keep the gates up. Make yourself . . . indispensable—" His voice broke on a cry of pain. When he spoke again it was through gritted teeth. "The school is your leverage now. Use it to buy your freedom. Your mind. Take the chancellorship if you have to." His eyes fell shut.

Lennon seized him by the shoulder, as if to shake him awake. "Dante!"

Dante opened his eyes, gazed at Blaine. "It's time. The house won't hold."

Blaine looked between Dante and Lennon, then nodded and reached for the latter.

"No," said Lennon, shaking her head. "Blaine, help him, please—"

A rafter on the other side of the room groaned overhead. Blaine caught Lennon by the arm and pulled her back just as a support beam fell between her and Dante. The chancellor's house—this cursed pocket of the universe that William had kept alive—was collapsing.

"Let me go," she shrieked, striking Blaine's chest and shoulders, even lashing out with her will, a series of sad attacks that Blaine easily deflected. She kept dragging her away, one-handed even as Lennon kicked and struggled, begged to be set free.

Plates of plaster flaked off the ceiling and a rain of bricks came down as Blaine dragged Lennon—thrashing and pleading—down the hall of memories and away from the bedroom. Through the clouds of dust, the falling detritus, Lennon caught a final glimpse of Dante. Somehow—despite his broken legs, despite the pain—he was on his knees, his head tipped back, palms up, a smile on his face.

She saw a flash of gold behind him.

Then the doorway collapsed to rubble.

Blaine dragged Lennon through the den as its walls fell around them, through the wreckage of the shattered chandelier, and out onto the front porch. They lunged for the green.

And the house imploded behind them.

58

DAYS LATER, LENNON opened her crusted eyes and took in the empty infirmary ward. The wind eddied in through the broken window. The day was bright, and the sky was a glassy blue. Lennon slipped out of her cot, tested her own legs gingerly. When she was certain she could stand, she left the infirmary, barefoot and wearing nothing but shorts and a hospital gown. Two nurses tried to stop her on her way out of the doors. She brought them to heel with half a thought.

The campus was in ruins. There were fallen trees and great gashes in the ground. Shattered glass littered the walkways, and a few of the buildings were only partially standing. Logos House had very nearly fallen in the worst of the quakes, and it wasn't the only building that had suffered significant damage. As Lennon approached Irvine Hall, she saw that the better part of its east wing had fallen to rubble.

"I want to start by saying this isn't a negotiation," said Lennon as she entered Eileen's office. It was the first time she'd spoken since

Dante's disappearance, and her voice sounded hoarse and strange, like it didn't even belong to her.

She looked toward Eileen, battered and bruised from the attack, seated behind her desk. Lennon knew that her standing at the school had changed, but she didn't grasp the full scope of her new power until that very moment, as Eileen gazed at her, startled and . . . *afraid*. Eileen, the most powerful persuasionist on campus, was afraid of her. "I'm going to talk and you're going to listen, and after you're done listening, you'll do what I say."

"You don't have to be this way," said Eileen, haltingly. "I don't intend to cause any trouble, and I can still be useful to you, to this school."

"You've done enough," said Lennon. "Here's what's going to happen next. You are going to relinquish the role of vice-chancellor, and if you refuse, I'll lower the walls of this campus so fast you won't even have the chance to beg me to stop."

Eileen went very quiet and very pale.

"I'm going to send you back to your home in Charleston, where you will remain until your son turns eighteen, at which point I'll send you to a remote location, a cabin in northern Wyoming, where you will remain for the rest of your natural life."

"*No—*"

"You will never harm your son, or practice persuasion against him or anyone else. When you walk through the doors of that elevator"—as Lennon said this, it appeared in the wall behind her—"your life, as you've known it, will end, and you're lucky that's all I'm taking after what you've done."

In truth, it wasn't out of mercy that Lennon left Eileen's memories of Drayton largely intact. It was to maximize her suffering, so that she would know, for the rest of her miserable life, exactly what was taken from her. So that she, like Lennon, would be forced to live with her grief.

Eileen's eyes filled with tears. "Lennon, please, let's just talk—"

Lennon lashed out with her will, and Eileen cut a cry of pain. Sparing no cruelty, Lennon ripped Eileen from her chair and made her crawl through the parted doors of the elevator, with spinal fluid leaking from her nose.

"You can't keep it forever," said Eileen, slumped against the back wall of the cabin.

"I can try," she said, and closed the doors.

Eileen would never step foot on Drayton's campus again.

It was the same with most of the faculty. Lennon was ruthless. She deposed Alec next, stripping his tenure, and threatening to lower the gates when he refused to go. That made it easy. The other professors—groveling and eager to prove their new loyalty—were quick to turn against him. In fact, Lennon didn't even have to expend the energy necessary to expel him from the college. They eagerly did it for her.

All of the jockeying and politicking made Lennon sick. But it had its uses too. Because Lennon found that in those early days, the faculty did the dirty work on her behalf. They turned on one another with relish, forming a kind of witch hunt in their haste to secure their own positions at the school. After a few months, only a small handful of the former faculty remained, and Lennon replaced those who'd left with a selection of alumni she knew she could trust. Emerson, who she named vice-chancellor, and Blaine, who she tenured. She gave Sawyer the library. Against her better judgment, she extended a professorship to Kieran as well, but he refused, preferring to brave the world beyond Drayton's gates.

With all of the positions filled and the campus restored to some semblance of normalcy, Lennon retired to Dante's house on the water, where she remained for the next few weeks, alone, with the exception of Gregory, who Lennon had found in the bushes outside of Irvine Hall just a few days after raising the gates.

Since her friends were distracted by their new roles at Drayton, Gregory became her primary companion. And Lennon took the liberty of withdrawing from the school completely.

She shunned all contact but kept a channel open via a permanent elevator, connecting Dante's home to the campus, allowing her power to flow through so that the gates would hold firm. But she herself refused to visit. The only reason she knew she'd been officially named chancellor was because a letter was mailed to her along with her diploma, informing her she'd been appointed to her new role by unanimous vote of the board.

Lennon burned the whole thing—the letter, envelope, diploma, and all.

Summer passed in a blur of heat and grief. Before Lennon knew it, the end of fall was approaching, and it was December again. In the weeks leading up to Christmas, Lennon fielded phone calls from her family and made excuses about school and stress and heaps of paperwork to account for her absence over Christmas. The idea of celebrating anything—while mired down by her grief—made her feel sick. So she spent that holiday alone, curled up in the living room, watching horror movies. She was half-asleep when the doorbell rang. She answered to discover Blaine, Sawyer, Emerson, and Kieran huddled together on her doorstep, clutching big foil catering trays of mashed potatoes and sliced honey ham, glazed dinner rolls and store-bought pies.

"You didn't have to do this," said Lennon as they shuffled inside.

"We kind of did, though," said Kieran, setting two large bottles of champagne on the countertop. "Blaine thought you might kill yours—"

Sawyer elbowed him in the ribs. "We didn't want you to be alone over Christmas."

They ate dinner on the floor of the living room by the TV light, gathered around the coffee table, pouring glasses of lukewarm champagne into overlarge wineglasses, downing one after the other. It was the first good night that Lennon had had since Dante's death. The conversation flowed well—thanks to the food and champagne—and for the first time in a very long time Lennon felt almost normal. More like herself than she had since William's death.

Over heaping plates, Lennon listened as Blaine, Sawyer, and Emerson spoke of the campus and all they were doing to improve it. More services for students. More regulations on persuasion. Better placement and support for graduates.

As vice-chancellor, Emerson had been presiding over future admissions, and had been combing through information of prospective candidates of the school, a shadowy process that involved a network of alumni casting out their psychic nets to harvest the best candidates. It sounded like exhausting work, but Emerson seemed to enjoy it. Lennon could tell she was happy; they all were.

And she resented them for it.

They had new lives and beginnings, but what did she have to show for her sacrifice? An empty house haunted by the ghost of the man who gave it to her? Gregory and grief, her newest and closest companions, now that everyone else had left her behind to start their new and promising lives?

Blaine reached across the coffee table to squeeze her hand, and it was only then that Lennon realized she was crying. "There is life beyond him," she said, in a soft voice. "You do know that, right?"

Lennon flinched. "I know that you want me to believe that. I know that I'd be happier if I could."

There was a long and awkward silence, the first one of the night. Sawyer, Emerson, and Blaine all exchanged long looks across the coffee table, as if some unspoken fear had just been confirmed. Sensing the awkwardness, Kieran got up to grab another bottle of champagne from the fridge, which was probably the smartest thing anyone could've done in the moment.

"Don't do that," said Lennon.

Blaine sipped foam off the top of a fresh glass of champagne. "Do what?"

"The theatrical concern," said Lennon. "You know I can't stand it."

"It's not theatrical," said Sawyer, waving Kieran off when he tried to top him up. "It's been months, Lennon. We're worried about you. You can't just hide away from the world forever."

"He's gone," said Blaine, trying to be gentle. "You have to accept it at some point. It'll hurt at first, but I promise you'll be better for it."

"They never found a body," said Lennon, and there was a long silence.

Only Emerson was brave enough to respond. "That's because there wasn't a body to find. The building imploded. What matter they were able to salvage from the wreckage—"

"You weren't there," Lennon snapped. "He was bleeding all over the floor. DNA isn't enough. I need something more than that before I'm willing to believe he's really gone."

No one challenged her.

That night they all slept together in the guest bedroom. Blaine, Sawyer, and Lennon all squeezed together on the bed. Kieran and Emerson insisted on sleeping on the carpet—in a nest of pillows and comforters—despite Lennon's assurances that there were other, more comfortable beds in the house. They said their good nights—drunk and pleasantly stuffed from dinner—and cut the lights. But long after the others fell asleep, Lennon remained awake, listening to Kieran's soft snores, and the gentle hush of the ocean. She thought of Dante in those final moments before the house imploded, an image she usually tried to cast out of her mind because it simply hurt too much to hold it there. But tonight, she allowed herself this painful indulgence, turning over that last memory she had of him, kneeling on the floor, palms up in surrender, smiling. She remembered too the flash of gold she'd seen behind him, a split moment before the wall collapsed. A warped bell ringing. Elevator doors gaping open.

59

THE FOLLOWING DAY, after her friends had gone, Lennon attempted to call an elevator to the past. With the Drayton gates a constant drain on her power, it wasn't easy work. In fact, the first elevator she summoned resulted in her seizing on the floor of her bedroom for the better part of ten minutes. It went on like that for days.

While Lennon struggled to summon the dregs of her power, she delved deep into Dante's past. Previously, he'd stated that his efforts to raise gates had only accessed a specific moment in time, one that was only important to him. If Dante really had called his own elevator as the chancellor's mansion was imploding, it stood to reason that it must've taken him back to that point.

But what was it?

Dante had been vague about the details of his past, prior to Drayton. So Lennon had to rely heavily on Carly's previous research into his life, piecing together a timeline of short-term apartments and the schools he'd briefly been enrolled in, the cities where he'd lived for little more than weeks at a time, the minutiae of a fraught childhood.

It was some months before she was able to open a gate to that crisp winter night when Dante had been freed from the prison. She'd chosen this night because, on all counts, it was one of the most significant of his life. The night that had changed everything, the night he'd been taken to Drayton.

Lennon stepped off the elevator cabin, and into the fresh-fallen snow. The Pendleton Juvenile Correctional Facility stood on a gentle hill, its few windows glowing dully in the cold dark. In the parking lot, a handful of cars were half buried under drifts. The whole night felt like it was holding its breath as Lennon approached the prison.

The lobby was empty, save for the security guard seated behind the front desk. "Visiting hours are over. You can try coming back—"

When Lennon didn't break pace, the man sprang to his feet, started to come from around the desk, but she raised a hand and the man went stone still, stopping midstep, and crashing—stiff—against the welcome desk. Lennon stole her memory from his mind a moment before he struck the floor.

As she walked, Lennon let her consciousness extend, roaming through the halls and the run of cells until she homed in on one that contained an essence that felt familiar. Dante's cell was in the solitary confinement block, and it took some effort to subdue the prison guards who oversaw the ward, the thick wall of bulletproof glass between them and Lennon making it difficult for her to extend her will and catch hold of their minds. Still, she managed to force them up from their seats and walked them down the hall, single file, into one of the only open cells on the block.

None of those under the force of her will so much as raised a finger in resistance, except one woman—visibly pregnant and terrified—who proved so contentious that Lennon had no choice but to drag her into a deep fugue. She slumped, comatose, against the wall, Lennon guiding her down to the floor.

The prison cell she sought was the last on the ward. It had a small slit for a window. Bleeding profusely now, her legs soft beneath her, Lennon stepped forward to look into the cell. It was empty, save for a small brown moth with tattered wings, throwing itself senselessly against the only light in the cell.

Lennon returned to the present, exhausted, crawling out of the elevator on her hands and knees, collapsing, spent, on the floor of the living room, her nose and eyes bleeding. It was some time before she managed to pick herself up off the floor, and when she did, she went out to the water, fully dressed, and waded waist-deep into the black surf. She stood there for some time, staring out toward the island, then she went inside, peeled off her wet clothes, and climbed into bed.

The next day, she rallied her strength and tried again.

This time, she went to a balmy Tuesday in the fifth summer of Dante's childhood. It was, by all accounts, a rather unremarkable summer, as summers went. Lennon stepped off the elevator and onto a wet street in Brooklyn. Children—their faces blurs of joy—ran barefoot and shrieking through an arc of water that spit from an open fire hydrant. The fat summer sun limned the mist, casting the whole scene in a bright and bleary sepia.

Across the street, there was a man sitting on a park bench. So little of who Lennon knew to be Dante was present in this hunched, gaunt figure, with the smile and the bleeding nose. But when their eyes met from across the street, she saw familiarity spark to life in his sunken eyes, like a firefly trapped in a jar.

Lennon crossed the street and went to him. She saw that there was a small brown moth clinging to his cheek. It was a tiny little thing with wrinkled wings, and as Lennon sat down on the bench beside him, it took flight, fluttering about the shell of his ear.

"Took you long enough," he said. Lennon noticed that his legs, broken the last time she'd seen him, had somehow been reset. A feat of persuasion, perhaps, and a painful one at that.

"I came as soon as I could," she said. "You didn't make it easy for me."

In the street, two brave little girls ran hand in hand through the water, so close to the hydrant's outlet that they were very nearly blasted off their feet.

"Are those your sisters?"

He nodded. "Beth and Eliza."

"Which one are you?" Lennon asked, nodding to the children. Any one of the boys could have been a young Dante—at that age it was hard to tell, and their faces were blurred so badly by the water and the golden light of the setting sun that even when she squinted, she couldn't quite bring them into focus.

Dante pointed to a window, three stories up, in one of the apartment complexes down the street. There was a small face pressed to the glass.

"Why aren't you playing with the other kids?"

"I was grounded."

"What'd you do?"

"I don't remember now," he said. "But I know I didn't really mind. It was enough just watching them." Here, his gaze returned to his sisters. "How are things at the school?"

"Things have changed. The gates held. I sent Eileen on her way."

"And the chancellorship?"

"It's mine now."

He nodded. A small smile touched his lips, and when it did, fresh blood streamed from his nose and spattered the concrete.

"Why didn't you tell me you planned to save my life?" Lennon asked. It was a question that had haunted her since the night she'd lost him. "You let me hate you. You let me think you'd betrayed me—"

"You would've stopped me," he said. "There was no other way."

"I didn't get the chance to say goodbye."

"This is that chance," he said.

"Well, I didn't come here to say goodbye, Dante. I came here to take you home."

Dante chose his next words very carefully. She could tell by the furrow that formed between his brows, the same expression he made in the classroom when someone asked a particularly difficult question. "I'm tired, Lennon."

"I know you are. But you can rest back in the present, where you belong."

Dante considered this for a beat. Silent.

Lennon tried to keep her voice level. "You don't want to come home, do you?"

"I haven't decided," he said.

"And that's what you're doing here? Deciding?"

"Yeah." He gestured down the street, toward the brilliant sunset. "I think if I go that way, I get to rest."

She wanted to stop him, of course. That was what she had come here to do. To pull him back from the brink, to save him as he had saved her. But now, alone in the past with him, Lennon knew she had no place. The choice of how and if he lived or died wasn't hers to make, no matter how much she loved him. And so it was out of love when she nodded, relenting, and stood up, feeling dizzy, and she could smell blood high up in her sinuses. She knew she couldn't stay there much longer. She was running out of time. The rest was up to Dante.

"Do you see that elevator across the street?" As she said this, it formed in the plexiglass wall of a bus stop awning.

Dante nodded.

"I'm going to go to it, and if you want to live, then you'll follow me."

Dante looked up at her, his eyes narrowed against the setting sun, which burned hotter and brighter by the moment. "And if I don't?"

"Then you'll stay here," said Lennon, "and I'll never forgive you for it, but I won't love you any less either."

"All right," he said, which might've been yes, or it might've been goodbye, but Lennon, bleeding from the nose, didn't pause to ask the question before turning her back on him. She walked across the wet street, listening for the sound of his footsteps behind her, hearing nothing but the laughing children. The elevator doors parted. Lennon stepped through them and turned to see Dante, standing in the street just a few feet behind her, the sunlight bright at his back, burning almost, as though he was on fire. He stepped forward on his weak and injured legs, almost fell but kept going. The doors began to close. Lennon threw out a hand to stop them, but they kept pressing inward, even as she fought to hold them back. Dante staggered—his face screwed with pain, his knees buckling—and fell into the elevator a moment before its doors sliced shut.

ACKNOWLEDGMENTS

I WANT TO thank my mom, whom I lost while writing this book, and everyone who helped me navigate the fraught waters of my grief. I'm especially grateful to my partner, my dad, my sister, my aunt, and my two cats, Edisto and Elijah (who actually really hated this book, as evidenced by their trying to stomp on the delete key multiple times while I was writing it).

Jenny Bent, thank you for being the best advocate I could ever ask for, and for making the harrowing experience that is publishing easier and less scary. Jessica Wade, thank you so much for helping me shape this story into what I always hoped it could be. I feel so lucky to have you as my editor. Gabbie Pachon, I'm so grateful for all of the hard work you do. I owe a huge thank-you to my amazing publicists, Stephanie Felty and Yazmine Hassan. I also want to thank Jessica Mangicaro and Hillary Tacuri for helping me launch this story into the world. Thank you, Katie Anderson, for creating such a stunning cover; seeing your designs is one of my favorite parts of the publishing process. To the rest of the team at Ace/Berkley: Thank you all so, so

ACKNOWLEDGMENTS

much. Three books in and I'm still so honored that I get to publish with you. I also want to thank my UK editor, Simon Taylor, and the entire team at Transworld for getting this book into the hands of readers across the pond. And to all of the other publishers who've put my books on shelves around the world: thank you.

Lastly, thank you to my readers. You've handed me my dreams by supporting my work. I'm immensely grateful to you all.